Mayhem With A
Capital M

Mayhem With A Capital M

Enjoy!
Marlene McNeil Chabot

MARLENE CHABOT

AUTHOR OF CHINA CONNECTION
AND NORTH DAKOTA NEIGHBOR

iUniverse, Inc.
Bloomington

Mayhem With A Capital M

iUniverse books may be ordered through booksellers or by contacting:

iUniverse
1663 Liberty Drive
Bloomington, IN 47403
www.iuniverse.com
1-800-Authors (1-800-288-4677)

ISBN: 978-1-4620-2363-9 (sc)
ISBN: 978-1-4620-2364-6 (ebk)

Printed in the United States of America

iUniverse rev. date: 06/18/2011

This book is dedicated to all my family and friends who I cherish so much.
Without their loving support I wouldn't be all that I am today.

I wish to express my gratitude to Angie Sanders for her friendship and her willingness to edit my book when she already has so many irons in the fire.

Chapter 1

Great Aunt Fiona on my father's side, who came all the way from Northern Ireland to this great continent our family now lives on, dispersed her *fantastic* gift, premonitions, upon another member of the Malone clan right before she croaked. Unfortunately, none of my siblings or cousins had the right type of blood when endowment time came, so her gift quietly fell upon my shoulders. My fate was sealed. Only a wee lad at the time, I didn't think it respectful to argue the outcome with an adult, an old, old, old adult at that. Besides, I didn't know a bloody thing about wiggling out of uncomfortable situations back then.

And now, well, I'm forty-some years old and, believe it or not, actually considered a true gentleman by a few people I know, so I'd rather not use foul language to tell anyone what I really think of the *gift*. Let's just say I regard it more as a curse. It hangs around me night and day, like my mutt Gracie, waiting for the right set of circumstances to drag me deeper and deeper into its folds. It's like an Albatross waiting for the exact moment to arrive, so it can plunge its body into the sea and capture its unknowing prey. Poor fish! I know exactly how it feels.

Of course, if I were to be totally honest with you, which I'm not likely to be because of the nature of my work as a private investigator, I'd have to at least acknowledge the fact that on rare occasions my sixth sense does work to my advantage. Take for instance two cases I solved, a year apart, which required my temporarily leaving behind the confines of the Twin Cities and Minnesota. The first investigation had to do with the pop bottling industry, and the other with property on which a new middle school was being built. Pretty sweet, huh?

Yeah, maybe to you it sounds great, but that dreaded curse does a big number on me when it's full blown. I get really nauseous and weak in the knees. Women who have bravely struggled through the first trimester of pregnancy know exactly what I mean.

Okay, okay. Enough of my whining. I should be thrilled that the premonitions only kick into high gear when things are in perfect alignment. Kinda like a solar eclipse or other similar phenomenon. Well, guess what? Today, New Year's Day, ended up being designated "D"day. That's right. You heard me. New Year's Day. And get this— in church of all places. Talk about miscalculated timing!

At approximately eleven-fifteen this morning, my immediate family and I, meaning mother, father, siblings and a few of their family members, were sitting in a well-worn oak pew at Holy Rosary Catholic Church in Northeast Minneapolis, patiently waiting for Father Mc Nealy to finish his long-winded ice fishing story, which he somehow worked into his sermon. Since I'm not the least bit interested in any type of fishing, I permitted my mind and eyes to stray for a moment or two. Well, it was either that or nodding off and getting whacked on the head by my dear mother.

As my head drifted slightly to the left, my eyes fell upon the six-foot marble statue of Mary holding baby Jesus that was created in Italy. The regal carving resides in an alcove above a small side altar near the front of the church. The altar itself was still overflowing with Christmas foliage, ten huge pots of bright red Poinsettias, to be exact, which should've been removed like the day after Christmas; their faded fallen petals were creating a new altar cloth. Too bad the petals didn't drop off a clump at a time instead of one by one, I thought. They would be a lot easier to clean up. Almost instantly, the collection of fallen petals brought to mind the old saying, "She loves me, she loves me not. She loves me . . .", and then kapow! My stomach felt like a huge rock had struck it. The curse wanted my undivided attention.

Luckily, I was sitting this time. I have been known to slip to the floor when an attack strikes and scare the living daylights out of whomever is around. I inhaled deeply in order to process what was occurring. This was the first time I had ever experienced the effects of my curse while attending any type of church service. What the heck brought the curse on in such a holy place?

Since I knew my mind had left the sermon before the attack came on, there were only two possible things to blame for triggering my darn sixth sense, the Mexican grown flowers or the statue. Mary and Jesus were too busy listening to countless prayers to bother with me, so that left the flowers. But why the flowers? I expelled the stale inhaled air and waited for the answer to reveal itself and the pain to subside.

After a couple minutes passed, the internal war in my body still raged on. I crossed my arms and clutched my sides. That position helps calm things down sometimes. There was no need to panic yet, I told myself, even though my stomach was doing double and triple time. I shifted gears momentarily to see what would happen. My thoughts were swiftly drawn away from the pain and focused on the flowers. The flowers merely reminded me of Mexico, and wasn't Mexico where I was going with my gorgeous girlfriend for our winter getaway this year? Yes, and in just two weeks time.

When the plane lands south of the border, all Rita and I plan to do is get ankle-deep in the hot sand and sample Margaritas and spicy foods. Although, I must confess, I might manage to squeeze in a siesta here and there if Rita gets the urge to wander off by herself in search of cheap trinkets.

What's that? No, I don't have a problem with my girlfriend going off by herself. You see, I belong to that select group of males who actually appreciate women who go off to shop for several hours and don't expect their significant others to tag along. That's when a man gets to do what a man wants to do, snooze.

So with only a carefree vacation planned, how could I possibly stumble into trouble, right? Poinsettias or no Poinsettias, this guy wasn't going to let stomach problems spoil his day. No way.

Oops. I forgot about you. I guess I shouldn't have passed my travel plans on so quickly. It's quite possible you're linked to an evil element somewhere out there in the universe I know nothing about.

Oh, well, now that my plans have been broadcast to the whole world, I can tell you're just dying to sneak more info out of me. Like, how does a person with a one-man PI operation, who usually squeaks by with just enough income each week to provide the bare necessities for his mutt and himself, scrape up enough dough for a trip out of the country? Asking that type of question is perfectly fine with me. Heck, it's only normal for one human being to wonder how another human being, with less income than he, can find ways to have fun. Right? Flights don't come cheap anymore, nor does gas for the car, for that matter.

The elderly Irish priest coughed unexpectedly now. "Sorry," he said, "I can't seem to shake this annoying cough." I didn't believe that story anymore than an overly exaggerated fish one. This priest's an old pro. The church bulletin I snatched off the small table before I entered the main part of the church today announced that Father Mc Nealy will be celebrating forty years in the priesthood. this March. That's more than enough time to learn how to regain the attention of those who become disinterested in his tales. Take me for instance.

I moved my head just a smidgen, so my eyes were settled back on the priest where they should've been all along. Hmm. As soon as I opened my mind to the man of cloth standing at the podium, my stomach problems magically disappeared. Shoot! I should've backtracked sooner.

Oh, don't worry. I haven't forgotten about your interest in me. I'd be more than happy to fill you in on how I can afford a trip on my tiny income, but right now I have to get back to the mass. Father Mc Nealy has finished his lengthy sermon, and it's time to stand and sing a song to Mary, *O Most Holy One,* found on page 356 of the church hymnal.

Chapter 2

Now that mass has finally concluded, I think it's time to fess up and tell you that a few members of my family, including myself, aren't as holy as you may think we are. We'd rather have skipped the holiness scene altogether and remained at home, but we didn't have a choice. Our seventy-year-old mother, a determined woman of French descent and a very devout Catholic, insisted that we all attend mass on New Year's Day, like she has for I don't remember how many years.

"New Year's Day is a Holy Day of Obligation," she always tells us in her most endearing voice. "You children don't realize how fortunate you are to have an extra church day created during your lifetime." Then she sighs and continues, "I still don't know why it took the church's upper hierarchy till 1970 to establish the holy day. It's in honor of the Solemnity of Mary and considered of greatest importance." With that final bit of information out of the way, she then adds, "Remember now, your significant others don't have to come if they don't want to," knowing full-well that two of her children are married to non-Catholics.

Fortunately for us, after appeasing Mom with our forced, hour-long holiness routine, it's on to secondary matters which certain members of our family consider of high importance too.

As usual after exiting church this time of year, we hop in our cars and drive straight to the home where we were raised and immediately begin to stuff our faces with high carb foods: cookies, candy, cheeses, sausages, meatballs, min-pizzas and whatever else can be made into miniature offerings. But, it doesn't stop there. Oh, no! After our plates are filled beyond capacity, we then enter the medium-sized living room, find a spot in front of or near the twenty-five inch Sony TV screen which will be broadcasting the Rose Bowl game, and park our butts for the duration of the afternoon.

You know, as much as our clan professes their dislike for anything winter and are so obsessed with the Rose Bowl, I've never really understood why we haven't jumped on a rental bus and headed to Pasadena, California where we could all broil in the sun and be a part of the live action instead. That would make a great trip for the Malone clan. We'd talk about it for years to come. Then again, maybe we wouldn't want to, depending on what happened along the way.

Oh, well. Since we're such diehard conformists, I guess I should just be grateful for the little things, like the fact that the Malone clan doesn't get their feathers ruffled when they hear that the Minnesota Gophers haven't made it to the Rose Bowl game yet again, when so many other fans do. Heck, our family doesn't need its home team on the screen to get riled up. Any two college football teams will do.

However, there is one itsy-bitsy drawback to watching a game at my folks' house on New Year's Day. Family rituals are followed to the ninth degree, one of them being we're only allowed to discuss non-football related topics during commercial breaks. So if you come to the Malone house to watch the game, you'd better bring your own tablet and pen to jot down anything you want to say at break time.

It's only a twenty-minute drive from church to the old homestead in Spring Lake Park, and we had finally reached our destination. Of course, if we had hit numerous red traffic lights or snow clogged roads, we'd still be another ten minutes away.

My folks led the Malone caravan home just as they had for many, many years. I often wondered what malady would befall my three siblings and me if we ever dared change that routine. Perhaps an alien would zap us to his ship, or better yet, a satellite sent out into space would hurl itself back to earth just in time to smash the car of the new leader. Hmm? I guess life's a lot simpler if you just go with the flow. Besides, common sense dictates that before my siblings and I park our cars in the long driveway, our parents' car still has to be put in the garage.

Dad cautiously maneuvered his Ford Taurus onto the blacktopped driveway now, making certain not to dig up any snow-covered grass running alongside it. Since he had already popped the double-car garage door up before entering the home stretch, he just continued on into the garage.

Time for the siblings and I to progress single-file style onto his property now. Like always, the Topaz and I brought up the rear. Nothing wrong with that. By sheer coincidence, I seem to live by one particular Bible quote most of the time anyway. "The last shall be first and the first shall be last." In this instance, I'll be the first one out of here tonight. No being held prisoner while others dillydally with long good-byes.

Coming from a family with extremely competitive nature, my siblings and I reached the entrance door to our folks' house at the same time. My brother Michael, the eldest of the Malone children, and I graciously stepped aside to allow Margaret, Mary, and my brother's wife, Helen, to enter first. "You three charming women go ahead," I announced, "us two ugly ducklings can wait."

Margaret's non-Catholic husband, Keith, whom she met while attending college in West Virginia and had made the decision to remain at my folks' place while the rest of us went to church, popped into the hallway entrance just as Michael and I walked in. "Where the heck have you guys been? Margaret told me mass only lasts an hour; you've been gone two." Then the football fanatic said, "They've already showed the panoramic view of the 94,392 people seated in the stands. If you two don't get moving, you're going to miss the kick-off."

I pulled the cuff of my winter jacket back and glanced at my new, silver wideband wristwatch purchased at Target with a Christmas gift card. "Calm down, Keith. The game doesn't start for another ten minutes."

Michael and I recklessly tossed our jackets on the nearby coatrack, one of those cheap metal ones that topples over when it reaches overload. Fortunately for us, Michael's family and my two sisters had taken their coats to the nearest guest bedroom, so we didn't have to worry about it falling over today.

As soon as my brother's jacket was hung, he dashed straight to the kitchen. I'm thinking for nourishment. Well, his stomach was churning quite loudly during the entire church service. Of course, he wasn't alone. You see, a true practicing Catholic avoids all forms of food an hour before taking communion at mass. Whether Michael is true to his Catholic roots I don't know. I've never felt the need to pry. Maybe he was just running late and didn't have time to squeeze breakfast in.

I, on the other hand, totally ignored the call of food for the moment and chose to remain in the hallway entrance to give my 6' 2" sandy-haired brother-in-law a mild dose of reality concerning driving time for Sunday service. "Keith, for future reference, it takes at least a good twenty minutes to get to the church."

"How's that? It's only two blocks from here. Margaret pointed it out to me the other day when we went shopping."

"St. Francis?"

"Yeah, I think that's the one. It has a huge spiked tower that looks like it skims the sky."

"The tower probably does touch the sky, but that's not the church the elder Malones attend. It never has been, and it never will be. Mom and Dad have been going to Holy Rosary Church in Northeast Minneapolis forever. Dad's parents went there, Mom and Dad got married there, and that's where we were taken every Sunday until we went off to college. Isn't that right, Mike?" Michael likes to be called Mike when he's around family.

My brother, who had managed to overload his plate with food in record time, had just zoomed in front of us and was attempting to reach the living room in zig zag fashion without spilling one drop of chow or beverage. "Hmm? Holy Rosary Church? Yeah, that's right. We got baptized there, made First Communions there, and we're confirmed there." Now he scratched his dark, black, thick head of hair with his empty hand. "Isn't it something how the years fly by? Gosh, how many years has it been since I was an altar boy? I mean altar server." Before I could let loose with a smart remark, he strolled off and found a spot by the TV.

Five seconds later, the rest of the of the family came pouring out of the kitchen too, like Lemmings. Time for Keith and I to get some grub, I thought. I grabbed his thick, football player like arm. "Come on. Let's see what they left us."

Even after entering the kitchen, my brother-in-law was determined to continue our church conversation. "Matt, there's something that doesn't make sense to me," he said while piling slices of cheese and sausage on his Styrofoam plate.

I managed to chomp down a raw carrot before asking, "What's that?"

"Well, I thought the Catholic Church was real strict about where one could attend mass. At least that's what I heard when I was a kid." He added meatballs and min-pizzas to his junk food pyramid and then finished the mixture off with ruffled chips before he continued. "Guys I hung out with said a person had to attend the church closest to their house or they'd be in deep trouble. The parish priest always knew when a person wasn't in the right church."

Mom had snuck back into the kitchen to get a cup of coffee just a few seconds before, so she overheard our conversation. "That was the rule," she said, and then she left the room without adding any more.

I chuckled. "One of those good old rules. A lot of them have been dropped since your childhood. Anyway, I think the one you're referring to had to do with tithing. The pastors wanted to keep the money in their own neighborhoods, so when their churches fell in disrepair they'd have the necessary funds to mend the problems." I crammed my plate with barbecued meatballs, min-pepperoni pizzas, dill pickles, and deviled eggs.

Keith set his plate on a counter now while he poured a large glass of diet pop for himself. "So you don't have to attend the church nearest your house anymore?"

"Nah. That went out with the big-reeled tape recorders. People are on the go now more than ever. They attend whatever church they want. It's kind of like open enrollment for schools–a smorgasbord of choice. And you know what? The change hasn't lost money for the local churches. People still give to the church where they're registered at. Of course, direct deposit helps too."

Chapter 3

Keith and I finally made our way to the living room now but I worried we had dallied too long in the kitchen over food and conversation and that my sports-crazed brother-in-law had missed the opening of the game. Unfortunately, we hadn't missed a thing, not even another terrible rendition of our national anthem, the *Star Spangled Banner*. Poor Francis Scott Key. His 1814 poem, written two years after witnessing the harsh reality of battle between our troops at Fort Mc Henry and the British ship, HMS Minden, was meant to be a joyous poem about America's victory, not a downer.

Since I didn't spot an available seat anywhere, I plopped down on the floor by my single sister, Mary, who was sitting on a folding chair near the hallway. I was pretty certain she wouldn't have stinky feet. Heck, she lives and breathes Avon products.

As soon as I got comfy, a middle-aged bald-headed referee stepped on to the playing field, ready to fulfill his task of asking the time-worn question heard at the start of every game. "Team captains, who wishes to make the call?" Then, "Heads or tails?"

The team captain of the Washington Huskies swiftly replied in a baritone voice, "Heads."

I hope he made the right choice because if he didn't, and the coin lands with tails facing up, the Purdue Boilermakers get to open the game. The pressure was on. Not only could I see it on the faces of the people who were sitting in the stadium where the game was about to be played out, but right here in the home of my youth.

The moment the coin was released in mid-air, I bit down on another raw carrot, Dad shoved a handful of shelled nuts in his mouth, Keith stuffed his face with chips, and Michael squeezed the life out of the can of pop he was holding.

What was it going to be? Would the Purdue Boilermakers win the toss or the Washington Huskies? The Huskies weren't as far from home as the Boilermakers, so even if they didn't win the toss, the momentum of their fans and family support would surely carry them along.

The referee, who was the shortest in stature of the three standing out there on the open field, bent down towards the rain-caked earth, carefully examined the coin resting by his feet, and then he made his proclamation. "Huskies won the toss!"

"Hot dog!" Keith shouted, forgetting the established decorum of the room. "I knew it was going to be the Huskies."

"Yeah," my small-framed brother who took after my mother's side of the family retorted, "you and about twenty thousand other people."

Dad gave my brother-in-law and brother the evil-eye. "Hush!"

Silence prevailed just in the nick of time. The referee asked the Huskies team captain if he wanted the ball. If he declines the ball, it goes to the Boilermakers.

The answer came swiftly, "We want the ball."

Of course, you and I both know, just because we've been told who gets the ball, it doesn't mean the game's ready to start. There's always those darn commercial breaks beforehand. Production people are so clever. They know exactly where to place the breaks to keep the tension going. Speaking of tension, I often wonder exactly how many people end up in the emergency room on game nights. I've heard the numbers are astronomical.

You know, as far as I'm concerned, there is only one good thing that comes from the New Year's Day commercials on TV. The Malones are free to talk about anything other than the game for a few minutes at least.

Michael left the leather hassock behind now that he had been occupying and came over by me. "When's Rita supposed to arrive, Matt?"

"In about twenty minutes, I hope." Rita Sinclair has been my girlfriend for about two years now. We aren't engaged, but I did happen to give her a pre-engagement ring, a blue Topaz stone I brought back from a working trip to Brazil and had placed in a setting. She works for a medium-sized ad firm downtown and often gets delayed when she's pressed to get a huge project done. Moving on now, I looked to see where my father was seated before I broached the next subject. "Mike, do you think Dad will make us wait till the games over to give us our travel tick....?"

The end of my question was firmly stamped out. The patriarch of the Malone clan clapped his short stubby hands and then he spoke. "Attention, everyone."

Since I was the only one who obeyed him at once, he fired off another round in Rock'n Roll decibels. "Quiet please!" His second appeal got excellent results. "Thank you. Kids, I know I've been keeping you in suspense since Christmas, and I plan to remedy that right now." Good, we're finally going to get the lowdown on our trips, I thought. About time. Dad looked away from us kids for a second now and sent Mom a short message via hand signals. She quickly grabbed the four white business sized envelopes that were sitting on the top of the piano and passed them on to dad.

Now my dad left his comfy lounge chair, went to the center of the living room and announced our names according to birth order, "Michael, Margaret, Matt and Mary." As soon as the eldest of the tribe joined him, he received an envelope. The clock was ticking. No, I mean literally. I could hear the old antiquated clock that joined our family when my great-grandmother died. It makes its home on the table near the piano. To me, the noise emanating from it sounds like a beating heart.

At least it wasn't beating off kilter like mine was right this minute. While I nervously waited my turn, I was overcome by memories of grade school, specifically report card day. My classmates and I would sit as straight as a ruler behind our desks, knees knocking and sweat pouring forth from every pore, as we waited for the principal to tell us to come forward for our card. My hands were sweating now, but my knees weren't shaking.

After Mary and I got our envelopes, we joined Michael and Margaret and huddled tightly together. There's strength in numbers. The four Ms. That's what we were called all through our school years. We were unbeatable. Nothing could stop us as long as we stuck to each other like manure or mud.

My father stared at the four of us for a second and then said, "Kids, at Christmas I told you the trip I listed in each of your cards was my way of saying thank you for helping out your mother and I during a difficult time, my heart surgery, and I meant it. But your cards never revealed the specific town you'd be flown to since we hadn't lined up the trips with the travel agent yet. Now they're all finalized. So I hope you've kept your trip a secret from each other like I requested."

Like the little children we once were, the four of us bobbed our heads in synchronized precision as we said, "Yes, Dad." Quite honestly, I had no knowledge whether my siblings shared with each other or not; all I knew was that I didn't feel one bit guilty about my response for once in my life.

I glanced down at my envelope, afraid to open it when the time came. After planning for the beach for the past eight days, I suddenly realized I might be flying to Mexico City instead. That would definitely end up at the top of my list of true catastrophes. Maybe it would be best to wait and open my envelope when Rita arrived. That way we could be shocked or surprised together. At the moment, I had no foreshadowing that my girlfriend had struck a deal with my father, and they had planned the Mexico trip together.

Michael, the most curious one in our family, probably because he's a mail sorter for the main post office in Minneapolis, tore at his envelope with a vengeance. "I don't believe it," he shouted as he ran his hand through his hair. After he settled down, he turned to face his wife who was still sitting on the couch. "Helen, you'd better brush up on your French. We're going to Montreal."

I was thrilled for them, especially since Michael shared at Thanksgiving that he'd like to go to Canada. My father's the one who stirred the pot that day. He said, "Where would you kids go on vacation if you had the means to do so?" I thought the question a waste of our time. We all know Dad's a huge fan of afternoon TV talk shows, so I figured his query had been merely influenced by either Oprah or Dr. Phil. Some guest probably threw out a variety of questions to get everyone to participate at meal time.

Not wanting to appear disrespectful, my siblings and I played along with Dad even though we had no clue where the discussion would lead us. Surprise, surprise. That was the most talkative meal our family has ever had together. Margaret said, "I've always wanted to go to the Caribbean," and my sister Mary and I both said, "Mexico."

Helen, a mixture of both Marilyn Monroe and Hilary Clinton, didn't seem the least bit affected by the news just delivered. She simply set her half-empty plate carefully down on the coffee table and became immoveable like a rock. Supposedly she's one of those people who requires a fair amount of time for information to soak in before she reacts. At least that's what my brother told me when he was first dating her.

Her oldest child, Rose, was not about to allow her to dawdle too long in her thinking mode. Drawing herself closer to her mother now, she softly tapped her on the arm. "Mom."

Helen immediately awoke from her mental slumber and went into overdrive. "I'm fine dear," she said to Rose. A broad smile swept across her face now as she swiftly catapulted herself off my parents' two year old leather couch, flew straight to Dad and wrapped her light-weight arms around him. "Merci, Archie," she said as she pecked him on the cheek. Of course, Helen kissed Michael too. When she was standing directly in front of my dad once again she said, "I can't believe you remembered, Pops."

"Remembered what?"the snoop in me asked, still pressing my unopened envelope to my chest like I was protecting the household from a poisonous snake.

Michael and Helen's family historian, eleven-year-old Rose, took it upon herself to blurt out the answer. "That Mom and Dad met in an introduction to French class at the University of Minnesota."

"Ahh, yes. The good ol' days," I said. "I had forgotten all about that. Good thing you're recording everything for prosperity, Rose."

"Thanks," she replied sweetly, too young to realize my comment was dripping with sarcasm.

"My turn." Margaret, the only member of our family besides me to have been blessed with the bright red hair of a true Irish person, ripped open her envelope in record breaking time. She was so antsy, shifting from one foot to the other every two seconds. I knew because I timed her movements.

"Tell me? Tell me?" Keith begged while crossing and uncrossing his legs. Yup, this couple's marriage was definitely no mistake, I thought. They were a match made in heaven or possibly some other place. "Come on hon, where are we going?"

My sister hurriedly took her itinerary out of the torn envelope and scanned it. "St. Thomas! Yahoo!" Now she hopped across the carpeted floor until she reached her husband who was sitting on the piano bench. "Our friends said it's a relaxing, fun island."

"Thanks, Archie." Keith squeezed Margaret tightly. "St. Thomas has great areas to snorkel, Margaret, and it's only a hop, skip and a jump from St. John's." I don't know about my sister's skipping and jumping abilities, but she certainly has the hopping part down.

It was my turn finally, but I suddenly had this crazy idea. I turned to my younger sister and said, "Mary, I have a strong hunch you're going to Mexico too, so let's just shout out our location on the count of three, okay?"

She shook her head. "Yeah, Matt, if you're certain that's what you want to do."

"You bet I am."

Chapter 4

I began the countdown. "One, two, three," and then Mary's and my voice belted out, "Puerto Vallarta!" The instant our destination was revealed sharp shooting pains ripped through my stomach. Was it the darn curse again? Or was I just nervous about my first trip with Rita?

Since I felt it was extremely important that Dad witness my reaction to his traveling plans for my sister Mary and I, I put the analyzation of my pain on hold temporarily and glanced over to where he had been standing, but he was no longer there. He had already returned to his recliner. Before I could think things through rationally, my feet brought me straight to his chair where I could display the *I've been deflated* look on my face up close and in his personal space.

As soon as Dad saw my dumb facial expression, his deep throaty laugh filled the 15' x 14' living room. "That's right, Matt. You and your baby sister are traveling to Puerto Vallarta together. Isn't that great?" I was so thrilled, I was left speechless. My father didn't seem to mind, he went right on. "Rita's paired off with you of course, but your sister still needs someone to share the fun with." Then he tapped his rugged chin with his index finger, "and I know just the person."

I didn't give two hoots who Mary was paired off with. It could be a stupid dill pickle for all I cared. I just didn't want to share any of my precious vacation time with her, even the same flight. This trip was supposed to be about Rita and me—the two of us. We hadn't been finding much time for each other, for the past four months, especially Rita, and this was supposed to be our long overdue, non-interrupted quality time together.

While I silently dwelt on my travel mess, my sister sauntered over to Dad's chair, her hips beating to the rhythm of some imaginary native music. "Who did you find to go with me?" she asked politely. My father's lips remained sealed like a clam's. "Come on, Dad, it's only fair that you tell me." When she realized she wasn't getting anywhere, she tried to enlist my help. "Matt, ask Dad to tell me who my traveling companion is."

I flapped my hand in front of me. "No dice." Mary could continue to badger Dad all night; I didn't want any part of this foray. My mind was focused on the sheet of paper in my hand. Somewhere in the fine print it contained the name of Rita's and my accommodations. A deep, suspicious inkling lurked in the far recesses of my brain. There was more than a flight to share with my sister. There it is, *Marriot Hacienda.* Armed with that pertinent detail now, I rudely cut off my sister's interrogation of Dad. "Hey, Baby Sister, where exactly are you staying?"

"Huh?"

Obviously my line of questioning hadn't succeeded in getting Mary's mind off her own problem, so I repeated myself.

Success at last. Fully detached from her previous endeavor at last, she twisted her medium-sized frame my way. "Are you speaking to me?"

"Yup."

"What do you want?"

"I was wondering where you're staying in Puerto Vallarta?" Pow! There it was again. Severe pain shot through me and my stomach flip-flopped. As I quickly clutched my mid-section, I hoped no one noticed how miserable I was.

"Ah, the Marriott—a timeshare thing." Darn it! If I wasn't already clutching my stomach with my hands, I would've slammed my fists on a nearby table. I thought Mary would ask why I wanted to know, but she never did. She was too concerned about her traveling companion. As soon as she was through answering me, she started in on my father again using a different tactic. She leaned into him and wrapped an arm around his shoulder. That's what she always did when she was little and wanted something really bad. "Daddy," she purred, "Why can't you tell me who's traveling with me?"

Poor Dad. Mary was going to continue until she wore him down, I thought, but I was wrong. He quickly lifted her lanky arm off his shoulder, gave her a hug and in a mellow tone said, "Sweetheart, your answer has to wait," and then he pointed to the TV. "Now, please increase the volume on the TV's remote."

Keith, who was ignorant of what just transpired between his father-in-law and sister-in-law, made up for the sudden silence hovering between them now. In his sport's stadium voice, he announced, "Hey, everybody, the games back on. Time to sit down."

The Malone clan instantly obeyed. As I dropped to the spot on the floor by Mary again, I thought how funny it was that when my siblings and I say something around the rest of the family, no one pays any attention, but let an outsider speak his mind and boom, the Malones all fall in line.

Ding dong! Don't get excited. The doorbell noise wasn't another TV commercial. Someone was actually at my folks' front door. Eyes immediately bounced from one person to the next, with shrugs turning them away at each glance. No one seemed to have a clue. Even me. I guess I was still so upset with Dad my brain had temporarily froze over the part about my girlfriend arriving soon.

Mom, the most virtuous among us, was the only one who dared to break the Malone rule of silence. Well, she could. Dad has never bawled her out for talking during a game. "Matt, dear," she said just above a whisper, "you're the closest to the door. See who it is."

I matched the decibels of my mother's voice now as I stood, "Sure," and then I briefly glanced at my watch. That's when it dawned on me, the new arrival had to be Rita. But even if I made the wrong call, I didn't mind missing part of the game—I've never really followed football that closely. I had more important things to do on Sundays and Mondays, like searching through the *Star Tribune* looking for work that was PI-related. My bread and butter.

Chapter 5

"Boy, am I glad you're here," I mouthed quietly to Rita as I swung the storm door out towards the steps to allow her access to the interior of my parents' home. "You're not going to believe what happened about five minutes ago."

Rita gracefully crossed the threshold now. "Ah, let me guess," she whispered back. "The game started?"

Obviously my girlfriend and I weren't on the same wavelength. Of course, I was disappointed but I decided to be polite and follow her line of thought. "Well, that too," and then I leaned into her and greeted her with a light but meaningful peck on the cheek.

"Why, Mr. Malone, thank you for such a warm welcome."

"Your most welcome," I replied, and then I quickly tended to the door before someone in the living room, namely Dad, yelled out a reminder to stop heating the outdoors.

While I was closing the door, Rita began anew. So much for my having the opportunity to straighten out what I was referring to. I'll just have to do it later. "So, who won the toss, Matt?"

I turned to face her again before I spoke. "The Washington Huskies."

Once the tiny interplay of football exchanges stopped, my girlfriend completely clammed up. Maybe she was using the quiet time to mentally prepare for my family. She rarely sees them. Probably wouldn't be a bad idea to keep my mouth shut too at this juncture, I thought. If nothing else, it would give Rita time to sort through her thoughts before entering the lion's den.

While I waited, my eyes silently took in the gorgeous view in front of me. Rita's petite hands stretched out in front of her as she slipped her black leather deerskin gloves off, the ones I gave her for Christmas, and then neatly tucked them into the slanted pockets of her red knee-length wool coat. With that done she now moved on to the coat. Her smooth, creamy hands began to slowly and methodically unbutton it, eventually exposing the casual wear hidden underneath. My girlfriend's body fit her top and pants to a T. *Matt. Your one lucky son of a gun. How did you ever manage to land another beautiful woman the second time around?*

Before I could respond to my own question, the silence surrounding us finally was shattered by Rita as she swiftly bounced back to the sport being watched on TV. "Speaking of football," she said, "when do you think the big boys, the Green Bay Packers, are going to build a new playing field? They keep talking about it, but nothing happens."

"I suppose when the Wisconsin politicians get involved."

My girlfriend was struggling to get her coat off now, so I readily offered my assistance. "Here, Hon, let me help you." I grasped the back of the coat, so her arms could easily slide out of it. With her coat in my arms now, I strolled over to the coatrack and hung it next to mine.

"Thanks,"she said, and then she fluffed her curly, dark chocolate hair to make it more presentable. After the love of my life, a slimly-built woman 5' 4" in height finished fussing with her hair, she started towards the living room where all the action was.

I barely caught her by the elbow before she left me in the dust. "Wait." There were issues that needed to be resolved now, not later, and definitely not in front of my family. "We need to talk in private," I said in a determined tone, and then I pointed to the room to the left of the living room, the kitchen. "Let's go in there."

Rita eyed me cautiously. "All right." Now she shifted her blue wool stocking-covered feet in my direction and flashed her luscious heart-shaped smile at me, exposing her pearly white teeth. The woman, my woman, was definitely in the wrong line of work, I thought. She shouldn't be writing ads for Tuttles and Gray; she should be in them. Why, with that high quality smile of hers and her emerald green eyes, she could convince people to buy a piece of land in Siberia or even the planet Neptune for that matter. Now do you understand why I want her all to myself?

Unfortunately for me, Rita's interest in what I had to share with her dissipated the moment we entered the kitchen. Her sharp emerald orbs swiftly darted from one food item to the next. "Your mother's been hard at it again, hasn't she?" I nodded in the affirmative. Her hand cautiously slid under a sliver of creamy fudge now that had been sitting on a small glass plate with other goodies on the mellow-yellow laminated counter top, and it soon disappeared into her creamy pink mouth. "Oh, my gosh. Her fudge is to die for, isn't it, Matt?"

I grinned. "You got that right, and so are all her other Christmas sweets.'"

My girlfriend glanced at all the treats again, and then she swept her arm across the counter where they were sitting. "How in the world does your mother get all this baking done?"

Forget the baking, I thought. *Don't you know all I want to do is crush you against my chest and kiss that sweet luscious mouth of yours.* With Michael's three kids lurking about though, the kitchen wasn't exactly at the top of my list of places for romancing that certain someone. Darn. Since Rita was still waiting for my reply, I quickly squelched any romantic notions and lamely said, "My mother hires a few elves to come in a couple weeks before Christmas. Isn't that what other women do?"

"I wouldn't know," Rita answered tartly. Whew. I didn't expect that little joke of mine to backfire. And, guess what? My girlfriend wasn't finished with me yet. "I'm never home long enough to bake, Matt. You of all people know that." Oh, she's so truthful. Luckily, that's one of the many things I like about her, probably because I have to lie so much in my line of work. A couple seconds ticked by in awkward silence now. Well, I sure didn't think I had anything to apologize for.

"Ah, perhaps you would like something to drink, Rita?" I said in a pleasant tone, finally breaking the spell.

Those few words warmed the kitchen up quite nicely. Rita immediately reverted to her sweeter side. "No thanks, Honey. Hey, did you have a chance to fix a plate of eats for yourself yet?"

I shook my head to signify *yes* and then quickly offered her a plate. Well, I couldn't afford to get on her bad side again, especially with our big trip coming up so soon. "Take as much as you want," I said, "Everyone else has visited the kitchen at least twice already."

Rita dove into the food with gusto after I gave her the green light. She stopped only once when she noticed something was missing. "Your mother's out of napkins."

Living alone for the past couple years, I've gotten pretty lazy when it comes to acting like a gentleman around the kitchen. Now, however, since I wanted to impress my girlfriend, I left my post near the kitchen sink and searched through the upper cupboards, one by one. Just as I was ready to throw in the towel and give up the hunt, I finally found extra napkins shoved into the corner of a top shelf. Isn't that the way it goes? When you're searching for something, it's always in the last spot you'd expect. I reached in the cupboard now, took the open package of napkins out and set them on the counter.

When Rita's plate was filled to the limit, she glanced up at me and batted her long thick eyelashes. Maybe she wanted to distract me, so I didn't notice how much food she had put on her plate. It didn't work. Her attention getter only threw me for a loop temporarily. Obviously my girlfriend still didn't realize that this guy didn't care how much food she eats. In fact, I actually relished the fact that we both had hearty appetites; it meant when we were married neither one of us would give each other a hard time about grocery bills being too high. I handed Rita a napkin and a set of plastic utensils now. "All right, Matt," she said, "What's on your mind? I know you've been dying to tell me."

My knees were still mighty wobbly from her flirtatious activity, so I braced myself against the counter before sharing. "Ah, yeah, I wanted to tell you about our trip. My dad gave us our travel info before the football game came on."

"Oh, great."

I forced enthusiasm into my voice. "Yeah. We're going to Puerto Vallarta." Okay, the good news is out in the open, on to the crummy part. As my palms began to perspire my throat began to tighten. How will she react? *Best to just get it over with, Matt.* "According to information I just received, Mary's going to Puerto Vallarta, and she's also staying at the same timeshare as us." Now my voice rose sharply. "Can you believe that?"

Rita drew herself next to me. "Ah, actually I can Sweetheart." The heat from our two bodies melding became intense. "There's no need to be upset," she calmly replied. "I knew about the plans, but your dad swore me to secrecy."

My "What?" bounced off the sunflower-colored painted walls. "What are you saying? You've known since Christmas where we were going?"

"Ah Huh." She grabbed my arm now. "Listen, there's no need to get worked up. If it weren't for me, your father would be forking out money for the timeshare too, and he certainly doesn't need to do that."

I was about to grill Rita about her involvement in the timeshare when the kitchen door swung open, and who should appear before us but my sibling, Mary. "Oh, here you are," she said sounding surprised. "Everyone was wondering what happened to you two. You're missing the game—the Huskies already made one touchdown. Well, not right at this minute. The station broke for a commercial."

I ran my hand through my hair. "Another commercial," I said in disgust. "They just had one."

"I know," Mary replied. "They must regulate them so they flash across the screen every ten minutes."

Rita, ever the marketing guru, plunged in, "Gotta sell those products. I'm sure you've heard how exorbitant TV ad time is." Mary pulled out a chair at the table now and sat. Rita and I joined her. "So, Mary, how are you?" Rita asked, probably thankful for the break in our conversation. "Are the little darlings treating you okay this year?" My girlfriend was referring to my sister's second grade students. Mary's an elementary school teacher in a northeastern suburb of Minneapolis.

My sister's thin, short-cropped jet black hair sparkled under the low mounted ceiling light. "So far my thirty students are behaving themselves," she sighed with relief, "but they continue to keep me very busy. Thank goodness for the holidays, huh? Speaking of which, did Matt tell you the three of us are traveling to the same destination for our vacation?"

Rita was slow to respond. "Ah, yes, he just mentioned it, but haven't you forgotten someone?"

Mary looked bewildered. "Who's that?"

"Why, the fourth person," Rita chirped cheerfully, "that friend of yours you've known since childhood."

My sister went ballistic. Her hands jerked wildly in the air as she screeched, "What?"

My girlfriend's orbs immediately bounced from my sister to the floor. "Perhaps I should explain."

"Yes, please do," I hastily begged, worried she might change her mind. "Two of the Malone children have been getting quite the run around from their dear old dad today. Isn't that right, sis?" My sibling's nodding head solemnly sliced the air in agreement.

23

Chapter 6

New Year's Day was over for another year. Thank God. I was totally wiped out no energy left for anything not even my lowly job. Sugar, fats and beer still circulating through my Emerald Isle veins were partially to blame. Then, also kindly stir in a spongy mind on overdrive due to unsolicited Malone clan comments regarding the Huskies-Boilermaker game (Huskies beat the Boilermakers 34-24), along with my father's delicate revelation about who was joining me on my trip, and, of course, added to that mixture was Rita's notorious involvement in above said vacation scheme.

"Crap! What a mess!" I cradled my unshaven face in my Minnesota winter cracked hands. I really didn't want to get out of bed this morning. However, when duty calls, even a sluggish PI must rise from bed at some point in time, especially if he has as demanding a mutt as Gracie. To get my attention, she sometimes clamps her jaws on the cuffs of my pajama top, and at other times she treats her teeth to my feet. But hey, as rascally as she gets, I have to admit she's a great companion. There would be a big hole in my life if she weren't around.

I didn't get my dog the usual way as a pup like most folks do. Gracie, an abandoned one-year-old dog, was brought to the Hennepin Humane Society by a good Samaritan, where she sat for several weeks before I showed up. I only stopped in there to try and get my mind off the untimely death of my wife, Irene, but once I saw the pathetic chocolate colored mutt sitting in a cell made of black metal my resolve began to melt away.

Of course, as soon as Gracie realized she had a captive audience, that made things even worse. She immediately began to put on a spectacular show for me. I didn't clap after her performance though. Instead, I found one of the Humane's volunteers and asked if I could take the dog for a short walk, the worst thing a person can do if you're not shopping for a dog. If any of your friends have gotten their pets from the Humane

Society, you know the rest. You handle the pet for awhile, and then bingo, you make the purchase. But when I'm out for a walk with the dog and people ask how I ended up with her, I never give them the real spiel. I simply state that the fates were more in her favor that day.

Today, Gracie had changed out her usual bugging routine for something new. She jumped over the footboard of my black antiquated double bed and smoothly edged her way up to me just enough, so she now stood smack dab over my reposed body. Unfortunately, I was in direct line with her wonderful doggie breath. "Phewey!" A dental check-up was definitely in order. Too bad it would have to wait. The cost is beyond what's in my wallet these days.

Gracie's stinky breath began to overpower me only after a few seconds. "Get away!" I warned., and then I took my hand and forcefully shoved her furry head to one side. The stubborn mutt stood her ground. Obviously, she came up on the bed for a reason, and she was going to see it through. As she continued to hold her face over mine, she began to claw at the wool blanket that was sheltering me from the unusually cool air in the room. "Ah huh. So that's your game plan. You want me out of bed."

Last night, because my thought process was a teeny bit out of whack due to the amount of beers I'd chugged down, I never gave the extreme temperature drop outside an inch of consideration. Normally when it's going to be in the sub-zero range, I set the apartment thermostat a little above my comfort level of 58 degrees. I know. I know. Fifty-eight doesn't sound comfortable to most people who live in the north country, but hey you gotta remember, I live on the fourth floor of the Foley Apartment Complex, and believe me—heat definitely rises. So, if you know anyone who wishes to take a test run of hell, just send them my way.

I decided to play nice and give Gracie another chance to shove off. Both of my hands were out from under the blanket now and I pressed them firmly against her chest. "Stop playing around, girl. I want you off the bed." Thankfully, she complied this time. With the mutt out of my way now, I slowly threw off the blanket and sheet that had been encasing me, allowing my body time to acclimate to the room.

While still in a prone position, I directed my eyes to the end of the bed where Gracie was now resting her head, and caught her brown pooled orbs studying me like a hawk. "Okay. So I forgot to say thank you."

"Wuff! Wuff!"

"And yes, you'll get a treat as soon as I find some clothes." As soon as those words leaped out of my mouth, the dog got busy. She bolted to the corner of the room where my dirty socks from yesterday were still laying, grabbed them up in her mouth and returned to the bed where she immediately dropped them by my hand.

"Thanks, but I need more than that. Like pants and shirt."

She shook her head from side to side like I was totally confusing her. The slobber that slid from her open mouth sprinkled on to my skin. Who said there was no such thing as a jiffy shower? The unexpected spray of water briefly brought to mind my upcoming vacation. "You're going to miss me, mutt. In eleven days I'm out of here. Then you'll have no one to be ornery to." The mutt ignored my blockbuster comments. She merely dropped her jaw and yawned. "Fine. Be that way, but you better not act like I didn't give you advanced warning when I drop you off at my folks." Gracie immediately snapped her mouth shut.

I swung my muscular legs gingerly off the side of the bed and then to the floor. Once my feet were settled on the carpet, I wandered over to the weeks worth of soiled clothes that were piled by my desk and hadn't quite made it to the laundry hamper in the bathroom yet and searched for something to wear. There had to be something in the heap I could put on. Methodically tossing each piece of clothing into another pile now, I picked through the mess and eventually found a pair of jeans that didn't look too shabby. Well, appearance is everything, right? At least that's what I've been told since birth.

"Pants, socks now the shirt, Malone." I opened the tiny closet in my one and only bedroom and grabbed the shirt that was nearest the door, an awfully faded royal blue sweatshirt from my alma mater, St. Cloud State University, that I just can't seem to let go of. Too much nostalgia perhaps. Beer buddies, Fall bonfires, professors who actually taught you something and old girlfriends that, well, enough said. You know how it is for us men. We can't seem to let go. Some things just linger way, way past their prime.

I tossed the sweatshirt on now, and then I ran my fingers through my hair, just to temporarily straighten out the mess on top of my noggin. Occasionally Margaret Grimshaw, the elderly neighbor who lives across the hall from me, comes calling early in the morning before I've had time to primp myself properly in the bathroom. Now, I glanced at my feet. "The heck with shoes; they can wait." I turned to Gracie. "Come on, girl. It's time for breakfast." That's all the mutt needed to hear. She flew through the bedroom door like she was on fire. So much for waiting for the master.

After Gracie got the Milkbones and I had put a sufficient amount of coffee and calories into my bulging stomach, I found my shoes and was ready to start the day. The mutt and I would head out to our usual location, Loring Park, where she would do her thing and I'd do mine, and then the two of us would once again return home. Of course when the temperature was way below zero, like it was today, we don't really dally too long at the park.

When we finally got back from our brisk morning walk, I took a quick shower and changed into different clothes—more office oriented. Now that the trip to Puerto Vallarta had been finalized and I knew I'd be leaving in less than two weeks time, I figured I'd better drive over to the hole-in-the-wall stucco building on Lowry Avenue that I used for an office and see what was cooking. Perhaps, if I was lucky, there would be a huge batch of phone calls requesting the services of a certain PI. With enough meat on them, I'd make plenty for the trip. Right now the small amount of cash snoozing in my wallet is barely enough to cover four beers and one, possibly two meals down south of the border, even with the difference in currency.

I jerked my winter jacket off the back of the kitchen chair where I had put it when I got home from the walk with the mutt, and then I made my way to the small table near the door and plucked up my key ring.

Gracie had watched while I retrieved my coat, and now she came up alongside me, thinking, I suppose, that we were going out again. I looked into her soulful eyes and gave her a military salute. "All right, Private Gracie, "I said, "you know the drill. You're to stand guard until I return. Remember, napping on the bed is off limits. The canteen, your favorite spot, will be open when I return." Then I popped out and locked up.

To reach the Foley's underground parking five floors below where I kept the Topaz, I could either ride the boring, no Muzak elevator or use my legs. Since the dog and I didn't have a long walk this morning, I opted for the steps. Another good reason for using the steps is that I avoid all the fuss and muss with other tenants in the building. I swear, no one in the building understands the job of a PI, not even Rod Thompson, a tall, lanky man of Norwegian descent who also lives on the fourth floor and happens to work for the FBI. He thinks being a PI is a big joke, that we don't know anything. Although I proved the guy wrong on the Delight Bottling case.

The daily taunts from others in the Foley are just as unreal. "Playing hooky, Malone, huh?" "What are you hitting, the tennis courts or the golf course, today?" "Must be rough having so much time off?" Well, you get my drift.

The basement door slammed shut behind me as I walked out onto the oil-stained concrete floor of the underground parking area. The slots in the tomb-like parking lot are assigned by apartment number, so no one gets to chose the widest berth by the exit doors. Besides, that spot is already reserved for the caretaker of the building. My car was about thirteen parking spots away from where I stood, but I could see it. As usual, the filthy white 1993 Topaz was smushed between two other apartment dwellers' modes of transportation, two black SUVs. How exciting. I don't think the SUVs have ever moved from their spots.

When I got to the Topaz, I barely managed to squeeze between it and the one to the left of it. Of course, getting into the car was going to be even rougher. It's like trying to force a sub sandwich into a toaster. But, as always, I eventually slid in and left the other mega cars in the dust.

In order to make my way to my so called *office* now that I had left the Foley behind, it was necessary to maneuver the Topaz in zig-zag like fashion throughout the downtown area until I reached Highway 65, also known as Central Avenue. From there, it was a straight shot to Lowry Avenue that is with a ton of stoplights in between.

On most of my routine trips to the office, I usually manage to make it through all the traffic lights without having to stop. I don't know if it's the miles per hour thing or not, but on this occasion I wasn't so fortunate.

Traffic was momentarily snarled at one of the intersections, and the light changed faster than I anticipated. Of course, to make matters worse, the cell phone began ringing. Since I didn't want an accident, I stepped on the brakes first. That was a mistake. The phone which had been lazily resting on the passenger seat immediately went airborne. My body lurched forward to catch it, but it was too late. It landed on the floor below my feet.

My cousin once shattered his foot, all because he leaned down, while in a holding pattern, and plucked his spilled mail off the floor of the car. Remembering that and not wanting to repeat the *delightful* incident all over again by another relative, I continued to hold my foot firmly on the brake while I leaned over and retrieved the small phone.

Now that I was accident-free and holding the phone in front of me, I didn't take time to check the number of the caller, like I usually do. Instead, I simply pressed the receiver button. "Matt Malone. How may I help you?"

"Hola! Me llamo Rita," the caller murmured in a soft, sexy voice."

"Well, hello to you too, Rita. So, you're practicing your Spanish. Nice. That means you can do all the talking when we're in Mexico."

"Not all of it, Mr. Malone. You promised to use what Spanish you learned from your friends during your college days. Remember?"

I laughed. "So, I did. I guess I'd better chase over to my folks tonight and search for those bar napkins I saved."

"Very funny."

The light finally changed to green, and I slowly moved forward. "It's nice to hear your voice, sweetheart. I really didn't expect a call from you with you being knee-deep in work."

"I needed a break. I've been gathering marketing data non-stop since seven this morning. Hey, Hon, are you getting as excited about the trip as I am?"

I gazed out the windshield now and stared at the filthy snowpacked mounds running along both sides of the street. "Are you kidding? I can't wait to expose my toes to the warm sands and leave this crappy weather behind."

"Bueno," Rita cooed. "That was the correct response, Mr. Malone. Just wait till you see the neat surprises I've packed for you."

My neck and face suddenly grew warm, and it had nothing to do with the heat in the car. Before I could find out exactly what type of surprises my girlfriend had in store for me, I heard another familiar voice in the background questioning her about where something was. The voice belonged to one of the owners of Tuttles and Gray Marketing firm. "Sorry, Matt. Gotta run. Adios."

"Chao," tumbled from my lips, but I think the line had already gone dead. Disappointed that Rita probably didn't hear me, I pressed the off button and tossed the cell phone back on the passenger seat. Three more blocks to go, and I'd be at work.

Chapter 7

My office isn't what you would call a fancy place. It's old, dilapidated and as small as a single car garage, a stucco hole-in-the wall building which doesn't serve any purpose other than to make some money for its middle-aged owner who has moved on to the sunnier climate of Florida. Even though the building I rent sounds like it's going to crumble when someone snaps their fingers, it offers free parking, and it matches the rest of the neighborhood.

Mail received at the office between the holidays is usually pretty scarce, as could now be seen by the two lone pieces of junk advertisement that had been stuck through the mail slot attached to the wooden door which barely hung on its hinges. I picked the ads up off the floor and tossed them in the overflowing trash can near the entrance door. While I remained bent over, I took the time to scan the floor. The dirty carpet was so worn it was splitting in several spots. A good vacuuming wouldn't make it any worse. "When was the last time I did that?" I asked aloud. Hmm, I couldn't recall.

I was the complete opposite of Miss Sinclair, my charming girlfriend. I never gave a fig about noting exact cleaning moments on a scrap of paper or a calendar. She did though. Had it all written down to the last detail when she washed the inside of her cupboards and shampooed the carpets. Well, as long as she only continues to be seen with Mr. Clean, it's okay with me. Who am I to stand in the way of her relationship with cleanliness. I stood now and strolled over to the massive desk of mine.

Before I turned my attention to the answering machine, I stole a quick look at the enormous amount of junk strewn across my ancient desk. I needed a cheap cleaning lady pronto, but I didn't even have enough coins in my junk jar for that. Besides, what woman in her right mind would want to tangle with my jungle? I quickly swatted the mess away from the message machine, so I could actually see it. It was blinking. Good. That meant there were calls to be heard. Hopefully, there would be something about a short job or two that I could handle before leaving the country.

At the same instant that my left hand clamped around the back of the beat up chair and the right reached out for the message machine, the phone dared to disturb the quietness of the moment.

"Malone's PI business. How may I help you?"

"Yeah," a rough chiseled voice said, "I gott'a talk to Malone."

A second ago, I had eagerly picked up the phone and rammed it against my right temple and ear, but now I switched it to the left side of my face which was much more comfortable. "Sir, you happen to be speaking to Matt Malone."

The man on the other end sounded surprised. "Oh? Sorry, Mr. Malone, I didn't recognize your voice. It's been awhile since I talked to you. This is Freddy Flat. Remember me?"

Without any hint, I didn't, but I still said, "Sure, sure. Freddy Flat. What have you been up to?" It helps make people feel they're important even if their not. You never know when they might use you again.

Obviously, the tone in my voice didn't convince Mr. Flat that I knew him because he now said, "You helped me out of a tiny jam a few years back, and I've carried your card around in my pocket all this time."

I smiled. That was nice to hear. At least my cards were being put to use. Freddy Flat? Freddy Flat? My mind was rewinding a mile a minute. Who was this guy? Ah, yes. Now, I remember. He was a janitor at a Minneapolis high school. The administration thought he was stealing tools and had him canned. I helped prove that he was innocent. "So what can I do for you, Freddy?" I asked, all the while hoping he had money to pay me this time.

"It's like this, Mr. Malone. My friend, Leonard, and I had a bit of a falling out yesterday if you know what I mean." He laughed nervously. "Anyway, this morning, I got to thinking about the stupid things I said to him and decided to pay him a visit and make amends. That's where I am right now."

Not understanding where Freddy was going with his story, I said, "That's nice. So why are you calling me? You should be explaining yourself to your friend instead."

Freddy hesitated. "I would, but there's a slight hitch."

I waited.

"Ah, well, you see, when I got here, Leonard's door was ajar, and he was laying face down on the carpet."

"Is he breathing?" While I waited for the answer, my free hand started sorting through the mess on the desk. One pile to keep—one to toss—one questionable.

"That's the problem in a nut shell. I can't tell. His stomach doesn't appear to be rising or falling. I suppose it would be easier to tell if he had a pot belly." He took a long pause before continuing. "This is one time working out doesn't pay off."

My winter jacket was still on, and I was beginning to get overheated, so I unzipped it. "Have you ever taken a person's pulse?"

Freddy Flat must not have thought my question was appropriate. He inhaled deeply, and then he said, "Heck, no. That's what they pay nurses for."

"Then hang up, Freddy, and dial 911," I shot back.

Freddy's fast reply came off like a sledge hammer hitting its mark. "No way! I ain't doing that. I've been in trouble before. The cops didn't buy my story then, so why the heck would they believe me a second time around?"

"I don't know," I replied rather too harshly. Then I retreated and said, "All right, Mr. Flat, take a deep breath and calm down." I had to think smart. Come up with a solution fast–a man's life hung in the balance. I raked my hand through my hair as if that would give me an idea. "Okay, where are you?" I quizzed and then began to scribble on the back of an envelope as fast as I could. When I finished recording the information, I put my pen down, folded the envelope and placed it in my jacket pocket. "Here's what I want you to do, Freddy. Close the apartment door, and then very carefully turn Leonard over on his back. When you're finished, find a towel and rub your prints off the phone. Can you handle that?"

"Yeah, sure, Mr. Malone. Sure."

"And, Freddy . . . ,"

"Yes?"

"Whatever you do, don't touch anything else. Just sit tight. I'll buzz the apartment twice, so you know it's me. Okay?"

His answer came in a low mellow tone now. "Yup. So How soon can you get here?"

"About ten minutes. I'm leaving right now." Then I quickly dropped the phone in its cradle, zipped up my jacket, spun in the direction of the door and walked out, making sure to lock up before climbing into the car. I don't really know why I bothered to lock the darn door. It wouldn't keep the criminal element out. One swift kick, and they'd be in.

Chapter 8

Freddy told me he was at the Happy Acres apartment complex off of old Highway 8 in New Brighton. That was just a few miles down the road from my office. I could either shoot over to Stinson Boulevard and then get on thirty-ninth and go over to old Hwy 8, or I could get back on Highway 65, take it to 39th and then get on old Hwy 8. Since there were too many traffic lights on Hwy 65, I chose Stinson Boulevard.

Happy Acres, like my office, was in an older part of town too, the newer being closer to the freeway and Highway 694. A friend of mine from college actually lived in one of Happy Acres' buildings for a couple years after graduation in the mid 70's. The complex was built in the early 60's. According to my memory, the outside of the buildings were already marred by time, dirty brown brick structures, black, faded, battered entrance doors and windows hidden by a few overgrown trees and shrubs.

I was on old Highway 8 now and Happy Acres was fast approaching. I signaled with my blinkers and turned left into the first parking lot. It looked as though renters parked wherever they pleased. The only vacant spot I could find, which wasn't a designated one, was between a humongous Oak tree and a huge, ugly green overflowing dumpster, so I parked there. Hopefully it wasn't trash day. Hmm. Apparently an apartment dweller thought the trash bin was for storing furniture not trash. Imagine that. The chair and table left behind were propping the lid up. Not a good idea. If this was a windy day, garbage would be plastered all over the neighborhood by now.

As I stepped out of the Topaz, I took time to survey the grounds systematically. More years of neglect since the 70's had finally taken their toll on the landscape. The once overgrown shrubs were ground to nothingness, and the trees stamped out the sky. The limbs, now pushed to their limits, pressed so tightly against the tenants' windows I expected to hear glass shattering any moment. Obviously, the owners of this complex didn't care two hoots about the property, they were only in it for the money.

I pressed the necessary buttons for apartment 202 twice, so Freddy would know that I had arrived. I already had prepared a story if I ran into anyone in the hall. Just a buddy visiting another buddy.

The buzzer's long horn blasting sound drowned my ear drums as the door let go of its lock mechanism. I immediately grabbed hold of the door handle and moved my body into the main lobby as fast as I could. I wasn't about to listen to that stupid noise any longer than I had to.

This building Leonard lived in was strictly for seniors. A posting on the outer door made that known when I first entered, but other signs in the lobby made you aware of that fact too. For instance, the huge bulletin board near the community room advertised all the senior activities, and a dozen or so walkers were neatly lined up outside the exercise room. The elevator sat idly by, so I hopped on and rode it to the second floor. On the way up I stared at the four bare walls which were covered in heavy quilted padding. I wondered if it was there to protect the elevator or the old timers.

When Freddy Flat gave me the location of Leonard's place, he told me the apartment was on the right, four doors down. I stepped off the elevator now and headed to the right. Supposedly there was a twenty-four inch ceramic statue of a boy in bib overalls and a straw hat standing next to Leonard's door. Yup, there's the statue by apartment 202. I drew up close to the door and wrapped lightly with my knuckles. A PI doesn't want to draw anymore attention to himself than he has to.

The door cracked open barely an inch. "Is that you, Malone?" a gravelly male voice asked from within.

"Yes, Freddy," I confirmed in a confessional manner, let me in."

Freddy, who was dressed in Rustler jeans and a dark blue flannel shirt, stepped to one side and swiftly swung the old wooden door into the interior of the apartment to allow me access. I stepped in cautiously. A PI never knows if a call for help is a set up or not, even if you've helped the caller in the past. It's the same for the police. "Mr. Malone, I'm glad you could get here so fast," he said as he closed the door behind me. Then without any warning he rushed an age-spotted chapped hand towards mine. I grabbed it and pumped it for a second or two.

Since Freddy didn't direct me to Leonard's location, I went straight to the kitchen. I presumed he was lying there because it was closest to his apartment's entrance. My assumption was way off kilter. He wasn't there. I spun around and faced the tall gray haired man who had followed in my footsteps. "Well, where is he, Freddy? You didn't move Leonard did you?"

Freddy Flat's body jerked slightly. "No, of course not. Why would I do that? Now he rerouted me with hand signals. He's down this short hall, in his living room."

As I stood in the doorway of the antiquated room, I felt like I had stepped back in time and had returned to my grandmother's Victorian style house. Two rose colored velvet chairs were separated by a dark walnut end table of which the top was inlaid with light shades of pink marble. Only a Tiffany lamp rested on the table. A grandfather clock stood at the back wall in the corner keeping time. Whoa! My eyes stopped flittering here and there the moment they sighted an item hanging on one of the walls in a gilt-edged frame. If my one and only art class, Introduction to Art, taught me anything it was to recognize pieces of work done by Picasso, Dali and Van Gogh. In this instance, the man who rented this apartment was displaying Van Gogh's *Starry Night. Excellent choice Leonard, even if the rest of your decor is outdated..*

Freddy must've seen the surprised expression on my face when my eyes caught sight of the painting. "You're not the first person to drop their jaw when they see what Leonard has in this room, Malone, but if you visit here long enough you get used to it. My friend was in the antique business."

"Is that so?" I replied nonchalantly as I tucked the information away for future reference. My eyes had lingered long enough on the Van Gogh, it was time to move on to the rest of the contents in the room, including Leonard. Ah, there he is. The supposed victim was laying smack in the center of the living room.

I strolled over to his lifeless body, dropped down on my knees and lowered my head. In a good position now, I placed my palm between the man's mouth and nostrils to check to see if he was still breathing. He was. I turned to Freddy for a brief moment and said, "Air's getting through." Unfortunately there wasn't any decent airflow around me. The garlic odor being expelled from Freddy's mouth about killed me on the spot.

"That's a good sign, right, Mr. Malone?"

"Ah, yes." Now I resumed my interest in Leonard. I pushed his left sleeve up on his charcoal colored knit shirt to check his pulse rate. While I held my fingers around the old man's wrist and counted, my eyes carefully examined his almost bald head. "He's got a knot the size of a quarter on the right side of his head."

Freddy leaned in for a closer look. "Where?" I pointed to the swelling. "Well, he didn't have that a while ago." I'd hoped Freddy would return to his previous stance after gazing at the lump on his friend's head, but he didn't, he steadfastly remained in his hunched position. And now, garlic stench was filling every available pore in my head. "Do you think someone broke in and tried to rob him?" With that said, he straightened his body and pointed to the painting I had been admiring just a few minutes before. "Knowing Leonard, he probably never had that picture insured."

I glanced at the picture briefly, and then I looked in Freddy's direction again and wondered why I wanted to punish myself even more. "Has your friend done anything since we spoke on the phone?"

"Like what?"

"You know, try to move or speak?"

Freddy rubbed his mostly gray, short cropped bearded chin. "No, sir, he hasn't even moved as much as a toe, but once or twice he made a bunch of garbled noises. I couldn't make them out."

I pushed my hair back off my forehead. "From what I've seen, I don't think anyone tried to rob your friend, Freddy. Nothings scattered about, no drawers have been rifled through, and the picture on the wall appears to be untouched. More than likely Leonard just had a dizzy spell and fell. He probably would've been all right if the coffee table hadn't gotten in his way and knocked him out cold."

Just as I completed my diagnosis, the unconscious seventy-something man began to stir. I immediately removed my hand from his wrist. "Take it easy, Leonard," I warned. "You've got a nice lump on your head."

Freddy's friend stared at me for a second. Then he lifted a hand to his head, felt for the swelling and said, "Who the heck are you? Did I forget about some meeting?"

"My name's Matt Malone," I rapidly replied as I began to lift the roughly 180-pound man off the floor by myself. "I've never met you before but I understand you know the guy standing by your Van Gogh painting."

Leonard Post tried to assist me in getting himself off the floor, but he wasn't able to. "Yeah, I know him, but we're not speaking to each other right now." Then he sliced the air with a couple expletives even this ex-service guy never heard before.

Freddy ignored his friend's childish outburst and swiftly came to his rescue. "Here, Malone, let me help," and then he bent over, grabbed Leonard's other arm and assisted him to his feet.

Once I was sure Leonard's feet were firmly planted on the living room carpet, I let Freddy guide him to the couch.

There was too much silence in the room. All I could hear was the ticking of the grandfather clock, but this PI could fix that. "Well, Leonard," I said, "maybe you'll change your mind about speaking to Freddy after you've heard what he has to say."

"I doubt it," the man said grumpily. "There's nothing he can say that will ever, ever change my mind."

"You old bear," Freddy snorted. "I'm going to explain whether you like it or not, and you aren't going to stop me," and then he plopped himself on the couch too. "You have no idea why I'm here."

Leonard crossed his arms. I think if he'd had earplugs he would've inserted them at that moment.

Freddy didn't let his friend's rude behavior deter him. "I came over here this morning to apologize for my behavior yesterday."

"Save your words," Leonard said in an angry tone, "You're lying. You've never ever apologized for anything in all the years I've known you. The word apology isn't in your vocabulary."

I swiftly interrupted. I didn't want to listen to this battle any longer. "Believe it or not, Leonard, Freddy told me the same story, so I'm thinking he's probably on the up and up." Perhaps if I left the room and gave the two old guys time alone, they might resolve their issues. The kitchen seemed the most obvious place to retreat to, not too close to the living room so the men thought they had their privacy and yet not that far out of range that I couldn't overhear their conversation.

Freddy gently punched his friend's arm. "You old geezer. Do you realize how lucky you were that I came by when I did?"

"And, why's that?"

"I found your apartment door wide open when I got here. That really threw me. As many times as I've come here, you've never left your door open for anything, even if the apartment is stuffy. But I just couldn't get myself to call out the rescue squad quite yet. Good thing too. I would've looked pretty silly. I said your name a couple times but you didn't answer, so I just assumed you were visiting a neighbor.

"Figuring you'd be back shortly then, I didn't think you'd mind if I hung out in your entryway. I wasn't about to leave here without first apologizing to you. After ten minutes slipped by though, and you still hadn't appeared, I finally flipped. Something was wrong. You once mentioned you aren't long-winded with your neighbors. So I made my move. No stone was going to be left unturned. I found you in here on the floor, out cold. Crap, Leonard! I thought you'd gone to greener pastures and I'd never have a chance to apologize."

The apartment owner sighed loudly. "Boy, let a person take one little fall, and everyone thinks it's over."

Freddy's serious tone increased in intensity. "Friend, if you had found me the way I found you, you would've been scared senseless too. I know you would. My gosh! You were on your stomach. When a person's in that position it's a little hard to tell whether they are breathing or not, and it didn't help that I don't know a fig about finding a pulse or giving CPR. Luckily, Mr. Malone, here, helped me out of a jam once before, so I called him."

Now that Freddy had finally gotten to the part about my being there, I decided to rejoin the two elderly gents. When I left the kitchen, I brought a glass of water and some aspirin I'd found in one of Leonard's cupboards. I figured he might appreciate some pain killer. "Here, Leonard," I said as I handed off the water and the headache medicine to him, "these should help."

Leonard received what I offered with a slight smile, "Thanks, but I'd rather have a shot of bourbon." He slowly bent his head back, tossed the pills in his mouth and then washed them down with the water. When his glass was finally empty, he set it on the table in front of him.

I remained standing on the opposite side of the coffee table while I questioned Leonard about what had happened. "What's the last thing you recall?"

Leonard brought his thin boney hand to his forehead. "My bedroom's so jammed with antique pieces I figured I'd take a few of the items down to the storage area." He moved his hand slowly across his head searching for the lump. "I opened the apartment door first. That way I only had to pick up the furniture once instead of twice. Then I came in here to grab the storage keys out of the desk over there, but as you saw, I never made it that far." He suddenly pulled his hand away from his head and flung it towards the floor. "This damn throw rug tripped me up." The rug he was referring to jetted out about six inches on each end of the coffee table. That was enough for anybody to take a tumble. "I'm taking that thing up and never using it again. I don't care what it's worth."

Freddy got off the couch now, came around the coffee table and clamped his hand gently on my shoulder. "Mr. Malone, I gotta tell you, you are one heck of a PI. You saved my friend and helped me out of a jam once again," and then he released his hand from my shoulder.

"What do you mean I helped you? You helped yourself," I said. "You were smart enough to call me, weren't you?"

Freddy snickered. "Yeah, right. Hey, Malone, would you mind doing one more small favor for me?"

"What's that?" I asked, not sure I wanted to hear what Freddy needed or to help him with anything else for that matter.

"Please," he begged softly, "don't tell Leonard what I really thought happened to him."

Leonard leaned his narrow shoulders against the back of his antique couch. "I suppose you thought I had gone on a drinking binge and passed out, right?"

I laughed. "You're not even in the ballpark, Leonard." Then I hastily explained. "He thought someone had broken in and tried to steal your Van Gogh." Leonard eagerly displayed what he actually thought of that tidbit. It was the exact response I expected from him. "I didn't have the heart to tell him it's only a copy, not the original."

Freddy smacked his hand against his leg. "What? You're pulling my leg, Malone, right?" I didn't respond, so he turned to his friend for an answer. "Then why do you always tell me how expensive the art piece is?"

Leonard laughed. "Well, it is—just not this one."

"You mean you have two of them?" Freddy asked.

"No, of course not," Leonard swiftly replied.

"Freddy," I interrupted, "the original isn't anywhere around here. If you want to see it you'd have to fly to Amsterdam. It's housed in the Van Gogh Museum." I wandered over to examine the Van Gogh painting again. "Whoever did this picture knows a thing or two about painting though."

"You bet he does," Leonard jumped in. "His father is a professor of art at one of the local colleges."

"Impressive. So where's this kid's studio? I'd like to have him paint a Van Gogh for me sometime if he doesn't ask too much."

"Have you ever seen the ads on TV and in the newspaper for the starving artists sales?" I shook my head up and down. "I wish they were held more frequently, but they only take place twice a year at selected hotels in Bloomington. Anyway, that's where I met the young fellow. His works are so close to the originals I was certain he must be an art major."

"Isn't he?" I asked.

"Heck, no. The kid said he only paints when the mood strikes him. His major is in chemical engineering. Go figure."

"Do you have any idea how I can reach him?" I asked.

"Of course," he quickly replied and then pointed to his dark roll-top desk I took a bunch of his business cards thinking I might want to pass them around to some antique associates of mine. They're in the middle drawer, the ones bundled with a red rubber band."

"Stay where you are, Leonard," Freddy insisted. "I'll get one for Mr. Malone," and then he walked over to where they were stored. Just as he opened the drawer, his friend's portable phone came to life. It was sitting on the upper portion of the desk.

Leonard quickly glanced at his wristwatch. "Freddy, will you get that? I'm sure it's my daughter. She checks on me once a day."

Freddy quickly slipped me a card and then picked up the phone. "Hello."

My fingers stung as soon as I touched the artist's contact card. What the heck? Then my stomach did a somersault. Premonitions–curses? At this point I didn't care what they were called. Enough is enough. Just be gone! I jammed the card in my jacket pocket and left.

Chapter 9

I felt a lot better by the time I got back to the Topaz. Maybe the dreaded curse wasn't the problem after all. Indigestion was to blame. Come to think of it, I was rushed earlier this morning, so perhaps my breakfast never had a chance to settle like it should've.

Now that I was inside the car, I turned the key in the ignition and allowed the car a few minutes to warm up. While I waited, I fiddled with the radio, searching for the weather station. In Minnesota, one never knows from one moment to the next what's about to descend on us. We could get torrential rains, a tornado or even a blizzard.

86.8 AM finally had what I was looking for. "South Dakota has been hit by a major snowstorm, and it looks as though it may move across the southwest and central area of Minnesota by tomorrow morning."

I ran my extremely dry hand across my bristly, one-day-old unshaven chin. "Crap!" I had planned to run a lot of errands tomorrow. The car was more than toasty now, so I backed it out of its makeshift parking spot and returned to the office. I still had to check the messages on my answer machine. Freddy's emergency phone call had kept me from that. Maybe, just maybe, someone somewhere needs a little assistance.

Once I entered the office, I charged straight through the clutter on the floor and massive desk to get to the answering machine, and then I pressed the *play* button. "First saved message from ten a.m. December 31st, 'Oops,' a very high pitched, Betty Boop style voice said, 'I thought I was calling the cleaners. Sorry.' Second message, twelve o'clock p.m. 'Yeah, hi Larry,' the deep masculine voice said. 'This is Mark, your neighbor. Give me a call when you get home, will yeah? I've got a leaky pipe under the kitchen sink again'."

I hastily mumbled under my breath,"Good grief," and then "What next? A joker calling to ask if my refrigerator's running, and if so I'd better catch it." The screwy messages I'd heard so far made me wonder why I even bothered to have a message machine hooked up to the phone. "Third message, December 31st, five o'clock p.m. 'I've got a problem here. Gas seems to be disappearing from my fleet of vans. The cops can't help. Not enough to go on and no extra men to spare. My name is Jake Ballad. You can reach me at (612) COFFEES.' There are no more new messages."

Now, there's a case that could make life bearable, especially if my client feels inclined to toss in a couple bags of free coffee to boot. No bombs, no guns, and no messing with angry husbands, a pretty easy job. I slipped my jacket off and slung it over the back of the chair that was residing by my desk. Since I've never been called upon to figure out what's happened to a tank of gas before, I didn't have a clue how long a project like that could last, but there was one thing I was certain of, it was going to be tough catching a thief who was randomly stealing gas from vans. Heck, the guilty party may have left the vicinity for better pastures already. I mean, who'd be that stupid to repeat the same thing over and over in an area that's heavily traveled. I ran my fingers through my hair. Yup, unless other people in the area are having gas stolen from their tanks, it's going to be darn hard for this PI to pinpoint the culprit.

Being desperate for any type of business at this juncture, I wrote Ballad's number down and then pushed it aside. Do I bother to respond or not? I shoved my hands in my pant pockets and allowed the loose coins to slide through my fingers as I wrestled with the question a while longer. The dark, ugly square clock on the wall in front of my desk was adding to the confusion. The big hand said, "Call the guy," and the small one said, "Don't bother."

Would I resolve the problem before I left on my trip? Probably not. Would I get paid if I solved the case? More than likely, yes. Ballad sounds like he has a solid business, but would he mind the spread of case time? I didn't know, and I wouldn't know until I called him.

Reluctantly, I reached for the phone and began dialing. "Yeah, hi, Mr. Ballad, this is Matt Malone. You left a message for me concerning stolen gas."

"Ah, yes. Mr. Malone, I'm glad you got back to me. As I mentioned in my message—the cops aren't able to follow through."

Now, just because I was on the phone didn't mean I didn't know how to multi-task. I can multi-task with the best of them. While one hand held the phone, the other shuffled things around on the desk. "I was wondering if I could stop by your office, say around five tonight? Or is that too late?"

Jake Ballad shot back full blast, "Not at all. I don't lock up until six."

Chapter 10

Jake Ballad's coffee business was about fifteen blocks north of my so called hole-in-the-wall office. He said it sits on the corner of Highway 65 and 37th Street Northeast. That's exactly where the boundaries of Minneapolis proper and the suburb of Columbia Heights begin to blur. Of course, the most efficient way to get there is to take Highway 65 even though it means getting caught up in rush hour traffic, squished between other motorized vehicles, and getting high on who knows what deadly fumes. Supposedly, those escaping the back of a bus are among the worst to breathe in. Which reminds me, there's another nice perk about my business location. At the end of the day, I get to head south into downtown on an almost empty highway while the rest of the working class drives bumper to bumper back to the burbs.

In my youth, I used to hang out in Ballad's neck of the woods. A couple blocks from his business on the other side of the street was the Heights Theater and a bowling alley. The theater, which was built in 1926 by Arthur Gluek, Gluek Brewery heir, was one of the most popular places to be on weekends and still is. Usually when my buddies and I went, we took in a war movie or saw the latest Disney flick.

The bowling alley held many fine memories too. In sixth and seventh grade, long before most girls were allowed to date, the guys and I would arrange to meet them there. Their folks never had a clue. Mary Jane was merely bowling with Susie.

A person couldn't miss Jack Ballad's coffee on wheels office even if he wanted to. A 4' by 3' sign displaying a coffee pot pouring liquid into a coffee cup was attached to a 24' metal pole. The intersection light turned green, and I swiftly pulled onto the property for Java to Go and immediately saw Ballad's vans, six altogether, lined up like ducks in a neat little row. Obviously this coffee business was booming. I parked my duck, the Topaz, alongside the bigger ducks and marched inside.

The building's lobby didn't have much to offer other than the strong rich aromas of coffee beans waiting to be ground somewhere in another room. No plants. No painted walls. And no pictures whatsoever. The black and white checkered linoleum floor just led to three gray metal card chairs that were parked by the lone window nearest the door and to a small counter set into the wall structure opposite the entrance. The room was totally void of customers. There was only one extremely exhausted looking, tall middle-aged man positioned on the other side of the counter and he had made immediate eye contact with me when I strolled in..

"Hi, can I help you?"

"Yeah, as a matter of fact you can," I replied, and then I slipped a hand in the back pocket of my pants, pulled out my wallet and handed him a business card.

After the man with brown crew-cut hair carefully examined my card, he offered me a strong hand, and I mean strong. His body was beefed like a football player's. There's no way I planned to ever meet him in a dark alley. "Nice to meet you, Mr. Malone. I'm Jake Ballad, owner of Java to Go." With our initial greeting out of the way now, Ballad stepped out from behind the stainless steel counter and pointed to the wooden chairs at our disposal. "Have a seat."

I unzipped my jacket and slung it over the back of a chair I'd selected, but before I could plant my derriere in it, I needed to find a new home for the multitude of coffee magazines littering the seat. I eyed the window ledge I'd seen when I first walked in, it ran behind my chair. A perfect spot to relocate them. There. Now, I just had one more thing to get out of the way before I riddled Ballad with questions. I poked my hand into my shirt pocket and whipped out a pen and a pocket-sized notepad. Yes, you heard me right. Notepad. I know there's more efficient ways of gathering info, so please don't waste time lecturing me. A palm pilot or other gadget may be great for you, but this PI still prefers the archaic methods the best. "Mr. Ballad, exactly how many entrances are there to your lot? I didn't get a chance to see if there was an alley running behind the building yet."

"There are three ways of getting in here," he answered. "One's through the alley. Another is off 37th." He cupped his chin with his hand now, "And then, of course, there's the one parallel to the building on Highway 65."

"The vans are parked out front tonight. Is that where you normally keep them?"

Ballad tilted his head in my direction and then crossed his arms. "No, not usually. It's more convenient to keep them around back where the guys load up their deliveries, but once I discovered someone was taking the gas, I thought it would be better to keep the vans out front, in the open. With non-stop traffic along the Hwy 65 corridor until late evening, I felt it was less likely there would be a repeat performance."

I quickly jotted a note to myself and then shot-off another question. "When exactly did you change the parking routine?"

"About a week ago, right after I reported the second incident, and the police told us there wasn't anything they could do for us."

"Did they give you a reason why they couldn't?"

"Apparently, there's a shortage of cruisers for the area, and they can't afford foot patrol."

I thought of all the crimes committed in other communities recently, and that's basically what cops in those neighborhoods said. "Makes sense. So how many men do you have working for you?"

Jake scratched his long thin nose. "Three at the moment. Mac Dougal, my fourth man, quit about three weeks ago. Said it was due to his wife's health. He's her only caregiver. I haven't had a chance to replace him yet."

Check to see if Dougal's reason for quitting was legitimate, I wrote. "And what about your other employees?" I continued.

"Well, there's my brother, his son, and a neighbor of mine."

I stretched my legs out in front of me. "Heard any of them say they are short on cash?"

"No, not that I can recall. Of course, while I'm here I don't spend time chewing the fat with the other men. Paperwork and phone calls keep me hopping, and the guys are busy with their deliveries. If you talk to them, you'll find out I run a tight ship. They're expected to be on the road by eight a.m. and be back around five p.m."

My eyes left Ballad's body for a moment and journeyed south to survey my grungy tennis shoes. It looked like my left toe was starting to wear a hole through the leather upper. Better buy a new pair of shoes before the trip too. With what money, pray tell? *You can charge it, Matt. You have a full month before the bill arrives in your mailbox.* I settled my eyes back on Ballad now. Not much to go on from what he told me so far, I thought to myself. Oh, sure, there's always the possibility of a disgruntled employee, but right now, the case feels more like someone's strapped for cash. "Here's what I think, Mr. Ballad. Someone needs a quick infusion of money. Either an employee or an outsider. At this time, I'm not ready to point fingers at any of your workers."

"Good," Ballad said in an even tone. "I'd like to think I can trust the men who work for me, especially since two of them are close relatives. So, what do you think, Malone? Are you interested in doing some work for me?"

"Well, your offer sounds more interesting than chasing down a deadbeat dad. The only thing is you've caught me at a rather bad time."

Deep wrinkles formulated on Ballad's forehead causing his eyebrows to almost fly off his face. "Oh? How's that? All of your time being consumed by a huge case?"

I waved his assumptions off. "Nah, nothing like that. I'm going on vacation in a week and a half, so it doesn't leave much time for me to keep on eye on your place."

Jake Ballad suddenly yawned. "Sorry. I got up earlier than I usually do. Had to drive my wife to the airport this morning. Good thing it's almost time for me to close." He stood now so I followed suit.

"No need to apologize," I said standing in front of him now. I always had a hard time getting up earlier than my normal routine called for.

Obviously Ballad liked my response, he grinned. "Look, Malone, don't be concerned about your vacation. I'll take whatever time you can put into the matter. Heck, maybe your watchful eyes over the next week will be all that's necessary to scare the person off permanently."

"Let's hope so," I said, already sensing that the job would take more than a week.

Chapter 11

I never thought to look at the time on my watch when I left Jake Ballad's business, but that didn't matter because my stomach told me all I needed to know. It had been begging for food the past fifteen minutes. To me that meant it was somewhere around six o'clock, my supper time. Shoot! I never took any meat out of the freezer. I guess tonight's meal will be another memorable one, like grilled cheese or peanut butter and jelly. But which of the two? I know, I'll just let a tossed coin make the decision for me, you know the way it does before a football game begins.

Now that I knew how my so-called evening meal was going to be selected for me, I wondered how the mutt's alarm clock was doing. Probably not much better than mine, and if that's the case—look out apartment. When Gracie doesn't get fed at the time she thinks she's supposed to, she's a bear. On nights when I've arrived home even just a few minutes late, I've found all the wastebaskets overturned and shreds of this and that dragged into various rooms of the apartment. Sometimes it's actually days before I find the unusual presents she's left behind for me. Such a nice dog. Since I didn't have wings to arrive home any faster than I could, I just hoped Gracie had contained herself and not done any major damage to the place this time.

Too tired to take the steps up to the apartment when I got back to the Foley, I hopped on the elevator at the garage level. Lucky for me, no one else was around. That meant I had a few extra moments of peace before facing the mutt.

The ride up was too swift, and before I knew it, the elevator door slid open for the fourth floor. I dragged myself into the hallway now, listened for a second until the elevator took off to another floor, and then I spun my weary body in the direction of my abode.

An elderly woman's voice rang out before my feet barely had time to leave their imprints on the ugly hallway carpet. "Ciao, Matt." So much for being by myself till I met the mutt, I thought.

I studied the hall where the cheerful voice came from and quickly framed my mouth with a smile. The woman was standing between my apartment and her own. "Oh, hello, Mrs. Grimshaw. I didn't expect to find you out here. You're usually eating supper by now."

"That's true. So where have you been, young man? This is the second time I've popped over to your place tonight."

"Really?" I ran my hand through my hair. "Well, I just finished getting info for a new case that I took on today."

The nonagenarian rubbed her small aged-hands together excitedly. "Oh, how interesting. Come for supper, and you can spill the beans."

Did she just say supper? Alleluia! No sandwich tonight. Of course I had planned to start my surveillance at Ballad's place as soon as I devoured whatever feast I ended up preparing, but I guess I could go a little later. I mean, who in his right mind is going to be stealing gas at seven p.m.? Besides, I'd be crazy to turn down a home-cooked meal just to eat something thinly spread on two dry slices of bread. "Okay," I said, hoping I didn't sound too eager to devour her homemade cooking. "I'll just get Gracie situated and be right over."

"All right, Matt," the elderly woman said as she slowly shuffled back to her apartment. "I'll see you in a few minutes."

***

Before I even stepped foot in Margaret's apartment, I looked and listened for any evidence of Petey. He's usually in the living room sitting on the back of the couch, talking to the TV. The parrot and I don't see eye to eye, so I breathe a little easier when he's not around. My dislike for the bird stems back to when I was in grade school and a friend of mine convinced me to hold his friendly parrot and the darn bird bit deep into my arm. Since then, I stay as far away as possible from any birds held in captivity.

Since I didn't hear or see Petey, I figured it was safe to go in, and so I headed straight to the heart of a home, the kitchen, where I knew I would find my neighbor. "Smells good, Margaret. What did you fix for supper tonight?" I asked as I continued to sniff the delicious aromas filling the room. "Another great Italian dish from your homeland?" My stomach started growling again. I tried to hide the noise.

I guess I didn't have to be concerned. Margaret didn't budge. She was too involved in her own thing, continuing to hover over her stove, tending to a huge kettle. I didn't know how long she'd stay that way. I suppose it all depends on what she's got cooking. I watched as the steam escaped the pot now and floated towards the ceiling. "Yes, it's an Italian, meal," she finally said, "but not one of my family recipes. I hope you don't mind that I borrowed another one of Mama D's instead."

Mrs. Grimshaw may be in her nineties, but that didn't stop her from dabbling in classes of all sorts, including cooking, and believe me, this neighbor was very appreciative of her culinary skills. "Are you kidding? After all these years of living near you, you should know that I like eating anything Italian, no matter who came up with the idea." Anxious to eat, I now turned my attention towards the dining room. "I see the table is already set. Is there anything I can carry to the table for you, Margaret?"

When she finally turned away from the stove to face me, her rose-patterned apron flapped in the gentle breeze she created. "Hmm, let's see. You could grab that bowl of mixed salad greens and the basket of dinner rolls sitting by the sink."

"Okay." I took the required steps needed to reach the items and then carried them to the dining room table. Once I had completed that task, I said, "That's done. Anything else I can bring in here?"

"Not that I can think of, Matt. Thank you. Why don't you just sit down. I'll be right there. I promise." Then Margaret focused all her attention on what was still in the pot on the stove.

"All right." I felt uncomfortable as I pulled a black lacquered chair away from the dining table and sat. Being from the old school as far as manners are concerned, I like to wait for the hostess to sit before I do, but when in Rome, you do as the Italian woman commands. "Oh, Margaret, I forgot to ask where Petey is? Is he here, or has he been loaned out for mating purposes again?" My hand automatically stretched for the bowl containing the salad mixture. Quickly realizing what I was doing, I put my hand back on my lap. It's hard waiting for the chef when food's already staring you in the face.

After two minutes passed, Margaret left the kitchen and joined me. She entered the dining room rather slowly. I assumed so as not to spill anything since she hadn't mentioned trouble with her legs. Margaret's had a lot of health problems over the years, but the soreness of her legs is usually due to Senior Mega Mall excursions. "Petey's not feeling too good so I put him in his cage in the back bedroom." Standing at the table now, she carefully set the mixture of meat and vegetables down next to my elbow. "Buon appetito."

"Thanks." I raised my water glass above my head. "The same to you." Then I hastily added, "To Petey's speedy recovery." Yes, I don't like the elderly woman's parrot, but I knew he was as important to her as Gracie was to me. Margaret finally approached the chair she was going to sit in, so I stood and pulled her chair out for her.

The tiny whitish-gray haired woman sat, and then I helped move her closer to the table. "Always such a gentleman, Matt." She shook her cloth napkin and spread it across her aproned lap. "Thank you. By the way, do you like veal? I never thought to ask."

"Lady," I said as I plopped myself back down, "I eat anything that comes out of your kitchen."

My hostess let go of one of her childish laughs before she passed the dressing to me. "Here, Mama D recommends this dressing for the salad. It's just vinegar and oil."

I took the glass cruet that was offered, drizzled the dressing over the mixture of greens, and then gave the cruet to Margaret. With that out of the way, I hungrily began to fill my fork with some greens, ready to munch away. Luckily, right before any salad actually had a chance to land on my tongue, I caught sight of a vegetable I wasn't quite sure of. "Ah, these green sliced vegetables don't look like the cucumbers I usually eat. Are they a new variety or something else?"

Margaret's olive green eyes danced for me as she asked a question of her own, "Exactly how often do you purchase fresh vegetables, Mr. Malone?"

"Rarely," I replied sheepishly. "The few times that I buy tomatoes, peppers, carrots or lettuce, I immediately toss them in the fridge's vegetable crisper never to think of them again, that is until a month or two passes and I suddenly have a craving for them. That's when I open the crisper and discover a drawer full of vegetables too disgusting to describe."

"Well, Matt, this green vegetable is very fresh, and it happens to be a zucchini, not a cucumber."

"A zucchini? Really? I didn't think you could get zucchini around here this time of year."

Margaret sighed heavily. I think she was contemplating giving up on me. "Zucchini, like other vegetables, is flown in from other countries during the winter months."

I felt like such an idiot that all I could say was, "Oh," and then I finally sampled the salad. "Mmm. This is really tasty, Margaret. I bet Rita would like this too. Hey, how about sharing the recipe with me, so I can fix it for her sometime?"

"Sure, Matt. I can do that."

After I took my second bite, I used my fork to casually point at the book resting by Margaret's left hand. So what's the scoop on the crossword puzzle book? I've never seen you leave one out while you're entertaining."

The elderly woman pushed a few, short stray hairs out of her eyes. "I'll be honest with you, Matt. I had an ulterior motive for inviting you here tonight. I'm stumped on one of the answers. I thought maybe you could help me out after supper." She picked up the puzzle book and opened it to a particular page.

I dropped my fork back in my salad bowl. "Me? The queen of crossword puzzles actually thinks I can solve a puzzle? You're joking, right? I haven't done a crossword puzzle in years. I get too frustrated."

"Oh, I bet you can figure this one out, Matt," my neighbor said as she closed her thick book. "Why, I believe you're the key."

Me, the key. Yeah, right. She's barking up the wrong tree for assistance this time, I thought. I picked up the platter of meat and vegetables and spooned an average portion on to my plate. "Ah, come on, Margaret, you've got so many intellectual friends, who'd be much more beneficial to you than me." Now I rested the platter on the table again.

My neighbor ignored her uneaten salad still sitting in front of her and gave me that *distressed damsel* look. Probably acting again, but I'll never know. She's gotten quite good at it. "But I don't need anyone else, Matt. I know you're the right person for the task."

Since I don't like to argue with elderly people—something to do with my compassion gene, I guess, I said, "I'm glad someone around here has got such confidence in me." Those magic words brightened Margaret's face considerably. Now that she appeared to be in a better frame of mind, I continued. "Remind me to take a look at it before I leave, okay?"

"I will," she answered, and then she took the half-empty platter of food sitting between the two of us and scooped a small portion of it onto her plate. "So, how's your lovely girlfriend, Rita?"

Chapter 12

"Good," I replied in a normal voice, and then it went sour from there, "now that our vacation is almost here." I lifted my teacup to my lips. Maybe the taste of tea would remove the irritation I was feeling.

"Hmm? Strange how you say that. Do I detect a little trouble brewing in paradise?"

I put my cup back on its saucer, and then I brought my left fist to my mouth and coughed lightly. "Ah, no. No, of course not. Well, not exactly."

Margaret lifted her tiny face so both of ours were in direct line with each other. Which is it, Matt? You know you can always speak openly with me."

"It's just . . ." I rubbed my hands on my pant legs. "It's just that Rita and I don't seem to find the time to get together like other couples do. Her bosses keep increasing her work load. Everything has to be done *pronto.* They keep telling the employees, 'If we want our firm to remain at the top of the pecking order, we have to put in the time. Make sacrifices.' That philosophy is plain crazy. Everyone has to have some time to themselves in order to remain sane."

My neighbor dabbed her almost invisible lips with her soft, wine colored napkin. "I agree, of course it is. I can easily empathize with the many young people in their forties and fifties who are so stressed out and yearn for the *good old days* when Sunday was actually a day of *rest.*" Now she moved her fingers towards the top of her head and rested them there. "If only we could turn back the hands of time."

"I'm all for that. The day they write a petition to turn back time let me know. I want to be first in line to scribble my name down." I brought my hands back to the table and encased my teacup in them.

Margaret laughed softly, and then she slowly pulled her fingers away from her forehead. "Don't worry; I'll let you know." The petite Italian woman picked up her teacup and let it gracefully skim her thin delicate lips as she said, "I'll be right behind you, mister."

"All right," and then I lifted my teacup in the air. "Say, speaking of turning back the clock, did I ever tell you where Rita and I are going on our vacation?" I took a sip of tea and set my cup back down.

Margaret nodded her head vigorously. "You did—Mexico, but if I remember correctly, you hadn't a clue where in Mexico you'd be going. Have you finally found out?"

"Yup. My father told me on New Year's Day."

"So tell me, Matt, what's your destination?"

"Puerto Vallarta," I happily announced, as my last forkful of salad dangled in front of my mouth.

"I've heard it's supposed to be a lovely vacation spot. One of my garden club friends told me the temperature there ranges between 80 and 90 degrees year around. Is that really true, or was she pulling my leg?"

"Nope. She knew what she was talking about. The other night when I searched a particular Internet site, I found the same information. Puerto Vallarta also happens to be one of only three destinations that's sunny three-hundred days of the year.

"Imagine that. I suppose Hawaii is one of the other areas?"

"Yup, and Sante Fe, New Mexico." I took a bite of veal now. It was cooked to perfection.

"I was in Sante Fe with my husband once. A nice place to vacation. You know, after my husband Joseph passed away, I used to think about moving to a much warmer climate, like Florida, New Mexico or even Arizona. There were no children to keep me here. As you know, we were never blessed with any. But I have so many wonderful friends here in Minnesota, and I realized I would miss them terribly."

"Yeah, that's the problem in a nutshell, isn't it?"

Margaret looked sullen. "Yes, it is." Then she turned her attention to the food she'd brought to the table. She reached for some veal, stabbed it, placed it on her plate and cut it up. "Speaking of problems, when I met you in the hall earlier, you mentioned a new case. What's that all about?"

"Oh, not much." Ever since I've known Mrs. Grimshaw, which has been several years now, she's been interested in the work that I do. Being an excellent listener, I frequently bounce ideas off her. Why, if she had a car to get around in and was a little spryer, she'd make a great sleuth partner for someone. Even though I know she won't repeat what I say, I still like to speak in generalizations. My clients' confidentiality is of the utmost importance to me. There's nothing on this earth that's going to make me lose their trust. I took another sip of green tea now before I continued. "Someone's siphoning gas out of cars."

"Yes, I know that."

"What do you mean you know that? I just met with the guy this evening, and I haven't told anyone about the meeting."

She looked at me rather strangely, like I was accusing her of lying. "Why, I learned about it in the paper the other day. There was an article about a man who was arrested for stealing gas from cars. Apparently he rigged his truck with pumps and tubes, so he could siphon the gas with just the flip of a switch."

"Hmm? I must've missed that article. Did the reporter mention where it happened?"

"I think somewhere in St. Paul," Margaret said. "I don't remember which suburb. Why do you ask?"

"Just wondering if it's related. That's all."

"Oh," my neighbor replied in a barely audible voice.

"I'm afraid as gas prices jump, we'll be seeing a lot more of that happening."

Margaret nodded in agreement as she set her empty plate aside. "You're probably right. I guess I should be happy that I don't own a car, huh?"

You and a lot of other people, I thought. No one likes to see a ninety-year-old person driving around town even if it's just to pick up groceries. "Yup," I answered, and then I pushed myself from the table and stood. After I was on my feet, I pulled the elderly woman's chair out and helped her up. Then the two of us cleared the dishes from her table and carried them to the kitchen. Once all the items were stashed away, I finally spoke. "Now what's troubling you, neighbor?"

"What do you mean what's troubling me?" Margaret repeated in a confusing tone. "Oh, yes, I see. How could I forget? You're referring to the puzzle, and I was supposed to remind you." She left me alone in her kitchen for a couple seconds, just to allow herself enough time to retrieve her crossword puzzle book and return to where I was standing. "Here's the page I marked, Matt. What's nine letters and means 'happy hour offering, maybe'?"

I touched my forehead like I was preparing to salute an officer. "You're joking? That's not really the one you need an answer for, right?"

"I'm serious. Why? What's the matter?"

I broke loose with thunderous laughter. "Ah, nothing's the matter," and then I tried to get serious again. "You were right. I actually do know the answer, Margaret."

"See. I told you." Margaret's gleeful giggles bounced off the kitchen walls now as she quickly grabbed a pencil from her kitchen counter, so she could write the answer in her puzzle book. "I'm ready."

"Two for one."

"Huh?" The furrows in Margaret's face became quite rigid as she turned deadly serious. She dropped the pencil she'd been holding and rested her hands on her hips now. "I don't get it. Two for one? You're certain of your answer?"

"Just try it," I said thinking of all the bars I had visited over the years. "I'll explain later."

Chapter 13

After leaving Mrs. Grimshaw's, I decided to take the mutt for a lengthy walk, one she wouldn't soon forget. The extended exercise was purposely planned to totally exhaust Gracie, so she didn't care one way or the other whether I was present at our abode later this evening or not.

Now since darkness settles in around four-thirty p.m. during the winter months in Minnesota, I don't make it a habit of traipsing all the way to Loring Park in the evening with the mutt. Heck, if I fell and got knocked unconscious, who'd find me? No one, probably, until the next morning when a runner stumbled and found me buried in three inches of snow. Besides that, I also didn't relish damaging anything major like Louie, my second cousin, no make that my third cousin, or is he my fourth cousin? Ah, it doesn't matter. The point is I don't want to suffer the consequences the rest of my life; he fell on ice ten years ago, and his back pain still persists.

But life is strange, and I felt I could change my way of thinking for just one night. Well, that and the fact that when Gracie and I strolled through Loring Park this morning, the walking paths seemed to be adequately shoveled, plus there were no signs of ice patches anywhere. Of course, keeping the dog out of the snow was another matter.

When we got to Loring Park, the sidewalks were still cleared like this morning, but the mutt refused to stay on the walking paths. Instead she planted her furry body in every mile-high mound of snow she could find. Even my yanking and repeating "No" didn't deter her one iota. The problem is she has a one-tracked mind like a lot of humans I know, and like them when she sets her mind to doing something, there's nothing on this planet that's going to hold her back, not even her master.

Our excursion lasted a half hour. As we stood under the lamppost light now which shined on the main entrance of the Foley, I studied Gracie's body. Golf ball size clumps of snow clung on every square inch of her four legs, underbelly, neck and mouth. I wasn't pleased. I had wanted to leave as quickly as possible when I got back to the apartment. Now I'd have to waste precious time melting the abominable snowman.

Once we reentered the apartment, I gave Gracie a firm command to sit tight. I needed a bath towel, and the nearest one I knew of was in the laundry hamper. If someone had been clocking the speed with which I returned to dry the dog off, I'm certain they would've informed me that I broke my old records by a landslide. Some snow resisted the terry towel no matter how hard I rubbed, but it would be taken care of shortly by other means. The dog's body heat plus the overheated apartment will melt the remaining snow off her in no time. Finished with my part of the drying process now, I proceeded to the kitchen to gather things for my all-nighter.

Waiting in the Topaz for an unknown gas thief could get awfully boring tonight, so I decided to bring enough stuff to keep me occupied for at least six hours. As much as I'd like to bring along coffee, due to it's great perk-me-up power, I decided against it. You see, I have a slight problem. black sludge passes right through me, as well as water and pop, so I'd end up spending more time visiting a Mc Donald's or Subway restroom than actually keeping watchful eyes on Ballad's vans. I did, however, pack a huge bag of potato chips, pretzels, Tostitos, Oreo cookies and a can of mixed nuts. For some reason, crunchy junk food works for me when I get drowsy.

Besides food, I also grabbed work related equipment that I store in one of the kitchen cupboards. Don't ask me why, but one of these days when I'm entertaining a visitor, I know I'll open the wrong cupboard door and nonchalantly say, "Can I offer you a cup of camera or perhaps a plate of binoculars?" The binoculars I selected to take with me were night-vison ones I'd borrowed from a relative about two months ago. I keep forgetting to return them. Drat! I feel so darn guilty about it.

Only a few minutes had passed since I'd begun to collect my paraphernalia. Now the articles were sitting on the kitchen table in front of me. "Okay. Looks like I've got it all." I shoved everything into a grocery bag, carried it to the door, and then set it down. Gracie had shadowed me, but I wasn't aware of it. So, when I turned around to tell her I was leaving, I almost tripped over her. I think she realized how close she came to having her paws crushed because she immediately sat down. "Here's the plan," I told her. "I spend the night in the car, and you get to stretch out on the master's bed. That arrangement work for you?"

"Wuff, wuff."

"Good. I figured it would." Now, I pointed in the direction of the bedroom. "Go lie down then." Shock of all shocks, Gracie actually followed through without giving me any guff for once. Hmm. Must've been the offer of the bed, although she was acting pretty worn out. Maybe the combination of the bed and the walk did the trick.

***

There were several cars parked on either side of 37th and Highway 65 when I arrived. Most probably belong to tenants who live above the businesses located at street level. Since I didn't want to stick out like an abscessed tooth, I parked the car facing north, one street ahead near the cross street of 36th and 37th, where I would have an excellent view of Ballad's vans. From this vantage point, I could also see anyone entering and exiting the alleyway.

The first couple hours went by rather quickly because I split my observation time between Ballad's coffee supply place and the cars entering and leaving the fast food joint directly across the street from it. But after midnight, activity cooled off considerably, and the hours dragged on and on. I should've anticipated that. Heck, it was a work night, and the majority of people needed their six or seven hours of beauty rest.

Every time I thought another hour had passed, I'd flick on the tiny flashlight that I usually stored in the car's glove compartment and discover the hands on my wristwatch had only moved another fifteen minutes. Disappointed, I'd then attack one of the many snacks I'd brought from home.

Well, guess what? By the time two o'clock rolled around, I found that I had eaten all of the chips, nuts and Oreos out of sheer boredom. Would this night ever end? I guess it didn't matter if it did or not. If nothing happened within the next hour, I'd have to repeat this same performance ten more times, and that thought wasn't gratifying in the least-especially if the Twin Cities got hit with sub-zero temperatures during that same time frame. I tossed the last Oreo cookie in my mouth and kept on watching.

After all that waiting, I finally got my first taste of action about five minutes after three. Someone magically appeared out of the blue and began slinking down Ballad's side of the street. Having friends who have worked the early shift at food places, I realized this early morning riser could be an *opener* for one of the fast food chains or restaurants in the vicinity, but I rather doubted it. It was a little too early. Since I didn't want to be discovered, I sunk deeper in my seat. The lone walker didn't move at a deer's pace but rather a toddler's. His head movement, though, reminded me of a snake or a drunken sailor as it jerked here and there and everywhere. Was it possible the person was looking for signs of a cop?

Even with my borrowed night vision binoculars, I couldn't distinguish the person's features or what sex he or she was. The large hood attached to the severely tattered winter coat was so huge it totally enveloped the person's head. The only thing I could actually report at this point, if I were asked, was that he or she was dragging along a light flimsy object. A garbage bag perhaps.

As the walker continued in my direction, he began to spin in all sorts of directions like a tornado, sucking up things as he went. But as soon as he was in direct line with Ballad's business, he stopped and stood like a statue for a few minutes. Then there was foot movement again. The person glanced up and down the street one more time before he actually strolled over to Ballad's trash dumpster and started rummaging through it. It looked like he retrieved several pop cans. Then the show came to a sudden halt. The dumpster lid slammed shut, and the person turned the corner and was out of sight.

Because the lone soul didn't hang around Ballad's business area all that long, and he had already been tossing items into his bag at different intervals along the block before stopping in my client's parking lot, I concluded he was either a harmless homeless person or an insomniac who collected pop cans for recycling, nothing more.

After that one suspicious person made an appearance at 37th and Highway 65, there were no other visitors straight through to my quitting time at five a.m., so I did what any PI in my position would do, split for home to get some much needed shut-eye.

Chapter 14

Despite ten more evenings of spying on Jake Ballad's vans, not one incident occurred to ruffle even a hummingbird's fine feathers. However, I did run into colder temperatures than I would've liked to experience a few evenings in a row. I'm talking cold like when a dog refuses to step outside to pee, but I made the best of it. Woolen blankets brought home from a four-year stint in the Air Force came in handy. Unfortunately, they smelled like mothballs because they had been in a storage closet at the Foley, but, hey, it was worth it. They kept me cozy. Ah, maybe sometimes a little too much. I caught myself nodding off now and then, not a good thing for a PI when he's trying to catch a thief, but in all honesty, I don't think I missed a thing.

I had a brief meeting with Ballad on the last day of my surveillance work before my vacation started. Due to Ballad's determined decision, I have to return to a boring gas case when I get back from my fun-filled vacation in Puerto Vallarta. True to his words on the first day we spoke, he still wanted me to continue my evening vigils. The venture was there all right but not enough was gained as far as I was concerned. My plan was to line my pockets with tons of silver before heading south of the border with the gorgeous Senorita Rita Sinclair. Now the only ones lining their pockets will be Señor Master Card and Visa as I rack up mucho charges while splurging on myself and my girlfriend. "Ah, caramba!"

Sun worshipers
Make way
We're coming to town.

Chapter 15

It was the third week of January, an arctic cold blast had just blown through Minnesota two days prior, and today the weatherman was calling for ten inches of new snow to fall on the Twin Cities. No reason to panic, I thought to myself as I finished hearing the latest forecast over the Humphrey Airport TV system. For the first time in my life, I didn't really care what dropped down out of the sky on Minneapolis or St. Paul, be it bird, plane or Superman. In exactly a half hour's time, I'd be going, *up, up and away in a beautiful Sun Country airplane.*

When the weather report was finished, I fixed my eyes on Rita's graceful legs once again, as she had been pacing back and forth in front of me for the past hour. I secretly wondered if she'd ever reveal what was on her mind. Perhaps she would, and then again maybe not. She keeps a ton of stuff bundled up inside her.

To give myself a break from my girlfriend's movements, I flipped the palm side of my hands down on my lap and studied my nails, and then I paged through a magazine I had purchased here at the airport. When I lost interest in both of them, I began watching her move to and fro again. She was definitely getting a workout. Whew! So was I. Someone get me a large cup of ice, pronto. The sensual ebb and flow of her silky rose-blossomed knee-length skirt against her exposed skin was getting to be too much for this male to handle. I felt heat surging above my neckline.

After Rita completed several rounds of pacing, she stopped smack in front of me. I was still sitting and gazed up at her politely, half-expecting some sort of explanation to finally pour forth, but still no words were uttered. Ah, the heck with it. Enough was enough. This man had reached his breaking point. I decided to take charge. "Rita, what's bothering you?" I asked in a soothing tone. "Are you nervous about flying?"

My girlfriend's emerald orbs reacted wildly. "Is that what you think? I'm afraid of flying?"

"Well, yeah. What other conclusion is there to make? Heck, you've been moving back and forth in front of me for the past hour."

"I have?" Rita took note of the time on her wristwatch. "Wow! Sorry. I guess I've been focusing on other things way too much." She leaned her petite body into me and then braced her arms firmly on my shoulders. "Mr. Malone . . ."

"Yes?"

"I just want you to know that flying doesn't bother me in the least."

"It doesn't, huh? Well, I'm glad we've cleared that up. So what is it, sweetheart? Did you leave an unfinished job behind at work?"

Rita sat down in the empty seat next to mine now. Her mouth formed a cute half-moon smile when she spoke. "Nope. I've got everything cleared off my desk that needed attention. It's just that I have this nagging feeling I've forgotten something–and there's no time to drive back home to get it."

I removed the *Sports Illustrated* magazine from my lap and set it on the blue plastic unoccupied seat on the other side of me. "That's a normal concern, but I'm positive you don't need to fret. Why, your organizational skills are off the chart. Heck, you're so organized you could have your own *Mission Organization* show on HGTV."

My sister, Mary, who had been walking around in circles for the last ten minutes, waiting for her friend to arrive, must've overheard Rita's and my conversation, because one minute my girlfriend and I are having a private, one-on one talk, and then bam, Mary flashes her passport and Visa card in front of our faces. "Hey, you two, lighten up. As long as we have these two little gems, who cares what else we need." She moved her two most prized possessions from in front of us now and placed them back in a zippered compartment of her medium-sized white leather purse. The purse seemed out of place since it didn't coordinate with the hot pink short-set she had donned for our flight. Once Mary's purse was shut, her eyes drifted to the huge window in front of us and the planes sitting on the tarmac.

"You're right," I swiftly replied, and then I nervously padded my short-sleeved cotton shirt pocket and the back pant pocket of my jeans, reassuring myself once more that I had the necessary stuff my sister had just displayed. Over the years I've learned one can never be too certain of anything in life.

Rita followed suit now and checked her belongings. She quickly unzipped her huge brown straw purse that was hanging from her slim shoulder and began rummaging through its contents. "Yeah, I guess I have the main essentials too. Sorry I've been such a nervous twit."

After Rita's apology, Mary shifted her eyes our way again. "Oh, please, Rita," she said as she waved her hand in the air, "you have nothing to be sorry for. Everyone worries about something or another leaving on a trip. 'Did I pay the bills?' 'Did I turn the gas off?' 'Did I toss the leftovers out?'"

Thanks to my sister's good-natured influence, my girlfriend's nervousness dissipated nicely. A loud laugh escaped her now as she added more to the list. "'Did I pack the right shoes?' 'Does a neighbor have my number in case of an emergency?' 'Did I pack enough clothes?'" She stopped sharing now and invited me to join the game with her gorgeous eyes. Such a caring woman. She didn't want me to feel like the odd man out.

It was a nice touch, but his guy wasn't about to bite. I held the ladies at bay as long as I could, and then I said, "I have no plans to extend the list of worries. You two are doing quite well without me." There's no way I'd ever reveal to the women in my life the one thing I worry about when I go on vacation, whether I packed suntan lotion or not. Thanks to the gene pool I received, I follow the traditional Irish fair-skin route, pale as a ghost until the first rays of sun turn me reddish-orange like a cooked lobster. I plucked my magazine off the seat now and laid it across my lap again. "So, Mary, when do you expect Elaine to show? Isn't she cutting it a little close?"

My sister took the empty seat the magazine had been occupying. "Don't tell me you've already forgotten what she was like as a child, Matt?"

"Heck, no!" I snapped. "How could I? She was always drumming up new ways for you two to bug me about this or that. You girls drove me insane."

Mary laughed softly. "That's because Elaine had a huge crush on you." Then she giggled again. Unfortunately for Rita and me, the grade school teacher's merriment spread like a flame for all to hear. "Whenever I'd suggest playing in the park, Elaine wouldn't hear of it if she knew you were hanging around the house. You know, thanks to you, I lost a lot of time on the swings and monkey bars. Come to think of it, according to all those mumbo jumbo psychology books out there, I should be deeply devastated by the loss of my childhood playtime."

"Well, forgive me if I don't feel too bad about that," I jokingly said, "but I think you've had plenty of time to make up for your loss. Let's see. How many days do kids attend school now? About 187, right? And of those 187 days, how many do you spend on the playground or in the gym with your little darlings?" Mary' mouth remained sealed. I quickly turned to Rita for additional reinforcement, but she wasn't offering any. All I got was an arctic glare. Luckily, I knew the coldness being sent my way wasn't triggered by the nonsense conversation I was having with my sister. Oh, no. This was one of her worrisome looks which usually meant, "*Is there a threat to our relationship, mister?*"

I dropped the magazine to the floor, and then reached out for Rita's hands. "Sweetheart, I didn't pay any attention to Elaine, believe me. I kicked the girls out of Sam's and my room every single time they tried to enter." Obviously those truthful words didn't generate any comfort yet. Rita's dirty looks continued to bore through my thick red head. I moved towards my sister now and pleaded for her assistance. "Come on, Mary. Tell her how it really was. Don't leave Rita in the dark."

My sister stood and lined herself up with my girlfriend. "That's right, Rita. He never, ever gave Elaine the time of day." Then she held her hand out like she was being sworn in by a courtroom lawyer. "And that's the whole truth. Nothing but the truth. So help me God."

If Mary convinces Rita of my innocence, I suppose I'll owe her big time. Oh, well, it'll be worth it. I don't want to spend seven days in paradise with an overly jealous woman.

After a few moments passed in quiet anticipation, Rita squeezed my hand tenderly. Good. The dampness between us had evaporated, but knowing her the way I do, she was too embarrassed to admit being even a tad jealous of Elaine, and less than thirty seconds later, I was proven right. Instead of explaining her behavior, she merely circumvented it. "Mary, you haven't answered Matt's question yet."

"What was that?" she inquired.

"He asked about your friend."

"Oh, Elaine's coming in her own good time. Ever since we were little, she's had a thing for cutting it close to the wire."

"You'd think she would've outgrown that by now," I said, all the while contemplating how I was going to behave once Elaine did show her face. So far, no one knew I had a secret interest in her during my senior high years.

My sister peered at her silver Timex wristwatch before continuing. "Give her about five more minutes. She'll show right when they announce to board the plane."

Rita looked Mary squarely in the eyes when she voiced her concern, "You're joking, right?"

"Afraid not," and then Mary plopped down again. "Just watch and see."

Chapter 16

"So," Elaine Best buzzed softly in my left lobe as she continued to nestle her elongated face on the back of my reclining headrest, "I told my husband, Frank, that he and Sam would be fine while I was gone. I left prepared meals in the freezer for them, washed their dirty clothes and even made sure their underwear was returned to their drawers." Out of breath now, she simply stopped talking and inhaled deeply.

Elaine was no different than any other Jill I've encountered. I knew she'd remain silent until this male responded to what she just said, so I set things in motion. First, I tilted my head up to the left just enough, so our two noses didn't rub tip to tip. You know, Eskimo fashion. There was no way I was going to get caught with my face snuggled up against another woman's with my girlfriend asleep in the seat right next to mine. I'm not that crazy. Then, after I was certain my head was positioned just right, I spoke in a low voice so as not to disturb Rita's slumber. "Elaine, take it from me, the men in your life will really appreciate what you've done."

"You think so?" I nodded politely. "Oh, Matt, you're such a doll," she cooed. Now the woman with the thick fluffed-up blonde hairdo took the liberty of ruffling my hair like a parent does when praising a small child.

Ouch! I took a gulp of stale air and bit my lip. Thank goodness Rita hadn't witnessed what just transpired between Elaine and me, she would've asked the captain to hand the blonde hussy a torn parachute and then push her out the nearest exit. "That's, ah, nice of you to say."

She took her hand off my hair now, and when she did I moved my head beyond her reach. "You know, Elaine, I still don't understand how you managed to have our plane wait for you even though the boarding gate was about to close."

The pilot's voice came over the intercom system before she had a chance to reply. "Passengers please return to your seats and fasten your seatbelts. We will be landing in ten minutes. A tip for those new to Puerto Vallarta, locals refer to this piece of paradise as PV. Thanks for flying with Sun Country. Enjoy your stay."

Elaine raised her head off my seat. "Well, I'd better do what the man said, sit down and put my seat belt on." A few seconds later, I felt a tap on my head. It was Elaine. "I didn't want you to think I forgot about your question. Catch me on the beach sometime, and I'll explain it to you."

"Sure," I said, knowing full well there would be no rendevous on the beach or anywhere else with her unless I wanted to lose Rita.

As soon as I heard my sister's friend click her seatbelt into position, I pulled my seat to an upright position, locked my belt into place and then nudged Rita.

She awoke with a start, but the tension that was on her face earlier in the flight had vanished. "What is it, Matt? Does the flight attendant want to know what beverage I'd like?"

"Nope. We're getting ready to land. You need to put your seat up in its normal upright position."

"Oh," she said somewhat surprised. Then she glanced down at the floral wristwatch decorating her left wrist. "Good grief! How long have I been out?"

I yawned. "Ah, shortly after takeoff."

Rita seemed hesitant to believe me. "Are you sure I was sleeping? I've never napped on a flight before."

"You did today. Maybe all that pacing at the airport wore you out."

"I suppose. So, did I miss anything important? Like a good movie?"

"Nah," I lied.

Now that Rita was fully awake, she quickly stowed the romance novel resting on her lap back in her purse, and then she pulled her seat forward. "Did the captain or crew ever say what the temperature was?"

"Yeah," Mary piped up from the seat behind her. "The flight attendant said it was 80."

Rita shaped her mouth like a small playful kitten just for me. "Mmm. Matt, you're one lucky man. I can model my new two-piece bathing suit for you as soon as we get situated at the condo."

"How about before we get settled in?" I said, and then I ran my fingers lightly over her arm that was resting between us.

Say what you mean to say,
Say what you mean to say . . .
John Mayer

Chapter 17

"Matt, what should we do first?" my sister eagerly inquired as she stood behind me in the plane's narrow aisle waiting for our turn to step off the plane.

I craned my head a smidgen to the left, so I could look over my shoulder at Mary. In the airport terminal back home I never noticed how much my sister's bright colored outfit made her look even paler than our Minnesota winter weather did. Oh, well, she'll lose that milky white color down here. After worshiping the sun for seven days, her skin tone will change dramatically. "I think claiming our luggage, should be at the tip of our list, don't you?"

"I don't know how Rita puts up with you, Matt," she said. Now without any warning, Mary's purse suddenly forced its way into the center of my back while the toes of her shoes began to claw at the heels of my tennis shoes. "Lighten up, brother. You take things too literally. I meant after that's taken care of." The newer closeness between the two of us didn't bother me. We were family after all, and besides, I knew she couldn't help it. It was the remaining rambunctious passengers on the plane that bugged me. I've never liked being pushed around by a crowd. It always made me feel like I was being vacuumed-packed in a tin of tuna.

I shrugged my shoulders in a lazy fashion when we were finally free of the plane. Heck, I never planned to come up with entertainment for the four of us, just my sweetheart and me. Luckily, my sister didn't press me again about our first day in PV, probably because conversation wasn't doable at the moment. You see, the other Minnesota vacationers, who followed us off the plane, buzzed in and out of us non-stop as they swarmed towards their one common goal, the airport terminal.

Even though we had been cooped up in the plane for about four hours and my legs cried out for exercise, I was delighted to learn that Puerto

Vallarta's International Airport, Gustavo Diaz Ordaz, didn't require much walking. After only a short jaunt, the four of us now huddled together in the carousel area where our luggage would soon be arriving off the conveyor belt.

Silence prevailed as we waited for the inactive carousel unit to wake from its slumber. I think we were all too scared to voice our main concern at the moment. The one thing airline passengers from Montezuma to the North Pole and all stops in between dread most is the disappearance of suitcases into *The Twilight Zone.*

My girlfriend was the first one to slice through the dead air. She took it upon herself to respond to Mary's question put to me earlier. "I think we should hail a taxi and go straight to the condo. There will be plenty of time to discuss meals or other topics once we're settled in."

"That's true," Elaine said as a yawn escaped her heart-shaped mouth. "I don't know about anyone else, but I'd like to take a tiny siesta before we start planning anything. I'm too darn tired to think straight."

Rita's eyes danced. Perhaps she was pleased to learn that the woman who sounded like a threat to her before was pleasant and actually very agreeable. "All right then, who wants to volunteer to hail a taxi while the rest of us collect the luggage?"

My sister spoke up before anyone else offered. "I'll go. My high school Spanish is a bit rusty, but I'm sure I can swing it. You only need a few words to catch a cab."

I was smiling on the inside now. Mary didn't know it, but her speedy offer got me off the hook. I never got around to digging out my Spanish notes written on those bar napkins, and so if the gals had voted for me to find a cab driver, I would've had to use sign language. "Thanks, Sis," I said, greatly appreciative of her generosity. "See you outside in about ten minutes then."

Mary winked. "Okay," and then she started off towards the exit.

"Oops."

"What's the matter, Matt?" Rita asked.

"I just realized Mary probably didn't have time to do research on Puerto Vallarta and its services. Vans pick passengers up at the airport, and regular taxis are used to travel around town."

"Oh, Matt," Elaine pounced, "you'd better catch her."

"Mary!" I shouted. "Wait!"

When my sister heard her name, she stopped abruptly, looked back at us, scrunched up her face and asked, "What?"

"Don't waste time searching for a yellow cab. The taxi drivers here at the airport only drive vans."

She gave me the thumbs up sign. "Gotcha." Then she disappeared into the crowd for a second time.

Now Elaine addressed me in a somber tone. "Matt, do you really think Mary will find a driver who understands her? I remember when she took her final exam for her high school Spanish class. It was an oral test. She said she flubbed it miserably."

Rita cleared her throat. She rarely does that. Perhaps it was a clue for me to defend my sister.

Taking it as a hint now to respond in a positive light about a sibling I didn't always see eye to eye with, I squeezed out as much honesty as I could possibly muster up. "Ah, come on, Elaine, that was years ago. Mary's a lot older and has tons of confidence in herself now. She'll be just fine." Then I placed my arm gently around Rita's shoulder hoping that was what she expected of me, and added, "But hey, if I'm wrong, we've got Senorita Rita here to straighten things out. Right, honey?"

My girlfriend gazed at me lovingly. "Sure, Matt," and then she slipped away from my embrace to catch Mary's luggage as it moved along the carousel.

The rest of our suitcases came around shortly, thank goodness. There are so darn many horror stories floating around about suitcases getting lost in limbo that I was worried I might actually have to shop for necessary essentials like underwear. Foreign sizes totally baffle me. My first experience with foreign shopping came when the Air Force sent me to Pakistan. I ended up purchasing things for my family that were never worn. The items were way too small for them. Now that we had collected all the luggage and regrouped, I counted the pieces. "One, two, three, four. All right, gals, time to find Mary."

"Shoot!" I said under my breath. As we stepped out into the warm humid air, I suddenly remembered what I had wanted to do before we exited the airport building, change out of my slacks and into shorts. Having flown before, I knew the confines of an airplane bathroom were too tight for my girth, but an airport bathroom is usually quite adequate. *You'll just have to keep your pants on a while longer, Malone. Besides, the cool van should be comfortable.*

"Does anyone see Mary, yet?" I inquired as I wiped sweat from my brow and thought about the wonderful invention of air conditioning.

"There she is, Matt," Rita said, "over there." Her finger pointed to the left at the edge of the solid brick airport building.

"I see her too," Elaine announced as she brushed too closely past me. "Good thing she's wearing her neon pink shorts outfit, huh?"

I chuckled. "Yeah, just think, if she'd chosen to wear white today instead, we'd have a heck of a time picking her out from all the other people roaming around."

When my sibling finally spotted us approaching in her direction, she waved her arms to get our attention. Obviously she had forgotten what she had on. "Perfect timing," she said the moment we stood in front of her with all our luggage, "and guess what? Our driver knows exactly where the condo is located."

Yay, I thought to myself. No zipping up and down tons of streets, racking up millions of miles in order to make more money off us ignorant gringos. A Roman cabdriver took advantage of me years ago, and I promised myself it wouldn't happen again. "Okay," I said, "show us the van, so we can get our luggage stowed away and take off."

Mary took her luggage from me first. "Come on. Follow me. It's the second van down this row."

Generous warning signs blinked on and off in my head now. "*Don't take. Don't take.*" Why I wondered? Soon as I caught sight of the van Mary had selected for us, I had my answer. Yup, we had a colossal problem on our hands. There was going to be no relief from the heat; the van's windows were all rolled down. PI that I am, I felt compelled to scan the windows on the other taxi vans lined up outside of the airport. Maybe Mary didn't have any other choice.

Darn! Just as I suspected, they all had air conditioning. How could she have made such a terrible decision? There were so many vans to chose from. As I pulled the hankie from my pants pocket and dabbed my forehead, I wondered when I'd have a chance to get even with Mary.

Not right this minute evidently. My feet stopped working within two-feet of the van. I've got to give them credit, as they were smarter than me.

Rita had already gotten into the van with the other women, but when she saw that I was frozen to the sidewalk, she became concerned and joined me. "Honey, is there anything wrong?"

"Nah," I lied. Then I quickly clamped my teeth on my tongue, afraid I might say something I'd later regret. *Mary got us a taxi, Matt, and that's all we asked her to do.*

'Come on, Matt," Mary chided. "Get your butt in here; the day is slipping away."

And whose fault was that? I said internally.

My girlfriend gently offered a hand to me, and my heat problems miraculously melted away.

When I entered the taxi van, our young male driver with a thick, full head of coal black hair grinned at me. "Lo lamento (sorry), señor. Van old, air conditioning broke down last week. No dinero to fix."

Of course not, I thought, as I drew the back of my hand across the upper third of my head and then swiped a glance at the name card, which was attached to the driver's visor, along with the three rosaries and St. Christopher metal that were dangled from the rearview mirror. *Okay, Virgin Mary, I get your message loud and clear. Since he's a pal of yours, I'll behave. I won't say one nasty thing to Juan. I promise.* I placed a hand in front of my face now, palm side out. "It's okay, Juan." Internally, I told myself to never, ever accept these conditions again. Then I added, "Casa not far?"

"Si," Juan swiftly replied now as he tore away from Puerto Vallarta's airport. His broad smile exposed the fact that he was missing several teeth.

Chapter 18

As soon as we were settled in at the condo, Mary and Elaine chose to escape to siesta land, but not Rita and me. We were too fired up to go that route just yet. So, what do two different worlds do when they are about to collide you ask? Well, I pulled my lovely sweetheart aside and suggested we explore the territory outside the confines of the four walls surrounding us.

Before setting forth however, Rita needed further clarification. "Are you referring to wandering the grounds of the Marriott Hacienda?"

"Nope," I replied. "I was thinking of escaping this oasis and checking out the white sandy beach. What do you think?"

"Fine with me, Matt. I'd love to wade in the ocean."

I slapped my hands together. "All right. Let's change our clothes and then skedaddle.

Before I entered the bedroom, Rita pulled a huge bottle of suntan lotion out of her straw purse and tossed it to me. "Here, Matt." I caught the bottle in midair. "You can spread some on my back after I put my halter top on, and then I'll do yours." Hmm, maybe I jumped the gun. There was plenty of adventure to be played out right here in our room. *Cool your jets, Matt. You'll see plenty of action later.*

Right before we left the grounds of the Marriott behind for our stroll along the beach, Rita examined the landscaped courtyard. "Hon, don't you think the combination of Hibiscus and grasses flow nicely together?"

"Ah huh," I answered lazily, feeling comfortable at last. It was the shorts I brought that did the trick.

"I'd like that kind of landscaping when we get married and own a home."

Marriage and home? Those two things weren't on my horizon anytime soon. Since I didn't want to stir up any trouble in paradise, I simply said,

"Sure, honey," and then taking Rita's hand in mine, I drew her to my side. I have to tell you, being here in PV with my special girl made me feel like a teenager again. Too bad euphoria doesn't last forever.

We had barely stamped our size seven and eleven footprints in the sand when a group of Mexican vendors began sizing us up. Apparently, they're allowed to hawk their wares up and down the beach, something I wasn't aware of when I told my dad I wanted to vacation in Mexico. Well, I hate to tell them, but they're barking up the wrong tree. They'll get nothing from this guy. I'd rather be knocked down by a thunderous wave from the Pacific Ocean than to be inundated by them. A person can move farther inland after they get hit by a wave, and they don't have to repeat, "No, gracias," a million times in Spanish.

The young children approached first while mommy and grandma waited in the wings, their mission, to sell foreigners cheap little trinkets. When that didn't appear to be going anywhere, the adults slid alongside us and tried to sell items like baby wear, dresses and hats.

As we attempted to continue our walk along the vendor bordered beach, I silently wondered what Rita thought of our shattered tranquility. Nice lady that she is, all she ever shared was an impish grin and that darn repetition of, "No, gracias."

Obviously she didn't mind the game the Mexicans played. My fuse on the other hand was growing shorter and shorter by the minute. The two of us were supposed to have a romantic stroll on the beach sans other people. With all that was happening now, we might as well have stayed at the condo and taken a nap. "No, gracias," I responded in a disgusted tone yet again, hoping this was the last time today those words would flow from my mouth.

When we finally ended up on a narrower patch of sand where the crafters' didn't pursue us, I turned to Rita and said, "Hon, what do you think about staying away from the beach and just using the pool at the condo while we're here?"

Miss Sinclair threw a throaty laugh my way. "Why, so we aren't hassled? Relax, Matt. This is part of the Mexican culture. If you want to learn about Mexico, you need to go with the flow. Experience it with all your senses."

"What if I don't want to? Their sales process is driving me loco."

"Come on, don't give up on the beach yet. We just got here. Besides, a friend of mine who comes down to Mexico quite frequently shared a beach trick with me."

"Oh, what's that?" I quizzed.

"You simply close your eyes when you're sunbathing, and the vendors move on."

"That's it?"

"Ah huh. Siestas are important to the people down here. The locals wouldn't dream of disturbing a person who is napping. Of course if you don't want to fake sleeping, there's always the wave of the hand and, "No, gracias.""

"See, I always knew there was a reason I wouldn't trade you for anyone else. You have all the answers." I gulped down my previous complaint, wrapped my arms around Rita's tiny waist and kissed her passionately. The beach was the perfect spot to let her know how much I loved her. Heck, no family was around to witness our necking on the beach, right? Guess again.

"Hey, you two, enough of that nonsense." I wish I hadn't recognized the voice, but I did. It was Mary.

"Ah, hi," I said after Rita and I unclinched our mouths and turned towards where the familiar voice had come from. "Where's Elaine? Don't tell me you lost her already?"

Mary fluffed her short, black wind-blown hair. "Nope. She's still snoozing. And Matt, before you ask, yes, I left her a note."

I denied what my sister suspected even though it was true. "I wasn't concerned about that. What do I care what grown women do? I only worried when Mom and Dad left me in charge of you."

Rita's eyebrows arched severely. Evidently she was deeply concerned about something. "Mary, do you think your friend is okay? I mean, she's not sick, right? None of us have eaten any food here yet."

Mary glanced down at her sandaled feet. "Nah, she's not sick. She's just totally wiped out from all the housework she did yesterday. She wanted everything just so for her family before she left." Now she raised her eyes to us again. "So, what have you two love birds been up to since you left the condo?"

Rita dropped my hand, and then raised hers above her eyebrows to shelter her eyes from the sweltering sun. "Not much. We've just been inundated by the Mexicans and all their wares."

Mary stared at my girlfriend for a second. "Yeah, I heard that's to be expected," and then she tossed her head my way. "Did you buy anything for Rita, yet? Like a piece of jewelry?"

Before I had a chance to comment, Rita fielded the question for me. "Actually there hasn't been anything worth purchasing."

"Oh, well, maybe the two of you would rather save your pesos for parasailing. I've seen them do that a little further down the beach. Heck, I might even get up enough nerve to try it myself."

"Wow!" I said. "You mean it, Mary, little miss whimp?" She nodded her head heavily for the affirmative. "Watch out, world. My sis is going to do something absolutely crazy for once in her life."

Rita came up alongside me and clasped my hand again. "Now, Matt, you promised to be nice to Mary. Remember?"

"Yes, and believe me I'm really trying."

My sister didn't appear to be upset by what I had said, probably because she was used to my teasing ways. "Oh, don't bawl him out, Rita," she calmly replied. "He's right. I always play it safe. I never learned to downhill ski, I refused to water ski, and I've never attempted to jump on a trampoline."

Rita consoled her. "Don't be so hard on yourself. Those things aren't necessarily the most exciting things in the world to do. How about skydiving?"

Mary shook her dark head of hair up and down. "Nope."

"Rollerblading?"

"No. One of my girlfriends broke her wrist right before I tried that. Seeing her in such pain scared me half to death."

"How about kayaking?"

I kindly butted in before my sister replied with another 'No.' "Hey, ladies, I have an idea. Why don't we skedaddle back to the condo and check on Elaine. She has to be awake by now."

The gals each latched on to one of my arms, and then they harmoniously chimed, "Brilliant idea."

My stomach growled quite loudly now. Embarrassed, I hurriedly patted my mid-section. "Sorry. I guess my stomach needs instant gratification."

Mary pinched my bare arm lightly. "Don't apologize, I'm starving too. I just manage to keep it on the QT. How about you, Rita? Are you ready to sample true Mexican cuisine?"

Rita grinned. "You bet'cha. What little I ate earlier this morning is long gone. I could go for some enchiladas, tostados, quesadillas . . ."

"Whoa!" I said as I stopped in mid-step. "Hold on there, Rita. If you keep talking like that, I'm going to have to split."

She dropped my arm as fast as she had taken it. "Why?" she said in a concerned tone. "What's the problem?"

I turned the pocket linings of my shorts inside out to expose them. "No dineros, Señorita."

My girlfriend stared at my empty pockets for a second, and then she began laughing loudly. "Come on Mary. Let's find Elaine and tell her lunch is on Matt." Then the two women took off running down the beach.

I stood gazing at the huge waves that were hitting the shore. Great. What do I do now? Rita thought I was joking. I rubbed the whiskers that were starting to sprout on my chin. It was a sure thing that manna wasn't going to drop from heaven anytime soon for me, so I did what any sensible male would do in my predicament, I took off after the women and let my Visa card do the rest.

Chapter 19

Eight o'clock this morning, as the four of us sat around the pool area at the timeshare finishing up the last bites of our Mexican style breakfast and sipping our final cups of dark black coffee, my darling girlfriend sweetly suggested that all four of us go parasailing.

"When do you want to do that?" I quizzed.

Rita dabbed her sensuous lips with her white cloth napkin. Then she smoothly replied, "Today".

I remained silent for only a second or two. It wasn't that I didn't want to try parasailing. Heck, when I was in the Air Force in my early twenties, I was forced to do many daring deeds, and I still do as a PI. It was just that... Well, I only wanted to do that kind of stuff with Rita—away from the glaring eyes of Elaine and my sister. Now I was trapped, thanks to Rita's brilliant idea. If I didn't agree about the foursome this morning, who knew the degree of friction that could erupt between us, and then this whole darn trip could blow up in my face. "Sure," came my not so strong response, "I'm game. How about you two?" I asked Elaine and Mary, hoping they'd decline. "What do you think?"

"Yeah, sure," Elaine replied. "I'm all for it."

Now, we just had to patiently wait for Mary. Would she go for it or not? Even though she brought the idea up yesterday, she also admitted she never has the nerve to do anything daring.

Two minutes lapsed by my watch, and then Mary patted her stomach and said, "Ah, gosh, I don't know. That Tortilla de Huevos (Mexican omelet) I ate had everything but the kitchen sink in it."

"Uh, huh," I said playing the devil's advocate, "and how exactly does that affect you, Mary? Are you trying to say you can't go parasailing on a full stomach? Well, I've got news for you, Sis. That activity doesn't entail swimming even though we fly over water. You take off from the beach and get dropped back exactly where you started. It's as simple as that."

Elaine hurriedly added, "Remember, Mary, it was you who enticed us with the parasailing idea in the first place, so no one's forcing you into this."

The four of us pushed our chairs away from the table now and then stood and formed a circle.

"I know," my sister replied in a downhearted tone. "I guess I'm just getting cold feet. What if I can't get down once I'm up that high in the sky?"

"You yank on the cords, silly," Elaine demonstrated. "That's what they're for. Then the men on the ground do the rest. There's nothing to it. Honest."

My sister shuffled her feet back and forth like she was practicing a tiny tap routine. "Sounds simple enough, Elaine, but you've gone parasailing before."

Rita drew closer to Mary. "Ignore them. If you don't feel comfortable about parasailing, don't do it. There's always something else you can try."

My sister nervously brushed her navy-blue shorts off as if getting rid of crumbs from the table, and then she inhaled deeply. "Thanks for the sound advice, Rita, but I think I should follow through with this one. As a teacher I'm always encouraging my students to try new things, but I don't take my own advice. I always chicken out at the last minute." She slapped her hands together now. "Well, not today. I'm going to be adventurous. Heck, life is too short not to sample new things, right Bro?"

I flung my arms in the air. "Hallelujah!" Now that our morning was planned, I took out my wallet and went back to the table we had just gotten up from. The gals immediately asked what I was doing. "Paying my share of the breakfast bill."

Rita scrambled over to the table. "Hon, put your money away. You don't need to pay anything."

Then it suddenly dawned on me. She's right. Our meals are added to the tab being kept at the Marriott like all the other amenities and then totaled at check-out time. I slapped my wallet closed now and shoved it in the back pocket of my pants. "All right gang, let's get our swimsuits on and head down to Playa Los Muertos Beach before Mary changes her mind."

***

The trip down the beach from the Marriott to the parasailing area was quite memorable. Three ladies ahead of me sashaying to and fro to the rhythm of the waves, while I slowly sauntered to the melody of the sand from behind, Rita's upper body partially covered with a thin, sheer white lace beach jacket and Mary's bottom half encased in some sort of tie-dyed scarf skirt. Only Elaine, who was the leader of the pack, was totally exposed, and what an exposure it was. Her lime green and black stripped bikini flattered her hourglass figure so perfectly. If I didn't keep close tabs on my emotions, I'd need to take a quick dip in the ocean before we got in line to parasail.

Our congo line lost a step or two now as we drew nearer our destination. It was all Elaine's fault, because she halted us abruptly. "Oh, great!" she said as she spun to speak to us face to face. "Look at the line of people already waiting. Couldn't they have found something else to do this morning?"

I stared at the line. "Not if they're like us," I said. "So, what do you want to do, turn around and try another day?"

"Are you kidding?" my sister bellowed. "Absolutely not. I've come this far, and I plan to wait it out. Besides, didn't we come down to PV for the sunshine?"

Rita kicked the sand with her brightly painted red toes. "We certainly did. I vote that we stick it out." Then she turned to Elaine.

Elaine looked at the rest of us. "I'm game if everyone else is."

"All right, tell you what, gals," I said without any hesitation, "I'll run ahead and get us a spot in line before it gets any longer. The three of you just enjoy the scenery."

"You're just so sweet, Matt," Elaine said as she gave me a bear hug. "Isn't he, Rita?"

Rita tartly responded, "Oh, yeah," and then she gave me the evil eye.

Chapter 20

When the gals finally caught up to me, my sister suggested what order we should go in. I was chosen to be first. Probably because I was the lone male, the under dog, so to speak. Then Mary said, "I'll follow Matt. Elaine's third, and then Rita, you bring up the rear." Good word choice, I thought to myself. It'll be fun watching my girlfriend bring up the rear. Although once the harness goes on, I won't get much of a view from the ground.

I had kicked off my tennis shoes the moment I got us locked into line, and I was beginning to regret it. The sand on Playa los Muertos beach was heating up rapidly as the morning wore on. At least there were only seven people ahead of us now instead of fifteen.

Luckily, their turns went fast and before I knew it the young man operating the parasail business was signaling me to get geared up. "Have you done this before, Señor?"

"Si," and then I demonstrated with my arm. "I pull on the cord and come down."

The short, young over-weight Mexican grinned. "Sí, buenos." He shouted to the boat driver now. "Okay, Jose," and then he threw his arm in the direction of the water. "Go."

I stared down at the waves of blue now as they gently rolled back and forth below me. What a sight. The tiny pin-dot of a boat I was being pulled by quickly maneuvered in and out of one-foot waves, acting more like a jet ski. When you live so far from any ocean, it's easy to forget little pleasures in life like this. If I had time and money to squander, I'd definitely parasail more frequently. As I was pulled in yet another direction now, I caught sight of El Pulpito, the pulpit shaped rock formation I'd heard of. It rests at the southern end of Playa Los Muertos. Geez, I wish I could stay up here forever. It's so exhilarating. A shrill whistle blew from below now. I tugged on my cord. Time to come down to earth both literally and figuratively.

Knowing my sister was as nervous as a chipmunk, I stepped out of the harness as fast as possible and handed it off to her before she had time to change her mind. "Now Mary," I said in strict brotherly fashion, "relax and enjoy the ride, and remember, as soon as you hear the whistle, tug on this blue cord right here," and then I showed her where it was. "It's really easy to do."

My sister nodded and then kicked off her sandals. "I hear you, Matt. I go up. I come down. It's as simple as that."

I bent over and scooped up her shoes now. "Yup."

Mary shared a brave smile as her feet were slowly swept off the sand. "Bye. I'll see you three in ten minutes."

"You better keep that promise," Elaine yelled, "because Rita and I still want to take our turns."

My sister waved now as she sailed high over the Pacific Ocean.

"You really think she'll be all right, Matt?" Rita asked as she cozied up to me. "She seemed pretty nervous even though she tired to put on a brave front for you."

I dropped Mary's sandals by my bare feet. It still hadn't sunk in that my sister followed through with her desire to parasail. "Yeah," I answered. Then I placed my arm around Rita's smooth shoulder to confirm what I stated even though my innards were telling me otherwise, namely my sister's ride might actually be pocked with danger. "She'll be fine. Just watch," and then I gave Rita a quick smooch on the cheek while Elaine's attention was diverted.

"Hey, you two," Elaine exclaimed in an excited tone, "are you watching Mary fly?"

"Yeah, yeah" we lamely replied.

"She looks like an old pro up there, doesn't she?"

I squeezed Rita's shoulder lightly, and then looked up at the sky and Mary. You couldn't miss picking her out against the backdrop of the scattered white clouds. She was wearing a scarlet red one-piece bathing suit. "You're right, Elaine, she does." Comfortable with the way my sister was handling herself, I finally expressed what I had been thinking earlier. "I still can't believe she did it."

Elaine didn't reply. She was too busy pacing back and forth in front of us now like a caged lion. Then "Darn!" suddenly flew out of her mouth.

Was she just getting nervous about her turn, I wondered? She told us she'd parasailed several times before. Was that a lie, or was there something more?

"What is it, Elaine?" Rita inquired with genuine concern. "Is everything all right?"

"Oh, it's nothing serious. I just wish we had a pair of binoculars. That's all. I'd love to see the expression on Mary's face."

That's what her parading back and forth was all about? A pair of stupid binoculars. I'd hate to be around Elaine when something truly serious rattles her cage. "Yeah," I nonchalantly agreed, "that would've been interesting."

Rita looped her hand in my free one now. "Well, maybe we can do something about that," she said trying to appease Elaine. "Hon, do you see anyone with a pair of binoculars hanging around their neck?"

"Nope. Not even a digital camera." Hmm? What's this sudden hand holding business all about? I wondered. Usually if my arm is laced around Rita's shoulders, that's sufficient contact. Is she staking her claim on me–worried that Elaine and her charming bikini are moving in? Or am I just digging too deep? Which was it?

"Oh, that's too bad," Rita said as she squeezed my hand. "I guess we'll just have to wait until Mary returns to see how she liked her new experience."

After several minutes elapsed, my girlfriend finally dropped my hand. "Matt."

"Huh? Yeah, what?"

"Your sister's time is almost up," and then she pointed to the new charm-like wristwatch she'd bought for herself before leaving on our trip.

"Yeah, so?"

"You should do a nice brotherly deed."

"Oh, and what's that," I inquired.

"Bring Mary her sandals and help her out of the harness."

I pondered her suggestion for a second. "I guess I could do that."

Now Rita poked my bare chest with her long fingernails. "You guess? What kind of talk is that?" Obviously, she was irritated with me. She went on. "I wouldn't want you as my brother."

"Good," I replied, "because I don't want to be your brother, just your boyfriend."

My girlfriend shook her dark head of hair. "You know what I mean," she said, her voice dripping cold like ice cubes.

"Hey, don't be so hard on me. I am thinking about my sister."

"You are?"

"You bet. Mary's single, right?" Rita bobbed her head up and down. "Well, I thought she'd appreciate the help of those muscle-bound beach boys who are just standing around doing nothing."

Elaine swiftly came to my defense. "Matt's right. His sister's a very attractive single woman—let her enjoy the limelight while she can."

Rita closed us out. She immediately folded her arms in front of herself. If this were an old-time movie and not a real life situation, you would've also seen steam pouring out of her fair ears. "Okay. Do it your way," she said roughly, "but just remember, if one of those Mexican guys happens to get too fresh with her, it's your fault."

Women! Why did God create them? To drive men crazy of course. I removed my arm from Rita's shoulder and said, "Tell you what," with a touch of sarcasm to my voice. "I'll stand where Mary's supposed to get dropped and keep my brotherly eyes glued to the men who help her. How's that?"

A tiny smile encased my girlfriend's lips as she permitted her arms to dangle by her sides again. She knew she had won this round, but I was a little worried. Would I hear about the way I spoke to her later, when we were out of earshot of Elaine?

"Here she comes, Matt," Elaine screamed. Then she made a mad dash to the section marked for take-off and landing.

I kissed Rita on the cheek, grabbed Mary's sandals, and then followed Elaine's example.

Chapter 21

The instant my sister's feet skimmed the sandy shore she was surrounded by a whirlwind of commotion. Young, handsome Mexican guys were closing in on her left and right, and none would let me anywhere near her. Probably thought I was another macho male competing for her attention. For the second time in my life, I was actually thankful I was hanging out with Elaine. She paraded right through the grouping, bringing me along for the ride. "So how was it, Mary?" she asked above the ruckus.

Mary couldn't stop giggling as the small band of men fought to help her out of her harness. You could tell she was enjoying the attention. "Oh, my gosh. It was the most exciting experience I've ever had in my entire life. All that expanse of water below and the never-ending sky above. I felt as free as a bird."

"Great," I said as I handed off her sandals to her. "We'll redeem your plane ticket, and you can don wings for your flight home."

"Ha. Ha. You think you're such a comedian, big brother."

Elaine was doubled-over with laughter. "You haven't changed a bit. You're still as funny as ever, Matt."

I knew Mary's comment was meant to be sarcastic, but I wasn't sure how to take Elaine's, so I ignored them both.

"Elaine," Mary said firmly, "You'd better stop laughing and get moving. Those guys aren't going to wait for you forever."

Elaine donned a serious face now. "Okay, okay. Adios, you two."

As soon as Mary's friend was out of the picture, she focused on me. "Rita's probably getting pretty antsy, huh? Everyone's had their turn except her."

"I don't know. She hasn't said. She's been too concerned about you."

"Me? Why, Matt?"

I shoved my hair off my forehead. "Ask mother hen when you see her. First, it was your nervousness before you went parasailing. Then, it was your maiden voyage. Oh, and don't forget all those muscle men on the beach who would be panting over you."

"Wow, you're right," Mary said. "She certainly sounds like a mother hen. Strange. She's never given me any indication she cares what's going on in this chick's life."

"Well, deep down she does," I replied as I hopped from one foot to the other. My feet were still bare, and the sand had gotten a lot hotter. "Even if she never says anything to you."

"Or could it just be her maternal instincts finally kicking in, Matt?"

"What the heck are you talking about, Mary?"

"Your girlfriend's in her mid-thirties; her baby clock's ticking. Maybe she's telling you in her own subtle way she's ready to get married and start a family."

I briefly thought about what Rita said yesterday concerning marriage and a home. "Nah. You're crazy. Her work is still too important to her."

"Wake up and smell the coffee, brother. We aren't living in the dark ages anymore. Women can raise kids and still have a career."

"Not Rita," I said so low only the ocean heard me.

Chapter 22

As I slowly made my way back to Rita, I began to mull over what my sister had just said. Surely she didn't have it right. The Miss Sinclair I knew wasn't ready for marriage and kids anymore than I was. At least she never gave me any indication that she was. Things were comfortable the way they were. Weren't they? Darn! I shouldn't allow Mary's rambling to get under my skin. What does she know about relationships anyway? Heck, she's in her mid-thirties and still looking for her first Mr. Right. Now, if she was Elizabeth Taylor, who supposedly has been married eight or nine times, I might be inclined to listen to what she had to say about relationships, but she isn't.

I swiftly swept my thoughts inward on the beach and found the love of my life staring in my direction. It was clear that she was studying me as I drew nearer. Shoot! Do my new white and black stripped swim trunks make me look that frightful? I never thought to look in the mirror after I changed. Of course, maybe her examination of me has nothing to do with the suit. Hopping all over this beach like a huge jackrabbit because my size eleven feet are on fire creates plenty of lunacy theories. "Ouch! I need my shoes."

My sister enjoyed seeing me suffer. "Poor Mattie. You forgot to slip your shoes on."

"Oooh! You shouldn't be making fun of me," I replied with no humor to my voice. "Oh, ouch! I'm the one who brought you your sandals, so the beach wouldn't torture you."

"Yeah, yeah."

My eyes scanned the beach again for Rita and her studious look. Apparently she had enough of me because her back was to me now as I watched her squat down.

"We're back, sweetie," I announced as I eased in beside her, even though I knew she had sensed we were upon her.

"I see." She quickly stood and handed over my shoes. "I believe you forgot these, Mr. Malone." She wasn't ignoring me after all. She was simply picking my tennis shoes up. Bless her little heart.

"I most certainly did. Thanks."

"So tell me, how did you manage to go off without your shoes?"

I ran my fingers through my hair and racked my brain for an answer. "I don't know. Either you were on my mind, or I was too lazy. Take your pick."

"I prefer lazy," my sister insisted.

Rita fluffed the sides of her hair. "Oh, no," she replied in a sexy tone. "I'd much rather think I was on his mind."

"Okay, you two," I said, "the teasing's over. Let me be." With that said, I plopped my butt on the hot, fine white sand, so I could clean off my feet. While I sat there, I thought about how easy it would've been to just slip my feet into sandals, but I refuse to wear them. My toes are too atrocious, so why expose them to the world? When my feet were finally clean, I then struggled to get my new white Nike tennis shoes back on. The heat surely was to blame for the fight now waging between my feet and shoes because the cold winter months in Minnesota never create such a problem.

While I continued to be preoccupied, Rita conversed with my sister. "Did you enjoy parasailing, Mary?"

My sister's voice was higher than normal when she responded to the question, probably because she was still feeling the adrenaline rush from being in the air. "Oh, yeah. Great. Wonderful. I'll never forget it. The ocean. The sky. Me up there swinging between the both of them. Lots of time to think about heaven and God."

When my sister mentioned God, I jumped up like my bottom was on fire and quickly brushed the back of my shorts off. I think it was the reminder of what the nuns said when I was in grade school about God being everywhere and seeing everything. A doubting Thomas, "Really?" escaped my lips accidently. I suppose I shouldn't have questioned my sister. Many people probably dwell on God and heaven when their lives hang in the balance over an ocean thousands of miles from their homes, but it's certainly not my cup of tea.

"Sure, Matt," my sister replied serenely. "Why, what did you think about?"

"Ah, I'd rather not get into that, if you don't mind."

Rita gave me a double whammy of her evil eye thing again or maybe it was her *meet me in the bedroom later* look before she pulled my sister towards her and politely asked, "Were you ever scared?"

"Yeah, but then I took a deep breath and told myself whatever happens, happens."

"Good for you," my girlfriend said and I knew she meant it. She never says anything she doesn't mean. Now me, that's a different story entirely.

Standing directly behind the two women now, I tapped Mary lightly on her back. "Bravo, sis. I'm really proud of you."

Mary spun around. "Thanks," she said and then she slugged me in the arm. "Those words mean a lot to me."

The minute Mary hit me I went into self-defense mode and swivelled in the opposite direction. With my back to the gals now, I watched the rolling ocean and Elaine's flight above it. "Hey, you two, Elaine's already coming around the bend."

Rita moved alongside me now and then cupped her hands around her eyes to shield them from the sun's glaring rays bouncing off the water. "The wind has picked up a couple notches, hasn't it?"

"Yup," I replied.

"The waves appear much larger now too," Mary added. "Hey, Matt, does a stronger wind make for better flying or worse?"

"A stronger wind makes it a little trickier for the boat to control the landing," I explained. Now my stomach did a double flip flop. It hadn't done that since my family and I were in church on New Years. Concerned for the safety of my girl friend, I took her hands in mine now and said, "Hon, do you really think you should go parasailing?"

"Yes, sweetheart. I'll be fine. The guys in the boat know what they're doing. If they felt the winds were too strong for parasailing, they would've announced it by now."

"Your right," I said, but my gut was still telling me she should be extra cautious. I looked to my sister, hoping she'd backup my concerns, but her eyes were glued to the sky and her friend.

"Elaine's done," she cried. "She just released her cord." Then she proceeded to give us a blow by blow account of her friend's descent. "Coming down. Oh, no! The wind's pulling her off course. She's heading for a thick clump of palm trees." Then she paused. "Okay, she cleared them. She's back on course now." Mary stopped reporting now and waved her arms in front of her. "Come on. I want to see if the men down here really do go gaga for blonde-haired women like I've heard."

"What do you plan to do with the information if it's true?" Rita asked while she dodged in and out of people trying to keep up with my sister.

"Why, I'll get my haired dyed tomorrow. The receptionist at our timeshare said the beauty shop prices are dirt cheap down here."

I couldn't believe what my sister just said. It was like someone let the snake out of it's glass enclosed home. First parasailing and then dying her hair. What next? A tattoo?

We were less than five feet from Elaine now and I finally had a clear view of her and the beefy men buzzing around her. From my estimate, she definitely had more men on her turf then Mary had. "Ah, sis, it looks like you'll be changing your hair color."

Elaine's mouth was frozen in a wide smile as she kept repeating, "Gracias, amigos," over and over while gazing over the men's heads. Was she searching for us? Did she want the three of us to save her from the onslaught of muscle-bound men who were wearing very little covering on their bottoms? I didn't have a clue. Sure, Elaine was a married woman, but other than a spouse, does one truly know how married someone really is.

My sister finally got close enough to her friend now to let her know we were within range. "Elaine, you want us to rescue you yet?"

Elaine glanced over her left shoulder. "Ah, there you are. Yeah, I need someone to tell them to back off."

Mary squeezed her way into the inner circle of men. "Perdone!," she said quite firmly, and then she reached for Elaine's arm and mentioned something about married. As soon as the cat was out of the bag, the dark skinned bodies wandered off.

Rita moved closer to the other two women now. "It looked like you had some tense moments coming down."

Elaine's smile evaporated now. "That's one way of putting it, I guess. The ride was definitely more challenging than I bargained for."

"Do you think Rita should go up?" I asked. The tables were turned now and I sounded like a mother hen.

A couple men from the parasailing business started to take the colorful harness off Elaine. "I don't want to spoil your fun, Rita," my sister's friend said, "but you might want to reconsider going up. There's always another day."

When the men finished with Elaine, they set the harness off to the side. I thought that was strange because they usually hold on to it, so the next person can slide right in. Less time lost–more money for their pockets. Maybe the parasailing was going to be cancelled for the rest of the day after all.

"Nope," Rita said with cool determination in her voice. "I don't plan to. As long as no one has said anything about refunds or cancellations yet, I'm going up."

The parasailing operators may not have been saying anything about money refunds yet, but they also weren't strapping Rita into the harness either. Lucky for my girlfriend, PIs have their ways of ferreting information out of people, and I was ready to put my skills to work. I ambled over to the younger man, who understood English, and asked what was up. "My brother brings a new harness from our truck," he explained. "It takes the wind better."

"Ah." I know his comment should've calmed my fears, but it made things worse. A newer harness to handle the wind? Are they crazy? My good vibes were shaking in their boots. Rita shouldn't parasail. Parasailing businesses located here in Mexico aren't insured. You do so at your own risk.

The brother arrived and handed the replacement harness to his father. The old man now signaled Rita to step up.

Before I permitted Rita to leave my side, I grabbed her and crushed her against my chest. With our faces resting against each other now, I whispered, "I love you," and then I gave her the most romantic kiss ever, hoping it would take her breath away.

It did. "Why, Mr. Malone," she purred, "what's come over you?"

"Nothing," I lied through my teeth, knowing full well that I feared my girlfriend might end up injured or worse. "Can't a fella wish his girl good luck?"

Rita sighed. "A huh. Just make sure you stash more of those good luck kisses away for later, mister." She unlocked herself from our embrace now so she could pull her long chocolate colored hair back and bundle it with a thin, ponytail binder that had been hanging around her wrist. When she was finished, she stepped into her harness and mouthed, "I love you too."

Mary and Elaine made haste and stepped out of Rita's path. I'd do the same once I was certain everything was secured correctly. There was no way I was going to let this precious cargo get away. One tragedy in my lifetime was enough.

The Mexican minutes get longer
and longer as the days go by . . .
Brooks and Dunn

Chapter 23

Once Rita was up and appeared to be okay, I rejoined Elaine and Mary and said, "Do you two want any thing to drink?" I was hoping they'd say "yes" because my nerves were shot and I really needed a beer.

"A coke would be fine," Mary said

"Might as well get me one too," Elaine added. Then as an after thought she said, "Want some help?"

Even though Rita was more than fifty feet off the ground and I know I would've enjoyed Elaine's company, there's no way I was I going to allow that to happen. I'm not that crazy. If Rita found out, there would be hell to pay. She'd ground me to a pulp. "Nah. I'm just going to that stand over there," I said as I pointed out a beverage hut. "Can't miss Rita's landing. She'd never forgive me."

The two gals corralled me the instant I got back. I quickly handed over the requested beverages, but no words of "thanks" were uttered. I thought that a bit odd, since these two women's manners were heavily ingrained in them before they even toddled around. Why, as far back as I can recall, my sister and Elaine have always shown appreciation for things done for them even if it was as tiny as an eraser smudge on a wall. Something wasn't right. I felt it deep in my gut. I suppose their ill manners could be blamed on their brains being fried by the sun, but then I should be behaving just as weird.

I uncapped my beer and tried not to analyze their strange behavior any further, but it wasn't easy. Neither woman was the least bit concerned about her windblown hair either. That seemed peculiar too. Up until right before I left them, they were both fussing with their locks. Well, they certainly had my undivided attention now whether they wanted it or not. I shoved my sun-glasses on top of my head to view their faces better and to hopefully capture a clue.

Nothing popped out except from my mouth. "All, right, Mary. What gives? Did you get a call from home about Dad?" Sure, the doctor said Dad was doing fine after his heart surgery a year ago, but problems can still crop up anytime.

Mary held her bottle of Coke out in front of her. "No, Matt. No one called." Her scarlet red swimsuit screamed at me. I quickly perched my sunglasses back on my nose. "It's just…."

"What?" I asked cautiously.

"We're worried about Rita."

Elaine's firm, "Yeah, Matt," snapped out so loud beachcombers within a mile-wide radius heard it. "Haven't you noticed how much stronger the wind has gotten since she took off?"

Of course I did. Did they think I was blind? There were only two possible directions to look when a person's walking along the beach—inland or ocean view. Common sense dictated that I, the boyfriend, focused my attention on the girlfriend who was soaring out over the ocean. Yes, she's in the sky, and I'm down here on the beach, but there wasn't a bloody thing I could do to protect her. Sometimes I hated my job as a PI, always having to uphold that tough guy image to the public. I sloughed off Elaine's question with a nonchalant, "Yeah," and left it at that.

She seemed surprised by my off-the-cuff response. "Wow, I can't believe how amazingly calm you are. If that was my hubby, Frank, parasailing up there, I'd be having a coronary about now."

Mary brushed her hair off her eyes, and then she studied my face for a moment. "You know what I think?"

"No, what?" Elaine asked as she pushed her windblown hair off her face too.

"It's the PI in him. He's not allowed to feel anything. How else would he be able to help people in such paralyzing circumstances?"

"I never thought of that. Makes perfect sense. So, is Mary right, Matt?".

I squeezed out a weak reply. "Not exactly. Look, Rita's a big girl, and she knows what she can handle. That only leaves one option open to me."

"And that is?" Elaine inquired as she screwed the lid back on her bottle of Coke.

"I wait and try not to fret." Then I glanced at my water resistant wristwatch. "Speaking of Rita's return, we only have two more minutes to wait according to this little gizmo on my wrist."

Silence engulfed the three of us now as we craned our necks and followed the flight of our fellow traveler.

The warning whistle blew. Then, a minute later it blew again and again.

Elaine's overwrought voice broke our tight grouping. "Oh, God. Rita's struggling with the release cord."

"Crap!" I said sharply. Why couldn't she have skipped the parasailing, I thought. She had nothing to prove. We could've come back another day. Heck, we have five more days in paradise. As I stood numbly by staring at the sky, I tried to send my thought waves to Rita. My grandfather was a strong believer in ESP, extrasensory perception. *Come on, Honey. Grab that darn cord and yank it with all you've got.*

Mary generated her own bit of noise now as she jumped up and down and excitedly announced, "She's all right, Matt. She's coming down! Yay! She's coming down!"

I ran the palms of my hands through my sweaty hair. "Yeah, but where exactly will she land?"

When the parasail drew closer to land, the wind toyed with it even more. Rita was being tossed like a volleyball. There's no way she'd land where she was supposed to now. I carefully scanned the area to see where else she might be brought in from. It didn't look good. Palm trees, statues, condos and several restaurants. My hands were clammy, and my stomach began playing hopscotch. A bad omen. My sixth sense was trying to tell me something, and this time it wasn't concerning a case. Is this what I was being warned about at church on New Year's Day? I said a silent prayer for my girlfriend like I sometimes do for Mrs. Grimshaw. Rita needed all the help she could get.

My plea appeared to be partially answered. Rita managed to clear all the sky high obstacles in her path, but the land was a different story. As soon as her feet slammed into the earth, her legs buckled, and then she was tossed on her butt. The parasail operators and I immediately rushed to her side. It took us a few minutes, but we finally got Rita untangled from the mess. I bent down and offered her my hands. I figured the slam dunk thing probably took its toll on her.

Rita refused my gallant offer. "I don't think I can stand, Matt. My ankle feels pretty strange, and it burns like heck."

How do I proceed now, I wondered? When my mother hurt her foot years ago, she was told the majority of injuries to the ankle are sprain related. The foot turns black and blue and is swollen for a while. That meant if Rita's ankle was merely sprained, Mary and I could ease her off the ground and help her hobble around. But what if my girlfriend was in the minority, and she actually had a more serious complication? Like say a fracture or broken ankle? Forcing her to stand could make the situation worse. I needed to have more information. "When you say your ankle feels strange, what exactly do you mean? Could it be broken?"

Before Rita could reply, the owner of the parasail business interrupted us. "Señor, I think it best if we move her out of the way until medical assistance arrives." Right. They don't provide any.

I didn't answer instantly. I was trying to decide whether I should get an ambulance to take Rita to the local hospital or have us go back to the condo. If her ankle was just sprained, all that was needed was an elastic bandage. I could purchase that at the Farmacia nearest our condo.

"Matt," Rita begged, "please don't call an ambulance for me. We're in a foreign country and we don't know what their services are like. It could be quite expensive even with our dollar worth more than the peso."

Still as practical as ever. Well, at least I knew Rita's head wasn't injured. What would we do without her super marketing skills? She's always analyzed situations from every angle, but for cry'n out loud, you'd think she could set those darn skills aside today of all days. "You have insurance," I said as calmly as possible, and then I motioned for the men to help me carry her to a quieter spot on the beach.

While we were moving her, Mary offered a speedier and cheaper alternative to an ambulance. "I could flag down one of those guys running around on a golf cart and offer to pay him to take Rita back to our condo. What do you think?"

My girlfriend clenched her hands into small fists. "Do it, Mary!" she commanded in a harsh tone. Oh, yeah, she was in serious pain all right. She's never spoken to anyone like that in the few years that we've been dating.

When Mary left to get help, Elaine sat down on the beach next to Rita. There appeared to be a nervous tension between the two women, probably because Elaine couldn't put her mother mode into practice and

Rita feared she might. I mean, can you picture a thirty-five year old woman wanting another woman, no relation to her, hugging her and saying her boo-boo would be all right? On the other hand, a boyfriend hugging his injured girlfriend and making baby talk was acceptable.

Not this boyfriend though. I've never been good at letting people know how much I care when they are hurting. True to my character, I continued a stiff soldier stance while keeping an eagle eye out for Mary's swift return.

Rita ignored Elaine, she turned to me for solace instead. "Matt, I keep rerunning that landing over and over. Was there anything I could've done differently?"

I scratched my head. "Not a thing, Hon. The wind's too strong. You couldn't have been in charge of your destiny even if you had wanted to be. I just wish I'd been there to catch you."

Rita spoke between sniffles. "Our trip is ruined now, thanks to me."

I put my hand up like a traffic cop. "Hush. Don't go there. We still have plenty of things we can do together."

Despite Rita's attempt to wipe her tears away, they kept flowing. "Oh, yeah. Right. Even if it's just a sprained ankle, I'll need crutches to get around. Toss out horseback riding, dancing, swimming, that tri-catamaran trip, and what's left?"

"You two were planning to go on a tri-catamaran outing?" Elaine asked in a surprised tone. "Gee, Mary and I didn't even discuss that option."

Now I treated Elaine like she was invisible too. Instead, I thought of all the tender moments Rita and I have shared alone in the darkness of the night. We could still do that. Unfortunately, I didn't pass my thoughts onto my girlfriend because Elaine was within hearing range, and I didn't want her to conjure up the wrong scene in her disheveled blonde head. I shifted my body slightly to face the direction we walked along earlier this morning. A bright yellow golf cart was heading our way. "Finally!"

Chapter 24

The Mexican man stepped on the brakes of his canary colored golf cart the moment he reached us, and then jumped off his cart onto the sand. For someone in his late fifties, he was fairly spry. His well-cropped jet black hair, thick like his exposed skin, was a stiff contrast to his wardrobe which was all white. "Hola! Me llamo, Juan. Americanos, sí?"

As I stretched my hand out to the stranger who was at least nine inches shorter than me, I wondered exactly who he was. "Sí," I hastily replied.

The man's solid hands firmly cupped mine. "Señor, your familia sent me to you. ¿Te ayudo?"

I had no hint of what he did for a living, but his grip was as strong if not stronger than mine. "Por favor. Sorry, I don't understand."

Juan's black mustache was as broad as his smile now as he repeated his words in English. "Can I help you?"

"Ah, sí, yes . . ."

Elaine interrupted before I could go any further. "Matt, he said your familia. What's he referring to?" She was the only one in our group who didn't know any Spanish. She had studied French in high school instead. Supposedly, it was because it was a more romantic language, but between you and me, I think she had her eye on the student teacher who was earning his degree in languages the quarter she signed up.

"He's talking about my sister, my family."

"Oh? Oh, I get it now. Familia–family."

And blondes wonder why they are the butt of so many jokes.

The driver of the golf cart continued now. "The pretty woman went back to where you are staying. ¿Quiubo (What's happening)?"

I glanced down at Rita. "Do you want to explain, or should I?"

She grimaced but her tears were finally gone. "You do it, Matt. I'm in too much pain. I can't think straight."

Elaine couldn't restrain her maternal instincts any longer. They were in full bloom now as she reached over, softly patted Rita's hands and said, "There, there. It'll be all right."

After Elaine's little emotional display, I thought it best to wait and see what developed with Rita before I told the owner of the golf cart about her injury. As much pain as Rita was in, she just might tell Elaine where to go in a not-to-lady-like fashion and then I'd have to settle things down pronto. When a couple seconds had elapsed and all was still sane with the world, I figured it was safe to pass the information on. "Eh, Señorita, torci el tobillo–twisted her ankle."

He gazed directly at my girlfriend. "Ah. You're in luck, Señorita, with bella verde ojos. I am a medico at the local clinic." Thank God, I thought. man with charm and smarts. His flattering remark about Rita's eyes ought to help her relax. Now he situated himself so he could speak to me. "Me permite?" The man must've assumed I was Rita's husband because he asked my permission to examine her.

"Sí, adelante," I swiftly replied.

The doctor squatted down near Rita's right leg now. "Don't worry, Señorita. I won't harm you. I will be most kind." Rita followed his hands as they gently moved below her knee. "Does it hurt anywhere else besides your ankle?" he inquired as his hands searched for other problems.

My girlfriend responded bravely. "No. As far as I can tell, it's all in the ankle area."

"Por favor, Señorita. Show me where it hurts the most."

Rita quickly pointed to her inner ankle.

"Ah, sí. You have more than a sprain. The bone… it is popped out. X-rays are needed."

I repeated the doctor's words. "X-rays?" If I wasn't expecting to hear that, I'm certain Rita wasn't either. "Why is that necessary? I thought all you do for a bone that's popped out is to get it back in place and then put a cast on."

"Sí, that is true if the break is clean, but we always take X-rays first to be certain of the damage."

I moved in closer to Rita. "Doctor, does that mean she'd need surgery if it wasn't a clean break?"

He nodded. "Sí."

Elaine released Rita's hands now and exploded. "Surgery! But Doctor Juan, we're only here on vacation for a few days. How's she going to fly back home?"

Rita got quite pale after Elaine's outburst. "Are you all right, Hon?" I asked, and then I handed her the bottled water I'd bought for her earlier. "Here, take a drink."

While Rita took a few swallows from the bottle, I drew my attention to the only other woman present now, the blonde with the tousled hair who looked like the bride of Frankenstein. "Elaine, control yourself. You can't worry about something we're not even sure of yet."

Her nervous hands flew to her mussed up hair. I suppose she was trying to make it more presentable. Too bad she didn't know it was beyond fixing. "I'm sorry I got so carried away, Rita," she said. "I wasn't thinking. You already have enough on your plate." When she was finished with Rita, my sister's childhood friend turned sharply to the doctor who was still squatted by Rita's feet and calmly asked, "What do you recommend we do, Doctor? Call an ambulance?"

Doctor Juan rose now and whipped his cell phone out of his shirt pocket. "Sí, I think that is best."

Rita's hands reached for mine. I generously offered them to her, and she clamped on appreciatively. "Matt, what if they make us pay right a way for the hospital services? I haven't got that kind of money on me."

"Hush, Rita I don't want you worrying about that." Now, I dropped to the soft, hot sand and positioned an arm around her shoulders. "Everything will be okay, Sweetheart. I'll call Tuttles and Gray and see what we can arrange."

Chapter 25

"Hola!" I said as I spoke into my cell phone for the second time this morning, forgetting, yet again that I was calling stateside. Luckily, the time here was the same as in Minnesota, nine a.m.

Mrs. Grimshaw's voice brimmed with excitement. "Oh, my goodness. Is that you, Matt?"

"Yup. Sorry I spoke in Spanish, Margaret."

"That's all right. I listen to the local Spanish radio station from time to time, so I know what the word means. Say, have you talked to your family since you left for Mexico?"

I dropped my eyes to the magazine I had just set on my lap. "No," I answered in a concerned tone. What was my apartment neighbor insinuating? "Is there a reason I should have?"

"No, not that I know of," she cooly replied. "I was just wondering if anyone had shared our weather report with you. That's all."

"Oh?" My shoulders relaxed now. "No, not a soul."

"Well, we got ten inches of new snow right after your plane took off."

"No kidding! I'll have to mention that to the women. Now, there's one more reason to be glad we're down here."

Mrs. Grimshaw sighed. "You four were fortunate to fly out when you did. I just hate being around all this snow. I wish I were ten years younger. Why, I'd fly somewhere warm every winter."

I got serious real fast. "Sometimes flying to a warmer climate isn't all it's cut out to be, Margaret."

Fortunately for me, my neighbor back home didn't pick up on what I was hinting at. Instead, she rambled on with her own thoughts. "Say, why are you calling me? Didn't you tell me you wanted to spend as much time as possible with Rita?"

I began to tap my fingers lightly on the magazine. What a difference a day makes, I thought. "I'll get to that in a moment," I replied in a tired tone, "but first, has anyone been looking for me?"

"Give me a minute to think about it," Margaret answered. "Let's see. Just Mr. Edwards, the caretaker. He said you'll finally be able to get into the driver side of your car without emptying all the air out of your body, whatever that means."

Yes, I said silently to myself. No more climbing over the front passenger seat to get to the driver position. I suppose I should act concerned about the guy who parked next to me for the last several years. "Is Mr. Franklin finally moving to a different floor?"

The elderly woman took a deep, heavy breath before she replied. "I guess you could say that. He dropped dead at work the day of the snowstorm. Just slumped over his computer. Can you imagine?"

"Nope. It must've been pretty hard on his co-workers. Did he have a heart attack?"

"I haven't heard, Matt. No one has stopped by his apartment to collect his things yet, but enough about the deceased Mr. Franklin. Tell me what your lovely girlfriend's doing while you're chatting on the phone with me? Is she down at the beach swimming?"

Yeah, right, if she only could. I cleared my throat before answering. "No, she's not swimming."

My neighbor spoke louder now. "What's with the stiff tone in your voice, Matt? Don't tell me you two had an argument? How is that supposed to draw you closer together?"

I took the medical magazine off my lap, tossed it on the low table in front of me where a variety of other magazines sat, and then I stretched my legs. The collection of magazines the hospital provided for visitors had filled a void for me. Ever since noon yesterday, I had been hanging out here off and on. "We didn't have an argument," I replied. "Honest, Margaret. Rita had a slight mishap, however, and I thought you should know about it before we come back home."

"Sweet Mother Mary and Joseph.," Margaret whispered into the phone. "What happened, Matt? Was she robbed? I heard that occurs a lot to Americans traveling in foreign countries."

I placed one leg on top of the other. "No, she wasn't robbed. Yesterday morning, the four of us decided to go parasailing.."

"Yes, go on," she insisted.

"By the time Rita's turn came, the wind had picked up considerably. Of course, I tried to convince her to go another day, but she refused to change her plans. As I've told you before, she can be quite obstinate. Well, her takeoff was fine, but when she returned to the beach she ran into problems. She veered off course, and her feet slammed into the sand."

"Oh, dear. How badly was she hurt?" Margaret asked sounding deeply concerned.

"She injured her right ankle."

Margaret let out a huge sigh this time. "My goodness. What was the diagnosis?"

There was no need to get into all the medical mumbo jumbo jargon with Margaret, I thought. A few details should be sufficient. "Bones supporting the inner and outer part of her ankle were broke," I explained, "and the only way to repair that kind of damage is with surgery. The doctor had to insert a thin, tiny metal plate and screws."

"Oh, no. How awful. How long will Rita have to stay in the hospital, Matt?"

I brushed a few stray strands of red hair off my forehead and stood. "The nurse told me she might get released before noon today."

"Are you at the hospital right now?"

"Yeah, I stayed here all night. I've been hanging out in the lobby for almost an hour now. Just waiting for the nurses and doctor to finish with Rita."

"You know as many times as I've been in the hospital for surgeries of my own, it seems like the morning is always shot before visitors are allowed into a patient's room."

"Well, the staff does have to follow routine procedures."

"Yes, of course they do. I understand that, but when you're a patient you just want to see your company and not be bothered with all the other stuff. Say, Mr. Malone."

"Yeah?"

"Take some friendly advice from a little Italian woman who's way past her prime. Pamper that girlfriend of yours to death, and for heaven's sake, ignore her when she tells you she doesn't need any help. We both know most people are too stubborn to admit when they need it, including me."

I began walking towards the elevator. It was a few steps from me. "Boy, did I ever learn that fact after my father's surgery."

"And, Matt."

"Yes?"

"Give Rita a hug from me and tell her I'm sorry to hear about her mishap."

"I will," I said as the elevator dinged, warning me that it was about to open. "Got to go. See you in a couple days."

"Arrivederci," my neighbor back home said, and then she quickly corrected herself. "Oops. That's Italian. I meant adios, amigo," and then her phone went dead.

The elevator door quietly slid open now. Six people stood like soldiers staring out past me, each engrossed in their own thoughts. The passengers must've gotten on at the basement level since the elevator was going up. I quickly joined them and pressed the floor I needed.

Chapter 26

A half hour before Rita was to be released into my care, I rented a wheelchair from the farmacia just kitty corner to the hospital. When I compared the rental price of crutches versus a wheelchair, I almost took the crutches. Then I got to thinking about Rita's taking just one misstep and the repercussions that would follow. Why, she'd be flat on her fanny and back at square one. She couldn't afford that. Nor could I for that matter. Besides, with a wheelchair at our disposal my girlfriend would probably feel less confined and be willing to take in a few attractions before our time was up here in paradise. At least, that's what I was hoping.

Of course, there was one significant issue that had to be addressed before today. How was I going to get wheelchair bound Rita from point A to point B without a car? Luckily, the Marriott readily resolved that problem. The hotel/timeshare chain down here offers free shuttle service for handicapped customers who need to travel twenty miles or less within the boundaries of PV.

"I'm so glad I'm out of that stuffy, boring overcrowded hospital," Rita said as she released her fourth yawn. "I simply don't comprehend why the hospital keeps people overnight. A patient doesn't get any sleep there. The nurses constantly disturb you for this, that and the other thing. 'Pill time. Let's check your vitals. Try sitting on the bedpan.' What finally drove me to the brink was that obnoxious pain system they have. 'How much pain are you in from 1-10?' I was asked that a zillion times. I wanted to scream, 'Who the heck cares?' just to get a reaction out of the nurses. Thank God you finally came to my rescue, Matt. I don't know what I would've done if you hadn't shown up when you did. Oh, that reminds me. I never asked you how many pesos you had to bribe the nurses with so they'd let me leave?" Then my girlfriend's mouth miraculously shut down.

What a relief. I was mighty thankful for the quiet interlude. Err, perhaps I should explain before you think the worst of me. I know there's a lot of men out there who envision stuffing their girlfriend's mouth with something to stop them from talking permanently, but believe me, that's not how I feel about Rita. She's normally a very thoughtful conversationalist—talks a little and then listens appropriately. Unfortunately, that's not the way it was playing out today. Right before her sudden meltdown, she was wired on overdrive in a one-way conversation going nowhere. Quite honestly, if she had remained that way indefinitely, I don't know how I'd behave. The meds the doctor prescribed had to be the culprit. I mean, what other explanation was there?

I wasn't present when the nurse gave her the stuff, so I had no idea what Rita was on. Valium? Oxycodone? Or Vicodin? Everyone reacts so differently to medication. I'll have to ask her later since her take-home hospital goodies were already packed in a solid white paper bag that was stapled shut.

I inhaled deeply and cleared my head of all thoughts of medicine now. Actually, when I got back to the pure silence sitting between the two of us, I realized I was missing a great opportunity. Here's my girlfriend on a once in a lifetime silent retreat, and I wasn't taking advantage of it. *Now's the time to get a few words in, Matt.* "By the way, Mary and Elaine are anxious to see you. They wanted to visit you at the hospital, but I told them you were only staying one night and you'd see them when you got released."

The words, "Good thinking," came out of Rita's mouth rather sluggishly. "No time to chat with all the poking and prodding going on. Besides, I was probably zoned out."

I thought back to yesterday afternoon. "You most definitely were."

"Well, I hope I didn't jabber about too much nonsense. I've never been heavily sedated before."

"You didn't," I lied. There was no way I was going to repeat any information she whispered into my ear, even if it was about an old boyfriend. Of course, I could use it for ammunition at a later date if I needed to. Nah, just forget that I thought about that.

When we were finally back at the Marriott, I gently glided Rita safely past the double glass entrance doors, in and out of the elevator, and straight down the narrow hall that led to our third floor condo. Once we were actually at the door of our condo, I busied myself with getting the key card out of my pant pocket and inserting it in the slot.

While Rita patiently waited for the door to get unlocked, she felt compelled to say something. "You know, Matt, you don't have to keep pushing this wheelchair. I've got two good arms."

Remembering Mrs. Grimshaw's bit of wisdom shared via the phone earlier this morning, I didn't allow myself to get irritated. Instead, I calmly said, "I know that, Sweetheart, but you've been through so much the past twenty-four hours. I thought the least I could do was lighten your burden. Besides, you'll have plenty of time to move yourself around when we get back to Minnesota." Now I placed the key card back in my pocket, and then I pushed the door open.

My sister flapped her small arms in mid-air when we entered the condo. "Elaine," she shouted, "come and see who just walked in." Then she strolled over to us and hugged Rita's shoulders. "I'm so sorry, Rita. If I hadn't suggested parasailing, you wouldn't be in this awful mess. Look at you." Mary's arms had served their purpose now. She allowed them to fall to her sides as she took a couple steps back.

Rita appeared paler after Mary had said her bit. "There's no way any of us could've predicted my injury, Mary," she said as she gazed at my sister. "If I didn't break my ankle on the beach, there's another million things that could've happened. It was in the cards."

"Yeah, fate," I said. "It's unpredictable. You can't control it. None of us knows what's going to happen from day to day."

Mary opened her mouth. "But still . . ."

Rita drew a finger to her luscious lips. "Shh, Mary, please. I don't want to hear another word about it. I knew what I was doing. There's no one to blame but myself."

Elaine traipsed out of the kitchen area now carrying two enormous margarita glasses filled to the brim with liquid refreshment. "Did I hear someone call my name?" When she spotted Rita, she almost dropped the drinks. "Oh, my gosh! You're right on time. I made these just the way I heard you liked them." Rita didn't reach for the wheels on the wheelchair to propel herself to the center of the living room, so I assumed it was okay for me to continue to do so.

"Thanks," Rita said rather sleepily as she accepted a margarita. "I was given a pain pill early this morning, and the effects have finally worn off."

"Well, I'm glad I whipped this up then," Elaine said with a cheerful grin. "I guess this is what you call one of those perfect timing incidents, huh?"

Rita permitted a weak smile to cross her face. "Most definitely."

Now that one refreshment had been claimed, Elaine scooted behind Rita's wheelchair to where I was standing. "Matt, I didn't know if you'd want a margarita or a cerveza. There's a couple Coronas chilling in the fridge. I can get one for you."

I kicked my tennis shoes off. "What you have there is fine," I replied lightly. "I really don't feel like a beer right now." After I took the margarita from Elaine, I sat down on the dark leather bench next to Rita's wheelchair.

"Elaine," my sister said with a slightly excited tone to her voice. "I hope you made enough margaritas for us too?"

"Sure, sure," the blonde answered. "Don't sweat it. I made a whole pitcher full."

Now Mary smiled broadly. "Wonderful. I'll get ours then." When she was halfway to the kitchen she inquired over her shoulder, "Anyone want munchies to go with their drinks?"

"Yeah," I swiftly responded. My stomach had been growling for over an hour already. "I'll take pretzels or anything else you have." Then I zeroed in on Rita's needs. "What about you, sweetheart?"

"Hmm? Yes. I suppose I shouldn't have a drink on an empty stomach. Breakfast-in-bed was served at seven-thirty this morning."

Mary giggled. "Oh, that's funny, Rita. Breakfast-in-bed. I've got to remember that one." Then she laughed again. "Well, I hope you won't be too disappointed by what I have to offer you this fine afternoon in our very chic Mexican style living room. My culinary delights haven't earned me four stars yet like the chefs at the hospital, but I hope they'll suffice. So, is there anything in particular you're craving?"

"Not really," my girlfriend said with a fatigued tone. "Fix whatever you want."

"That makes it easy enough." Now Mary quickly invited her friend to join her with a wave of her hand. "Come on, Elaine. I can't carry snacks and our drinks too."

Elaine whirled past me in her tight fitting jean shorts and bright purple halter top. "I suppose not," and then she gave us a wink.

I was going to wait until the snacks came before I took a taste of the margarita, but I was afraid if I held the glass any longer, I'd accidently jar it and spill the lime colored contents on the lush white area carpet running beneath my bare feet. "Hmm, not bad. Elaine did a good job of mixing it up. Did you taste yours yet, Rita?" She replied with a slow back and forth motion to her head. If my eyes were picking up on my girlfriend's cues right, she wasn't in any shape to do anything, not even sipping on a drink. "Sweetheart, you don't look very comfortable. I think I should get you out of that wheelchair and settled on the sofa, don't you? The nurse said something about your foot needing to be elevated for several days to reduce the swelling."

"You're right, Matt. There's been so much commotion since you wheeled me in, I'd forgotten all about that." Now, she licked salt off the rim of her glass and sipped some of its contents. "Umm, Señor Malone."

"Yes, Senorita Sinclair?"

"You didn't rate Elaine's bartending abilities correctly."

"I didn't?"

"Absolutely not. She didn't do a good job, she did a super job." She handed her drink off to me now. "Here, set this down someplace safe, will you? I'm afraid I might drop it."

I got up, took her glass, said "Ah huh," and then I placed both our drinks on the white wicker side table nearest the sofa. "Ready to get out of the chair now?"

Rita didn't reply. She merely shifted her buns to the edge of the chair and stretched her arms out to me.

"What's this mean?" I said as I mimicked Rita's arm placement. "Are you trying to tell me you want a hug or a lift out of the chair? I'm having a hard time interpreting your movements, Lady."

"Mister, you know perfectly well I want help getting out of this chair." Then she paused. "Of course, if you want to give me a hug afterwards I won't give you any grief."

I leaned towards her and slowly eased her out of the wheelchair now. "Remember," I said, "don't stand on your right leg, just your left."

"Roger, Captain, I've taken your advice under consideration." Rita dug her painted fingernails into my arms before she placed her left foot down and hopped twice to reach the couch. I could tell she was scared. Now that she was at her destination, she sat down gently and allowed me to help her get situated.

"Straighten your legs," I suggested, "and I'll put a throw pillow under your right ankle to prop it up." Then I grabbed one of the bright blue pillows resting on a wicker chair and placed her heavily gauzed foot on it, making darn sure it was situated correctly. According to the nurses at the hospital, her foot needed to be higher than her heart. "There, comfy now?"

"Mmm, yes. Much better."

"Great." Before I stood, I brushed Rita's hair off her eyes and kissed her softly on the forehead. "Hon, don't you think you could use a catnap? You look exhausted."

Rita let go of several more yawns. "I don't think so. I'm fine." She wasn't fine in my book. She was fighting sleep, anyone could see that. Why was she denying it? "I'll be all right, Matt, really. I've already missed spending a whole day with you?" That's what it was. She didn't want me out of her sight. Rita allowed her head to relax against the curved arm of the couch now, and then she said, "I can't afford to lose another one."

Okay. If Rita didn't think she was ready for a nap yet, I might as well go along for the ride. I reached behind her and retrieved her drink from the wicker table. "Here you go, Senorita Sinclair. Drink up. The day is young."

As I held her drink in front of her, Rita's eyes flickered rapidly. She was sleep deprived. all right. Not only couldn't she keep her eyes open, but it took her a few moments of deep concentration before putting a hand out for her glass. When she finally did, she treated her drink like an annoying fly and swatted it away. "No, gracias, Señor. I told you food first," and then she drifted off to sleep.

Chapter 27

Mary and Elaine began their return to the living room now humming a catchy Mexican tune. Luckily, I caught their attention before they had come too far in and woke Rita. "Shh," I whispered in their direction, "she just fell asleep."

"Sorry it took us so long," Elaine said softly. "We couldn't decide what you two might enjoy munching on."

I quickly pointed to the square, glass-topped dining table situated at the other end of the room that overlooked the pool on the ground floor outdoors. Mary and her friend understood immediately. They carted the food and drinks to the table and set them down.

Even though we were a fair distance from the couch and Rita now, we still continued to speak in confessional voices around the table. "So, how long do you think Rita will be out, Matt?" my sister inquired.

"No clue. When we left the hospital, Rita said she didn't get any sleep last night."

"Of course, not," Elaine interjected. "I dare you to find me one person who says they actually had a goodnight's sleep while they spent time in a hospital." She held a finger up in front of her. "Just one."

My sister swayed her head. "Quite honestly, I don't think it's possible."

"I totally agree," I said. "Remember Dad's stay in the hospital, Mary, after his heart surgery?"

"Ah huh. His room was a zoo. People in and out around the clock."

Elaine picked up a piece of cheese nacho and encased it in her mouth. Then ignoring dining etiquette, she said what was on her mind. "Do the surgery and then send the patient home where they can recuperate in peace and quiet in their own bed. Just think of all the people who wouldn't have to be hooked up to those stupid monitors."

"Amen, to that," I quietly replied as I reached for something to put in my stomach.

Mary picked up her glass, took a sip of her margarita and swallowed. "Matt, I think you should do something for yourself while Rita's napping."

"Like what?"

"Oh, stepping outside and getting some fresh air for one thing."

I shook my head vehemently. "No, way! That wouldn't be right. I can't go gallivanting around town without Rita. What kind of boyfriend does that?"

"Matt, I'm not suggesting you spend several hours out and about doing whatever you please, just one or two. Surely Rita wouldn't mind. Besides, she'll probably sleep the whole time you're gone."

I stared out the window. "Nope, I'm not leaving even if it's just for two hours,"

Mary wasn't about to give up on her idea just yet. She raised her fancy crystal glass off the table a few inches. "Hear me out. What if Rita decides she doesn't want to do any sightseeing from a wheelchair the rest of her stay?"

"Yeah," Elaine edged in. "Your whole vacation would be shot."

I shook my head again as I reached for a few pretzels and dunked them in cheese dip. "Ah, I don't know. The plan was to fill my hours doing things with Rita."

"Well," Mary said, "it just so happens Elaine's been dying to purchase a few paintings of Mexican scenery to take back home with her, and she needs someone to barter in Spanish for her."

Elaine tossed her blonde head to one side. "Oh, yeah, Matt. That would be great if you could help me out. I heard there's quite a few artists selling their wares at a market just a couple blocks from here, so we wouldn't be gone too long." She tugged on my arm. "Please, please say you'll do it," and then she spread her lips into a luscious smile the way she did when she wanted something from me when she was younger.

Warnings went off in my head. *Be careful, Matt. You may get in trouble with this woman.* But as fast as they came they went. I finished my margarita and set the empty glass down. "I don't know, gals. I feel guilty leaving Rita behind."

My sister tried to make me feel better. "It's not like you're leaving Rita by herself, you know. I'm going to be right here."

I bent my head towards my glass and mumbled into it, "Yeah, right," but I wasn't really satisfied that Mary would keep an eye on Rita. She tends to get distracted easily.

"Come on, what do you say, Matt?" Elaine wiped her hands with a napkin, and then she lightly touched the top of my hand. It was resting on the table. Sparks ignited, but I controlled my innards. I remained heavy and salty like the Dead Sea. "It'll do you good to get out of here for awhile," she continued. "You were cooped up in that horrible hospital all last night and part of today. You need a change of venue–have some fun."

Not if the girlfriend finds out, I thought to myself. I quickly wiggled my hand out from under Elaine's and then I turned to face my sister who was just emptying her glass of its cool, lime colored liquid content. "You promise to stay right by the couch until we return?"

Mary held up her fingers like she was taking an oath for a scouting organization. "I do. Now scram. Get out of here. I don't want to see either of your ugly faces until you have some paintings in hand. Comprehendo?"

"Sí," Elaine and I replied as one.

Chapter 28

As soon as we started making our way along the shop-filled street, Elaine said, "I hope you don't feel I'm infringing on your time with Rita, Matt."

"Don't worry about it. Like Mary said, she'll probably be out for several hours and I don't have anything else to occupy my time with."

"Still...."

I paused in front of one of the shop windows now and studied it intently. "End of discussion, Elaine. Just drop it."

My companion scrambled down the cobblestoned street now and left me in the dust. "Come on, Matt," she shouted over her shoulder. "The open market I was telling you about is around the next corner."

"Give me a sec, will yeah?" I was trying to decide what I could possibly purchase for Rita to cheer her up. Unfortunately, nothing in the window was crying out to me. I tore my eyes away from the colorful window displays now and focused them on the blonde-haired woman who was several steps ahead of me. "Slow down, Elaine. I want to enjoy the sights and sounds of PV as much as you do but at a more leisurely pace. Who knows when any of us will get back this way again."

Just as I finished saying that, a short, elderly woman, around the age of a great-grandma, poked her pure white head out of one of the shop's open doorways and stared out at me. She quickly released a smile, exposing some missing teeth. Perhaps she thought her winning grin was all that was required to reward her business with a few of our American dollars.

That's one great thing Mexico has going for it, the weakness of its peso to our dollar. Towns up and down the coastal regions, as well as some centrally located ones, have progressed nicely as the years have gone on, like Puerto Vallarta, where people were supposedly here as long ago as 580 BC, but the Mexican money has never caught up. Why? The country's monetary woes have always been wrapped around political corruption and probably always will be.

Sadly, what's become one man's Achilles' heel becomes another man's jackpot. Americans and other nationalities get more for their buck in Mexico than they can in their own backyards.

Elaine shifted her head in my direction before she spoke. "I have," and then she still continued at a steady pace.

How does one confuse rushing with leisurely, I wondered. Maybe the word leisure was never added to this blonde's vocabulary. Once I realized my sister's friend wasn't about to slow down anytime soon, I put myself into speed walking mode, so I wouldn't lose her. When I eventually caught up to her, I was breathing haphazardly. "Exactly what are you looking for?" I asked. "An original watercolor matted and framed or a velvet painting like that?" Now, I pointed to a middle-aged native who was sitting cross-legged on the ground next to samples of his work.

"I'm not sure, but I'll know it when I spot it."

I wasn't a bit surprised with what Elaine just said. It was one of many brainwashed comments females use excessively. It's like cracking open a fortune cooking and reading the same fortune over and over, or watching Bill Murray who plays the main character in the movie *Ground Hog Day* repeat the same day over and over again. Will the poor guy ever get out of the rut he's stuck in? So too with women. They just know, it and that's that. Well, what if the gal I'm with doesn't see it? Does that mean I'll be hitting more markets in town? I'm not up to that. My feet couldn't handle it, nor could I. I hate shopping as much as the next guy.

A tiny child dressed in bright blue shorts and a t-shirt beckoned me to her mother's stall which displayed shawls woven in many choices of color. I shook my head and said, "No, gracias." The little girl acted disappointed and scrambled into her mother's open arms, I felt bad, but I couldn't buy everything that was being sold. Feeling the heat now from the mother's and child's glaring eyes, I traveled on.

The next stall offered all types of silver items: jewelry, rings, necklaces, belt buckles, buttons and hair clasps. A pair of silver barrettes to hold Rita's long hair behind her dainty, vanilla-scented ears would be nice, and they would certainly compliment her dark chocolate hair. Before I could make a final decision, my shopping partner grabbed my hand and whisked me away.

"What's going on? Are you afraid you'll lose me?"

Elaine pushed her long straight bangs to one side before answering. "Of course not. I found some paintings, Matt, and I want your honest opinion before you start bartering with the artist."

"Okay."

When we arrived at the stall containing the paintings Elaine was interested in, I eased my hand from her grip. I figured she didn't need my macho hand any longer. The sales area was small, but no Mexican artist was present. Perhaps he went off to get a meal from one of the street vendors. Actually, not having him here worked perfectly. Elaine and I could discuss the paintings without offending him or her.

Even though the artist wasn't in his stall, two young college-aged men dressed in light-weight khaki pants and white loose-fitting cotton Mexican shirts were socializing with what I assumed was a newly married couple. Well, they were hugging and kissing to the extreme. That's usually a telltale sign. Embarrassed to be around such mush, I turned my attention to Elaine and asked, "So, where are the paintings you're interested in?"

"Over in that corner," she said, and then she pointed to the left of me.

I looked, but I didn't see a darn thing. The two men were directly in my line of vision. Thinking of Rita, and therefore not wanting to hang around any longer than I had to, I selfishly decided to infringe on their intimate conversation. "Excuse us," I said. "We'd like to get to the pictures behind you."

"Oh, sure. No problem," the shorter man with the sandy-brown hair that was two shades lighter than his tan answered. I wonder if he got his tan here or before he flew down to PV. I guess it didn't matter.

"Okay, Matt," Elaine said as she neared the pictures, "it's between these three, right here. Do I buy the three-foot one which encompasses all of PV—the water, mountains and tower of Our Lady of Guadalupe Church, or do I buy the smaller ones which just depict a man and a woman in festival garb?"

I rubbed my hands together as if that would resolve Elaine's dilemma. "It's up to you. I have no decorating sense whatsoever, but I'm sure my sister's made you aware of that a long time ago."

Elaine sighed. "Ah, come on, Matt. Don't wimp out on me. Just because you're a bachelor doesn't mean you don't have an opinion. Everyone has an opinion."

I've never liked being classified as a wimp. I immediately caved in and squatted down to take a closer look. "Well, there's definitely more detail involved in this larger piece than there is in the smaller ones. I guess it all depends on what colors are already in the room you'll be hanging it in and if it captures the theme."

You're so cute, Matt. I could just squeeze you." I held my hand out to ward her off. Elaine laughed deeply. "Don't worry; I won't. You didn't mean theme."

"I didn't?"

"No. Theme is like for a party: Halloween, birthday or wedding shower. You meant my style."

I ran my hand through my red hair. I do that a lot when I'm uncomfortable. "Whatever. It's all the same to me."

"Well, it doesn't have to be. If you just watched a little HGTV every night, you'd have the terms down in no time. Why, I bet more men watch the decorating shows on that channel than women."

Elaine stepped back a ways to take a better look at the pictures. "Actually the colors don't matter, Frank and I plan to repaint some of the rooms in the house when I get back from this trip."

I ignored Elaine's patter. Instead, I picked up one of the smaller paintings to examine it more closely. "Not as many brush strokes on this one, and the strokes aren't as heavy." After I said that, I stood and held the painting away from the sun. "You know, Elaine, I think two different artists did these paintings."

"You're right!" It was the voice of the sandy-haired individual who spoke to me a few minutes before. His speech pattern sounded like a Midwesterner. I just couldn't pinpoint which state. He shoved his hand out in front of me. "Hi. I'm Darryl Hunt."

The moment I grabbed his hand I felt like I had been given a one-two punch to the stomach. Either I snacked on something that didn't agree with me or I was coming down with a bad case of Tourista, I thought. Here's hoping it's the former because I certainly didn't want to spend the rest of the day sitting on the throne in the condo. Stupid me! Not only was my body on vacation, but my mind too. I didn't even occur to me that my stomach problem could be related to my sixth sense.

As soon as I dropped Darryl's hand, he continued. "Sorry, we couldn't help you when you first arrived, but we were just finishing up a sale."

Surprised to learn that the paintings weren't done by a Mexican artist, I said, "Oh, that's okay. She was looking for something done by a local artist anyway. You know how women are."

His mouth formed a devilish grin. "Yeah, very particular. Well, you're in luck. My friend and I have been coming down here since high school. He was born right here in Puerto Vallarta." Then he loped his lanky arm around his friend's shoulder.

Now the other twenty-something man with jet black hair joined in. "Darryl forgot to tell you one small thing. The only reason he's here is because I know the language and we can stay at my grandparents for free."

"That's the way to do it, I guess," I said. "Otherwise, you wouldn't make much money after you put out for hotel accommodations."

I was getting ready to set the small painting back down when Darryl reached for it. "Here. Let me take that from you."

"Thanks," I said as I handed it off to him.

Darryl's partner went on. "If you're really not into Mexican scenery and such, we can show you samples of other work we've done. All we have to do is plug in our laptop and bring up our Web site."

"Oh, that won't be necessary," Elaine interrupted. "The velvet paintings would work better. The interior of my house is fashioned more on the Spanish style of architecture. It was popular twenty-five years ago. I'm sure you know what I'm talking about, dark woodwork, high ceilings with wood beams stretched across, and arched doorways. The only thing the previous owners didn't do was stucco the house and put clay tiles on the roof." Elaine paused for a moment. "My problem is I can't decide which painting would work best."

"Well, perhaps I can help you make a decision if you show me what else you were looking at. By the way, I'm Pedro Hernandez." The young man totally ignored me and went straight for Elaine's hand, so I stepped aside.

My companion enjoyed the selective attention so much that if it were dark out, her smile would've shone the way. She took the hand offered to her and said, "Nice to meet you, Pedro. I'm Elaine." With that out of the way now, she strolled back to the other two paintings she had just shown me.

Pedro ambled behind paying close attention to the exact spot Elaine was speaking of. When he reached the location, he moved the two pictures away from the ones they were leaning against. "I'll tell you what, "he said to Elaine as he held the pictures out in front of him, "for you, and only you, I will sell all three for the lump sum of seventy-five dollars. Is that a bargain or what?"

I glanced at Elaine to see if she still wanted me to play the barter game.

The slim woman totally ignored me. Instead she raised her right hand to her mouth and chewed on her perfectly painted nails. "I don't know. I'm afraid my husband might think that's a little too steep," and then she gave me a quick wink

The two young artists glared at me. Crap! How many more dirty looks am I going to get today?

Darryl, who seemed to be extremely rough around the edges, anxiously cut-in. "Seventy-five dollars is too steep for three masterpieces? You've got to be joking? You wouldn't believe the kind of money we get back home for our work."

Pedro immediately tried to make amends. "I'm sorry my friend sounds so harsh, but we really are starving artists. Why don't you two think about the pieces a little bit. We can set the paintings aside for you. If you don't come back by evening, we'll put them out for sale again."

Elaine wiped her lips delicately with her finger. "Well, all right. I would like a little more time to discuss the price with my husband." Then she clutched my arm and pulled me down the street in the opposite direction. Great! She was passing me off as her spouse now. What will she do next?

After we were a small distance from Pedro and Darryl's stall, Elaine finally commented. "Can you imagine?"

"Imagine what?"

"That those guys actually believed you were my stingy husband."

I chortled softly. "You've got to be kidding? Of course, I guess it's better than them thinking I'm your escort."

"Escort?" My companion almost choked; she was laughing so hard. "That's hilarious."

"What?" I asked. "You mean I would never pass for one?" secretly relieved that no one would ever suspect me of that.

"Not on your life," Elaine replied still giggling. "You have to dress and walk a certain way to carry that off."

"Well, good. I couldn't afford to maintain a hefty wardrobe anyway. Just give me jeans, and I'm in heaven." I had reached the first street corner ahead of Elaine and stopped abruptly. We wouldn't be able to cross just yet with so many cars and buses zooming by. I looked back at Elaine. She was just about caught up to me. "Can we please head back to the hotel, now?" I pleaded.

"Not yet. I want you to help me decide whether the three pictures are a good deal or not. Perhaps we could check out one of the bars around here and chat there."

I frantically waved my hand in front of me. "Oh, no. No bar. Rita's a wonderful woman, but if she found out I went there with you, there's no telling what kind of hot water I'd be in."

"Okay. No bar. How about a Coke or cup of java then?"

"Which ever you prefer is fine."

My sister's friend didn't offer a comeback. Her attention was momentarily drawn to other things. "Matt, look. Something's going on over there." My blonde companion pointed across the street to a particular shop where large groups of people were coming and going. "Must be a pretty popular place, huh? Care to see what's up?"

I glanced across the way. "Are you talking about that rustic clay building on the corner?"

"Yeah."

"Sure. Let's take a look."

The two of us joined up now like Siamese twins and scurried across the cobblestone street and then continued on to the doorway of the shop. Right before we entered, I tilted my head back a bit to read the sign hanging over the entrance. I wanted to make sure I knew what we were getting ourselves into.

Elaine quickly moved a few steps to my right and then braced her hands on her hips. "What are you staring at, Matt, a sea gull?"

"No. The shop's sign."

Who ever said Tequila was so fine?
I'm going to shoot them.
Now won't that be divine.

Chapter 29

"Oh, great!" the blonde boomed as she placed her slim hands on her solidly packed hips. "It says Tequila. Well, we both know how dangerous that liquid refreshment can be. I suppose that means we can't go in?"

I shook my head. "We can take a quick peek, but I'm warning you, if the place turns out to be a bar, we're out of there." Now I played the perfect gentleman and held the door open for her.

"Hey, this is a cool place," my companion said in a library voice. "It isn't at all what I expected."

"Me neither," I whispered into her ear. Even though the shop had only two small windows and the interior was darker than I would've liked, it appeared to be warm and friendly. I stepped from one shelf to the next now, admiring the huge quantity of liquor on display. "Man, there's a wide variety of tequila to chose from. I didn't realize they made flavored tequila, did you?"

Elaine bent her head slightly and copied what I was doing: reading the labels on the bottles. "Nope. I've made plenty of Margaritas and Tequila Sunrises over the years, but none of the bottled tequila I used was blended with anything else."

From time to time the various shaped bottles gave way to more interesting things, like a flock of people gathered in a circle.

"What do you think that large group is doing in the corner over there, Matt?

"Haven't a clue," I said rather loudly, and then I craned my neck to see if that would help, but the group was too tightly knit.

Just then, a neatly dressed elderly male sales clerk who had been watching us out of the corner of his eye decided to fill us in. "Those people, Senor, are tasting the different flavors of tequila we make."

My sister's friend flipped her bangs to one side. "Really?"

He opened his hands wide. "Sí. The cruise ships bring many people here. We are busy all the time. If you like, we can explain the history of tequila and share samples of our famous brand with you when these people are finished. As you can see, there are many to try." Without waiting for our reply, he then disappeared behind a counter.

Elaine faced off with me now, her high forehead exposing deeply embedded furrows.

"I …. I don't know, Matt. What do you think? Do you want to learn about tequila?"

I glanced at my watch. I didn't want to go beyond the two hour limit I'd set for us.

"We've got plenty of time, right?"

"Yeah. We've only been gone a little over a half-hour."

My sister's friend started to back pedal now like someone had pushed her too far. "But . . . , but what about the free samples? No bar, remember?"

Why was Elaine doing such a fine job of playing the devil's advocate now all of a sudden? Was Rita messing with her mind from a distance somehow? "Look, we've already established that this place isn't a bar. Besides, when something is free you don't get much. I bet the samples are less than a half a shot-glass worth if that." At least that's what I hoped after giving my stamp of approval.

Once the blonde heard my reasoning, her demeanor changed drastically. "Senor," she said excitedly, drawing the attention of the clerk who had just spoken to us, "put us down por favor. We'll wait."

The man nodded, "Sí. Bueno."

With that arrangement out of the way, Elaine swiftly turned her attention to me again. "Now about those paintings …"

"There you two are," Rita said in a gingerly fashion, still sitting on the couch in the same spot where I'd left her, but her injured foot was elevated then, now her foot was cradled in an ice pack. The nap did her good, I thought. She doesn't look like a sleep deprived person anymore. "Mary and I were seriously considering sending out the Mexican militia. If anyone could find you, we were certain they would."

I chuckled at the thought of the Mexican militia tracking down Elaine and me. What would've been even more hilarious would've been the suggestion to hire a private eye to hunt down a private eye, but I didn't share that joke. I kept it to myself.

Rita's babysitter, my sister, was resting at the dining room table, a romance novel clutched in her tanned hands. She probably had been dreaming about some swash-buckler sweeping her off her feet. "Yeah, that's right. That was our plan until I reminded your girlfriend that a woman was shopping for a picture and a bachelor was helping her select it. Great duo, don't you think?"

"Funny," I said as I continued to remain at the entrance door with Elaine.

"Come in. Come in." Mary said as she left her book at the table and entered the living room from the opposite end. "What's holding you two back?"

I offered a clipped response, "Nothing, absolutely nothing," leaving no room for Elaine to speak.

I think my sister sensed something was amiss because as she drew closer to Elaine and me, she stopped and stared into the recesses of our eyes. Fortunately for us, she didn't reveal whatever she thought she saw. She just continued on to one of the wicker chairs instead, eased herself into it and then said, "Rita and I were just discussing what we should have for supper right before the two of you walked in. So if you have any suggestions, they would be deeply appreciated."

"You can fix—anything youse wants," Elaine said now as she struggled by herself to reach the center of the room, inch by inch. Giggles followed each footstep. For some reason, the Leaning Tower of Pisa came to mind. If my memory served me correctly, I'd have to say the tall blonde leaned a lot more than the Tower. My sister's childhood friend may have been the star attraction at the moment, but she was also on a collision course with the coffee table.

Luckily, my conception of things was still pretty sharp even though we both had equal shares of various flavored tequila. Of course, tests have proven men's bodies can handle a whole lot more liquor than women's. I quickly went to Elaine's rescue and helped steer her towards a chair. "Thinks, Matt. I mean thanks," she said much too loudly. "I always told Mary you were a real gem. Oops. Shh, shh. I forgot." Then she placed her index finger on my open mouth. "Shouldn't say stuff like that, right? Don't want your girlfriend to hear me."

Upon hearing all that Elaine had to say, Rita's arms flew into a crossed position. "Well," she said in an huff, "I see you and little Miss Muffet here found time to imbibe alcoholic beverages while you were gone. Isn't that quaint?" Without waiting for any explanation now, my girlfriend's snake eyes fired venom through my chest. Grand! When Rita spreads her poison around, it usually takes several days for both of us to recover. Might as well forget enjoying the rest of our vacation together. Unless I can get through to her some way.

The situation could be a lot worse, I suppose. How you ask? Well, I never told Rita or anyone else about Elaine's and my summer fling the end of my senior year of college. The two of us had promised to keep it a secret, and so far we both had succeeded nicely.

Elaine had just broken up with some hotshot from her high school days and my latest gal friend had just dumped me for a navy guy. We ran into each other accidently at the movies, and before you could whistle Dixie, bing bang, we were an item. Unfortunately when summer ended, I joined the Air Force, and the rest is history like they say.

After I got Elaine situated in one of the wicker chairs, I went straight to my honey and tried to make amends by giving her a kiss on her forehead. I figured that might soften her up.

My plan backfired. "What do you think you're doing, Mr. Malone?" Rita sharply asked me before she turned her head to the wall behind the couch. Yup, she was demonstrating all the signs of a classic brush off.

Well, if that's the way she wanted it, I wasn't about to beg. I can be stubborn too. I strolled to the bench by the couch and dropped my weary medium-framed body down.

For some reason my sister seemed oblivious to the strong tension that now existed between Rita and me. Maybe it's because she's never had a serious relationship or because she sees so much friction between the little ones on a daily basis. "So tell me," she said, "what else did you two do besides have a few drinks together?"

I kicked my tennis shoes off wishing that the drink situation could fall off as easily as my shoes. "Elaine bought paintings for her house."

Mary clapped her hands together now as she turned to her friend. "That's fantastic, Elaine. Did you find them in that little market around the corner?"

My sister's friend leaned forward in her chair and almost slipped out of it. There was no way I was going to be a knight in shining armor this time. "Yup," she slowly replied and then she held out some of her fingers for us to see. "Three," and then she giggled again. "Jus wait till you see em."

My girlfriend decided to rejoin us now. "So, where are the pictures you bought?" she fired back.

"That's right," Mary said. "They weren't carrying anything when they came in, were they?" She stood up and made her way towards the door now. "Did you forget them out in the hall, Matt?"

"No," I snapped. "Don't bother looking there."

My girlfriend smartly replied, "Because the woman never bought any, right? Why, I bet her shopping spree was just a ploy to get you alone."

"What?" my sister said in a stunned tone. "Is that what you really think of my friend? For your information, it was my idea that Matt help Elaine purchase some paintings, not hers. He's familiar with the Spanish language, and he knows how to barter."

Somehow Elaine managed to magically toss her silliness aside for the moment like it never really existed. "I did to buy three velvet paintings."

The words "prove it," swiftly escaped Rita's harshly formed lips. Oh, oh. Double, maybe triple trouble's brewing now. The envelope was being pushed a little too far. Why was my girlfriend so agitated? Had an alien invaded her body while we were gone? The real Rita we know and love is kind, fair, understanding and listens to others. This gal wasn't giving anyone a shot. If she was, she'd realize she sounded like a butcher looking for just one more piece of meat to hack up.

The temperature was not only rising sharply in the room but on the nape of my neck. Yes, Rita had a right to be upset by what she saw in front of her—two adults who had a little too much to drink—but she hasn't even asked us to explain. If my mind's not too fuddled, I believe the saying still stands, *innocent until proven guilty.*

Elaine continued, "They're supposed to be dropped off at the main desk later."

Mary moved over by her friend whom she had just stuck up for and began to pace in front of her. "Exactly how much later, Elaine?"

My sister's old childhood friend flipped her hands up in the air. "I don't know. What did Darryl say, Matt?"

I brushed my hair with my hand. Why couldn't I be invisible? Invisible would be nice. "Ah, I'm afraid I wasn't paying attention, Elaine. If Darryl was speaking in Mexican terms, he meant mañana—tomorrow," and then

I swiftly tried to turn the conversation in a different direction. "Hey, I picked up some fresh avocados at the market, does anyone want one?" Now I pulled the fruit out of my pockets. "Did you gals know that sixty percent of all avocados grown come from Mexico?"

Rita hadn't lighten up one iota, but she was first to respond. "No. I thought those ugly green things were just grown in California."

I stole a glance Elaine's way, hoping she wouldn't make any other stupid blunders the rest of the evening. I didn't need to plunge any deeper into hell than I already was. Her perky mouth opened slowly. *Please, God, keep what she has to say brief.* "Hmm? I always thought they came from Florida," and then she rubbed her hands back and forth on her bare legs before she shared more. "Matt and I sampled blue tequila today at Cava Antiqua, a perfectly charming tequila shop just down the road. The blue tequila only comes from Mexico. Nowhere else. Isn't that right, Matt?"

I swiped my hair with my hand again. Why couldn't she let the drinking part of our outing be dropped? Did she have a death wish? I didn't have any choice. I had to answer. "Ah, yeah. We discovered the shop quite by accident, a very popular place. People in and out of there all day long. We were told it's a real hotspot for cruise ship travelers."

My drinking companion wriggled a little in her chair, and then she crossed her legs. "The bad news is blue tequila isn't allowed to be exported to other countries."

Curious now, Mary asked, "Why not?"

"Because Mexico wants to keep it all for their people."

"Well, it wasn't their people drinking it today," Rita said as she threw several daggers my way.

"Oh, tourists are permitted to purchase a couple bottles of tequila to take back home if they so desire," Elaine explained.

"Yeah," I hastily added without thinking of the repercussions that would surely follow, "and you can sample all the tequila you want for free too."

"Is that so?" Rita exclaimed in a bitterly raw tone.

Elaine smoothly volleyed back with, "Ah, huh," and then she hiccuped six times in a row.

All I ever do is work, work, work.

Chapter 30

Things were never quite the same between Rita and me in PV after Elaine's and my side excursion to the tequila shop. Oh, sure, she politely accepted a few side trips about town with me before we left—one being an outdoor lunch at El Nogalito's deep in the heart of a rainforest where parrots and other birds observed your every move and swooped down on you when you'd least expect—but the deep hot passionate feelings she had for me no longer existed.

Now that we were in Minnesota again and had returned to barely time for each other, I had no clue how I was going to resurrect what we lost in PV. All I knew was that I had to take definite steps before all that was between us unraveled for good. Something on a grandiose scale. "Yes." Something that truly demonstrated I only had eyes for the gorgeous Miss Sinclair, and her alone. The problem was the only mucho grande thing that came to mind was the proposal of marriage, the actual setting of a wedding date. I nervously ran my hand through my hair as I pictured the scene in my head. Rita's shocked at first, but then she wraps her arms around me tenderly and says, "Yes, Matt. Those are the words I've been waiting to hear. What took you so long to ask them?" Unfortunately, when I finally came back down ro reality, my gut instincts told me that's probably not how it would play out.

The phone rang now, the one sitting on the ancient desk in my office on Lowry Avenue. It immediately stamped out all thoughts of Rita and marriage that were cluttering my mind. "Matt Malone. How can I help you?"

"Oh, good, Matt, you're there. I was hoping our snowstorm didn't delay your return to Minnesota." It was Jake Ballad. "Just wanted to check and make sure it was still on with you to play security look-out at my business." Shoot! I thought I'd luck out and he wouldn't need my services anymore. I didn't relish the thought of reverting to sitting in a freezing car lit by stars.

"Yup. I plan to continue the arrangement we made before I left for Mexico." As much as I didn't want to return to this case, I didn't have much choice. I dropped more money in Mexico than I originally planned. Well, we had all agreed to pay our own way before we left, but being a male trained in chivalry, I frequently found myself picking up the tab. That, and I didn't expect to be purchasing several presents for Rita related to an injury. I took a Bic pen off my desk now and squeezed it near the breaking point, and then I let it slip from my hand. "Actually, Jake, I plan to start tonight again."

"Great. That's what I wanted to hear. Knowing you're on duty means I can finally get some much needed sleep."

What did Ballad mean by that last comment of his? Was his loss of sleep due to his obsessive concern over the disappearance of gas in his vans' tanks? Or did he … "Jake, you weren't keeping vigil over your vans while I was gone were you?"

The man on the other end of the phone coughed before he answered. "Ah, yeah. I know it wasn't the smartest thing to do, but I thought the person might return when you were out of the country. Of course, he didn't."

"It sure wasn't," I agreed. "You shouldn't have been watching your place especially when we don't know what kind of criminal element is out there. Besides, someone might have mistaken you for a burglar and reported you to the police."

"Well, the same thing could happen to you," the owner of Java to Go business speedily replied.

Before I rebutted my client's snappy comment, I examined my small, ugly office from ceiling to floor and wall to wall, cross referencing his business space as I did so. His put mine to shame, no matter which way you sliced it. Why, a wrecking ball could smash through this place right now, and I'd never know it. Visions of dollar signs suddenly danced in my head. Yup, I'm definitely torching this place when the money starts rolling in. Besides, it doesn't hurt to start fresh from time to time. With the matter of my office now settled in my head, I finally said, "It's different for me. I have police connections, and I can flash my PI card if need be."

"Ah, geez, I never thought of that. Well, I suppose I'd better let you get back to your daily routine. You must have tons of catching up to do."

"What? Oh, yes," I lied. "There's always a lot to do when I get back from vacation. Before you go though, I was just wondering if you have anything more to share about your employees. Something perhaps you didn't think about before?"

Ballad yawned into the phone. "Nope. Sorry. Nothing else has come to mind."

Our phone call ended now, and I moved on to more important things—like sorting through the mail to see if somebody, somewhere could use the services of a smart, upstanding debonair PI, namely me. After approximately ten minutes of filtering out the bills from the other mail, I was left with two items: an ad for an oil change at Johnny's Lube Shop near downtown and a note from the telephone company soliciting additional add-on services for my work phone.

Neither was of interest to me, so I decided to toss them both in the trash.

As I slowly released the ads from my grip and watched them sail into the wastebasket, I wondered how smoothly Rita's first day back at work was going with the added challenge of a wheelchair to maneuver. Knowing her boss, she was probably sitting hip deep in work.

When the phone rang for the second time, I wondered if this was any indication of how the rest of the day would fare. "Matt Malone. How can I help you?"

"Hola!" It was Mrs. Grimshaw. Darn! Our flight got in so late last night that I didn't bother letting her know we made it back okay.

"Well, hello, Neighbor. It's sure nice to hear a familiar voice."

"So how does it feel to be at work again?"

"Pretty good, I guess, but I haven't accomplished much yet."

"Oh, why is that, Matt?" Margaret asked. "Is your stomach reacting to all the Mexican food you ate?"

"No," I answered sleepily. "My stomach is made of iron."

"Then what's the problem?"

"Oh, I've been wasting time going through the mail."

"Ah, yes, and most of it's probably junk. Am I right?"

"Of course. By the way, I'm sorry I didn't call and tell you I was back in town."

"That's all right, Dear," Margaret said. "I didn't call about that. I just wanted to know if you felt like coming over for supper tonight? I figured your refrigerator was probably bare."

I dragged my hand through my hair. "It is, but I can't take you up on your offer. My mother suggested that I eat with her and Dad since I have to pick up Gracie."

"Your parents?" Margaret sounded like she had been rejected by a suitor. "Oh, dear, dear. Well, you go along to your parents' house then. You mustn't disappoint your family."

"Oh, I'm sure I wouldn't be disappointing them if I didn't show up, but they've babysat Gracie long enough."

"Did she behave while you were on vacation?"

"Oh, yes. Her manners were perfect, but why shouldn't they be, Margaret? Mom and Dad spoil her rotten."

My neighbor giggled. "I probably would do the same."

"Sure, you would. You love Gracie as much as your Petey."

"Matt."

"Yes?"

"Do you think you can come by tomorrow night, instead?"

My legs felt heavy. I sat down now. "Ah, yeah, that should work." Of course it would–especially since I make it a habit of not turning down any free meals.

"Good," the elderly woman said, "because I want to hear what all you did while you were in Mexico."

My mind hurriedly shifted to PV. It was supposed to be a romantic getaway, and ended up being a nightmarish one instead. "Ah, there's not much to tell."

"Really? Well, then, at least come with a hearty appetite."

"No problem," I said as I shifted my weary feet under the desk and thought about all the wonderful gourmet meals my neighbor's created for me. "See you tomorrow night, then."

"Si. Adios, amigo," Margaret cheerfully submitted, and then she hung up.

Day is Done
And dusk has Come.
All flee town now as One,
Like the fallen sun has already Done.

Chapter 31

Not much to report on the home front, my parents' home that is. Mom and Dad's serious faces rapidly transformed into cheerful ones the minute I stepped into their kitchen. It's always nice to know that I can still count on my family to appreciate me. Unfortunately, the same didn't hold true for Gracie. If ever a dog knew how to bypass a warm welcome, she certainly did. Unlike the folks, she totally ignored my entrance and continued to chow from her messy silver doggie dish that sat on the floor by the trash can. The mutt's lack of interest in me didn't phase me in the least. I knew how to handle that. The minute I offered Milkbones for her dessert, she'd attach herself to my body like she was an overgrown appendage.

Mom served up a scrumptious salad any host on the Food Channel would give four stars for and a delicious beef stew, including the doughnut-sized dumplings that melt in your mouth. It had been a long time since I'd had this particular meal. Maybe not since my late wife, Irene, was alive. That would be about three years ago. I'm certain Margaret Grimshaw never made it for me; her meals are always Italian oriented. Well, it's what she grew up with after all. When the serving bowl filled with stew reached me, I inhaled the deep, subtle use of the herbal enhancement, bay leaf. Yup, Mexico was definitely behind me. I was back in the good old Midwest where hot dishes and stews filled the stomach, and the sun didn't shine three hundred days of the year.

Conversation during supper flowed gently, mostly talk of how much snow I missed while gone, until that is we hit a huge bump in the road–Rita–and it suddenly came to a head. Evidently, Mary took it upon herself to inform my parents about the slight shift in Rita's and my relationship. How kind of my sister to do so without consulting me.

"Matt, I just don't understand it," my mother said as she stared at the empty spaces on her plate where food had been just moments before.

"Why in heaven's name would you go off with a married woman and to a bar at that?" Obviously, Mary only gave her bits and pieces of my Mexican fiasco. Funny how she found time to share tales of woe but didn't disclose her part in it. Some people just never grow up.

Besides salad and stew, my mother had thoughtfully placed freshly baked slices of white bread on the table so we could sop up the stew juices left on our plates. I grabbed a piece of bread now, pretended it was my sister, and swiftly dragged it back and forth across my plate several times. "Mom, Rita had just come back from the hospital. She couldn't go anywhere."

"So, that means you can take someone else out for a drink instead? What kind of boyfriend does that?"

"You don't understand. It wasn't like that." I placed the heavily saturated bread in my mouth now and swallowed hard. "It was Mary's idea. After Rita fell asleep, she suggested I take a break and help Elaine shop for paintings for her home. And we never went to a bar."

Dad's face tightened considerably. "Son, what do you call drinking tequila? I believe it's still considered a liquor even in Mexico."

I wiped my mouth with a red and white napkin Mom had bought in abundance for the New Year's Day get together, and then I brushed my hand through my hair. "Look, it was a tequila shop, not a bar. The owners cater to the tourist trade. All they offer to the public is free samples of various tequilas they sell on site, including blue which isn't exported.

"How do you explain Elaine's behavior then?" my father inquired.

"She doesn't handle liquor that well, which I wasn't told till after the fact."

"What I want to know," my mother now said in a kindly tone, "is how you're going to rectify your problem with Rita? You know how much she means to this family."

I pushed my plate aside and bounced my eyes from one parent to the other, trying to decide whether I should share my marriage plans with them. Nope. It's too early to say anything, I decided. So I just said, "Elaine's and my detour to the tequila shop was an unfortunate incident, but I'm sure Rita will soon realize it wasn't worth getting so uptight about. You have to remember she was taking some pretty strong drugs that day. They can affect a persons thinking."

"I hear you, son," my father said in an empathetic voice as he set his half-empty cup of coffee down. "I know how short my fuse was when I was taking all that medicine. Perhaps you're right about your girlfriend. We'd hate to see your relationship with her destroyed over a simple misunderstanding. She's such a good fit for you."

I closed my hand over my dad's calloused one for a second and then dropped it. "You're not the only one," I said.

My mother casually glanced up at the wall above the stove. That's where she's always kept a few knickknacks and the kitchen clock. "Matt, didn't you say something about a stake out?"

"Yeah," I answered, wondering what she was driving at, and then it dawned on me. Instead of checking the wall clock, I shoved my shirt sleeve up and exposed my watch. "Oops, I didn't realize it was that late already. I've got to run. Sorry." I pushed my chair away from the table now and stood to take my leave. As I walked towards the front door with Gracie in tow, I thanked my folks for caring for the mutt, and the great dinner, and I promised to resolve my problems with Rita as soon as possible.

On the drive back to the apartment I was feeling pretty crummy, but Gracie was her usual ecstatic self. She knew exactly where she was going even though her master didn't, but who wants to be in perpetual motion? The darn mutt had taken over the front passenger seat without my permission, and there was no controlling her now. She'd stand, then sit, and then stand again, throwing in an additional lick to my face from time to time for good measure.

"Gracie, you're okay," I said, trying to calm her down. "We'll be at the apartment in a few minutes, and then you can prance and pace to your heart's content." The only word that managed to make it through her thick skull was apartment. Her odd shaped ears shot straight up now. "Yes, you heard me," I said, and then I repeated, "apartment" again. This time her soft pointy ears almost went through the roof of the car. "Well, I'm happy to see you haven't forgotten our abode even with all the spoiling the senior Malones have lavished on you."

Gracie answered with, "Wuff, wuff," and then she gave me an unexpected smack on my right cheek.

I pushed her messy mouth away from my face. "Keep your slobber to yourself. I hate those yucky kisses of yours."

The huge entrance door of the underground parking at the Foley Complex gave access to the Topaz now, and I quickly slid into my assigned spot, and then Gracie and I excited out the side door of the building, so she could take a short jaunt around the block to tend to her needs.

I felt guilty about trimming the dog's evening walk time, but there wasn't anything I could do about it. I needed tonight's income to keep a roof over our heads. No one wants to sleep on a park bench, especially me.

When we finally retreated to our own home, sweet home, I hauled out the necessary supplies for spying, and then I broke the bad news to Gracie. "I know we just got reunited, mutt, but I have to pull an all nighter. I'm really sorry." The dog seemed to understand the information I just fed her and pranced straight to my bedroom.

Just to be certain Gracie had really settled in before I left, I jingled my car keys once and said in a loud voice, "Okay, I'm leaving." Then I waited for her to reappear, but nothing happened. So I knew it was safe to slip out.

It was a lot colder than the last time I sat in the car waiting for the thief to appear, and I was grateful that I had borrowed an old sleeping bag from my folks. My mother, bless her heart, felt sorry for me and had also sent along a bag of sweets for me to snack on. The only thing missing this evening was a huge thermos of coffee, but like I said before, when I'm in spy mode, it's not good for me to be drinking that stuff or any other liquid refreshment.

The parking spot I selected for the Topaz this time was actually on 37th, only a stone's throw from Ballad's Java place. I did note however that there was one minor problem with the choice of stake out location for tonight. The car was lined up with Sally's twenty-four hour fast-food joint, and the smells wafting into the Topaz were tying my stomach in knots. Why would the smells drive this PI's stomach crazy? Because my stomach craves anything deep fried, and Sally's was notorious for greasy food on overdrive. No matter. I planned to stay right here, so my stomach will just have to adjust.

After several hours of inhaling Sally's gourmet delights while quietly killing time within the confines of the car, I decided this evening's stake out was going to end up being a complete bust, but I was wrong. Quarter after one rolled around, and then BAM, a dark truck pulled into Ballad's parking lot. Once there, the driver permitted the truck to sit still for a full two minutes before he flicked the truck lights on and off several times, and then peeled out. Was the commotion with the truck lights done for his partner's benefit? You know, signaling the other guy that the coast was clear to loot the gas from the vans, or perhaps the flash of lights was used as a distraction to keep anyone in the vicinity from actually seeing his accomplice leave the truck.

Chapter 32

Anxious to see if my theory was accurate concerning an accomplice, I picked up the night goggles resting on the front passenger seat now and firmly pressed them against my forehead and cheeks. They'd help me find anyone lurking in Java to Go's parking lot. I opened my eyes wide, ready to peer into the dark, but that's as far as I got. "Born Free," my cell phone's new ringtone disrupted my plans. Strange how I had selected that particular song right before I left on vacation. Talk about self-fulfilling prophecy.

I shoved my parents' well-worn Coleman sleeping bag off my lap and dug deep into my winter jacket's inner pocket and retrieved the cell phone. "This is Matt Malone."

"Hi, Big Brother, it's Mary. I was hoping you were still up."

Just the person I wanted to avoid. "Yeah, I'm still up," I replied sarcastically. "I'm doing a stake out. What's your excuse?"

Mary stammered. "I… I don't know where to begin, Matt. I … I did a terrible thing, and it's been preying on me all day."

I knew exactly what she was referring to, but I wasn't going to let her off the hook that easily. Oh, no. Let her conscience bother her a little longer, I thought. "Really? And what was that pray tell?" I asked as if I had just dipped my tongue in honey. "Did you finally snap and yell at one of your little students?" My sister was an angel with kids; she'd never let them rile her up.

"I, ah, told Mom about Rita's and your rift."

"What?" I said, faking anger. Too bad Margaret Grimshaw wasn't here to witness my performance. She would've been so proud of me. She displays her acting talents so well, that I even get caught up in believing her from time to time.

"Oh, Matt, I feel awful. I didn't mean to say anything, honestly. It just slipped out. I had no right to tell Mother what's going on in your life. Can you ever forgive me?"

I felt spiteful. Mary needed to learn stay out of other peoples' business. I so wanted to tell her I was in the hot seat tonight because of her, but I wouldn't. Instead, I'd let her sweat it out another five more minutes before I responded to her request. "Forget it, Mary. Just go to bed. Those second graders need a wide awake teacher tomorrow not a zombie."

My sister sighed into the phone. "Thanks for being so forgiving, Matt. I don't know if I could be. Does that mean you'll still talk to my class about your profession?" While we were on vacation Mary happened to ask me if I'd be interested in speaking to her students. Her darling second graders were going to read a fictional story about a young boy who solves crimes with the help of his trusty mutt. Of course, being the nice brother that I am I told her I would. Now, I wished I hadn't.

I adjusted my body so I could take a good look out the car's front window now. Oops. It had begun to fog up during our chit chat. I'd better end this conversation before my vision was completely blurred. "Yeah, twelve o'clock sharp, next Monday. Good night." Now, I bent my head temporarily to find the cell phone's end button.

When I finally lifted my head again, I thought I caught sight of something moving by the side of Jake Ballad's building. A house pet? Possibly, but my instincts were betting on a human. Unfortunately, Ballad's huge coffee billboard didn't offer much help. It didn't shine far enough over for me to decipher what exactly was out there.

Chapter 33

I finally got tired of waiting for man or beast to be exposed under the lethal rays of light beaming from Ballad's billboard and decided it was time to escape from my comfort zone to take a closer look. Besides, the stretch would do my legs some good. They felt like paperweights and were starting to go numb. I yanked the keys from the ignition, stepped out of the Topaz and locked the car door.

"Brr." It was chillier than I thought. Before I moved an inch from the quiet street and set foot on the path that led to Ballad's business, I zipped my jacket all the way up and analyzed the situation further. The Topaz was parked about six car links from Ballad's parking lot. If I wanted to catch anyone and still act like I was going home from work or what not, I needed to speed walk, not run or jog. Now, the only other problem that needed to be resolved was the heavy snowpacked sidewalk. It would offer major resistance no matter what speed my legs went. Broken bones came to mind, and I suddenly thought of Rita. There was no way I wanted to end up like her. "Malone, stop sweating it," I told myself. "Your size eleven tennis shoes will keep your feet firmly grounded. Now get going!"

When my feet safely planted themselves at the darkest corner of Jake Ballad's building, the words "Stop, or I'll shoot," rang out in a loud angry voice. Not wanting to die in the middle of a case, I did what I was commanded. "Okay, now put your hands behind your head and turn around slowly."

Relief flooded over me as soon as I faced danger head on. "Why … good evening."

"Don't you good evening me," the man's deep baritone voice answered back. "Do you live around here?"

"No, sir," I said somewhat amused.

"Then you'd better have a darn good reason for being in this neck of the woods this time of night," the six foot roughly two-hundred pound police officer said as he continued to hold his gun at waist level.

I moved my feet a smidgen—hoping I didn't get in trouble for that too. "I do Officer. I'm a private investigator. Jake Ballad, the owner of this business, hired me a couple weeks ago to keep on eye on the place after hours. A couple of his vans were depleted of gas. Perhaps you heard about it? Ballad said he reported the theft to the police."

Just as the officer nodded acknowledgment of what I said, a squad car pulled up alongside of him. The window on the driver's side rolled down halfway, and then a cap-covered head swiftly emerged from the car's interior into the crisp night air. "Do you need any help, Bill?"

"Not sure," he said to his fellow officer. "Hang around for a minute or two if you can."

"Sure, I'd be happy to," and then he slid his window up and parked off to the side.

Bill turned his attention back to me now. "Keep one hand behind your head and slowly pull your identification out."

I reached in my back pocket for my wallet. Once I had it, I opened it and flashed my PI card at him.

"Mr. Malone, I'd like to see your drivers license too. That way I can make sure you are who you say you are."

"Of course, I understand. Anything you want." I quickly pointed to where I kept my license. "It's tucked behind my PI card."

Officer Bill slid my license out and then walked over to the waiting squad car and motioned for the driver to roll the window down. "Ralph, run this through the system, will yeah?"

Ralph took the card and said, "Okay, Bill." Then we waited. After a few minutes went by, Ralph opened his car door and shared what he'd learned. "He's as clean as a whistle, Bill."

The cop holding the gun on me bent his head for a second and stared at his shoes as if they would give him an answer. "All right then. False alarm." Then he straightened up and waved at the other officer. "Thanks for the back-up, Ralph. Might as well call it a night."

Ralph didn't argue. He backed up his squad car, turned it around and then headed south on Central Avenue.

"You can put your hands down now, Mr. Malone," Officer Bill said as he placed his gun back in his holster. "Sorry, if I frightened you."

I laughed nervously. "I was only scared when I thought a druggie wanted money and was going to leave me for dead. So what's going on Officer? Was a crime committed in this part of town tonight?"

He cleared his throat before answering. "Yeah, we got called in on a robbery two blocks back. We think the suspects took off in a truck."

I rubbed my hands together; my fingers were tingling. In my haste to get out of the car, I'd forgotten to put gloves on. "Was the truck open in the back or enclosed?"

Officer Bill cupped his bearded chin. "We believe it was open—easier for them to toss the goods in. Why do you ask?"

I continued to rub my hands together. "Well, a dark truck, maybe a GMC, pulled into this parking lot only a few minutes ago. The driver flashed his lights on and off a couple times and then took off. I thought maybe he was having trouble with his truck."

The cop standing in front of me got excited. "Do you think you could identify the driver?"

I shook my head. "Sorry, no. The truck was here in this dark perimeter of the lot."

"Well, Mr. Malone, I'd better get out of here so you can get back to your surveillance."

I started following the officer off the premises. "Oh, I don't think there's any chance anything else is going to happen tonight, not with two officers on patrol."

"You're probably right," he replied, and then we went our separate ways.

Chapter 34

As one advances in age it's only natural to feel like life is flying by faster and faster, but today's disappearance of hours for me was unreal. I had only five hours of slumber before I had to get up and work another eight hours. Now here it is evening again, and I am standing in front of the mirror primping for my dinner with Mrs. Grimshaw. My body was on overdrive begging for mercy. As I shaved away the few remaining whiskers on my face, my mind drifted back to the days events, trying to recall what actually took place.

Early this morning after much number crunching, I discovered my checking account wasn't as deep in the toilet as I previously thought. It was only sunk midway, and there was more good news to come. By the time morning rolled into noon, I had received three inquiries into my services, one of which promised to put a very substantial amount of money in my pocket. I rested my shaver on the sink for a second. "Okay," I said to my mirror reflection, "Now you have two good reasons to put your wedding plan into action."

Those, of course, were the positive things in my day, but with good comes bad, right? My brain cells scurried to the negative now. My attempts to reach Ms. Sinclair were fruitless. On top of that, there was yet another night ahead of me to spend alone in a cold car, one in which only a polar bear or a penguin could appreciate.

I picked up the new aftershave cologne my mother gave the guys in the family for Christmas. It was manly enough, but I didn't know if I liked the idea of putting something on that was called Black Suede. What kind of name is that? Sounds like a jacket. I tilted the wide bottle until fluid reached my fingertips. When I felt the liquid had moistened them sufficiently enough, I gently slapped the cologne on my face.

The aftershave was the last step in my preparations for the evening. I recapped the bottle and returned it to the toilet tank. I knew the tank top wasn't the most practical place to keep it, but when you have a mushroom-sized bathroom, you use every conceivable inch of space you've got. "All right Malone, time to go. The lady is waiting."

As I gingerly stepped from the bathroom and continued on towards the entrance, the mutt spied me and began to whine. "I know, Gracie, I keep leaving you behind, but I don't do it on purpose. Mrs. Grimshaw's a lonely person. She was never able to have any children, and I'm kind of her substitute son. Why, she's taken us under her wing so many times, I'd feel guilty if I refused her an hour of my company tonight." The dog lifted her right front foot like she wanted me to shake her hand. I gripped it. "Good. I'm glad that's settled," and then I dropped her paw. "Oh, by the way, I have night watch again, too."

When that last bit of news passed my lips, Gracie's demeanor changed dramatically. All I saw now was her jowls scraping the floor as she silently padded off to the bedroom.

Oh, boy. I felt like a parent who had just told their child they weren't going to Disney World. My mutt made me feel like I was the worst pet owner on this planet. If she had her way, I'd be tossed in a dungeon forever. But darn it; life isn't fair. Too soon this dog forgets, me thinks. Wasn't I the one who saved her from euthanasia at the hands of the Humane Society? Wasn't I the one who made sure her shots were current, that she had adequate food and exercised regularly? If I could talk to her in doggie language, I'd remind her of those facts. She wasn't wandering the streets with a pack of dogs after all. She had a nice, warm comfy home and plenty of people who cared and shared my love for her. Sure, I didn't like leaving her alone this much, but during tough financial times, a guy has to do what he has to do to survive. There are no second chances in my line of work, only firsts.

Well, I'll take that back. If I was married and had to be on duty at night, my lovely wife would be here to provide good companionship for Gracie and vice versa, but that's not an acceptable reason to tie the knot.

"Okay, enough's enough," I said to the entryway walls that were surrounding me. "Put the guilt trip hysteria behind you, Malone, and get on with it." I plucked my keys off the small table in the hallway now, locked the door and walked across the hall.

Margaret must've been keeping watch for me through her peephole because her door swung open just as I was getting ready to rap with my knuckles.

"Ciao! Come in. Come in," she said enthusiastically. "I'm so glad you could make it, Matt." I knew she was telling the truth because her grayish-blue eyes sparkled with delight.

I entered her abode slowly—looking and listening for Petey's whereabouts. You know how dearly I love him. Besides, I had more than my share of parrots at the open-air restaurant Rita and I dined at in Mexico.

My neighbor noticed my timidity at once. "You don't have to worry. Petey's on loan tonight."

I felt my body relax instantly. "Great! I mean, that's good for you. Every little bit of money a person can make these days helps, right?"

Margaret padded the bottom of her floral apron. It was hiding part of her below-the-knee green skirt. "Yes, that's so true. You know, you and I are a lot alike. We both take whatever comes our way." I nodded. "Well, the table is set—go make yourself comfortable. I won't be but a moment."

Just as I inhaled the aromas floating in from the kitchen, my stomach grumbled. I'm going to hold Margaret to that timetable, I thought to myself. "All right." I went and sat at the place setting that was furthest from the kitchen. Since Margaret had a tendency to pop up and down during a meal to retrieve things she had forgotten to place on the table, I felt she should sit nearer the kitchen. "So what are we having tonight?" My nose couldn't figure it out.

"Italian cole slaw, asparagus parmesan, mashed potatoes and fried scampi," the answer readily came from the kitchen.

"Scampi's shrimp isn't it?" I casually asked not wanting to raise any red flags concerning the dinner menu. I couldn't bear to eat clams or oysters—too slimy for my mouth.

"Ah ha."

Margaret's tea kettle suddenly whistled. That usually means all is ready and my stomach is finally going to get fed. My neighbor emerged from the kitchen carrying a tray with three medium-sized bowls on it. There should be four. Apparently there wasn't enough room. Although, maybe the elderly woman planned it that way and wanted to bring the teapot and the meat out at the same time, so they didn't get cold. I offered to make the second run to the kitchen. "How about if I get the rest of the stuff for you, Margaret? I've been sitting all day and could use the exercise."

Usually my neighbor would have been offended by the mere offer since she tries so hard to appear self-sufficient, but tonight was different. "All right," she replied. "My feet have been rather sore the last couple of days."

"Really? From dancing too much?" I inquired, and then I slipped the empty tray from her frail hands and scooted in and out of the kitchen in nothing flat.

Margaret waited till I returned to answer me. "No, Matt, I haven't gone dancing in over a week. My feet problems are probably old age related." She placed her hand out towards me now. "Set the teapot by me will you, Dear? The meat can go anywhere."

I did what she asked, and then I said, "Well, if I was a nonagenarian, my body would be beyond sore. It would be dead weight splattered on a La-Z-Boy recliner somewhere."

Margaret gave way to an impish laugh. "Why, isn't that where I usually find you when I come over for a late night visit?"

I brushed my hand through my hair. "Very funny. It's a good thing I don't take you too seriously."

My hostess stopped laughing now and started passing the bowls of food. "These are some more of Mama D's recipes. They're pretty similar to what I grew up with in Italy." After the fourth bowl left her hands, she said, "How was your day at work? Are you getting anywhere with your case involving the disappearing gas? I remember you were working on that before your vacation."

I flicked my left hand from side to side, the right occupied with the glass bowl Margaret had just given me. "So, so," I replied. Before I continued further, I quickly scooped a spoonful of fried scampi from the bowl, and then I set the half-empty bowl back in the center of the table. "I ran background checks on the four guys that work where the gas was stolen. Nothing yet, and I received calls about possible jobs. If a certain one materializes, it could be quite lucrative for me."

Margaret tilted her head towards me. "Oh? Tell me more."

"Well, it would involve searching for a long lost cousin."

"Why do I have the feeling you're not telling me everything?" she said as she poured hot tea for the both of us.

I punctured the scampi a couple times with my fork, watched the moisture run out and then stirred the teeny pieces into the asparagus. "You do know your way around sleuthing, don't you Miss Marple?" I jokingly said.

"Only what I've learned from reading Agatha Christie and from that rascal across the hall who calls himself a private investigator."

"Is that so? Hmm. And here I thought no one ever listened to me. Well, in this case a will happens to be involved."

The little woman smiled. "Ah, money, the root of all evil."

I grinned. "It can be, can't it?"

"It most certainly can, Dear." Margaret watched me as I finally placed my first bite of scampi in my mouth and chewed it. "Well, what do you think? Do you like the dish?"

I picked up the blue cloth napkin that she had provided for me and wiped my mouth. "It's seasoned with just the right amount of garlic. I don't like food that reeks of it."

"Me neither. Actually, too much garlic ruins the dish."

"I didn't know that. Maybe that's why some of the dishes I make don't taste like they're supposed to." Then I raised another forkful of scampi to my mouth. "So, what's the other seasoning you use in this recipe?"

"Oregano. Almost every Italian dish calls for it. Of course, it's also used in stuffing and other meals too." Now Margaret's right hand gripped the handle of her gold-rimmed tea cup. "Tell me, how was Mexico? I've been dying to hear."

I reached for the bowl of asparagus parmesan now and dipped a serving spoon in it. The vegetable dish was so gooey that when I went to place the contents on my plate it almost skidded off into oblivion. "Funny, I've been dying to forget it."

"Oh, come now, Matt. You must've shared some good times with Rita despite her broken ankle."

"It was minimal. My sister and her friend were in our faces most of the time."

"I'm sorry to hear that. I know how much this trip meant to you. "Well, why don't you tell me about the beaches, first? Are they as nice as I've heard?"

I took the delicately painted tea cup that had been recently filled and held it in front of me with both hands. "Puerto Vallarta, like a lot of other popular vacations spots, has dozen of beaches, but the closest one to our timeshare was Playa Los Muertos. That's where most of the locals hangout."

My neighbor shook a little like one does when they've been chilled to the bone. "Los Muertos? Why, that means the dead. I hope that wasn't the beach Rita got hurt on."

"The one and only. We wanted to go parasailing, and this particular beach offered it."

"Why on earth would the Mexican's pick such a terrible name for a beach?"

I set my teacup down without ever tasting the smooth blend of mango and black tea leaves. "Apparently, a battle broke out between pirates and local miners ages ago. When it was over, dead bodies covered the entire beach."

"How gruesome!" Margaret remarked as she pushed her empty plate aside and rested her arms on the table.

"Actually, it wasn't." My hostess gave me a cold stare. She probably thought I had no heart. I placed my hand half-way between my head and the table now. "Honest. What I told you is only a legend. There never were any miners in Puerto Vallarta."

"Even so—just the thought of sunning yourself on a beach pertaining to death sounds so morbid."

"I agree, and so do a lot of other visitors and PV locals. For years they've been trying to change the beach's name to del Sol–the sun, but for some reason the old one still endures."

A timer in the kitchen suddenly went off. "Dessert's ready," Margaret announced as she stood. "Excuse me, Matt. I need to get it out of the oven, but when I get back, I want to hear if this trip to Mexico strengthened your relationship with Rita like you hoped it would. You haven't said a word about that yet."

Shoot! I was hoping I wouldn't have to get into that tonight, but I suppose there's no way of escaping it. Just then my cell phone began to play its now obnoxious tune. I'd have to get up and retrieve it. It was tucked in my jacket which had been tossed on Margaret's couch when I first arrived. Perhaps the person calling would give me the out I was looking for.

Chapter 35

Midway through the tune's cycle, I managed to wrap my hands around the phone. Unfortunately, I didn't recognize the number displayed on the cell's tiny screen. If I had, maybe things would have played out differently for Rita and me down the road. I pressed the talk button now, thinking the caller could possibly be one of the potential business clients who had tried reaching me earlier in the day. "Good evening. This is Matt Malone. How can I help you?"

"Matt, it's me."

Even though the woman was calling from an unknown number and her voice was distant and troubling, there was no denying who *me* meant. "What's going on, Mary?" She'd better not still be fretting over telling Mom about Rita and me. That issue was settled last night, or so I thought. "You sound like you're in a vacuum. Where the heck are you? Are you all right?"

"I'm fine Matt. Elaine's the one with the problem."

Holy sh… Here we go again. My sister just doesn't get it. I'm already in quicksand up to my waist, and now, thanks to her, sinking faster and faster. Before you know it, I'll have disappeared completely. "Elaine!" I shouted across the phone lines minus any expletives. Remember when I said nasty bold words weren't in my vocabulary? Well, the way things were going lately they soon may be. "She's home now. Her husband can help her with any problem she has."

"That's just it. He can't."

"Ah hem, I think a little clarification is necessary. He can't, or he won't?"

My sister raised her voice to match mine now. "He can't, and he shouldn't."

I was getting angrier by the minute. "And why not?"

"Because it's a situation you're all too familiar with."

"Yeah, right. Okay, spit it out, Mary. Give me the gritty details."

My kid sister sounded exasperated. "Someone broke into Elaine's house and knocked her husband unconscious. Is that spelling it out good enough for you now, mister private eye."

"Settle down, Mary. I didn't realize the situation was as serious as that. Has anyone called the police? How about Frank? Has he come to yet?"

"I don't know about the police because I just got here, but Frank's conscious now, and Elaine's tending to him."

"Do me a favor. Ask Elaine if she's called the police."

I could hear Mary mumbling something to her friend. Then she came back on the phone. "No, the police haven't been notified yet. Elaine says she wants you to come over and see the mess first. She trusts you."

Now what do I do, I wondered? "You're putting me in an awkward position, Mary, and you know that. I shouldn't go anywhere near Elaine's, especially when I haven't resolved my situation with Rita yet."

Mary raised her voice a notch higher. "Matt, my dearest and closet friend is shook up and asked for you, no one else. You have to help her."

I pressed my hands firmly against my forehead. I could lose my girlfriend over this, or my sister could stay angry with me the rest of her life, and then I'd have my mother's constant wrath to endure. Either way I couldn't possibly win. What it really boils down to is my job. It comes first. "Mary, where did you say Elaine lived? I've forgotten."

"In Columbia Heights. 3901 Walnut Street. Turn left by the Dairy Queen. She's in a cul-de-sac. Just a minute, Matt. What's that, Elaine? She says to tell you theirs is the only house with lights on each side of the entrance door."

"All right. Tell her not to touch anything. I'll be there as soon as I can." I shut the cell phone off now and slipped it back in the inside pocket of my jacket. Then I threw my jacket on. As I spun around to face the dining room table again, I found Margaret standing in her kitchen doorway holding a metal pie pan. Steam was rising from its contents.

"What is it, Matt?" My neighbor asked. Her face looked as crestfallen as Gracie's did earlier. "Did I say something I shouldn't have? When I asked you to dinner tonight, you said you could spare an hour or two."

I stared at the pie she was holding. The honey-brown crust was slightly peeking above the edges of the pan. Darn! Dessert is my downfall. My stomach wanted to stay and have a slice of whatever was hidden beneath the crust no matter who was in trouble. "I know I did, Margaret, and I apologize for leaving this way, but something unexpected has come up."

The woman's brows furrowed deeper into her forehead. "Not your father?"

'Oh, no," I said to defray her concerns. "It's my sister, Mary. Her friend's home was broken into this evening."

My neighbor finally set the pie on the table. "Goodness gracious. Well, shouldn't her friend call the police?"

"That's what I said. You know how I don't like getting on the bad side of the police, Margaret, but apparently Elaine wants me to see the way things are first."

"Did you say Elaine? Why, wasn't that your sister's traveling companion in Mexico?"

I shoved my hand in my pant pocket and dug for my car key. "Yeah, that's the one. The gals have known each other since grade school."

"Well, then, don't let me detain you, Matt. Get going. We can eat the dessert another time."

"I hope so," I said, and then I started to make my way to the door. "Thanks again for the scrumptious dinner."

"You're welcome. Oh, Matt," Margaret called from behind me.

"Yes?"

"Just leave the door open. I thought I'd check on Mrs. Nelson down the hall. She's been feeling under the weather."

"Sure. Good night."

Chapter 36

If I had allowed Elaine Best's address to sink into my weary brain at the time Mary gave it to me, I would've realized she was practically neighbors of Java to Go. As it turned out, it wasn't until Jake Ballad's business came into view, twenty minutes later, that it dawned on me the business I was working for and my sister's friend were only two blocks from each other. Could the break-in at Elaine's be related to the situation that occurred last night? I made a mental note to get the lowdown from my pal, Sergeant Murchinak, who works in a police sub-station on the northern fringe of downtown Minneapolis. He and I go back a long ways. If anyone can sniff through information without outing me, Murchinak can, especially if I bring him a box of donuts.

My sister's directions were impeccable. Of course, coming from an elementary school teacher, they should be. Can you picture a classroom of seven-year-olds trying to follow a teacher's orders without clear directions? Utter chaos would ensue.

I made a left off thirty-ninth, a sharp right towards the cul-de-sac on Walnut, and then drove onto the lightly, snow-covered driveway of the two-story framed house that had identical, black metal lights flanking each side of the entrance to the home. The turquoise painted front door took me back a couple decades. Now-a-days, people are into gray, black and white doors, or if they're real rebels—even bright red.

I parked the Topaz next to Mary's navy blue Volkswagen and then made my way to the front door. Before I announced my arrival, I carefully examined the exterior of the wood door. No evidence of foul play. Maybe the burglars got in through the back door. Ready to let them know I was there now, I took off my thick winter gloves and pressed the tiny, smooth silver doorbell. The ding-dong could be heard instantly, and then a mixture of voices came next, followed by light footsteps, a woman's, I'm guessing. Although they could belong to Elaine's son, depending on his age. I never quizzed her about that.

My first guess was correct. A woman greeted me. My sister Mary to be exact. "Matt," she said as she quickly threw her bulky sweater covered arms around me. "It's just awful what those criminals did, knocking Elaine's husband out and ransacking most of their house. Looking for what God only knows."

Well, at least she's got that right, I thought. God would be the only other one to know what the scumbags were up to. I mean, since Sunday School days, most of us were taught that God was all knowing. He knows every step we take, every thought we have and every word that's escaped our lips. Sadly, somewhere along the route from childhood to grown-up, a large number of people have forgotten what they learned in their formative years. Otherwise, why would there be such an increase in prisons throughout the world. I certainly haven't changed my opinion of what God can do since getting older, but I still want to know why he allows senseless, destructive acts to occur to people who live by the Golden Rule, like my beloved Irene. Why couldn't God warn the good people ahead of time, so they could change the outcome.

"Where's, Elaine?" I inquired.

"In the other room with her husband and son," Mary replied as she pointed to the room off to the left of the small foyer where we were now standing.

The floor beyond the five-by-three-foot light beige tiled floor I was on was covered with a thick off-white carpet. Obviously the home was designed with Minnesota weather in mind. The tile floor offered visitors or family members a place where they could easily leave their muddy shoes or snowpacked boots behind before treading on the carpet. I bent over now and quickly slipped out of my tennis shoes.

"You don't have to do that," my sister insisted as she stood there watching me still wearing her black slip-on shoes. "Elaine doesn't mind."

"Well, it's done now," I said under my breath, and then I set my shoes next to the cluster of shoes already lined up in a neat row.

As soon as Elaine saw me enter her living room, she got off the brown leather couch where she had been sitting with her husband and came over to greet me. "Matt, thanks for coming so quickly. Frank and I were just discussing what the burglar might have been doing in our house."

I glanced over at her husband for a second and acknowledged him. He nodded back while continuing to hold a cold compress to the back of his head. Then I checked out Elaine's son who was keeping himself busy playing on the carpet with his metal cars. Could be about seven, I suppose. With that out of the way now, I drew my attention back to Elaine. "Mind if I chat with your husband before I take a look around the house?"

Elaine fidgeted with her hands. "No, not at all."

Since my sister's friend didn't seem too interested in returning to the couch any time soon, I decided I'd take up residency there. From this new vantage point, I noted that Elaine had definitely picked herself a winner. Not only was Frank a head taller than my 5' 11" frame, he was extremely muscular and had a full blown bushy brown beard that hid his round face. Of all his features, I was the most envious of his professor like beard. Over the years I've tried to grow one like that, but my hair never fills in around the mouth like it should. I tucked my jealousy under wraps now and introduced myself. "Hi. I'm Matt. Mary's brother."

Elaine's husband gave me a firm grip with his free hand. Nothing lost there even with a bump on his head. "Yeah, Mary's mentioned you on and off over the years. Sorry, we finally meet under these set of circumstances."

"No need to apologize, Frank. Look, do you feel up to answering a few questions? I understand you received quite a blow to your head."

"I did, but the old noggin doesn't hurt as much now. I think the painkiller Elaine gave me finally kicked in. Either that, or the ice pack has frozen my brain." He attempted a smile, but it came out more like a grimace.

The Best's little boy took a break from playing with his Match Box cars now. "Are you a policeman?" he asked as he stared at me with wide-eyed innocence. "You don't look like one. Where are your special clothes?"

I gazed down at the boy, and softly replied, "I'm something like a policeman, but I'm called a private investigator. We don't have to wear special clothes." Now I scooted to the edge of the couch cushion I was on, so I could get closer to him. "My name's Matt. What's yours?"

"Samuel, but everybody calls me Sam."

"Nice to meet you, Sam." I said as I unzipped my jacket. "I've come over to help your daddy."

The boy continued to keep his saucy hazel eyes on me. "That's good because somebody mean hurt him."

"I know. Were you and your mommy home, Sam, when it happened?"

"No," he answered in a serious tone, "Mommy and I were gone." Sam's interest in me waned now. He picked up his toy cars and began playing with them again.

Since our conversation had ended, I moved my body back, so it rested against the rear of the couch. "Any idea what the burglar was looking for, Frank?"

Elaine's husband shifted the cold compress slightly before he spoke. "I think it was my computer stuff. I just got a ton of new computer equipment delivered to the house this morning."

I reached inside my jacket and pulled a notepad and pen from my shirt pocket. "Equipment for personal or work-related use?"

"Work. I work from home twice a week."

"Any of your neighbors home during the week like you?"

The man who was somewhere between mid and late thirties thought about my question for a minute or two. "Don Strand at the end of the block has been selling insurance from home for several years."

Elaine interrupted us. "And Helen Snyder in our cul-de-sac is a stay at home mom."

"I've never seen her though," Frank added. "The family only moved in about a month ago."

"Anyone else?" I inquired.

"Not that I can think of," he stated in his broadcaster voice. "Why do you need to know?"

I scribbled the two names down before I answered. "They may have seen something or could possibly be involved." Now I continued my line of questioning. "What about work? How many people knew you were going to be receiving a shipment of computer equipment?"

Elaine's husband stole a look at his black corduroy slippers. "The department I work in is tiny. Six of us all together, and that's including my boss. We're all allowed to work from home, so it's not like my co-workers couldn't get a hold of the same equipment if they wanted it."

Probably a dead end there, I thought to myself as I rested my pen and notepad on my lap, but there's one more thing I needed to ask before I eliminated his job completely. "Is your work top secret, Frank?"

Elaine's husband tensed up. "No way! My work has nothing to do with the government. We write educational software."

Oh, oh. It looks like I'm going to have to calm Frank down if I wanted him to continue. "Sounds like pretty interesting work."

"It is. The kids really like the games we create for them."

"Were you home when the burglar or burglars intruded, or did you happen to walk in on them?"

Frank closed his eyes. "Just a minute, Matt. Elaine, Honey, can you please put this ice bag back in the freezer?"

"Are you sure you don't want it?"she asked in a concerned tone as she crossed the room and took the package of peas from her husband. You could tell there was mutual love between them.

"Yeah, I think I need it off my head for a while." His eyes opened now just in time to see the quizzical expression on my face. "We didn't have any ice on hand," he explained, "and frozen vegetables are the next best thing supposedly." Then he gazed lovingly at his son who was still absorbed in his world of cars. "I had gone downstairs to search for the tools I needed to connect all my new computer equipment. While I was in the basement, I heard footsteps overhead. I didn't give the noise much thought. I just assumed Elaine and Sam were back from running errands, but I was wrong. I had forgotten that Sam was also being signed up for Cub Scouts this evening."

"When I finally came upstairs, I didn't see anyone in the kitchen, so I continued on through the rest of the house. A few things were out of order in the dining room but not enough to make me question that something was wrong. Curious to know where Sam and Elaine were, I entered Sam's bedroom. I didn't find them, but Sam's dresser drawers were l pulled out, and clothes from his closet were strewn across the carpet. The room looked like someone had just had a major temper tantrum.

Worried now for the safety of my family, I headed to the next room—my office. I was knocked on the head the moment I stepped into the room."

"You never saw the perpetrator then?" I inquired in a solemn tone, regretting the fact that there was no face to the criminal.

Frank shook his head. "Afraid not."

I glanced over at Mary who had remained silent during my entire inquisition. She was sitting in a comfy blue and gold floral chair by the brick fireplace which was about four feet from us. I signaled her with a shake of my head that I didn't have a clue. Then I focused on Frank again. The man was wiped out. There was no point in questioning him any further. "All right, Frank, you just sit tight. I'll have your wife show me around." Now I stood, went over to where my sister was sitting, and in a hushed tone I said, "Mary, make darn sure Elaine reports the break-in to the police. They have to be notified."

Chapter 37

As the tall blonde-haired woman and I made our way along the narrow hallway that led to the other rooms in her home, I offered some light conversation. "Boy, you really meant it, Elaine, when you told those artists your home was decorated to represent a Spanish style casa."

"We didn't have anything to do with our home's Spanish appearance," Elaine confided as we stepped into the dining room. "It was done long before we bought the place." We stopped in front of the dark walnut triple-doored buffet that was pushed up against the outer wall of the house now. "Someone pulled this heavy piece of furniture away from the wall and also messed with the few pictures that we have in here." She pointed to the pictures decorating the wall. "See how lopsided they are, Matt." I nodded. "Low flying jets can't be blamed for that. They've never had an affect on our wall decorations before." Something on the dining room table beckoned to Elaine now, and she bent over to take a better look. When she straightened herself back up, a few strands of hair fell across her mouth making her look so fragile. My soft side ached for her. I wanted to clear the hair from her face, but she's married so I kept my distance.

Elaine eventually resolved her hair issue. She swiped the strands with her hand. "Matt, I didn't want to alarm Frank or Sam anymore than they already are, but I think these guys were looking for a wall safe."

"But how many people living in a middle class neighborhood have safes? Okay, that was a stupid question. I forgot about all the hunters who stash their guns in safes now-a-days."

"Forget the hunters," Elaine said. "You'd be surprised how many homes around here have been passed on to the next generation, and when the son or daughter cleans out the home, he or she actually finds a nice goldmine of jewelry, paintings or money in what you'd call a *unique* hiding place."

"Really? You wouldn't care to point me in the direction of one of those homes would you?"

Elaine was so preoccupied with what had taken place in her home only an hour or so ago that she totally ignored my lightheartedness and returned to the hallway. "Frank's office is next." I followed close behind her gyrating hips. The view was fantastic. Too bad I had to keep reminding myself it wasn't meant for my eyes.

I quickly did what I knew I had to do. I cleared my mind of all thoughts not associated with the house. "Hey, Elaine, I haven't seen the paintings you bought in Mexico. No time to hang them up yet?"

"No, no. That's not it. We're going to be painting several rooms, so Mary offered to keep them at her place until we're finished." We entered Frank's office now. It was definitely meant for a man. There was dark wood paneling on the lower half of the walls and deep blue paint on the upper half.

"Oh?" Now I did a three-hundred and sixty-degree panoramic tour of her husband's office. Two huge boxes of computer equipment weren't even open yet. If this is what the burglars wanted, surely they would have waltzed out the door with them. Frank's computer desk and two file cabinets had been pulled away from the walls, the same as the dining room buffet. The closet door was ajar. It didn't seem to contain much—a few winter blankets on the floor. I'm betting they were on the upper storage racks before.

Elaine watched me as I poked my head deeper into the closet. "Is any of Frank's shipment missing?" I asked as I stepped out of the closet now.

"Not as far as I know."

Not finding one darn thing that could be useful in Frank's office, I suggested we move on to Sam's room. "Come on, maybe we'll find something in your son's room."

Sam's room was delightful for a small boy. There was nothing Spanish about it. The walls were painted a soft blue to coordinate with the navy blue carpet. The scattered upper-wall bookshelves were painted bright white. A miniature train set was nestled in the corner by the only window in the room. As Frank mentioned earlier, the boy's clothes were strewn across the carpet and dangling from the edges of the pulled out drawers of his tall white dresser. I wasn't sure where to step; I didn't want to mess up the clothes further. What the heck would someone be looking for in a kid's room, I wondered. Surely there was nothing worth snatching in here.

Elaine made her way to the center of the room and just stood there, lost in her own thoughts. I studied her medium tanned face. No emotion was betrayed in her eyes, but I had a feeling she was on the verge of crying. I couldn't let that happen. You know how much I hate crying.

"Looks like Sam's a Vikings fan," I said trying to break the thoughts that were putting a strain on the woman standing next to me.

Elaine finally woke from her slumber. "Huh? How did you know? Are you psychic or something?"

No, I said to myself. Just have a sixth sense that hasn't been working too well lately. Not wanting to leave Elaine hanging any longer, I quickly pointed to the familiar logo on a few of Sam's shirts.

"He has a signed football too, a collector item. It's mounted in plexiglass and wood. My dad got it for him."

"Who signed it?"

"I think Fran Tarkenton and Chuck Forman."

"Wow! Two top Minnesota players?" Football memories came flooding back now as I momentarily forgot what I was here for. "Geez, Elaine, do you think I can take a look at it for just a sec?"

Sam's mother quickly turned her back on me. "Let's see. It should be up there," the blonde said as she pointed to the shelf nearest the ceiling. "Oh, no! It's gone! Sam will be devastated. How could they take it, Matt?" Tears formed at the corner of her eyes and eventually tumbled down her cheeks. "Why our house?" she asked through her sobbing. "Why our house?"

Of course, I thought to myself, a mounted football. That's probably what was used to knock Frank on the head. "It's going to be all right, Elaine," I said in a soothing monotone. "We'll find the guy or guys that did this. I promise." Feeling at a loss for what else to do, I swung my arm over her shoulders. "Come on now; dry those tears. You don't want Frank seeing those. He needs you to be the strong one tonight."

Elaine smiled a bit and then went and grabbed a tissue from the blue box on Sam's dresser. After she blew her nose she said, "Thanks. I'm okay now, but is my face red and blotchy, Matt?"

There were no mirrors in the room, so I could lie. "You look great. Let's go and see how Frank's doing, shall we?"

As we began to trace our steps back to the living room, Elaine said, "By the way, Matt, I forgot to tell you our painting projects will be done by Friday and we've invited a few friends and neighbors over to help us party Saturday evening. Why don't you and Rita join us?"

I ran my hand through my hair. "Oh, geez, Elaine. I don't know. Rita's pretty tied up with work, and I haven't had a chance to sort things out with her yet."

"Well, come even if she can't. I know Frank and Sam would like to see you again, especially after this."

"I'll see what my case load looks like." I already knew what it looked like, zilch, but I didn't want to be around Elaine anymore than I had to especially if I wanted to save my relationship with Rita.

Chapter 38

I left Elaine and Frank's at eight-thirty p.m. no further ahead than when I arrived an hour earlier. Oh, sure, I did discover that the burglar didn't have to force his way in. Elaine had seen to that. She simply left the back door unlocked when she left to run errands with Sam. It's not attached to the garage.

Sneaking into a person's house through the back door during daylight hours is not only easy but makes perfect sense. A robber has no nosy neighbors to contend with. The neighborhood watchdogs are so busy viewing every inch of movement on the street side, they have no time left for the backyards. Yup, rear entrances are a whole different enchilada, amigo. Not only are they not being spied upon by inquisitive neighbors, they are generally camouflaged with nasty overgrown shrubs or a trellis smothered in thick thorny twisty vines.

Speaking of thick things, I was really bummed out about Sam's missing numbered, autographed football. "Find the football, Malone, and you'll have the perp. No doubt about it. Case closed.

Hey, maybe this particular burglar steals nothing but sports memorabilia. A person can make quite a bundle selling items on E-bay or Craig's List. At least that's what I've heard. I snapped my fingers. "That's it." I should start looking there. Oh, I know Elaine and her husband didn't hire me on, but it doesn't hurt to do a little investigating of my own. Who knows, I might just uncover something of great interest.

When I finally dropped my body behind the steering wheel of my filthy Topaz, I decided it was time to buzz Rita again, certain she was ready to talk now. I mean, how long does it take a woman to decide that she was in the wrong? Five minutes, two hours, three days, a week? I pulled the cell phone from my jacket pocket, selected her number and waited. The phone on the other end just rang and rang. Eventually, I gave up trying when I realized the phone wasn't going to kick into the voice-messaging system. She must've forgotten to hook it back up when she got home from vacation.

Where could she be? I stared at the phone as if it had all the answers neatly stored away. Work? She's so darn diligent about staying on top of things. Couldn't she let things slide just once for our sake? I turned the cell phone off and dropped it on the seat next to me, and then I pushed my jacket sleeve up to peer at my Casio watch. Not late enough to start the night shift at Ballad's java place and not sufficient time to return to the apartment and hop on the Internet highway. Hmm. I suppose I could just find a place that offers coffee and dessert. Bridgeman's, two blocks from Ballad's, ought to do the trick.

"Well, hi, Sweetie," said the plump, sixty-something woman with streaks of orange shooting through her thin dry hair. My Aunt Irma had a cat with hair the color of hers. She called the cat Fireball. The waitress continued, "Find yourself a seat, and I'll be right with you."

I acknowledged her, and then I glanced around the restaurant. Most of the tables and booths were already taken. Where should I sit, I wondered. I didn't want to sit by the booth containing a trillion teenagers. I can't take all that raging hormone juice, especially since I've never been a parent. Fortunately, my seating arrangement was finally chosen for me. Chairs scraped on the worn wood floor, and then two teenagers, a boy and a girl, stood and began putting their coats on. Okay, their small table for two works for me.

As soon as they moved away from the table, I walked over and sat down. One empty malt glass with two straws, one quarter-filled coffee cup and two dirty plates stared up at me. Oh, and let's not forget the three shiny quarters that were left behind, such a big tip. Their waitress will surely jump for joy when she spots her present.

The waitress who had greeted me when I first entered the restaurant appeared at my side in under two minutes. She gave me a smile the size of an apple and then handed me a huge booklet. "Here, why don't you take a look at our menu while I clean the table for you," and then she quickly slipped the tip in her apron, set the dirty dishes in a plastic dishpan and wiped the table. When she finished her task, she carted the dishpan back to the kitchen.

Now that the woman was gone, my fingers continued to dance through the massive menu, skipping all appetizers and entrees and getting right to the nitty-gritty, the desserts.

It's a good thing I took the shortcut through the menu booklet because my efficient waitress didn't believe in allowing dust to collect under her feet. She returned to my table under six seconds if that. "Okay, then, so what can I get yeah? Did you want our special of the evening or something else?"

"Something else, "I cooly replied as I stared up into her pale olive green eyes. They were a sharp contrast to her hair. "I'd like a cup of steaming black coffee and a slice of your famous peach pie."

"Good choice." Then she took the heavy menu from me, tucked it under her arm and continued. "We just received a new shipment of those luscious Georgia peaches this morning. Mmm, mmm. They're really good. You want that pie topped with a scoop of our creamy vanilla ice cream?"

The long boring night ahead flashed through my head. There would be no snacks to munch on because I had forgotten to pack any. "Sure. Why not?" Then I placed my hand on my slightly bulging stomach and patted it. "There's always another day to watch my diet."

The woman helping me rolled her olive green eyes away from the menu in her hand now and set them on my face. "All righty. I'll be back in a snap, or my name ain't Mary Jane," and then she turned and sashayed her way to the order counter.

Before she got too far out of hearing range though, I managed to say, "No rush. I've got plenty of time to spare."

The peach pie and ice cream came a few minutes later, and they slid down as smooth as gin. So did the hot coffee, but just barely. I guess the dessert wasn't necessary. Mrs. Grimshaw's Italian dinner was still tucked in the confines of my stomach somewhere. Now that everything had disappeared in front of me, I needed to take a hike to the men's room. There was no way I was going to hold on to that coffee all night.

Just as I was passing my waitress and another waitress, double her size and girth, I heard Mary Jane say, "You should've seen the young man I had earlier this evening."

"What was wrong with him?" her fellow worker asked. "Was he on drugs?"

"No, but he was a total jackass. Nervous little twit too. Something wasn't quite right, but I couldn't put my finger on it."

"What did he order?"

"All he ended up getting," Mary Jane replied, "was a single cup of coffee."

The other waitress scratched her bleached blonde hair. "What was wrong with that?"

"When he first came in, he said his pal was going to be joining him shortly and they planned on ordering two full meals."

"Did his friend ever show up?"

Mary Jane shook her head vehemently. "Of course not."

The blonde yawned. "I don't suppose he left you any kind of tip either?"

"Of course not," Mary Jane replied disgustedly.

"Excuse me," I said in a low tone.

My waitress turned to me and said, "Oh, I'm sorry, sweetheart. Are we in your way?"

"No. Not at all."

"What is it then, Sweetie?" Mary Jane asked as she smoothed out her white and red apron. "Are you ready for your bill?"

"No. Your conversation has intrigued me. I'd like to butt in if you gals don't mind."

"Honey, a good-looking guy such as yourself can interrupt us anytime. Ain't that right, Lola?"

Lola acted like I'd caught her in the act of a serious misdemeanor. "Ah, what? I don't know. It depends. Are you planning to make a complaint to management about us?"

The thought of my telling tales about what one waitress discussed with another left me in stitches. Of course, I didn't permit the women to see the humor in it; only my serious side showed through. "Nope," I answered, and then I whipped out my calling card and handed it to them.

Mary Jane's and Lola's eyes about flew out of their sockets. "No way!" Lola said in utter shock. You're a real PI?"

"Yup."

Mary Jane wagged her finger at me. "I knew there was something different about you, Sweetie, the minute you walked through the door."

"We get cops in here all the time," Lola went on, "but we've never met a private eye. So, come on. Tell us what's so special about Mary Jane's story."

I ran my hand through my hair. How much do I repeat, I wondered. "A friend who lives in this vicinity had her house broken into tonight right before dusk."

Mary Jane made the sign of the cross with her pudgy fingers. "Oh, my God. You mean I could have been serving the burglar?"

"Perhaps," I replied in a tone that I hoped calmed Mary Jane's nerves. "All I want is a description of the fellow you were talking about. Do you think you can do that for me?"

Before she could respond to my question, a deep voice yelled from the kitchen, "Order up."

"That's mine," Lola announced. "Gott'a go." But before she hustled back to the counter to pick up her order, she turned to Mary Jane and said, "Go talk to him. I'll cover your tables for you."

Mary Jane looked over her shoulder into the kitchen. "Thanks, Lola." Then in almost a whisper she said to me, "Let's sit at your table. It's far enough from the kitchen and the cook if you get my drift."

Chapter 39

Mary Jane was quite cooperative, and to show how much I appreciated her generosity, I dropped a substantial tip on my table. I figured at least one of us should finish the night being happy. Actually after the tip this PI gave Mary Jane, I can picture her volunteering to do anything a future Bridgeman's customer requests of her–including cartwheels.

Money was leaving my pockets left and right, but nothing was flowing back in to fill the huge gaps left behind. Maybe I should consider being a part-time waiter. Heck, tips could help with a few bills, and I'd get free meals to boot. As swiftly as that thought came I waved it away. Nah, I couldn't put up with the customers. There's too many fussy people out there. They'd drive me insane.

After I left Bridgeman's, I drove north two blocks to begin my all-nighter spy duties. Maybe if I prayed to St. Jude, saint of hopeless cases, something would develop tonight. If it didn't, it just meant he had bigger fish to fry. Honestly, he and St. Anthony haven't let me down yet. Why, they've found house keys, my wallet and even important mail for me (bills).

Unfortunately, this evening ended up being like all the rest. No criminal element crossed the path of my nightscope. Six hours of sitting behind the wheel of the Topaz, and St. Jude hadn't delivered. Darn! He must've been too busy with an emergency elsewhere. All I got from my spy work was one very frozen butt.

Wasting my precious evenings of sleep was driving me crazy. I really didn't think anyone was ever going to show up. As a matter of fact, if I were Ballad, I'd cut me loose right now and shove my losses under the rug or floorboards. End of story. Perhaps, Mr. Malone, he's on the fringes of proceeding in that direction very shortly. "Which means you better do some-thing pronto."

Hmm? Approach the stolen gas from another angle. "Yeah." I pinched my chin with my cold fingers. "That's it." Interview Ballad's employees and recent ex-employee. Ready for bed now, I turned the engine on and left Ballad's business behind.

***

This morning I decided to try Rita again, right after I took a quick shower and chowed down on a bowlfull of Cheerios. I couldn't afford to let the issue of Elaine's and my outing fester any longer. Time always seems to have a way of blowing existing problems out of proportion. I glanced at the clock on the kitchen stove. My girlfriend's day at the office had already begun. I'll call her there. She can't ignore the phone on her desk. "Rita Sinclair, please."

"This is Rita."

"Oh, hi, Rita. It's Matt."

"I know it's you, Matt," she said in cool, mediocre tone. "I don't want to talk right now."

When she said, *right now*, I took that as a good sign. "Oh, sure, Honey, I understand. You're swamped with work. How about if I pick up Chinese from our favorite place, Fu Yu's, and bring it over after you're done with work? We can talk then."

Rita stalled. Not a good sign. "That's not going to work, Matt. I'm training in the newest member of our team, and I have no idea how late I'll be."

Unperturbed by what she said, I continued in a pleasant manner. "Ah, that's all right. I can find plenty to keep me busy. Just give me a jingle when you're ready to leave work, okay?"

I heard a young male voice interrupt Rita. I didn't recognize the speaker. "That's okay, Lee, I'm hanging up now." Rita never responded to my last question. All she said was, "I have to go," and then she clunked the phone down hard without even a good-bye.

"Well, that didn't go well," I told Gracie who was sleeping on the floor by my feet. "She hasn't softened up one iota yet." The dog raised her head now. "How am I going to get through to her?" I poured myself a cup of dark coffee, and then I swirled it with a spoon. The whirling motion drew me inward like it's done a thousand times before.

Send her flowers? If I do, don't reveal too much in the attached message. The fewer the words the better. This PI's been in enough offices to notice co-workers sneaking a look at the message card once the receiver of the bouquet is out of sight.

I stopped stirring now and began tapping my fingers on the kitchen table. It's nine-thirty. Floral shops ought to be open. I picked up my spoon and carried it to the counter by the sink. After I set it down, I opened the drawer directly below–my junk drawer. It was crammed full of crap I never used: bread bag twisties, screws, a couple of buttons, a box of matches, a few chewed off pencils, a broken switch plate, a choke chain Gracie had outgrown, and of course the current phone directory for Minneapolis and surrounding communities.

I carried the heavy book back to the table, flipped to the yellow pages and immediately let my fingers do the walking. There were plenty of floral shops to chose from. I selected Tooties and Nancy's Flowers in Bloom. It was the closest to Tuttles and Gray where Rita worked. Now, I picked up the phone again. "Yes, I'd like to order a bouquet of daisies. No, it doesn't matter what color. Could you tell how much something like that costs? Thanks. The message? To the only person for me. No, that's it. You can charge it to my MasterCard. You have a good day too. Thanks."

With the flower order out of the way, it was time to do a clean-up act in my tiny kitchen. The breakfast dishes had been accumulating since getting back from Mexico, and the dog's food dishes, as well as, the off-white linoleum floor were in dire straights too.

Forty-five minutes later, the kitchen was all spiffed up except for one small dirty spot on the floor that still needed to be scrubbed. I had every intention of taking care of it, but then there was a light knock on my apartment door. Since I didn't want to be caught cleaning, I quickly tossed the rag, a pair of worn out briefs, behind the tall wastebasket snuggled up against the stove, and then I escaped to the entryway.

When Gracie saw me on the move, she trotted alongside me. Knowing her, she probably didn't want to be left out of the action.

"Well, hello," I said in a cheerful tone to the person out in the hall. "I didn't expect to see you again this soon."

Mrs. Grimshaw's wrinkled mouth instantly flipped to a grin as she shifted her rose-colored slippered feet slightly so they were lined up with mine. he slippers matched her long—sleeved floral cotton blouse she was wearing. I guess a woman can never have too much pink in her wardrobe.

165

Both the top and the slippers were a nice contrast to the solid knit black slacks she had on. "Well, I felt like chatting," she said, "and we never did have a chance to eat our dessert last night."

My stomach began to rumble even though I had eaten cereal less than a half-hour ago. I hope Margaret didn't hear it. She'll think I never eat under my own roof. My eyes moved now from my neighbor's face to what was in her hands. The dessert was encased in a solid colored Tupperware container—no hints there, but that's okay. I remembered seeing a pie pan in her hands last night before I left. "Would you like me to take that from you?" I offered.

"Why, yes, Matt. That would be nice." As soon as I had the container in my hands, Gracie moved her body, so it was stretched across the doorway. Margaret bent a little and patted the dog on the head. "Good morning, Gracie, and how are you?"

Gracie's tail went wild instantly, letting me know at least someone was paying attention to her. "Wuff, wuff."

Embarrassed by the dog's total lack of manners, I decided to let the mutt know who was in control of this household. I yanked on her collar and said, "Gracie, back up. Let Margaret in." Amazingly, she actually obeyed me for a change and stepped back a few paces. Luckily, Margaret's a thin person and squeezed her way into the dusty hallway entrance.

With the dog issue resolved now, I focused on my company again. "Madame, my clean kitchen awaits you. Please follow me."

Margaret giggled nervously as she stepped into the kitchen. When she reached the center of the room, her old eyes began to slowly examine every nook and cranny with the help of her silver-framed trifocals, probably because she expected to find a sink full of dishes. "My, my you really have been busy, haven't you?"

"Yup," I replied, proud of my success. "Just finished cleaning up when you rapped on the door. If you're through searching for hidden dirty dishes, have a seat." I set the dessert in the center of the well-worn, round wood table now before I gathered plates from the cupboard.

"Where would you like me to sit, Matt?" she inquired pleasantly.

"Ah, anywhere you want," I replied with my back to my visitor. Then I heard a noisy scraping sound. When the plates were finally in my hands, it dawned on me to offer a beverage. "Margaret, how about a cup of coffee to go with the pie?"

A couples of hisses traveled to my ears but no words. I swiftly turned to face the woman at the table and caught her in the act of releasing the lid from the dessert. "What was that you said, Matt? I was preoccupied."

I permitted my mouth to form a small smile. "Yes, I can see that. How about something to wash the pie down with?"

My neighbor laid the lid on the table now. "Oh, yes, some coffee would be fine, but only if it's already made. Otherwise, tap water will do."

"You're in luck," I said as I pointed to the coffee pot. "There's exactly enough for one cup."

Now, I returned to the table with two plates and the coffee pot. The pie was out of its container and sitting out in the open. "Man, that looks good." The crust was hiding the insides completely, so I still didn't know what kind it was, but my mouth was drooling anyway. "Just have to get the silverware, a spatula and a mug, and we'll be all set," I announced.

"Matt, how did it go at Elaine's?"

I had the coffee mug and spatula in hand but still had to get the silverware. "Didn't accomplish much."

"Was it as serious as they thought?"

I returned to the table with the rest of the items. "Big time. A burglar got in their house through an unlocked door, and Elaine's husband was knocked unconscious."

"Oh, dear," Margaret said.

"Exactly." I pulled out a chair to sit.

"No, you don't understand," the ninety-year-old woman said with arched eyebrows. "I was referring to the fact that we don't have any napkins. The apple pie is quite messy."

"Apple Pie! My favorite." Too lazy to get up, I slid my chair back far enough to reach the counter and grasp a few napkins from the napkin holder. "There, now we're all set."

Now, Margaret began to slice the pie, and I quickly held a plate out for her. As the first piece slid on to the plate, she said, "So did the burglar manage to steal anything at Elaine's?"

"Oh, yeah," I replied as I set the one plate down and picked up another. "An autographed football."

"That's it?" I nodded my head. "My goodness. They were very lucky, weren't they?"

"Yup."

"Oh, by the way, Matt, guess who called me after you left for Elaine's last night?"

"I'm not even going to venture a stab at it," I said. "I'm quite sure I'd be wrong."

Margaret's eyes twinkled. "Tom."

I gave her a wink. Tom is one of the gentlemen Margaret goes out with from time to time. "He did, did he? And what did he have to say?"

She smiled impishly. "You won't believe who he stumbled upon last night at your favorite Chinese restaurant." Now, she settled her slice of pie in front of her.

I slipped a quarter-size portion of pie on my fork and then I held the fork out in front of me. "Fu Yu's? Gee, I can't imagine, but knowing Tom, he probably ran into the Archbishop of St. Paul or a celebrity from WCCO TV." With that said, I placed the sample of pie in my mouth and pulled out the empty fork.

"No, you're way off the track. He saw Rita. She was with some guy in his thirties who looked like he was pumped up on steroids. Blonde hair–kind of boyish looking–smooth dresser. Of course, Tom didn't know about Rita's accident, so he had to let me know she was in a wheelchair."

What the heck is going on here? I thought to myself. I asked Rita if she wanted Chinese and she said, "No." he could've just said she ate at Fu Yu's last night and not even mentioned the fact that it was with a stranger.

"Matt, is everything all right? Your fork is dangling in mid-air."

"Huh. Oh, yeah, I'm fine. Just thinking."

"Work?" Margaret asked as she slid her first bite of pie on her fork.

"Ah, no," I replied too fast for my own good. Margaret's a pretty smart lady; she'd soon figure things out. Best to get her mind off me. I put another piece of pie in my mouth now to quiet things down.

"Well, whatever you were thinking about seemed pretty serious." She set her fork down and took a sip of coffee. "You know, you never really talked about Rita last night. What's that all about?"

I jabbed the rest of my pie with the fork but didn't partake of any. "Sorry, if you felt I left you hanging, Margaret. I've been avoiding the topic."

My neighbor shook her small oval-framed head. "Non capisco!" she muttered as she slapped her coffee mug down. "I don't understand. What's going on between you two lovebirds?"

My cork was about to blow. There's no way I can keep it in check much longer. Well, maybe I shouldn't. I recall some extremely wise person saying it wasn't good to keep all that stress bottled up. Who was it? Dr. Freud or Dr. Phil? I tapped my forehead with my chapped fingers. Ah, forget it, it doesn't matter anymore, Malone. Let it all hang out. I dropped my hand to the table. "Rita got extremely upset with me while on vacation, and I'm trying to rectify it. That's it. Period."

Margaret reached for my hand that was nearest her. It had been snaking its way along the wooden table. "Matt, haven't we been friends a long time?"

"Yes," I replied softly, and then my shoulders slumped forward.

"Well, surely ,you remember the promise I made to you. Whatever you tell me in private stays inside me. No one ever finds out."

I chuckled briefly. This sweet elderly woman wasn't aware that four people already knew what was going on in my love life. It didn't matter who she blabbed to. "My mother and father know thanks to my *dear* sister, Mary. She still hasn't learned to keep things to herself."

"Okay, then, here's your chance to get if off your chest once and for all. You'll feel much better, and who knows, maybe I can even help you."

I took a long deep breath. Did I want to repeat the whole story once more? Not really, but I began anyway. "Rita was exhausted from her stay in the hospital and fell asleep shortly after I brought her back to the condo. My sister suggested that I go to the market with Elaine since I had been cooped up for a day and a half already. Her friend, who didn't know Spanish, wanted to buy a few paintings and needed someone to barter for her. After saying 'No way' several times, I went.

"Elaine found three fabulous pictures but wasn't convinced they were a bargain. We decided to find a quiet spot away from the artists where we could discuss the prices. Elaine mentioned a bar. I knew that could only produce trouble, and I didn't want any part of it. We finally found a quaint shop and decided to venture in. The store only sold bottled tequila, but shoppers were allowed to sample as many varieties as they wanted for free."

"Ah huh. I see where you are going with this," the little woman politely replied. "No need to finish." She released my hand now and waved her petite hand in front of herself. "You and Elaine came back from your shopping excursion feeling extremely happy, and then the green-eyed monster entered the picture, right?"

I brushed my fingers through my hair. "Give the lady a gold star."

"I keep telling you I'm a good detective. It's all those shows I watch." The tiny Italian began to drum her arthritic fingers on the table now. "So, when do you plan to hash out your differences? Like hot water for tea, it's not good to let problems boil too long." Then her table music stopped abruptly.

I lifted my head and shoulders. "I know. I tried contacting her yesterday, but her answering machine never picked up, so I waited and called her at work this morning."

Margaret's almost invisible gray eyebrows peaked like Gracie's ears do. "Did you catch her?"

"Uh huh. I suggested I pick up Chinese for tonight's supper. She said she was too busy."

My visitor finally got back to the half slice of pie still sitting in front of her. "That's what you were thinking about earlier. She had Fu Yu's last night but wasn't interested in it tonight. Please tell me you're going to keep on trying to get through to her."

The last piece of my apple pie went into my mouth. "Mmph." Then I swallowed. "You know, you sound just like my parents, Margaret."

The elderly woman plopped her frail elbows on the wood table. I could tell her brain cells were whirling overtime. "Matt, there's only one solution. You're going to have to do something super, super special to get Miss Sinclair's attention."

"Did that right after I talked to her," I hurriedly replied as I pushed my empty plate out of the way.

Margaret's eyebrows twitched excitedly. "Well, good for you. That's the spirit."

"Yup. Right before I cleaned up the kitchen, I ordered a bouquet of daisies. They're supposed to be delivered before noon today."

My neighbor clapped her hands. "Perfect. Matt, did I ever tell you about any of the crazy things my late husband did while courting me?"

I shook my head. "No, I don't believe you ever have. All I seem to recall you saying over the years is that he was a perfect gentleman."

The woman sitting next to me winked as she brought her mug of black coffee to her lips. "Someday when we have nothing better to do, ask me to share a few priceless gems with you. They really make your nonsense pale in comparison."

The two of us stared at the table now engrossed in our own thoughts. The only noise that could be heard was the tick-tock of the clock and Gracie's nails striking the linoleum floor as she padded back and forth looking for a few measly crumbs.

Chapter 40

Mrs. Grimshaw kindly volunteered to take Gracie to her apartment at the conclusion of our morning chat. She said the dog deserved more human contact than I was giving her the last couple days, but I had a sneaky feeling she had a much different reason for doing so. She was missing that darn bird of hers. He had been loaned out for mating purposes again.

After she and the mutt left, I put the dirty dishes in the sink, and then I delved right into my work plans for the day. Numero uno—call Jake Ballad and get his employees' work schedules and obtain the phone number and address of his ex-employee: Mac Dougal. He should be the easiest to track down since he was acting as full-time caregiver for his wife. With my plans firmly set in my mind now, I left the kitchen and went in search of my wallet which held a business card for Java to Go and dialed the number listed on the card.

Ballad gave me much more than I asked for regarding Mac Dougal, which was helpful. I like having as much background information on a person as I possibly can before I question him or her. "He used to live in Columbia Heights up until a couple years ago. When his wife lost one kidney and the other began to fail her too, he felt it was time to move closer to the hospital. Running a person back and forth for kidney dialysis three days a week really takes a toll on the caregiver.

"I suppose so. So, where does Mac live now?" I quizzed.

"In a bungalow just a stones throw from Universal Hospital in Fridley."

With Mac Dougal's number in hand now and my cell phone, I swiftly made my way down to the underground parking and the Topaz. Since I wanted to make sure Mac Dougal was available for me, I decided I'd call him from the car before hitting the road, so I did that now. He answered in a washed out tone on the fourth ring. "I'll be here all day," he said.

"Good. I should be there in about twenty minutes." I pressed the cell phone's *end* button now and then shot out of the Foley like a cannonball.

To get from point A, the Foley Complex, to point B, Mac Dougal's home, I had three routes to chose from. I could take University Avenue or Highway 65, both of which requires attention and patience due to all the stop and go traffic. The speedier alternative was Interstate 35W. Since my daily work routine revolved around Highway 65, one of the longer routes, I opted to stick with what I was familiar with. Besides, it was a sunny January day—the Wells Fargo bank signage I just passed said it was 18 above zero—and I wanted to take advantage of the heat penetrating through the closed car window.

Taking the long way around to get someplace in the winter on a sunny day is a great lift for one's spirits, but there is a down side too. Tooling along at 30 m.p.h. with the added intrusions of traffic lights gets darn boring, and before you know it your mind wanders aimlessly. That's what happened to me when I stopped at my third red light.

Unlike other days when I drive this particular route, my brain cells didn't automatically shift to any futuristic or fantasy situation. Today it stuck to realism. So far, this day was starting off as a darn good day in the weather department and in other ways too. Margaret dropped by with my favorite pie and took Gracie home, and then for the first time in four long years, I didn't have to suck the breath out of my body in order to get into the passenger side of the Topaz. Hallelujah! Of course, being a decent fellow, I felt a teensy tinge of remorse about that long—standing issue. A nemesis of mine died, making room for me to finally get in and out of the Topaz on the driver side. *But you didn't help him succumb to death, Malone. He did it to himself.*

Speaking of doing things to oneself, I hope Rita will call today and say she wants to smooth things over. That would be a major miracle. The light finally changed to green now, and it was time to continue.

Columbia Heights and Hilltop, which had finally disappeared from view, along with Fridley, which was coming into focus, were all part of the first ring of the Minneapolis area. It's not hard to figure out where one town cuts off and the city limits of Fridley begins once you know which clues to look for. A few minutes after driving under the Interstate 694 by-pass, which runs east and west, you're there.

As I stepped on the brakes to prepare for another light change up ahead, the obligatory Minnesota History class I attended years ago at St.

Cloud State University swiftly came to mind. Professor Anderson, a frail elderly man, was writing on the chalkboard and speaking at the same time. "In 1879, the city of Fridley was named after Abram Fridley, the first territorial representative for the area. If someone can tell me what the town's original name was, you'll get extra credit," and then he turned around to face the class.

A friend of mine, who always sat in the front row in any class he took, a brown noser through and through, piped up, "I don't know the name, Professor Anderson, but I bet it was taken from the Ojibway Indians since they covered most of this region at one time."

"Yes, the name came from an Ojibway word," our instructor replied reluctantly, and then he locked eyes with each one of us again. "No one's brave enough to take a stab at it, huh? I'm truly disappointed." Not wanting to waste anymore class time, he then filled us in. "Land in Fridley, Columbia Heights, Hilltop and Spring Lake Park were all part of Manomin which means wild rice." He scribbled the word on the board now. "Like a lot of other Native American Indian words European settlers borrowed, they dropped a letter from the Indian spelling: double o."

I tapped my fingers on the steering wheel now, keeping beat to an old Duke Ellington tune playing on the radio. Well, I never saw wild rice growing in Fridley. I'm certain my folks would've shown it to us kids when we came this way to visit relatives since it was so noteworthy. I shook my head to jog stale memories locked in my brain. Nope. The words wild rice never slid off anyone's tongue, but then again, a lot changes in a hundred years.

Time to move on. I curbed the thoughts rattling through my head and moved my eyes from side to side along the road. Fridley's welcome sign soon greeted me with open arms. *A city since 1957. Population 27,449.* It wouldn't be much longer now before Mac Dougal's block would be popping up. I quickly glanced at the passenger seat where I'd tossed the scrap of paper I'd scribbled his address on: 7220 Madison Street.

Hmm? I wonder if that's near where my parents purchased a small parcel of land around the late 1940's. That's when land was still reasonably priced out this way. They only kept the property about five years. A down payment on a bigger house was more important at the time. My head began to ache when I thought of the money they would've raked in if they had kept the land for ten more years. By the 60's, young and old alike were swallowing up land faster than a person could wink, wanting to be free of the pollution and busyness of the big city.

There was another ten blocks to go before making my first left off of 65, but I already saw the sign for Universal Hospital which was located on Osborne Road, the exact spot where Madison street intersected. Osborne ran east and west, Madison north and south.

Being almost thirty minutes from the hubbub of downtown Minneapolis now, I relished the quiet of the area I had just entered. Although, Fridley has been known for some not so quiet times, the summer of 1965, for instance. Two F4 tornadoes blew through here. Thirteen people were killed, and one out of every four homes was destroyed or damaged.

After an ambulance zoomed passed the Topaz, I was finally able to make my turn onto Madison. Jake Ballad said he thought Mac Dougal's house was towards the middle of the block. Since most streets are set up in such a way that odd numbered houses are on the left and even on the right, I expected to find Dougal's on the right.

Mac Dougal's bungalow must have been one of the rare homes untouched by the storms. It looked exactly like the ones built in the 1930's that I saw in an architectural magazine recently; wide overhanging eaves, shingled roof, bricked front facade and an enclosed porch. Once I parked the Topaz along the curb in front of the house, I walked up the narrow walkway, stepped onto the porch and rang the doorbell.

A white haired man with a generous girth, around seventy-something, immediately filled the doorway. His upper lip was partially hidden by a thin mustache the same color as his hair. His face wore a solemn look. "Yes?" he said in a stern manner.

Clearly the man was irritated by my presence so I wasted no time in letting him know who I was. I quickly handed my calling card over to him and introduced myself. "Matt Malone."

The elderly gentleman stared at my card for a second and then gave me access to his premises. "Yes, yes. Won't you please come in," he said more gently now.

The door that was attached to the house and not the porch opened directly into the living room. There was a fireplace on one short wall and two tall, dark overflowing bookcases flanking the arched opening of the larger wall which more than likely separated the living room from the dining area. I say more than likely because I wouldn't be going back there to see, but I knew that's how this style of house was supposed to be situated. There was also plenty of furnishings to fill the room: a pair of men's worn slippers, a couch, coffee table, two end tables, two chairs, a magazine rack, oddball knick-knacks, and two oxygen tanks.

I looked at Mac Dougal now, waiting for him to tell me to sit. He didn't. So, I chose a faded, overstuffed blue and green checked chair which was positioned against the windows to the porch.

The owner of the house still remained in the center of the room. "Martha's having a rather bad day today," he announced softly. If you don't mind, let's keep our voices down."

"Sure," I agreed softly, and then I got my notepad and pen out.

Mac Dougal walked over to the bluish-green couch now and prepared to sit, but then he suddenly straightened his body out. "I'm sorry. I'm just not thinking today. If Martha were up, she'd bawl me out about my manners. Mr. Malone, would you care for a cup of coffee or tea?"

I swiped some lint off my navy corduroy pants and said, "No thanks. I had breakfast right before I left home."

The old man sat down now, folded his hands in front of him and waited.

I cupped my mouth with my right hand, and then cleared my throat. "Sir, what is your wife's prognosis if you don't mind a stranger asking?"

"Son, at one time it might have bothered me to be asked about her condition, but it doesn't anymore. Martha's been on kidney dialysis for over a year now, and a couple months ago she started having trouble breathing." He pointed to the oxygen tank. "She has to have one of those darn things connected to her at all times. It's a terrible way for a person to live, but she doesn't complain."

I gazed down at my badly scuffed up black dress shoes now, feeling guilty for interrupting his precious time with his wife. "Geez, Mac," I said, "I'm really sorry to bother you with all that you've got on your plate."

The man sitting across from me slapped his hands together like Mrs. Grimshaw frequently does. "It's all right," he replied. "It's nice to talk to someone other than a doctor for a change."

"I understand. My father had heart surgery performed on him last year, and my mother really appreciated when visitors dropped by." I paused for only a minute and then went off in a different direction. So, do you feel comfortable discussing your previous employment with Java to Go?"

Mac Dougal whisked his hands in front of him. "Sure. I have nothing to hide. I liked working for Jake Ballad. He's a fair man. He understood my concerns about Martha's health condition."

I tapped my Bic pen on the notepad which was resting on my knees. "So, what was your impression of the other three guys who worked for Jake?"

The man I was speaking to shifted his weight on the couch before answering. "I didn't see much of them. We had a time schedule you know. I'd say a few words to them while we were loading our vans in the morning and then wish them goodnight when we clocked out in the evening." He rubbed his double chin. "That's it. The youngest fellow, Ballad's nephew, seemed a bit too cocky for me—but maybe I just don't understand that age group anymore seeing as how our kids are grown and we never had any grandkids."

I stopped note taking. "Have you heard the recent story about gas being stolen from cars?"

"Yes," he replied sharply. "I caught that story on the news the other day." His thick white eyebrows raised a notch now as he continued. "I just don't understand what this world's coming to. Crime is on the rampage. I thought it was settling down for awhile there, but it hasn't. I hate to say this, Mr. Malone, but I'm glad Martha's too ill to know what's going on out there." He swiftly pointed to the world beyond his living room now.

"Mac, has anyone shared that gas was siphoned from Ballad's vans recently?"

The man threw up his hands. "What? Not him too? I told Jake he should put a fence up around his property."

"When was that?" I rapidly inquired.

The owner of the house glanced around his crowded living room. "Let me see. About a year ago I guess. That edge of town was beginning to absorb the criminal element, druggies and what not."

From what little we had discussed so far, I already had the distinct impression Mac wasn't involved with the gas theft. How could he be? He had no motive, and he had no time to do it. I caught a glimpse of my wristwatch now. Enough of this man's precious time had been devoured, it's time to cut him loose. I slipped my notepad and pen back into my shirt pocket. "Well, that wraps up what I came here for."

Mac appeared to be taken unaware by my short interrogation. "You're finished already?"

"Yup." Now I forced my body out of the deep chair and took a few steps to the couch where the master of the house was still sitting. "But I would like to call and follow up on other information I may gather down the road. Is that all right?'

"Hell, yes! Don't mind a bit. I'd be happy to help you capture those slimeballs who are ruining the good name of our communities."

Chapter 41

Now that the interview with Mac Dougal was over, I planned to drive back to Columbia Heights and catch up with one of Jake Ballad's present employees: his neighbor. I would've preferred to stop at my folks first and have a cup of coffee with them since they only live a couple blocks north of the hospital, but according to my watch, it was just about time for Al Stone to have lunch. Darn!

Supposedly, interviewee number two's daily routine includes lunch at the Mc Donald's on Highway 65 (Central Avenue) closest to Java to Go. Ballad had given me an age bracket for Al, but since aging a person can be quite challenging and I didn't want to fight the lunch crowd trying to figure out which guy I was looking for, I called him beforehand to get a brief description of what he looked like.

Stone was to the point. "Just look for a middle-aged guy wearing a purple and gold U of M Gopher's cap, a dark navy quilted vest and brown khaki pants."

Skip the age, the jacket and pants. Finding someone from the neck up was much simpler for me. Sometimes the person I'm looking for has a birthmark, a tattoo, heavy make-up or even rings adorning his face. Then there's the outlandish hair-dos. But I'm not going there. Thankfully, the particular cap Stone mentioned should really stand out from the crowd. This Mc Donald's doesn't cater to the U of M students. The college is quite a distance from here.

I drove into Mc Donald's parking lot now. Even though it was the bewitching hour, I actually found a vacant spot right away, and quickly parked the Topaz.

I passed through the double glass doors of the fast-food place and immediately saw a man of Al Stone's description standing in line two waiting to give his order. I strolled over to where he stood, let him know

I had arrived, and then got in line three to place my own order. I selected the number six combo—the double-decker cheeseburger, fries and a large Coke. While I waited in line, I kept my eyes peeled on Stone, so I'd know which booth he selected to devour his food in.

"Combo six is ready to roll," my order taker shouted from behind the front counter. He must've thought I went off to the bathroom or something.

"Excuse me. That's me," I said as I casually eased my way up to the counter and quickly grabbed my tray of food. The supply counter was next on my agenda. The person filling my order neglected to provide me with a few necessities like a straw and napkins. I placed the items on my tray now. Okay. I had everything I needed. I was ready to meet with Al Stone.

When I finally reached Stone's table, he was bent over his chicken sandwich and getting ready to chomp down on it, but then he suddenly stopped in his tracks. He must've sensed someone was hovering over him. His head straightened slightly, and then his eyes locked onto mine. "Have a seat," he ordered, and then he put his messy sandwich back down in its Styrofoam container.

I silently set my tray down, slipped into the bright red booth, and said "Matt Malone," and then I automatically extended my hand.

Al Stone jerked his head up but didn't offer me either hand. I was thankful. Both were messy from the condiments that had oozed from his thickly stuffed sandwich. "When you called a few minutes ago, you mentioned there was something important you needed to talk to me about. With my personal life or work?" he asked with a voice that was rough around the edges, "because I don't share much about my personal life. It's nobody's business if you get my drift."

I put his nervous mind at ease instantly. There was no way I was suffering from indigestion because of the foul mood I may have placed him in. "Don't worry—what we're about to discuss isn't personal. It's work-related."

Stone relaxed his tall frame against the red cushioned booth now. "That I have no problem with," he replied. Then he clutched his chicken sandwich between his large hands again and asked, "What exactly do you want to know?"

I unwrapped my double-decker cheeseburger. The smell of onions and cheese drifted to my nostrils. "Do you think someone has a beef with Jake Ballad?"

The man sitting directly across from me quickly swallowed his first bite. "A what?"

"You know," I said, "a tiff—a disagreement."

His hazel eyes opened wide like a child's on Christmas morn. "Oh, I got yeah. Not that I'm aware of. Jake's an all around good guy. Why, that man would give you the shirt off his back if you needed it."

I stared at him intently waiting to hear more.

"A few years back, Schwann's home delivery service was cutting drivers, and I was one of the guys let go. Jake heard about it and was nice enough to create a position for me at Java to Go. Not everyone looks out for another human being like that, but Ballad does." Now he took the plastic lid off his tall beverage container and drank straight from the ice and pop-filled glass. When he had enough liquid refreshment, he set his glass on the table and went back to his three-fourths eaten sandwich.

Hmm, maybe I'd better have a bite of my own sandwich before it gets cold. There's nothing I hated worse than eating a cheeseburger with cold congealed cheese. I hoisted my heavy burger in the air now and quickly chomped on a corner of it. After my teeth ground it up good and I swallowed what little remained in my mouth, I carefully pitched a couple loaded questions Al's way. "What do you think of Ballad's brother and son? Are they as hard of workers as Mac Dougal was?"

The man sitting across from me smacked his lips. "Talk about someone who didn't goof around—I miss Mac. He may be in his seventies, but he sure could heft those bags of roasted and ground coffee into his van. Nice fella. A little *old fashioned,* but I was sorry to see him go. He's the one who trained me in when I started working for Ballad." Now, Stone tugged on the visor of his cap before continuing. "Chet, Jake's brother seems, all right I guess. His personality is pretty similar to Jake's: low key, but his adopted son, a high school dropout, travels in his own space if you know what I mean. Arrives late, never catches up, and is as rude as hell to say the least. If you ever get the chance to speak to him within his personal space, take a look at his eyes. They're real glassy."

"Into drugs?"

Al swallowed his last bite of sandwich. "I'll leave it up to you, Mr. PI, to figure out. Let's just say I don't think it's allergies."

"Fair enough," I replied in a more serious fashion, and then I slid a French fry in my mouth and pulverized it. Once the mushed up fry had passed my throat, I quizzed Al again. "So, what's your take on the gas siphoned from the vans, Al?"

"A teenage prank."

"Really? What makes you say that?"

Jake Ballad's employee shoved his empty food containers off to the side now. "You've been at Java to Go, right?" I nodded. "Well, then you know it's surrounded by tons of fast food places—or what I call teenage heaven."

I slowly moved my Coke in front of me. "Interesting. I see where you would suspect teens."

Stone reached for the left cuff of his blue flannel shirt and pushed it up just enough to see his wristwatch. "Gott'a run. Is there anything else you wanted to ask, Malone."

"Yeah," I said, "just one more thing. Where were you the two evenings that the gas disappeared from the vans?"

Ballad's employee gave me an icy stare. Had I tuned him out? I waited patiently for a response. It finally came. He stepped out of the booth, yanked on his stiff cap visor, said, "At my brother's playing poker with a couple of his buddies," and then he stomped off.

Done with lunch now too, I wiped my hands and mouth with a couple napkins, crumpled them into a ball and tossed them on the tray. "All right. Two down and two to go."

✳✳✳

After the short luncheon meeting with Al Stone, I decided to drive over to my office on Lowry Avenue, which was closer to Java to Go than my apartment, and see what prospects might be lurking there before I had to meet with Chet Ballad and his son. You know, the more I thought about it, it was probably a good thing I was going to plant my body inside the confines of the office's four walls for more than an hour today. The place always looks like a tornado has ripped through it, and as of yet, no Merry Maids have ever popped in to offer to clean up for me.

As usual, once I arrived at the building known as my office, it took me forever to open the rotten entrance door with the key even though we both know one good swift kick could've done the job. Why, you might ask, do I make life so hard on myself? It's a Catch 22 kind of thing. You see, if I gained entrance the easy way, I'd have to shell out a bundle of bills to buy a new door, which I never seem to have. I swung the door open now and was greeted by the mail. Thankfully, I haven't been forced to provide a mailbox for the mailman yet, so my mail continues to be slipped through the slim, metal slot set in the door. Being a weekday, the mail naturally consisted of all bills. Saturdays, in Minnesota, seem to be the appointed delivery day for junk mail.

Deciding to deal with the phone messages first, I plopped the mail on my overloaded desk and pushed in the message machine's play button and listened. "Matt? Matt, are you there?" It was Mrs. Grimshaw's voice. What the heck would she be calling me for? We just saw each other a couple hours ago. Oh, no! Something serious must've happened, I thought. My ears perked up to hear what was coming next. "Please pick up." Silence. Then she mumbled to herself, "He's not there. Okay, Matt, I'll say this fast, so you get the whole message. Unless these old eyes were deceiving me earlier, your underwear was poking out from behind your kitchen wastebasket this morning. You might want to remove them before you think of entertaining anyone else. Arrivederci."

I smacked my forehead with my hand. "Crap!" How could I have not noticed that? I was so sure the underwear was tucked out of sight. Well, let's hope this little tidbit is something my neighbor keeps under her hat. I wouldn't care to have everyone on the planet, meaning my fellow apartment dwellers, know what I do with my worn-out underwear.

Message two. "Yes, this is Mrs. Phillips," the perky, upper-crust sounding female voice said. "I didn't hear back from you yet and wondered whether you were interested in taking the job on the hunt for my long lost cousin. Please call me back no later than tomorrow at 218-877-2423. Thank you."

I picked up the Bic pen laying by the phone and quickly jotted the number down on the back of a bill envelope before I forgot it. Then, as an extra precautionary measure, I drew three huge asterisks in front of and after the number, so I didn't throw the envelope away by accident. Now with that taken care of, I pressed the button on the voice mail machine one more time to make sure I hadn't missed anything. Nope. Only two calls had been left.

"Okay, Malone," I said as I took a three-hundred-sixty-degree turn around my tiny hole-in-the-wall office, "What's it going to be, tackling the bills or cleaning?" Both demanded a lot of attention. Since I wasn't certain I had enough stashed away to pay all the bills, I chose the lesser of two evils first: cleaning. I strolled over to the one and only closet in the building now and dragged out the Dirt Devil upright vacuum that was running on its last leg. It's just about ready for burial because I picked it up at a garage sale for a steal and have been dragging it back and forth between the apartment and here for several years already.

Even though I don't vacuum as frequently as I should at my business residence there is a huge difference between using the Dirt Devil here versus the apartment. At the office I don't have to put up with anyone knocking on the walls or ceiling to let me know they can't stand the horrendous noise the bright red, cleaning machine makes as it sucks the life out of the carpet. I ran my hand along the vacuum's rather paltry handle until it came in contact with the on-off switch and flipped the button to the on position.

I had barely started zipping around the office when a cloud began to engulf everything, and I started sneezing uncontrollably. Luckily I knew what the problem was. I hadn't changed the dirt bag in at least six months. I stooped down now and unlocked the chamber that hid the dirt bag. Yup. Just as I suspected. The bag was bursting at the seams. I quickly removed it and tossed it outside the door. Then I pulled my swivel chair towards the door and braced it open to get rid of the dusty haze. No more vacuuming. I neglected to purchase more bags. Of course, I still had plenty of cleaning to do. Darn.

Fortunately, the invigorating January air sweeping through the office propelled me on now with what I had already started. There was no need for a general's stern look today. Waste-baskets needed to be emptied, and then it was on to rifling through the stuff on my massive desk.

Five minutes later, I closed the entrance door and reclaimed my swivel chair. Talk about feeling like you're living in a freezer. Well, at least no one could say I was sleeping on the job. With my chair scooted up to the desk now, I sat down and began scanning the items laid out in front of me. The calendar was partially covered by bills. Curious to see what my schedule entailed, I tugged at it till it sat squarely in front of me. No engagements marked down for the end of January. Zippo. I flipped the calendar to February. Nothing for February either. Oh, man. Valentines day already. Now, I really have to scramble and get my situation with Rita straightened out. There's no way I was going to let that day arrive, the second anniversary of the day we met, and not be able to celebrate it with great fanfare.

I thought about the engagement ring safely tucked away in my dresser drawer again. Maybe I'll get a chance to give the ring to Rita after all—then I began to whistle an old lovey-dovey Frank Sinatra tune, *Something Stupid*. It happened to be a favorite of mine.

The rest of the day went by rather fast even though I never managed to get through the mess on my desk. A minor dent was made in the bill pile. And I could see the phone again now that everything had been shifted away from it. Actually the phone was to blame for my not completing my desk cleaning. Every time I'd pick up a bill or a document of some sort, the phone rang. My mother called to see how my day was progressing and tried to worm out of me what Rita and I were up to. I succeeded in keeping the latter to myself. Margaret called again and wanted to know how the coffee case was going and also whether I was going to hunt down the long lost cousin we talked about, something which was tempting but I hadn't made a decision on yet.

"You know Matt, helping you find a long lost cousin would be fun. I even have some ideas on where we can search for information."

"Whoa. Take it easy, Margaret. I don't know if it's such a good idea to be searching for someone right now. An out of town job like this one could be very time consuming, and I'm still trying to get back into Rita's good graces." I didn't care to burden my neighbor with other things that were factoring into whether I took the new case or not, such as only a mere pittance of a retainer would exchange hands—nothing more. If I put all my energy into the case and had nothing to show for it in the end, I'd be back at square one.

After I ended my conversation with my neighbor, I got to thinking about my sixth sense and where it had been hiding lately. I mean, let's face it, this would be the perfect time for my curse to kick in, but it just wasn't cooperating It had left me adrift in my own *field of dreams*. I was the captain of a football team being pressed into making the right decision for the team. "What's it going to be? Heads or tails?" My palms started sweating. Just like a football game, so much was riding on what I decided to do. My income or Rita? Which would it be? Without one, the other didn't matter. Maybe I should just call *time out*.

I diverted any other incoming thoughts on Rita and the new case now and settled my attention elsewhere, like the disappearance of the sun's rays and the rumbling of my stomach. It's got to be time to close up shop, I thought. I slid my shirt sleeve up past my wrist to expose my watch: Four-thirty. "At least my internal clock hasn't disappointed me yet." The small pile of papers I'd had a chance to sort through got moved to the right corner of the desk. The larger stack I didn't examine yet got shoved next to the phone. Now, I collected my jacket and locked up.

Chapter 42

Jake Ballad was sitting behind the counter bent over an old-fashioned adding machine crunching numbers just like he was the first time we met. Probably fretting over whether he was going to reach this month's sales quota or not. As soon as he heard the door shut, he broke from his work and greeted me. "Oh, hi, Matt. I suppose you're here to interview my brother and nephew?"

"Yup." A wave of freshly roasted coffee swiftly filled my nostrils. It wasn't the same blend as before. French roast perhaps? Whatever it was I really wanted to taste it. Before I got off track big time and demanded a cup of coffee this instant like a caffeine crazed jerk, I rushed out the words, "Are they back from their rounds yet?"

Ballad brushed his hair off his eyes and looked at the wall mounted clock above his work station. "Should be pulling in any minute. Would you care for a cup of today's special blend? I still have a half a pot left."

Pleased that my caffeine needs were going to be filled without blurting out demands after all, I succumbed and said, "Sure. Might as well."

Ballad left his seat now, went to the small table where the coffee pot sat and filled a Styrofoam cup for me. When he finished, he came over to the counter that divided the business side from the lobby and set my coffee down. "I suppose you'd like complete privacy when you're ready to interview the guys, huh?"

I thought about his question. It was probably best if he wasn't around to influence anyone. "That's right."

"No problem," Ballad said. "I've got plenty of work in the back to keep me busy."

I took my steaming cup of coffee off the counter now. "Do you think you could find something to occupy Nick's time as well? I'd prefer to interview the men one-on-one."

"Sure. Nick's always hungry. I'll scrounge up a snack for him in the back room."

"Great!"

Just as I finished the last drop of my coffee, Chet and Nick came barreling through the door that led to the roasting room and beyond and quickly hung their van keys on a pegboard invisible to anyone who felt obligated to peer through the building's front windows. I kept a low profile and let the owner of the business do what he thought necessary.

Jake remained in his desk chair where he had returned after pouring me a cup of his special brew. "Guys, Mr. Malone, the man in the lobby, wants to speak with you." Chet, who was wearing a cap with the Vikings logo on it, shot a curious glance in my direction and then nodded politely. Jake stood now, swung his arm over his nephew's slim shoulders and said, "How about I buy you a Coke and a bag of chips to snack on, Nick, while you wait your turn?"

Nick didn't attempt to answer his uncle. He just ran his young hand through his long, stringy shoulder-length blonde-streaked hair and allowed himself to be steered out the door he had just come through only moments before.

Chet didn't join me until the door firmly closed behind Jake and Nick, and even then he stepped into the lobby cautiously. Was he worried? Perhaps. I mean, the guy had no clue what I did. I could be an undercover cop or even work for the mob for that matter.

"Have a seat, Chet," I said in as light a tone as possible, and then I pulled a chair away from the wall for myself and turned it towards him. I couldn't get over how much the two brothers looked alike. Chet, however, was the younger of the two. When he was finally settled in I began with normal chit chat first. "Nice Vikings cap."

Chet grinned. "Thanks. It's getting kind of worn. I've had it a while."

"So, are you into the Viking scene big time or just as the season rolls around?"

"I guess big time. I collect Vikings memorabilia off E-bay from time to time."

"Really? So does my older brother," I fibbed. Okay, Malone, now that you have him in your pocket so to speak, it's time to tell Jake's brother what's up. "I suppose you're wondering why I requested to speak with you, Chet?"

Jake's brother stretched his long neck and shook his head. "You got that right."

I gave him my business card now. "I own a small private investigation business here in the Twin Cities." Chet's body was no longer relaxed; it had become rigid like steel. Was he guilty of something or was he just worried about what was to come next? I ignored his body language for now. "Your brother asked me to look into the gas theft."

"But, but," he stammered, "that took place weeks ago."

"I know. I've been on the case for a while now."

He leaned forward in his chair. "Really? I wonder why Jake didn't fill me in."

"Probably because I asked your brother to keep my involvement under wraps." I sat back in my chair now and watched for any other signs of nervousness on Chet's part.

Jake's brother shook his elongated neck. "Mr. Malone, I don't mean to offend you, but why hire a private investigator? Cops should handle a theft. Heck, our taxes provide for their services."

"Your brother spoke with the police before hiring me, Chet," I explained, and then I glanced down at the floor while he processed my information. After I felt sufficient time had elapsed, I focused my eyes on him again. So far, I wasn't getting any vibes from him that he might have been involved in the theft. "I don't know if you are aware of it or not, but there's a shortage of manpower at the police station and they can't afford to assign anyone to the task. The good news is, since I started watching your brother's place, there hasn't been any more gas siphoned from the vans. However, there still remains the question of who engineered the heist? That's why I'm taking the time to question Jake's employees."

Chet began to fidget with his large hands. "I . . . I don't get it. Exactly what kind of answers do you hope to obtain from me?"

"Where you were on the two evenings the gas disappeared from the vans."

"Jake probably didn't mention that I have another job besides this."

"Nope. He didn't. So, what else do you do?"

"I play in a band." He stretched his legs off to the left side of his chair now.

I scratched my head. "Ah? What instrument do you play?"

Chet slid his hands back and forth along the upper portion of his jean clad legs. "Drums."

"So, you probably need to be on stage for just about every number?"

"You got it," he said permitting the first smile to engulf his face.

The unpadded hard plastic chair was beginning to make me feel uncomfortable, but I trudged on. "Did you happen to have gigs both nights the gas was stolen?" I asked.

"As a matter of fact, I did. We play three nights a week at a bar down on Hennepin Avenue. Perhaps you've heard of it. Sluggers?"

Everyone in Minneapolis knew Sluggers. It was one of a handful of bars that had a wild reputation to uphold. Sluggers gained its right after Prohibition. Nowadays the bar was as tame as a pussy cat. Checking on the band's gig dates should be a cinch. Most entertainment is lined up a year in advance, so managers have to keep a pretty good record of who is expected when.

"Does Nick play in the band too?" I innocently asked knowing full well where I was going with this line of questioning.

Chet Ballad laughed. "My son? No way," he offered hastily not understanding what I was really fishing for. "Nick can't stand music from the 50's and 60's."

"Oh? What kind of music is he into?"

"Hard rapper stuff." Then as if a lightbulb magically turned on in his head, Chet's voice changed dramatically. "Whoa! Just hold on there, Malone. Are you insinuating that my son may have had something to do with the theft?" I kept quiet. "Because if you are, you can forget that. You're dead wrong. Sure Nick's a little on the wild side, but underneath he's a solid kid. Don't tell me you've forgotten what it was like to be young and carefree?"

"I wasn't implying any such thing," I lied. "I just wondered if he was at the bar with you those two evenings. That's all." Now I ran my hand through my hair before continuing. "And no, I haven't forgotten what life was like as a twenty-year-old. It goes by way too fast. Before you know it, partying is given up for more mature things like mortgages and children."

Hearing my reply seemed to loosen the bad vibes Chet apparently thought he was getting from me. He folded his hands in his lap now and said quite soberly, "You know, you're an all right guy for a PI, Malone. Nick wasn't with me that night. I … I don't have any idea where he was."

I was finished interrogating Chet, now it was time to hear what his son had to say. I asked Chet to send his son out to the lobby.

Ever since I was a wee lad, I was taught not to *judge a book by its cover*. Years later when my sister, Mary, became a school teacher she said, "The worst thing a teacher can do is to judge a student by the previous teacher's comments that are conveniently tucked away in the student's file folder. Ignore them. Make up your own mind." Then there's the old adage, *appearance isn't everything*. Unfortunately for Nick, when he entered the lobby, I found myself immediately judging him according to Al Stone's assessment, not his father's.

Jake Ballad's twenty-year-old nephew was tall and thin. There wasn't one ounce of muscle or fat on him. He reminded me of the fictional character Icabod Crane. Although to Icabod's credit, he would never have been caught wearing two silver rings through a nostril, three attached to his earlobe and another protruding his lower lip. I got goose bumps just looking at his decorated head. How can a person possibly eat with a ring attached to a lip or a tongue? There's no way I could. Of course, knowing diet fads, someday a doctor will announce it's a good way to lose weight. I wondered if the kid had unexposed parts of his body pierced too, but I didn't think it appropriate to ask.

My eyes examined the young man's body next. His upper torso was completely covered by a navy blue sweatshirt emblazoned with the words "Coffee, Rap or Nothing." The lower half of his body was clothed in stone-washed blue jeans that hung loosely on his hips. The material surrounding the knee area on both pant legs was totally obliterated, leaving his knees to an early start on tanning. There was no denying Nick was nervous. His pacing resembled the attitude of a trapped mountain lion.

"Relax, Nick," I said in a soothing tone. "There's nothing to be anxious about. Grab a chair and sit a spell."

"No, thanks," he swiftly replied. "I don't like sitting anymore than I have to."

Wanting to make him think I had empathy for his predicament, I said, "I can understand that. I'm sure if I drove around town for a living I wouldn't want to sit anymore than was absolutely necessary either."

My words seemed to console Nick. He stopped shuffling his feet and crossed his arms. "Uncle Jake said you're a PI?"

"That's right. Your uncle hired me to figure out who stole the gas from the vans. Some of the people I've already spoken with have thrown out a few scenarios, and I was wondering if you'd like to take a stab at it. What do you think happened?"

The young man's arms immediately sprung into active duty. They flew out to his sides now. "Haven't a clue, but, if I was going to siphon gas from another vehicle, I'd pick one of those huge over-the-road trucks that you see at all the rest stops."

I wasn't sure if I believed him or not. His words flowed too smoothly. They were too pat. Most people require a bit of time to reflect before they pronounce a thought or opinion. Was this simply an answer he prepared in case he got pushed into a corner?

Since Nick was standing directly in front of me, I took Al Stone's suggestion to heart and scrutinized his hazel eyes. They didn't appear to be glassy and distant. If Chet's son was a hardline addict, his eyes certainly wouldn't change from one day to the next.

Chet's son began to shuffle his feet again. "So, is that it? Are you done with me? Because if you are, I'd like to take off."

"Oh, I suppose you're getting together with a few of your buddies after work, huh?" Nick shook his long head of hair. Strands flew everywhere. "Something like that."

"You're lucky you still have friends who have time for you," I said. "Usually after high school everyone seems to go their separate way." Jake's nephew didn't agree or disagree with me. I stood now. Might as well be on level ground with him when I ask the next question, I thought, otherwise he might attempt to kick my chair out from under me. "So, where exactly were you the two evenings gas was stolen from the vans?"

The young man's medium-toned voice rose sharply. "What? How the hell am I suppose to remember that? It wasn't like I was doing a gig or something."

There was something swimming underneath this kid's hard exterior, but what was it? I took my jacket off the back of my chair now and started to put it on. "Tell you what, Nick. Why don't you give it some thought and then give me a call when you've figured it out. Your uncle has my number." Then I turned and strolled to the door. The minute I stepped out into the frigid night air, I took a quick glance over my shoulder and saw a paralyzed Nick Ballad standing right where I left him, by the windows in the lobby.

Chapter 43

Saturday finally arrived, and things still weren't peaches and cream between Rita and me. The daisies I had delivered the other day hadn't packed the punch I'd expected them to. Oh, sure, Rita responded to her gift, but it was just a short, curt to-the-point message left on the answering machine. "Got the daisies." Nothing more nothing less. No words of endearment or even, "I'll see or chat with you soon." To be blunt, if Rita doesn't change her four-star general tactics soon, she's going to discover that her relationship with a lowly private, me, has crashed and burned. Just because I'm a man doesn't mean I lack feelings. That cold shoulder treatment of hers is getting to be a bit much. It's making it harder and harder for me to go through with my marriage proposal plans. Maybe everybody was wrong, and we weren't meant to be together. The trip to Mexico was merely an eye-opener to help us discern that.

In half-dressed attire, I stood gazing at the four bland walls in my bedroom for a moment, and then I glanced down at the small white crushed-velvet box in my hands. Time to put it away. This quarter carat diamond ring wasn't leaving my apartment any time soon. I snapped the lid shut. It was a nice ring, and I didn't even have to purchase it. Margaret presented it to me some time ago. I said, "No," but she insisted. You see, I took the place of the children she never had.

"Matt," she said the day she offered it to me, "my husband gave me so many expensive pieces of jewelry over the years, but this diamond ring means the most to me. If I don't do something with it now, it will be stashed in my casket or pawned off to pay nursing home bills. Let me have the pleasure of seeing it on your girlfriend's finger instead."

After I heard my neighbor's reason for wanting me to have the ring, I couldn't deny the nonagenarian that tiny bit of happiness, but now a smidgen of guilt ran down my spine. The little Italian woman may never live to see that day all because of Elaine's and my immature behavior in PV. I slipped the ring box back in the top dresser drawer under my undershirts now and then shook my head. I really shouldn't be going to Elaine's and Frank's party tonight—but what else was there to do. Sit in my La-Z-Boy and mope? My sister would be there, as well as, some of the Best's neighbors. Maybe I can work the PI angle. As far as I knew, Elaine reported the break-in, so there was no harm in being inquisitive about that particular day.

The bedroom phone rang, and Gracie, who had been resting on the bed, about jumped out of her fur. "Don't worry. It's not for you," I said in a calming tone. The mutt circled the top of the bed a couple times and then plopped down again.

I moved to the nightstand and caught the phone on the third ring. "Hi. Yes, I'll be there in just a few minutes."

As soon as I dropped the phone in its cradle, I finished dressing, and then I went to the hall closet to hunt for the only dress coat I owned, a trench coat left over from my Air Force days. After a little searching, I finally found what I was looking for. The long, dark navy blue lined coat looked a little wrinkled, but it would keep my dress pants dry if it started to snow. I pulled the coat off its wire hanger now and slung it over my arm. Then I locked up and strolled across the carpeted hall to Mrs. Grimshaw's.

Her apartment door sprung open immediately. "Right on time," she announced as she joined me in the hall. She was wearing her long black wool coat, a rose colored neck scarf and black leather gloves. As she stood in front of me, her eyes swiftly examined me from head to toe. "My, my. Don't you look spiffy tonight," and then she sniffed the air. "Is that a new cologne you're wearing, Mr. Malone?"

I took her apartment keys from her hand and locked her door. "It was a Christmas present from my mother. All of us guys got the same thing."

"Well, it has a real nice smell to it."

"Thanks. I'm surprised you don't recognize it. I've worn it before."

"Oh? When was that?"

"The last time you invited me to dinner."

"Really? Sorry. I must've had too much on my mind that evening to notice."

Now that the elderly woman's door was locked, I led her to the elevator which was a short distance from our abodes. Before I had the chance to select the down button for us, the elevator door slid open and out popped Rodney Thompson, the tall, blonde headed FBI agent who lives next door to me. He's gone so much we rarely see each other. "Wow! Where are you two going all slicked up like that?" he inquired.

Margaret gave him a wink before explaining, "A party."

"Oh, a senior thing?"

"No," I said as nicely as I could. Rod liked to dig daggers into me whenever he got the chance. "We've been invited to the home of a friend of my sister's." The elevator door jerked to close now, and I reached in and pressed my hand on the hold button. "Come on, Margaret. We'd better go." My neighbor glanced at Rod one last time, and then she followed me into the elevator. As the door began to close in front of us I said as politely as possible, "See you around, Rod."

"Ditto," he replied.

Now that the elevator door was closed Mrs. Grimshaw turned to me and gave me a stern look. "You two don't see eye to eye, do you?"

"No, we don't," I confirmed, "and I don't suspect we ever will."

"That's so sad. I just don't understand why you men can't be nice to each other." When I didn't answer, the small, thin woman standing next to me hastily changed the subject. "By the way, I've never had a chance to thank you for inviting me to Elaine's party. I was hoping I'd meet her someday."

"Why," I teasingly asked, "so you could lecture her?"

Margaret clutched the top of her winter coat now. "Oh, no, Dear. I would never do that. It was purely out of curiosity. She is your sister's childhood friend after all."

"That she is."

When we reached the underground parking, I told Margaret to stay by the stairwell door and I'd bring the car around for her. I was concerned about her safety since she was wearing one-inch heels, not her usual flats, and my car was almost at the other end of the building. Two minutes later, I pulled the Topaz up in front of my neighbor, put the car in park, got out, opened the passenger door and helped her in. "Thank you, Matt. You're a man of impeccable manners. Your mother taught you well."

"So you keep telling me. Now you know why I asked you along." I shut the passenger door and went around to my side and slid in. "Speaking of manners. I want to clear something up. You know that underwear you saw peeking from behind the trash can when you were in my kitchen the other day?"

"Ah, huh."

"Well, that was Gracie's doing," I lied. "She tore them out of my hand when I was putting my clean clothes away." Now I relaxed my head against the headrest and waited to see if my neighbor swallowed the story. That one I didn't mind if she passed around.

Margaret eyed me cautiously. "Silly animals. You never know what those pets of ours are going to do next, do we?"

Yay! She bought it. I cleared my throat now before answering. "No you don't," I replied as I kept my fingers firmly planted on the steering wheel and my head staring out the windshield. There's always a long wait before the monstrous garage door swings up, and I was worried that if I didn't remain seated the way I was I might give my true self away.

Chapter 44

This morning the meteorologist on WCCO radio promised a couple of inches of snow by evening. As of yet, nothing was happening, and I was relieved. Having another person in the car during stormy weather always places extra pressure on me to drive even more cautiously.

When we finally arrived at Elaine's and Frank's house, a number of cars were already situated in the cul-de-sac portion surrounding their home, so I hastily honed in on their narrow driveway instead. Only one white Toyota Camry was taking up space. I pulled up behind it, parked and then helped Margaret up the front steps. As soon as she was safely inside, I backed the Topaz out of the driveway and hunted for a spot along the street. I could've left the car in the driveway, but I hate juggling my car once it's parked, and I sure as heck don't like forcing someone else to move theirs if I'm ready to leave before them.

Soft salsa music and strangers greeted me when I entered the house. Feeling awkward about making a move in any direction without someone I knew inviting me to do so, I remained glued to the foyer's tile floor hoping someone would come to my rescue soon. Luckily it didn't take too long before I finally recognized a familiar head mixed in with all the others. It was my sister Mary's, and she was heading down the hall straight for me.

"There you are, Matt," she said in a singsong tone. "I've been looking everywhere for you." Then she quickly pointed to the living room. "If you're wondering where Mrs. Grimshaw is, she's already sitting on the couch in there."

I peered in the direction my sister's hand was signaling and found my neighbor all nice and cozy, a beverage in one hand and pleasantly chatting with the other. Typical Italian. Their hands are never quiet.

With the whereabouts of my neighbor noted, I decided to go and let her know her escort was finally inside, but our hostess kept me from proceeding with my plan. "Matt, I'm so glad you decided to come," Elaine said as she came up behind me, grabbed my elbow and pulled me aside. "Mrs. Grimshaw, your neighbor, seems to be enjoying herself."

"So I see. Thanks again for letting me bring her."

Elaine smiled. "We aim to please," she replied in a syrupy tone. "I'm just glad you decided to come," and then she slowly slid her hand below my elbow, making my body tingle irreverently. Before this noted gentleman permitted inappropriate thoughts to whirl around in his head, the words, "Pick your poison, Señor. Corona or a margarita?" interrupted me.

Dredging up memories best forgotten of that now infamous day in Mexico when Elaine and Mary mixed drinks for Rita and me, I decided not to go that route again. "I think I'd better steer clear of the margaritas and have a Corona since I'm Margaret's designated driver."

Elaine laughed lightly. "Matt, you are too funny. You always have such clever come backs. That's exactly why I wanted you at our party, to keep everyone in stitches."

"Oh, oh. The pressure's on. I sure hope I don't disappoint you. You may have been better off hiring a comedian."

"See," she said still giggling slightly, "Now, that's what I"m talking about." As soon as Elaine regained her composure, she released my arm. "Well, I'd better go place your order with Frank before you decide to take a hike up the street to the local bar," and then she started moving towards the kitchen.

"Elaine, wait."

My sister's childhood friend's feet were in mid-step when she stopped. "Yes?"

"Where's your son? I was hoping I'd get another chance to talk to him tonight."

"That's so sweet of you, Matt, but he's spending the night at his friends across the street." The blonde haired woman twisted her upper torso halfway and pointed to the front door with her long, tanned delicate hand.

"Probably a good idea," I said after having observed the people marching back and forth in front of me carrying plastic cups filled to the brim with alcoholic beverages that were decorated with sombreros. If I were a parent, this definitely wouldn't be the type of atmosphere I'd expose my child to either.

Once Elaine disappeared, I squeezed my way through the living room archway. In the process, I interrupted a good-looking couple dressed in matching Mexican garb who were having an intense conversation. Hmm? I took a look at what I was wearing. Someone dropped the ball. I was never told to dress for a Mexican fiesta. Oh, well. I'd much rather be wearing comfortable clothes than some twenty-dollar costume that had to be returned in the morning.

As I neared the leather couch now, I found my sibling, another woman and Margaret gazing at a painting on the wall behind them. They had no idea I was in the room. Before I made my presence known, I stopped in front of the coffee table to get a better view of what they were staring at. It was the large Mexican painting Elaine purchased in Puerto Vallarta. It really was made for this room. After waiting what seemed like eternity for the women to turn back towards the coffee table, I finally gave up and decided to voice my opinion on what they were looking at. "A very colorful picture isn't it?"

Only the middle-aged woman on Margaret's left turned to respond. "Yes, it most certainly is," she earnestly replied. Could she be one of Elaine's neighbors I wanted to speak to?

Since only the stranger had made an effort to chit chat with me, I gave up on Margaret and Mary and continued my conversation with her. "I don't think it would've looked as nice against white walls, do you?" That comment got Mary and Margaret's attention now. The two women immediately straightened their bodies around and tilted their heads my way.

"Oh, I agree completely, Matt," my sister hastily replied, and then she leaned into Margaret to share more. "Elaine and Frank just painted the living room walls pale green this week."

"Oh, really? Well, they did a nice job," Margaret answered softly, and then she lifted her cold beverage to her lips.

"I see Mary's taken good care of you, Margaret?"

The ninety-year-old immediately moved the drink away from her lips and hoisted it in the air. "Oh, you mean this? It's a virgin margarita. Tastes good. You should try one, Matt."

"Ah, no, thanks. I'm waiting on a beer," now I spoke to my sister. "Any idea where Elaine hung the two smaller pictures, Mary?"

"Nope."

"Well, I suppose I can put the question to her when she returns with my beer."

"Say, Matt," my sister said, "have you met Susie? She lives at the other end of the street."

I released a grin now and then extended my hand to Susie. "I don't believe I've had the pleasure. Nice to meet you, Susie." Even though she lived several houses down, she may have seen someone strange in the neighborhood the day Elaine's and Frank's house was ransacked. I'll have to touch base with her later when she's by herself, unless Margaret weasels information out of her before that.

"Nice to meet you too," Susie volleyed back as she eyed me this way and that. It was bad enough she held my hand way too long, but to be put through the examination process was more than this guy could bear. If I was a mean person, I would've shook my hand loose as soon as possible and then made some lame excuse about having to move on. "My, my. Your sister never told me what a handsome brother she had." I waited politely till she stopped drooling before I came up with a wise reply.

It was obvious Susie was yet another older woman on the prowl. So sorry, lady, but as far as I knew I still wasn't available. "Me? Oh, you must be referring to our other brother. Mary has two you know."

"No way?" Susie said with her hand held to her breast. "Mary grew up with two brothers?" I bobbed my head. "Lucky her."

"A-hem," Mary said in response to Susie's remark. "Sometimes. Like, next week Matt's going to speak to the kids in my classroom, right, Big Brother?"

"Yup, I said I would."

Margaret set her drink down on the coffee table now and gave me a little wink. I think she noticed my discomfort. "Matt, don't feel you have to babysit me. Move around a little. Mingle."

"Yeah, go on," Mary chimed in. "Susie and I will make sure no one makes a move on Margaret." All three of the women on the couch laughed loudly now. I wouldn't be surprised if Margaret's virgin drink was actually spiked with a little something extra, especially since I know she loves her evening glass of wine.

Thankful for my quick pardon, I said, "Okay. I can take a hint. I'll move along then." Now I moved a few feet away. Not having to worry about my neighbor anymore gave me the flexibility to meander through the house and eavesdrop on conversations. Just what I wanted to do all along. Why, if I'm lucky enough, perhaps I'll even catch someone discussing the break-in.

Too bad my plans were a bit premature. As I was about to start up a conversation with some other folks, I saw Elaine working her magic and easily snaking her way through the crowded room to bring me my requested beer. "Here you go. Your Corona, Señor."

I took the beer from her soft hands now. "Gracias."

"You're welcome, Amigo," Elaine said casually and then she switched to a more serious side. "Matt, there's lots of friends and neighbors here and I'd like you to meet them. Do you think you're up to it?"

"Sure. Margaret and Mary told me to get lost right before you showed up."

She released a deep laugh. "Really? Well, how nice of them." She grabbed my free hand now. "Come on then, I'll start introducing you around."

"All right." All I had to do now was remember who lived where.

As we winded our way out of the living room and into the hallway, my sister's friend said in just above a whisper, "Matt, I got the strangest call the other day."

Those words engaged my PI inquisitive side instantly. I wanted to know all the gritty details. "Oh? How so? Did you forget something in our rental unit?"

The blonde ran her hand along the top of her forehead and then flipped her bangs to one side before she answered. "No. I didn't forget anything. The man who called wanted to know if the pictures I purchased arrived home safely."

Not knowing exactly what to ask next, I simply waited it out to see if Elaine gave me more details. Which she did. "Remember how impressed I was when the people at the front desk offered to wrap the pictures in bubble wrap so the velvet wouldn't get torn on the long flight home?"

"Yeah. We thought their customer service went way beyond what they were expected to do."

Elaine sighed. "Exactly."

"So, what's bothering you? Were you uncomfortable about the call?"

"To be honest, Matt, I'm not exactly sure how I felt. The call seemed odd and caught me off guard. It came only two days after our house had been ransacked."

I rubbed my forehead. "Did the man you spoke with happen to give his name?"

"Yes," she replied, "but it could've been phoney."

"That's true," I said in a matter-of-fact tone. Why would someone from the Marriott call her, I wondered. "Elaine, let me ask Rita for the number to the Marriott," I blurted out without thinking through the consequences. "Then we'll know if the call was legit."

My sister's friend reacted like a heavy burden had been lifted from her bosom. "Oh, Matt, you'd really do that for me? You're such a sweet guy. I can't believe Rita is still giving you the cold shoulder?"

I put my hand out like I was pushing something dangerous out of the way. "Let's not go there tonight, okay? I want to enjoy the evening."

"Sure. My mistake. Sorry I even mentioned her. It won't happen again," and then the blonde turned back to the topic at hand. "Well, thank you for offering to check on that for me. I know I'll sleep a whole lot better at night knowing if the call was on the up and up."

"Elaine."

"Yes, Matt?"

"You said you'd sleep better. What about Frank?"

"Oh, he's got enough on his plate right now with work and all. I've kept the call to myself."

More secrets. They always seem to bite you in the butt when you least expect. Moving on to a new topic, I said, "By the way, where did you hang the two smaller pictures you bought in Mexico?"

We stopped just short of the dining room now, so Elaine could respond. As she talked, I watched the people in the room sample the various snacks spread before them on the dining room table. "Frank and I couldn't decide if the little ones should go in the dining room or in the living room with the bigger picture, so for now they're stashed in our bedroom closet. Why so curious about the paintings, Matt?"

"Oh, Mary and I just wanted to see how they fit into your decor," I lied. Actually, that call Elaine received from Mexico had my sixth sense strung tighter than a guitar not to mention how destructive it was being to my stomach.

Chapter 45

At the stroke of eleven, Margaret and I departed Frank's and Ela
Mexican fiesta. I had already brought the Topaz up the Best's drive
so it was just a matter of me safely escorting my elderly neighbor to
passenger side of the car.

No words were uttered between Margaret and me when we le
driveway behind, and I had no problem with that. Being a woman th
I knew she was just itching to tell me about her evening. You knov
women are. Gott'a be yaking all the time. Perhaps my neighbor just
I needed a few moments of quiet to focus on finding the main ro
of this unfamiliar neighborhood. Whatever her reason was for ren
quiet I appreciated the silence.

Too bad all good things must come to an end. The peacef
was enjoying shattered after only a whole five minutes. But guess
wasn't the weaker sex who reconnected the communication bri
no. It was the male. "Some party, huh?"

Not receiving any sort of response from the woman riding
me, I pivoted my head to the right so I could view her face. (
That explained it. Margaret's eyes were half-shut. Poor thing.
used to keeping such late hours. No wonder she didn't jabber
we left the party. It took a couple seconds before my neighbo
was talking to her. "Hmm? What's that you said, Matt?"

"Nice party, wasn't it?"

A partial yawn parted the elderly woman's lips. "Most
Then she raised her hands to loosen the rose-colored scarf
properly around her thin neck. "A little too many people fo
up with though. How did you fair?"

I lifted my right hand off the steering wheel and waved
said in a tired tone. I was beginning to feel the effects of th

the snacks I had. As soon as the coast was clear, I made a quick turn on to Highway 65. From there, it's a direct shot to downtown and the Foley Complex. "Did you chat with my sister for very long?"

Margaret patted her mouth to cover yet another yawn. "No, not really," and then she pressed her white-haired head into the cushy car seat. She was too short to relax her head against the headrest like average-height and taller people do.

"Oh, why not?"

"Elaine interrupted us. She asked Mary to help her keep the drinks flowing, as well as, the appetizers."

The car's windshield was getting spotty now from the light snow that had just started to fall. I flicked the wipers on to keep the window as clear as possible. "Sorry to hear that. If I would've known Mary got pulled away from you, I would've gladly returned to your side. I was your escort after all."

The petite Italian woman flapped her leather-gloved hands at me. "It's all right, Matt. I wanted to give you a chance to talk to others. At least I met Frank and Elaine, such a charming couple. They seem to be a perfect match."

"My sentiments exactly. If Rita could've been there tonight, she would've seen that too."

"You're absolutely right, Matt." She loosened her scarf more now. "Oh, I did meet one other interesting person while you were making the rounds."

My eyes wandered from the road to Margaret for a split second. "Care to share?"

The nonagenarian straightened her body a smidgen. "No, not tonight," she said as we approached the Foley Complex. "I'm too tired. I'll tell you all about it in the morning."

When I finally pulled up near the south edge of our apartment building, I stepped on the brakes and allowed the car to slowly inch its way towards the garage door. As soon as everything was lined up correctly, I pressed the garage door opener. "All right, just don't forget," I said.

"I won't," Margaret replied as she fought to control a much larger yawn.

***

After I dropped Margaret at her apartment, all I could think about was crawling under the covers and getting a good night's sleep. I hadn't been getting much sleep since Rita and I went into our own separate orbits when we got back from Mexico. Unfortunately, my thoughts of dreamland were totally demolished before I even got the key in the lock. It was the cell phone that disturbed my plans first with its insufferable tune of *Born Free*. Yes, I've had plenty of time to change it. Maybe I just didn't want to. I don't know. I wasn't quite sure what the answer was. Perhaps I should call Dr, Laura. She seems to have all the answers these days. "Darn, I've got to get Gracie outside one last time." She must be about ready to explode. I dug my cell phone out of my winter jacket with my left hand and opened the door with my right. Who says men can't do two things at once.

When the door swung open, Gracie almost bowled me over with her exuberance. To keep her at bay, I held the cell phone out in front of her and said. "Slow down," and then I pressed the incoming button. I really hoped the caller was Rita and not a wrong number. Now that the answer button was set, I molded my free hand to represent the dog command for *sit*, and spoke into the phone. "Matt Malone."

"Matt, this is Frank, Elaine's husband." His voice sounded strained. Probably just weary from this evening's entertaining.

"Oh, hi, Frank. Sorry I had to leave your party so soon, but my neighbor, Mrs. Grimshaw, has an early bedtime."

"I understand. With all that's happening, I kind'a wish we were in bed already too."

Knowing that he was still entertaining, I didn't think anything of his remark. Being a PI, I should have. Frank may have been holding the phone on his end, but I could hear Mary's and Elaine's voices in the background. It sounded like they were saying, "Tell him, Frank. Go on. Tell him."

I thought back to my time at Elaine's and Frank's house earlier this evening, and I didn't recall leaving anything behind. "Is that the gals interrupting you, Frank? What's so important that you need to take time away from your guests to call me?"

"We've been robbed," his troubled voice announced into the phone.

I ran my hand through my hair. "What?" I was having a hard time understanding what I'd just heard. "I left your place not more than ten minutes ago."

Elaine came on the phone now. I could picture how she whipped the phone out of Frank's grip. She was a forceful lady when she wanted to be. "The lights in the house were cut off for about six minutes, Matt." She inhaled deeply, probably to steady her nerves. "Frank and I just thought a couple fuses blew with all the stuff we had plugged in. Before we had a chance to check the fuse box though, the lights came back on. That's when Mary noticed our big picture from Mexico had disappeared."

I rubbed my head in frustration. I should've stayed at the party longer. "Is that all that seems to be missing?" I asked, concerned the smaller pictures she purchased and more of her son's football paraphernalia might be gone as well.

"As far as we can tell," Elaine said in a subdued tone. "Matt, how could our house be robbed with all of our friends here?"

I heard my sister's voice again. "Tell him we want him back here, pronto."

"Did you hear what Mary said, Matt?"

"Yes. I'll be there as soon as I can." Now I tucked the cell phone back in my pocket, snapped Gracie's leash on, and out the door we went.

Chapter 46

By the time I got back to Frank's and Elaine's, there were only a few cars standing around. I suppose after the guests realized what had happened right under their noses, they were too scared to stay. The Toyota Camry happened to be one of the cars to take its leave, so I pulled onto the newly snow covered driveway now and parked the Topaz close to the house.

Since the mutt wouldn't be coming in with me, I let her escape the confines of the car just long enough to piddle by a tall oak near the street. If the snow continued the way it was, whatever mess she made should be washed away before daylight. Time ticked away as I patiently waited for her to be finished. By the count of five, Gracie was done. A record for her. Now I gently yanked on her leash to get her attention. She needed to get back to the car. Of course, Gracie wasn't having any of my nonsense, she pulled in the opposite direction instead. "No. You can't go in that house," I stated in a tough tone. Elaine and Frank had enough going on in their home without a hound adding to their misery. After one more round of tug of war, I finally succeeded in getting the mutt back in the Topaz. As I prepared to close the car door on her, I patted her on the head and said, "I won't be too long, girl. I promise."

Gracie whined, but I stood my ground. "Hush. If you're good, I'll sneak you a snack. I'm sure they've got tons of leftovers."

I shouldn't have mentioned the word *snack*. The dog went bonkers. "Yes, you heard me. You like snacks, don't you?" Gracie ran her head and shoulders under my hand. I ruffled her thick fur coat, and then she settled in.

Now I locked the car, quickly approached the front steps and rang the doorbell. The outside house lights were still glaring brightly.

Frank let me in.

I immediately crossed the threshold and stepped into the warm entryway. The collection of shoes that were covering the floor earlier had disappeared like the cars and the painting. At least I didn't have to worry about walking out the door in someone else's shoes.

I bent over and started to take my shoes off. Frank stopped me. "Don't bother, Matt. We've got a huge clean up ahead of us in the morning anyway."

"Yeah, that's the downer of throwing a party, isn't it? The mess the next day. If only a person could wave a magic wand and it would all vanish."

"Like the picture," Frank added and then coughed. Perhaps he realized too late he shouldn't have said that with his wife standing within earshot.

Three seconds later Elaine and Mary joined us. Elaine didn't seem to be at all affected by her husband's comment. She simply said, "That's what people use Merry Maids for."

I neatly dovetailed her comment with, "Except too many of us can't afford to use their services."

"Amen to that," my sister replied. "Heck, for the amount of money they charge, I should've left the teaching profession long ago."

Elaine patted her hand. "Now, Mary, you're too good a teacher to think like that. What would the second graders do without you?"

"I don't know," Mary hastily responded. "Should I quit and find out?"

We were drifting too far afield of what I was called here for, so I decided to end the discussion at hand. "Hey, you two, I was asked to investigate a robbery not listen to prattle about how good a teacher Mary is. Leave that for another day. Okay."

My sister batted her thick eyelashes at me. "Sorry, Big Brother. You're right. You came here to talk about something quite serious. We'd better let the man do his job, Elaine."

The blonde-haired woman didn't say another word. She just glanced down at the floor like a child does when she's been scolded by a parent.

"Thank you. So, what do you think happened?" I asked.

Frank motioned to the living room. Apparently, he wanted us all to go in there. "Elaine, would you please bring some coffee for us?"

The blonde eyed her husband for a moment, and then she replied, "Sure, Hon. Right a way."

"None for me," I said as I waved my hand in the air. "Caffeine keeps me awake."

"Make it three then," Frank said tiredly.

Elaine smiled slightly and then sailed off to the kitchen.

"Are your guests all gone now, Frank?" I asked as I approached the couch. "I noticed a few cars still on the street."

"Everyone left right after the lights came back on. The cars on the street belong to a few of our neighbors."

I sat down now in the exact spot Margaret was occupying earlier in the evening. "Good. That makes it easier to talk. By the way, you did report the first break-in incident, didn't you?"

Frank finally chose a comfy chair by the fireplace. "Of course. Elaine told me she called right after you left that evening."

After Mary plopped herself into the chair directly across from the couch, she stared up at the blank wall above my head. "They haven't reported tonight's episode yet, though."

I couldn't believe the couple had delayed reporting an incident to the police a second time. "You know, if I was a cop, I'd think you two had something to hide."

As Frank's face puffed up, it turned crimson. If I had poked him with a pin, he would've exploded. Thankfully, he sucked in his feelings and dropped his eyes to his bare sandaled feet instead. "Well, we don't! Elaine just wants your gut impression first like the last time."

Wonderful! Not only is my girlfriend not speaking to me because of an incident with his wife, but now I'm getting dragged into some unknown force at work in their household besides. How am I going to explain this to Rita if I ever get the chance? My stomach started doing somersaults now. Was there no way of escaping that crazy curse of mine that I inherited from Great Aunt Fiona?

Mary began to fidget with her hands as she brought her eyes in contact with mine. Her eyes seemed to be telling me to be careful where I treaded. "Matt, you don't look too good."

I brought my hand to my cheek. It felt warm. My pain was being broadcast to everyone in sight. At least Frank didn't know what was going on. I played it cool. "Huh? Oh, yeah, I'm okay. I think I mixed too many hot food groups together tonight. That's all."

My sister hadn't swallowed my blatant lie. She quickly turned Frank's way now.

Luckily, Elaine interrupted the conversation, waltzing in now carrying a tray with three mugs on it but no sugar or cream. Obviously, Frank likes his black too. After she handed Mary and Frank their coffee, Elaine took one from the tray for herself, and then she sat cross-legged on the floor next to her husband's feet. "Have I missed anything?" she quizzed.

My sister answered. "No, not a thing."

Trying to forget about my stomach troubles now, I turned my attention to Frank and Elaine. "I know you're not going to like my line of questioning, but have either of you ticked anyone off lately?"

Elaine threw me a stern look. Perhaps she thought I was including my girlfriend, Rita, in that inquiry and was warning me that this was not a good night to open that can of worms. I gave her a silent nod in the negative to calm her fears.

The owners of the Spanish-styled home now looked intently at each other for a few moments. When they were ready to reply, they answered like a well-tuned chorus, "No, not that we are aware of."

"Did either of you pick up any comments in regards to the break-in?"

Frank dropped his eyes on his wife. "I was fixing drinks most of the evening. The only one I recall asking anything was our next door neighbor. After I told him the police hadn't come up with anything yet, he suggested that we start a neighborhood watch group."

Elaine stared straight at me. "I didn't hear any buzz in regards to the break-in. I guess I was too busy making sure everyone met everyone else and that they had enough to snack on."

Nothing the couple said was of any use yet. I could feel my eyebrows inch up higher and higher on my forehead now. "Did any of your friends arrive with someone you didn't know?"

Both Elaine and Frank shook their heads. Then Elaine said, "Well, of course we didn't know your neighbor, Mrs. Grimshaw."

I cleared my throat instead of laughing. "I think we can eliminate her from our worries. She's involved in a lot of things and has many friends, but she's as dangerous as a goldfish. Besides, she rode with me, and we were gone before your lights were tampered with."

"Lighten up, Matt," Elaine said as she waved her hand at me. "I was just answering your question."

"Just think a little harder," I begged. "There's got to be somebody else who didn't belong here."

Frank ran his thick hands through his tousled hair. "Sorry. I'm drawing a blank."

I looked at Elaine. "So am I," she replied sleepily. "Maybe something will come to me in the morning."

My sister was the only one who hadn't offered anything. I straightened my head and gazed at her now. "How about you, Mary? In the course of the evening, did you happen to overhear something that didn't sit right?"

She tilted her head slightly. "Nope."

I got off the couch now and pulled it a short distance from the wall. Nothing amiss except the hook the painting had been hanging from. It was on the floor. I slid the couch back and then turned to face Elaine and Frank again. "Well, I haven't got a clue. You'd better call and report the robbery to the police," and then I moved towards the entryway. When I reached the front door, I glanced over my left shoulder and said, "Mary, make sure to leave my phone number with Frank just in case something comes up."

"I will," she replied from her seat in the living room.

Frank had gotten up the same time I did and had followed me to the door. Before I had a chance to say good-bye, he asked, "How much do we owe you, Matt?"

I braced my rough chin with my hands and thought about his question. There was no way I was going to charge them for my services even though I could use the money. "Let's see? Nothing for me, but would you happen to have any leftovers for a hungry mutt sitting out in my Topaz? I kind of promised her I'd bring her something if I could."

Elaine overheard my request and said, "Sure. Wait right there, Matt," and then she rushed to her kitchen. When she returned, she was carrying a small see-through throw away container. It was filled to the brim with cold cuts. "This ought to satisfy Gracie's hunger pangs."

I examined the container she offered me. "Thanks," I said in an appreciative tone. "It ought to take care of her for a couple days at least." I grasped the doorknob now and turned it. As I pulled the door inward I banged my knee rather hard. Probably have a bruise tomorrow, I thought. Since I had a bit more to say before I left, I ignored the pain and pressed onward. "Sorry I wasn't any help, but please do call me the minute either of you has something to share."

Frank nodded his head. "We will. Good night," and then he shut the door behind me.

Chapter 47

I was pretty frazzled this morning due to last night's events at Frank's and Elaine's, but I knew there was nothing I could do regarding PI stuff on a Sunday. The only people I'd be able to contact were the police, and I had no intention of messing with them. They'd like nothing better than to blow off this PI, so I decided to do something to please my mother instead. I put on my Sunday best and joined my parents at Holy Rosary Church for the hour-long worship service. Today, I was determined to be good and not allow anything to distract me during the priest's sermon like I did on New Year's Day. With as much trouble as I get into, there had to be some minute message I could glean from the priest and actually put into practice.

But when it came time to listen to Father Mc Nealy's sermon, I again found my mind straying. The same statue of the Blessed Virgin that drew me away from the priest's talk on New Year's Day was distracting me again. Mary, who was so serene and pious, draped in a beautifully painted blue cloak. *No, that's wrong, Matt. Mary wasn't the culprit. Think back.* My memory dug deep to seek the answer. *Oh, yeah. Now I remember. Mary's altar was decorated with tons of potted Poinsettias.* Those darn Mexican plants set my sixth sense into motion, not Mary. I didn't think to look further because I was going to Puerto Vallarta and that was that. Boy, I sure wandered down the wrong path that day. "It's been mayhem with a capital M ever since," I said in what I thought were inaudible words.

Obviously, they weren't. My mother swiftly jabbed my rib cage with her bony elbow.

"Sorry," I whispered in her ear while still gazing at Mary's altar. Nothing's that simple is it. I wasn't a fortune teller. Nothing indicated to me that Rita would break her ankle the second day in Puerto Vallarta or that I'd be spending any one-on-one time with Elaine either, and I never

ever received any inkling about the green-eyed monster that would claim my girlfriend or that Elaine would enlist my aid when we got home.

Enough about what's happened Matt. Get a grip. Pay attention to the mass. You did say you were going to do that today. I straightened myself out now and focused on the man clothed in a green vestment who was standing behind the pulpit

When church service was over and we were walking out to the parking lot, my mother kindly asked if I'd like to join her and Dad for breakfast at Perkins just around the corner.

Now, I love food more than almost anything else, as any person can attest to by looking at me, but for some reason I declined the invitation. Maybe I was afraid what the topic of discussion would be: Rita and me. "Ah, no, thanks. Not today. I've got a lot of stuff on my plate."

"Like Rita, perhaps?" my father hurriedly queried as he swivelled his long body into the driver side of the Ford Taurus and turned the ignition on..

My bare hands were starting to feel numb from the sub-zero temperature now so I slid them into the side pockets of my winter jacket. My right hand wasn't as snug as the left. It had run into a bit of interference, a folded piece of cardboard. Nothing jarred my memory, so I let it ride. "Well, yeah," I nonchalantly replied. "As a matter of fact, I plan to call her later."

My mother leaned over my father now and said, "Glad to hear that, Matt," and then they drove off.

As I hurriedly walked to my car, I pulled the irritation from my pocket. It appeared to be a business card. I unfolded it. Oh, yeah. I had forgotton all about this little card. Freddy Flat had handed me this at Leonard's apartment after I mentioned my interest in the artist who painted Leonard's superb Van Gogh fake. I examined the card now. It actually had two names on it. "What the ...? My jaw almost dropped to the ground and hit the snow-packed parking lot. "I'll be damned." There was more on my plate today than I ever bargained for. I jumped into the Topaz now and flew out of the parking lot like a tornado out of control.

Chapter 48

When I arrived home from church fifteen minutes later, I was greeted by one very ballistic mutt and a tiny, bright red blinking light which was emanating from my answering machine. I quickly slipped my jacket off and tossed it on a nearby chair. Which gets my attention first, I asked myself, as if I really needed to think about it. Life has taught me that if there's a dog involved versus an inanimate object, the dog wins out every time.

Since I had taken Gracie out to do her duty right before I left for church, and she had done plenty of it, I figured her problem must be in a different area of her life—food or water—so I wrapped my hand around her plain brown collar, a K-Mart Blue Light special, and gently tugged her in the direction of the kitchen now. "Okay, girl. Show me what you want."

True to the nature of this beast, the dog remained in the center of the kitchen floor and was not about to let go of her hyperactivity.

I took the bull by the horns and pretended to be a dog. Where would I move my dishes to in a kitchen? There weren't many places to stash them. My doggie eyes spotted the blue square plastic food dish fairly quickly. It was under the kitchen table and hadn't been touched, so that wasn't the problem. Where's my water bowl? I love pushing it all around the kitchen floor. My master never knows where he'll find it next. Frankly, being a dog wasn't all it was cracked up to be. "Enough of this dog stuff. Time to be human again, Matt. That's it. Your thirsty, Girl, right?" No reply.

The dog it seemed was not about to give me any hints on the whereabouts of her water dish, so I continued to scan every nook and cranny the kitchen floor had to offer until I finally found the small, stainless steel bowl wedged between the stove and fridge. I strolled over to the appliances and unstuck the bowl. As soon as it was jarred loose, water went flying everywhere, including on me. "There you go. You've got your water now, Gracie. Hurry up and lick it up."

She still didn't budge an inch. Instead she gave me this *what a dumb master you are* look. Then she raised her head proudly, pranced out of the kitchen and jumped into my La-Z-Boy recliner.

I rubbed my wet hands on my pants good clothes as I watched her depart. "Well, I'm glad we were able to resolve that minor problem. Let me know if there is anything else you need help with your royal highness." I moved to the counter now, grabbed some paper toweling and wiped up the mess. After I finished, I left the kitchen behind and went back to the answering machine. There were two messages.

The one from Mrs. Grimshaw said, "Ciao! Where are you, Matt? I know you couldn't possibly have gone to church. Did you forget that I told you I had something to share with you today? Anyway, grazie molto. I really enjoyed last night's party. Please return my call when you get back from wherever you went. Arrivederci!" Beep. Next message. "Matt? Matt are you there?" Ah, huh! No wonder Gracie was bonkers. She didn't want her water dish. The mutt heard two familiar voices but couldn't find the people. There was a short pause before the second woman spoke again."It's Rita. Pick up." Another pause. "If you're there and you just don't feel like picking up, I understand. I'm really sorry I've been ignoring you lately. Look, we need to talk. I'll be home all day." Click.

Rita called. I felt giddy. Was it possible for an Air Force trained guy, turned PI, to feel this way? Who cares. Don't analyze the situation to death, Matt. Just let your fingers do the walking. Nothing else.

My palms were sweating, my right hand was resting on the phone, all signs were *go* for takeoff, but then there came a knocking on the door. It was a gentle knock, the kind that leads you to believe a woman was standing on the other side. Then again, it could just be a child playing in the hallway. I waited.

"Matt. Matt, are you in there? It's Margaret, Mrs. Grimshaw."

"One minute," I called out. Then I removed my hand from the phone, spun around and went straight to the door of my abode. When I reached it, I flipped the mechanism to unlock, stepped back and permitted Margaret to shuffle in.

She was wearing an expensive-looking olive-green two-piece wool suit with matching pumps. Why women want to wear such strange colored shoes is beyond me. Give me a pair of brown or black shoes any day.

They go with everything. Now that I was finished studying Margaret's ensemble, I noticed the small brown paper bag she was holding out to me. Before I could comment on the bag, she said, "Buongiorno!"

"Good morning to you too," I said. Then I raised the bag above my head and asked, "What's this? Doggie food for the pooch?"

My elderly neighbor patted my hand that was dangling alongside my body. "No, Dear. The youth of my church were selling caramel rolls after the seven a.m. service this morning."

I brought my arm down now. "I suppose the money they make goes back into the church coffers?"

"No. The teenagers are raising funds to see the Pope when he comes to Washington, D.C. next spring."

"Oh?" The smell of fresh baked caramel rolls permeated the air. My stomach roared. I tried to ignore it as best I could. "Well, good for them and good for me," I said as I continued to hold the bag. "I was invited to Perkins this morning."

"Really? Are you saying you have no interest in those rolls then? Because I can easily find another neighbor to give them to, or I'm sure Mr. Edwards our caretaker would take them off my hands." As soon as Margaret finished, she peeked around the corner into the living room. "Ah, there you are Gracie, all nice and comfy. I wondered where you were hiding. So tell me, where was your master when I called earlier, huh?"

Gracie shifted her half-opened eyes from Margaret to me and back to Margaret again, and then she started whimpering

"Margaret, you misunderstood. I'm not turning your gift of rolls down." I glanced over at Gracie now as we entered the living room. "Gracie, go back to sleep you're not involved in this conversation." The mutt obeyed. She shut her eyes and went off to dreamland again. I pointed to the furniture now. "Have a seat, Margaret." Then I set the brown bag on the coffee table.

My neighbor glanced around the room for a second or two before deciding on the couch, and then she slowly made her way there. Once she was seated, she began questioning me. "Well, Matt, are you going to tell me where you were when I called?"

I ran my hand through my matted hair before I allowed myself to sit in the one and only chair that matched the couch. "You probably won't believe this, but I actually did go to mass."

"You're right," she answered softly. "I don't. So, where did you go?"

"The ten-thirty service at Holy Rosary with my parents. Call and ask them if you want."

"My goodness. You really are telling the truth. That's the first time you've told me to verify something with your parents." A cheerful glow spread across the elderly woman's face now. "I knew you'd go back to church. It was just a matter of timing, that's all."

"Whoa!" My hands flew out in front of me. "Hold on there. Don't go jumping to such serious conclusions. I only went because I had nothing better to do."

"Even so, it's a start, and I'm sure your parents were pleased. I suppose it was your parents who invited you to Perkins?"

"Yup."

She quickly glanced at her tiny silver wristwatch. "Hmm. According to my calculations you should still be at Perkins eating breakfast. What happened?"

"I declined the invite."

Wrinkles on Margaret's forehead really protruded now. "Matt Malone gave up a free meal? Are you loco?"

Gracie's sleep had been disturbed yet again. Her eyes jerked open and she stared at the two people who had made the jarring noise. After a few seconds, she determined what she must do. She jumped off the La-Z-Boy, crept over to where Margaret was and laid down by her feet.

I threw her a icy stare. "Traitor."

"Oh, Matt," Margaret chided, "Don't call this nice dog such a mean name."

"Ah, she knows I'm just teasing her."

"Are you sure?" The elderly woman gently patted Gracie on the back now. "There, there. Your master said he didn't mean what he said." The mutt responded to her soothing words and licked her hand.

"Women," I said melodramatically, and then my stomach growled again.

Margaret must've caught my stomach talking to me too. She stopped petting Gracie now and shoved the bag my way. "Here, take one. I don't mind."

I caved in at once. "All right," I said, and then I opened the bag and took a roll out.

"You probably want a napkin too."

She was right as usual. My fingers were already sticking together. "I know I've got a box of Kleenex around here somewhere. That works too," I said, and then I quickly stole a glance in this direction and that, but I never found the tissue. *Forget it, Matt. You're in your own home, and a man's home is his castle. The heck with Kleenix or napkins. Lick your fingers if you want to.*

Margaret had been craning her short neck this way and that too, but after a few seconds she gave up on the search for the Kleenix box too. "So, what was the real reason you didn't go out for breakfast, Matt?"

"You know me too well, Margaret. It's scary. I think it's time for me to move to another floor or another city."

The nonagenarian's eyes grew huge, and then she let go of a youthful laugh. "You'll never move, Matt. You like it here too much. Now spill the beans."

"Okay, you win. I knew my parents would ask about Rita and me and I had nothing new to tell them."

Mrs. Grimshaw brushed invisible lint off her wool skirt. "Oh, for heavens sake, Matt. You young ones worry about way too many things. Life is too short for that."

My head immediately sunk to my chest. The little Italian woman's words can humble a big man pretty quickly.

"On the other hand," she added, "if I was in your shoes, perhaps I would've done the same thing."

I lifted my head slightly. "You would have? You don't know how much I appreciate you saying that, Margaret." Then I tilted my head towards the phone. "You weren't the only one who left a message on the phone this morning while I was at church."

The elderly woman tugged on her skirt. "Care to tell me who else called, or am I supposed to guess?"

I sat forward in my chair. "No, no. No guessing games. Just write this down in your journal. I don't want you to forget it. Miss Rita Sinclair called."

I thought Margaret would be as ecstatic as I was, but all she said was, "And?"

My heart started racing. "She asked me to call her back."

Now my neighbor's eyes lit up a bit. "Well, have you?"

I flicked a real piece of lint off my black dress pants. "Nope. Haven't had time."

Margaret's eyes went from happy to frail in nothing flat. "I know the last thing you want is a meddling old lady to give you advice, but I'm giving it anyway because I like you. Forget that I'm here. Snap to it Soldier. Pick up that phone and call her this instant."

"Is that a direct order?"

The old woman's head bounced like the sing-along-dot did on the silver screen when I was a lad. Her reply came through loud and clear.

"Yes, ma'am," I said, and then I clicked my heels and saluted her.

Chapter 49

I quickly excused myself now, and headed to my bedroom to make that call to Rita. Our conversation lasted three minutes at the max, but I felt it went well. When I finally emerged from the bedroom, I found Margaret firmly perched at one end of the couch and the dog resting next to her. What a Hallmark moment, I thought.

As soon as my neighbor caught sight of me, she bounced a little. "Well, what did she say? Your face doesn't look like its been splashed with toilet water. Is all forgiven? Are you two lovebirds an item again?"

"A what? What kind of jargon is that?"

"An item. I thought that's the terminology your generation used."

I scratched my head. "First I heard of it."

"Forget that then. Just tell me if all is forgiven, Matt?"

"Beats me," I replied, and then I sat down in the leather recliner.

The little woman's aged eyes were all afire as she scooted to the edge of the couch. "What? You didn't make her angrier, did you?" I turned my head this way and that. "What's wrong with Rita, then?" I shrugged my shoulders. "Well, if you ask me, I think you two need some sort of intervention."

"What precisely do you mean by that?" I asked in a slightly raised tone. "Like what happens for an alcoholic or a dope addict?"

Margaret ignored my mood. She's seen me in worse ones than this. "Of course not. I only thought if you two met in a neutral place, say my apartment for instance, and talked things out with a third party present, like me, you could work out your problems." Now she slid herself further back on the couch and folded her hands. "Everyone knows how much I like entertaining. It would be a good way to get Rita over for dessert or even supper. Let me do that for you, Matt. I see how much this separation is tearing you up inside."

"Thanks for the offer, Margaret. I appreciate what you're trying to do, but the intervention isn't necessary. Rita actually suggested we get together tomorrow night at Fu Yu's."

The little woman who began her life in Italy some ninety years ago acted as though she had just received a blow to her chin. "Oh, I see. Well, hopefully that will do the trick. Si?"

"I would think so. I mean we're meeting at our favorite restaurant. What could possibly go wrong there?"

Margaret started to come around slowly. "Probably nothing, Matt. I guess Rita wouldn't have suggested the restaurant if she didn't feel it was a safe neutral territory."

"Exactly."

Gracie decided to add her input to our conversation. She jumped off the couch now and began wagging her tail.

"See, even the mutt agrees with us," I remarked, and then I went over and joined my neighbor on the couch. Okay, I'm all yours, Margaret. What was it you were too tired to share with me last night?"

Chapter 50

"You know, Matt, I think I'd like a piece of that second caramel roll if you don't mind. Your eating has given me hunger pangs too."

"Care for anything else with that?" I asked. "A glass of water? A cup of tea?" I didn't want to get a few things from the kitchen now and then have to retrieve something else from there in a few more minutes, especially if we're in the middle of a serious conversation.

Margaret shook her oval-shaped head. "No, just the roll."

I got off the couch and went to the kitchen to collect a couple napkins, a knife and a small saucer, and then I returned to the living room and my guest.

My neighbor took the roll out of the bag now and placed it on the plate I'd set in front of her. "Cut me just a smidgen, Matt. That will tide me over until lunch." Since Margaret can afford the extra poundage and I can't, I ignored her request and cut a much larger piece.

"Matt, a smidgen means a fourth not a half."

I laughed. "Darn, I never could get those fractions right." Now I placed Margaret's piece of roll on a napkin and gave it to her. Okay, are you ready to spin your tale?"

Margaret had just taken a bite of the roll, so my question caught her off guard. At first she responded by bowing her head, but after she swallowed what was in her mouth, she let loose. "It was the lady you met when you first arrived at Elaine's."

"That would've been my sister," I replied wondering where this conversation was headed.

The woman sitting next to me scooped up an unused napkin and wiped her small thin-lipped mouth with it. "Not Mary. The one sitting on the couch with Mary and me."

I rolled my shoulders. "I don't know. I met so many people at Elaine's party last night. I can't possibly recall them all."

"Believe me, you couldn't have forgotten this woman. You just need your memory jarred."

"If you say so." I had the urge to run my hand through my hair, but my fingers were still sticky.

My neighbor continued to prod me with facts now. "She was surprised to learn that Mary had two brothers. Does that help?"

I snapped my fingers. "Of course! Susie Boyle. I just gave her an itsy-bitsy spot in the darkest corner of my brain."

"Why did you do that, Mr. Malone?" Margaret asked as she batted her hand in front of her like the southern belles did with their fans.

Because Miss Scarlett, I don't like to recall women who are on the prowl for a man, especially if they're fifteen to twenty years older than the man." I paused for a moment, and then I said, "Be honest. Do you think she ever found an available prospect last night?"

"I don't know," the elderly woman politely replied, "but she certainly had some interesting information to share."

"She did, huh? Enough for Miss Marple and her other pals to work with?"

Margaret grinned. "Oh, yes, indeed."

"Very good sleuthing, Grimshaw. Fill me in."

"Well, early in the morning on the day of the break-in, a young clean-shaven college-aged lad came to Miss Boyle's door and asked if she needed any yard work done. She lied and told him her husband did the mowing and such." Margaret put her hand to her mouth. "It's sad to think a single woman has to be so careful these days. Anyway, the young man didn't give up so easily. He asked if she knew any neighbors who could use some help. Susie didn't see any harm in suggesting the elderly couple three doors down from Elaine's. At least there were two of them. After she shared that, he went up the street towards their house. She didn't know whether he ever spoke to them or not."

I was pleased to get this information since I never pursued Ms. Boyle after introductions. The reason I didn't was a short one. If I started questioning her, I'd have an unmarried woman breathing down my neck the rest of the evening. No thank you. With Margaret's good luck, I still didn't have to worry about any in-your-face contact with her. All I have to do is pick up the phone and get a description of the young man. Easy enough.

"Matt, what's going on in that thick head of yours? You haven't said one word about what I uncovered."

My mental wanderings evaporated into thin air as quick as they came. "What? Oh, sorry. I didn't mean to leave you hanging. You did great. I'll contact Susie later and get a description of the guy."

My neighbor let her hands fall in her lap now. "I love helping you solve crimes, Matt. Remember how much I helped you when we took that little trip to North Dakota last year?"

I permitted a slim smile to slide across my face now. "Yup, you were a terrific asset. I'll never forget the quality time you arranged for me with Rose Jenson, your Mandan Indian friend. Thanks to my visit with her, I was able to sew up two cases quite nicely."

Margaret smiled broadly. Even though she was a nonagenarian, she still appreciated compliments. "Well, that was all I came here to tell you," she said as she stood. "I really should get going. Sorry it took me so long to share."

I got off the couch now too. "Don't you go apologizing for the time you spent here. You're welcome to stay as long as you like. Nothing exciting ever happens here on Sundays. Heck, thanks to your visit and the teens at your church, I got the most important meal out of the way already, breakfast, and I've got a half a roll left for lunch besides."

A smile softened the wrinkles on my neighbor's face. "It's nice to know that you want me to stay longer, but I need to wash my morning dishes and straighten up the kitchen. I never know when someone might drop in."

"Like one of your many boyfriends," I teased.

My neighbor's facial skin tone changed dramatically. She had been pale when she entered my abode but not now as she readied herself to leave, her cheeks took on a deep red beet color. I'm sure they'll stay that way for a while. Margaret started towards the entryway and then suddenly stopped. Turning to face me again now she said in a serious manner, "It's terrible when your memory isn't as sharp as it used to be." No kidding, I thought to myself. I'm already starting to forget things. "I didn't ask you for Elaine's phone number. I'd like to thank her and Frank for their wonderful hospitality last night."

Oh, my gosh! "Speaking of memory, I can't believe I never told you what happened after I dropped you off at your door last night."

"What did Gracie do now? Piddle on the kitchen floor or stash your underwear behind the trash container again?"

"Nothing like that," I replied in a controlled tone, and then I strolled over to a small Mission-style antique desk that was purchased on our first anniversary by my now deceased wife. It was situated in the hallway against the wall leading to the kitchen doorway. I opened the one lone drawer and pulled out the slip with Elaine's number on it, and then I grabbed a pad of sticky notes and jotted the number down. When I was finished, I looked up from what I was doing and explained further. "Frank called and asked me to return to their house."

My neighbor's face quickly turned quizzical. "Non capisco. Mi scusi. I don't understand."

I handed Margaret the sticky note. "Of course not. Neither did I at first."

Her tiny hand flew to her mouth as she suddenly realized she might know the reason Frank called. "Don't tell me he heard about Elaine's and your escapade down Mexico way?"

I laughed sheepishly. "No, thank God. One angry person is quite enough."

The old woman appeared to be growing frustrated with me. She began to make a fan out of the small piece of paper I gave her. "Now who is stalling, Matt? How much time are you going to take before you spit it out?"

"Okay, okay, I'm getting there," I said. My neighbor was right. I do have a bad habit of drawing things out too long, but it makes my work sound so much more interesting. "A few minutes after we left the party, the lights in Frank's and Elaine's home were cut off, and I don't mean due to an overloaded circuitry. When the lights came back on, my sister noticed that their large painting from Mexico was missing."

"How could a huge painting disappear with all those people around?" Margaret bent her head in thought for a minute. "The break-in was supposedly a random act since other burglaries had been occurring in the same area, and the only thing taken was football-related, correct?"

I jerked my head to confirm she was on the right track.

"Now, the painting disappears. Hmm, I wonder? Matt, was the painting in the house when the break-in took place?"

"Nah. Mary was holding onto the three pictures until Frank and Elaine were done painting the rooms in their house." At that bit of information, Margaret's lips began to part. I didn't give her a chance to continue her line of questions. I just told her, "I know what you're going to say next."

She crossed her arms in front of her. "You're that positive?"

"Yup. You want to know if I think the person who got into Elaine's house the first time, was actually looking for the painting? Well, that thought crossed my mind. At the party Elaine confided in me that she received a rather strange phone call from a Marriott Hacienda employee in Puerto Vallarta. He asked if her pictures arrived safely."

"Oh, dear Matt. I hope she told Frank about the call."

"Nope. She said since Frank had already been through enough with the break-in. She wanted to fly solo."

"I suppose she asked you to check out the authenticity of that phone call then?"

"Yes, but I don't think I'm going to be able to do that."

"Why not?

"Rita has to get the timeshare number. Her boss let us use his place."

Margaret stared at me. "Oh, dear. That does complicate things, doesn't it." She braced her cheek with her fingers now. "I know. Let me call Rita. I'll tell her a friend of mine is interested in staying in the hotel part of the Marriott."

I hugged Margaret. "Mrs. Grimshaw, you're a genius. Just don't call Rita today. She's a smart gal. She'll put two and two together real fast. Wait till after my date with her."

My neighbor sighed deeply. "I hope you know what you're doing, Matt. If Rita gets wind of your continued involvement with Elaine, she's not going to be walking down any aisle with you."

"Just pray that my tongue won't slip, and things will be resolved quickly and quietly."

The nonagenarian appeared drained now. Probably too much excitement for her in an hour's time. She patted me squarely on the back, softly offered "Buona fortuna," and then lazily shuffled out the door and across the hall to her abode.

226

Chapter 51

This day came faster than I anticipated. I planned to get up an hour earlier to prepare for the onslaught of silly questions the children in my sister's class were sure to ask me today, but I blew it. I slept through the alarm. Now, I had only thirty minutes to play with. At the moment, I was sitting at the kitchen table in my white boxer shorts sipping on a steaming cup of coffee and jotting down answers to inane questions as fast as I thought of them. Good thing I knew what age group I'd be speaking too. If my memory hasn't totally failed me, kids in second grade were either seven or eight years old, depending on what time of year their birthdays fell.

When I was seven, I didn't know much about the world around me other than my friends' names and what games they liked to play. The three games I played the most were space cadet, marbles and cowboys and Indians. As far as television viewing went, I watched a few cowboy and wrestling shows. Actually, we didn't have too many choices way back when. Kids nowadays, with over a gazillion channels to chose from, would call that a boring life, but it wasn't.

Of course with computer usage and all the other technology being introduced to children as early as three years of age, there was no telling what kind of database a current second grader had going for him or her.

Maybe it would be best for me to assume kids didn't know much about detectives or such. Unless that is, their parents allowed them to stay up later than my folks did. "Geez, I wish Mary had given me a copy of the story her class was reading. It would give me an idea how fanciful or real the information was that the second-graders were going to glean from me."

Up until a second ago, Gracie had been patiently standing by waiting for me to give her the usual two Milkbones she gets every morning, but now she was through waiting. She wandered over to where I was sitting and began whining.

I gave her my *not now* look. It didn't do the trick, so I stroked her knobby head and gave her some instant insight instead. "We're going to see little kids today, Gracie. Pretty cool, huh?" Like she really understood.

The mutt cocked her head this way and that and then began whining again but much louder this time.

"Shh, girl," I said without glancing her way. "Only I need to hear you not all the other apartment tenants. Just let me jot down one more thing. There." Now I dropped my Bic pen on the writing tablet and glanced at Gracie. "Hey, girl, I've decided to tell the boys and girls how brave you were when I hunted down Mr. Harper in the woods last year. They'll like that story, especially the part about your being friendly to the bad guy. My friends thought that was hilarious when I shared it with them."

Gracie stopped whining now and tried another tactic, she began tugging on my arm. "What's that? You'd rather have me tell the kids how you helped me discover the terrible virus that was inside Delight's canned pop. I don't know. The children might not be interested. The majority of them probably aren't allowed to drink pop yet." Now I shoved my chair out from the table and went to the cupboard under the kitchen sink. That's where I store the mutt's food. After I had two Milkbones in hand I said, "There you go. Now make darn sure you are on your best behavior at school today because my sister's job is at stake."

Since the dog forced me to move, I thought I might as well get cleaned up, but before I could even lift one of my size eleven feet off the kitchen's linoleum floor, my stomach reminded me that it needed to be fed too. "Okay. A bowl of Cheerios it is." I took a partially empty box of cereal out of an upper cupboard and then grabbed a clean bowl that was still sitting in the drying rack from a couple nights ago. Yes, I do eventually put clean dishes away. They either disappear into the fridge or end up in the sink to be washed again.

I filled the bowl almost to the brim, making sure to leave enough room for milk to be added, and then I found a clean spoon and began feeding my stomach. Of course, since I had food in my mouth now, I needed to get rid of the aftertaste, so I poured myself another cup of java. "Ah, that's much better." When I finished, I carried the dirty dishes to the sink, and then I gazed up at the wall clock. "Ten o'clock." That can't be right. I checked the clock again. Geez! I stewed over those questions a lot longer than I thought.

I flew from the kitchen to the bathroom like a bat on a night mission, armed only with a freshly washed face cloth and bath towel, ready for the refreshing effects of warm water that would stream down my rugged body on this frigid day.

Gracie wanted to see what I was up too, but I wouldn't give in. "Don't worry. You're next Mutt. I'm not bringing a stinky dog to school with me. No way."

Two hours later, Gracie and I were walking down the hallway of Washington Elementary smelling like fresh picked daisies. Well, maybe that's pushing it a bit. Anyway, I was wearing this silly laminated sign the size of an index card with the words *Visitors Pass* emblazoned on it. It was strung on a cord that looked like a shoelace and was meant to go over the head. Fortunately for the mutt, she wasn't forced to wear one. Evidently, the school officials were pretty positive a lone dog wouldn't get very far with a kid.

We were in front of Mary's classroom now, so I stopped and rapped twice gently. I didn't want the kids to think the principal had come to visit.

A cute little girl with huge blue eyes, a head of solid brown curls and a pink polka-dotted dress opened the door just wide enough to stick her head out into the hall. She flashed me this adorable smile, exposing a gap or two between her teeth. She must've lost some baby ones recently, I thought. I wonder if Rita was this cute when she was this age? Probably. I'll have to ask her mother to pull out Rita's grade school pictures the next time I'm there for a visit. If there is a next time.

"Hi. I'm here to see your teacher."

The tiny girl's smile remained while she said, "Are you her brother?"

She was going to knock the socks off some guy when she became a teenager. "Why, yes I am. Can Gracie and I come in?"

The girl turned toward her classmates and screamed, "They're here! They're here!" Then she stepped out of the way and permitted Gracie and me to enter. As she closed the door behind us she said, "I'm Margie. I'm in charge of the door this month."

"Nice to meet you Margie. I'm in charge of the door at my house all the time."

"Oh?" Margie said, and then she returned to her desk. Obviously, my being in control of my door at the apartment didn't impress her in the least.

Mary finally looked up from her desk and came over to greet me. "Sorry. We're not quite ready for you. The children got in from recess, and as you can see, some of them really take their time getting their coats and boots off."

"No, rush. The mutt and I are used to cooling our heels; aren't we Gracie?" Gracie opened her mouth wide and yawned. "See. So, Miss Malone, did you have to go out in the bitter cold and watch the kids play during lunch hour?" I asked as I studied her face intently. "Your nose and cheeks don't look rosy."

"Oh, no. For the last couple of years, we've had parent volunteers supervise noon playtime. It gives the teachers a chance to prepare for afternoon lessons."

"Oh, that's nice."

"Not so nice. We only get about fifteen minutes." Mary turned towards her students now. "Children our visitor has arrived. I'd like you to gather up front in a semi-circle that way everyone will be able to see Mr. Malone and his dog up close."

"Good idea, Teacher," I said just above a whisper. "Kids in the last couple of rows always feel like they've been left out, you know, cheated of some privilege."

"And you know this, how?" Mary asked in her normal tone of voice. "From previous experience perhaps?"

I quickly ran my hand through my hair. "Maybe."

Mary left me now and went up front to join her students.

I turned to Gracie and said, "Time to show off. Heel, Girl." The mutt surprised me. She actually remembered this command and matched me step for step. When we finally reached the blackboard in the front of the classroom, I threw another command out. "Sit, Gracie," and again she minded. I couldn't believe it. Maybe she just needed kids around the apartment to show off for. Unfortunately, I didn't feel like going through the trouble of parenthood at this time in my life if I wasn't going to be with Rita. I patted the mutt on the head now. "Good girl."

"Good afternoon, boys and girls. My name is Mr. Malone, and this here is my dog Gracie."

In unison the children dragged out, "Hello, Mr. Malone. Hello, Gracie."

Now I grabbed a metal chair that was sitting off to the side and sat. "I understand you've been reading a story about a boy who solves crimes with his dog. What are their names?"

The kids hands flew up.

I pointed to a blonde-haired kid who was on the chunky side. "The boy's name is Charlie, and his dog's name is Sam."

"Can someone give me an example of the kind of crimes Charlie solves?"

A girl with a very pale face and dark black pigtails raised her hand.

"Yes?" I said.

"A GI Joe figure was missing from his friend's treehouse."

At least I now had an idea of what level of crime fighting Charlie was involved with.

Another child raised his hand. "Mr. Malone. Mr. Malone."

"Yes, what is it?"

"Do you dust for fingerprints in your job?"

"Sometimes I do . . ."

"Charlie's dog dug up the GI Joe," a small boy interrupted. He was wearing thick plastic glasses and a huge milk mustache. "The wind blew GI Joe off the window ledge and down into a big pile of leaves. Does Gracie dig up clues for you too?"

"Well …"Right then a piercing sound emanated from the classroom's intercom system. The children looked from one to the other. I glanced at Mary. Her hands flew up in the air.

"Good afternoon, Boys and Girls. This is your principal, Miss O'Dell. Superintendent Crane has brought some surprise visitors to our school today. Teachers, please bring your students to the gymnasium immediately."

Mary stood. "Okay, Children, you heard Miss O'Dell. Line up quickly," and then she turned to me and said, "I didn't know anything about this, Matt. I'm so sorry. Can we do a rain check?"

I was in a bind now. I didn't want to do a rain check, but, on the other hand, I couldn't act like a jerk and say "No" with her students standing right there. I smiled bravely and said, "Sure. Give me a call and we'll set something up." Then I stood and tugged on Gracie's leash.

"Children, Mr. Malone and Gracie are leaving now, but they promised to spend time with us another day. Say good-bye to our visitors."

"Good-bye, Mr. Malone. Good-bye, Gracie." Then Mary's students left their classroom in silence and in single file.

"Well, Gracie, it looks like it's just you and me, Girl. Maybe we'll have better luck at the office." I strolled over to Mary's desk, removed my visitors pass that had been dangling from my neck like a piece of jewelry and placed it on her desk, and then headed to the nearest exit with the mutt in tow.

Chapter 52

Even though it was mighty gloomy outside this afternoon with the gray sky foreshadowing a terrible snowstorm approaching Minneapolis soon, the inside of my hole-in-the-wall office was far gloomier. I had unresolved cases waiting to be tidied up and a messy desk to boot. As I mentioned earlier, I'm not a neat person at the office, but when I know a client plans to stop by, boy, can I make this place spin on its ear. Lucky for me, this century is all about letting your fingers doing the walking first. All my clients call before they come sit down with me. What's on television shows is a bunch of hooey. I've never ever had a client show up at this PI's doorstep out of the blue.

I turned a full 360 degrees now and stared at everything visible to the naked eye. The interior of this building looked like a war zone. Only a bulldozer could handle it, and I knew that was never going to happen while I rented the space. So, I did the only logical thing I could think of to brighten the room. I flicked on the switches for the overhead light and the desk lamp.

My agenda was filled with a long list of things to take care of once I got situated, but the numero uno priority was to check out the phone number on the card Freddy Flat handed me a couple weeks ago. I wanted to see if I recognized the voice on the other end. I had a strong hunch Elaine's missing painting was connected to one of the artists listed on the card.

I dropped this morning's copy of the *Star Tribune* in the middle of my desk before I charged over to the thermostat and cranked the heat up. There was no reason this PI had to freeze his tush off while laboring at his desk.

The mutt had been traipsing behind me ever since we arrived, instead of settling down like she normally does. Now when she made her move to follow me to the thermostat, I finally had enough. I pointed to the south side of the building and spoke in a harsh tone, "Gracie, go lay over in that corner." She quickly hung her elongated head and made haste in the direction I showed.

After the thermostat was set to seventy-five degrees, I rubbed my chapped palms together and spoke to the stale air. "All right. Now, I can get down to the nuts and bolts—business matters." I plopped my derriere down on the chair resting by the antiquated desk, unzipped my jacket and reached for the phone. As the phone on the other end repeated it's ring tone, I planned my strategy. I'd allow the owner of the number to say, "Hello" a couple times before I'd either speak up or hang up.

"Hello. Hello? Is there anybody there?" a crisp, clear, young male voice asked. "Hello?"

I wasn't at all surprised by the voice. I had heard it several times in PV. I decided to let the guy dangle one more "hello" before I pounced on him. Hopefully, my sixth sense can cue me into something. "Hi, Pedro. This is Matt Malone. I met you when I was vacationing in PV. Remember the guy who was chaperoning a beautiful, tall blonde about town?" Then I paused for effect. "She bought three of your paintings."

"Oh, yeah. I remember you both. The lady couldn't decide if she wanted to pay our asking price, so you left and then came back later. Did her paintings survive the flight?"

Hmm. If Pedro was the one who called Elaine pretending to be a Marriott employee, he sure was one cool dude, meaning his tracks were being covered very nicely. "Yes, they did," I answered just as cooly, "and they are already decorating her walls." I didn't feel he needed to know that the two smaller ones were still sitting in Elaine's closet, especially if he was involved with the theft and wanted to return to the scene of the crime to finish the job. Now I finished with, "The paintings really took on a life of their own once they were displayed."

"Great. It's always nice to hear that. As a starving artist, I never have any idea what kind of decor my paintings are going to end up in."

"So, are you and Darryl back in school full time now?"

"Yup, we've officially settled in for the duration. Second semester starts Monday."

The office had finally reached the temperature I set for myself earlier and now I desperately needed to take my jacket off. "I suppose your brushes and canvases have been stored away then," I continued as I cradled the phone between my chin and shoulder, and then carefully slid my jacket off. When it was removed, I placed the phone back in my hand again. There was no way I was going to allow the phone to drop on the desk. Margaret Grimshaw has done plenty of that to me over the years, and that loud clunking is really irritating to the ears.

"Mine are—but Darryl always seems to find time to fit painting into his heavy schedule. Of course, I do help out at the Minneapolis Institute of Art whenever I can."

"You do?"

"Yeah, it's good for me to stay in touch with the art scene around town. I learn a lot about what type of paintings people like and dislike. So, Mr. Malone, is there some particular reason you're calling? You didn't show any interest in purchasing any of our paintings when we spoke in Mexico."

I scratched the stubby hair growth that was popping across my chin like newly sown grass. "Well, it's the funniest thing. I was actually given the business card you and Darryl use long before I vacationed in PV, but I never took the time to look at it. The day I received it I was in such a rush, I just stashed it away in my jacket You know what they say, 'out of sight, out of mind.' Anyway, I'd seen the very realistic Van Gogh you painted for Leonard Post, Starry Night, and when I mentioned I'd like something similar to hang in my apartment, Mr. Post was kind enough give me your card. Would you believe I just found it this past weekend? Small world, isn't it?" I said in an amused tone. "Anyway, I was wondering if you had any other Van Gogh works for sale, or if I have to place an order?"

"Oh, geez. I could really use the money, but I don't do Van Gogh paintings, Mr. Malone. That's Darryl's specialty. Well, he does other artists' works, as well, but, hey, if you want a knock-off of a Picasso or Cezanne I'm your man."

"Sorry. I'm a real Van Gogh fanatic."

"Oh, well, in that case, would you like me to ask Darryl if he has any Van Gogh paintings on hand?"

"That would be great. You can leave me a message on my home phone. It's 612-724-PEYE."

"Got it. I'll call you back as soon as I reach Darryl."

"Thanks, Pedro." I stole a glance at Gracie now. She was curled up in a ball like a baby snoring away. Must be nice not to have any worries. Darryl Hunt? Could he be the one behind the theft of Elaine's picture? Susie

235

Boyle told Mrs. Grimshaw a young unknown college student was recently looking for work in her neighborhood. I clamped my fingers around the phone piece so tight I thought it might crumble in my hand. Not needing to pump Pedro for further information at this time, I added, "I appreciate your help," and then I casually ended our conversation with, "Good luck with school."

"Yeah, thanks." Click.

Chapter 53

When I dropped the newspaper on the desk earlier, it landed near the phone. Now as I set the phone back in its cradle, I hastily glanced at the front page. I wanted to make sure I didn't miss out on any major news events that happened in the area that I service. Sometimes I luck out. I'm able to drum up business off a particular article–like Sherlock Holmes did.

> *"Huge collection of Impressionist and Post impressionist masterpieces on display at the Minneapolis Institute of Arts the entire month of February."*

"What?" My stomach lurched so violently I thought it was having convulsions. The curse of course. I threw my arms around my mid-section thinking the warmth from them might help control things, and then I continued to read on.

> *"Revenue brought in by visitors should help the ailing hotel and retailers in the downtown area significantly. Because of the large number of people expected to view the masterpieces, the art board discussed additional security measures at their last meeting, but it was decided the amount of security already in place was sufficient."*

Could there be a connection? Original art—Fake art. "Hmm? Stealing an original and selling it on the black market, if handled right could fetch a tidy sum." My mind quickly reeled through stuff stashed in my brain. There was a newspaper article, not too long ago, about the easy theft of a Picasso piece. The guy takes a taxi to the Le Fevre Gallery in London, asks the driver to wait, then waltzes into the gallery, steals the Picasso, and makes his getaway in the cab. A year ago, when Rita was doing a marketing blitz for the Minneapolis Institute of Art, she told me Picasso was the world's most stolen artist. Second and third in line were Miro and Chagall.

Pedro works at the Institute. Both men paint near perfect replicas of famous Impressionist paintings. So, which guy was involved with the theft of Elaine's painting? Pedro? Darryl? Or both?

Taking original paintings down to Mexico and switching them out and bringing forgeries back into the United States was a clever way to move stolen art work back and forth. Anyone could easily place a painting between another already framed canvas. The heavy backings used to protect the painting would provide protection as well as a good hiding spot. "Very convenient." Who's going to question a Mexican style painting that's going to the states. They're pedaled everywhere, even on street corners in Minnesota during the summer months.

So, was there going to be a switch at the Minneapolis Institute of Arts? Is that why someone needed to get their hands on Elaine's painting so soon after it entered the country? "Too many questions, Malone, and no answers."

I stretched my arms out and yawned. Margaret Grimshaw promised to speak with Rita tomorrow, but tomorrow could be too late. Maybe I should just throw caution to the wind and ask Rita for the number to the Marriott tonight over supper. Nah. No way. I'm not getting paid to help Elaine; the phone number can wait.

What I should be doing is trying to resolve the gas theft at Jake Ballad's place, another brick wall. I scratched my head and rolled my eyes towards the ceiling. How do I do that with no eye witness and the incident not occurring again? *Matt, you're batting zero, and you've got bills coming due.* "I know, I know."

The phone rang now unexpectedly and shook me from my discouraging thoughts. If that was Pedro calling me back, that could mean Darryl was probably present when I called. On the other hand, it could be Rita calling to cancel our date. Not sure who was on the other end, I took my time picking up. "Matt Malone, available for a variety of PI services."

The person on the other end began to chuckle. "Oh, Mr. Malone, you're such a card. You haven't changed one bit since I last spoke with you."

Since the female caller failed to enlighten me in regards to her identity, I now had the task of trying to remember where I had heard that loud, sweet melodic voice before. The name sat there on the outer fringes of my brain. I was certain it would come to me in due time.

"My father requested that I place this call for him."

Father? Who worked for her dad? After a few seconds more, her name finally came through my memory bank. "Oh, Carol, for cry'n out loud. It's been sometime, hasn't it?

The woman agreed. "It sure has, but we still talk about the good job you did for our company."

"So, are you still looking for the perfect man?" Actually, it was the other way around. Carol was a sweet individual, but she was so overweight no man gave her a second glance.

"Nope. I got engaged last year."

Her announcement blew me out of the water. "Why, that's great news." I shuffled through casework notes on my desk while trying to guess who the heck the lucky guy might be.

Carol Welch sounded ecstatic. "You can say that again. Actually, Matt, if it weren't for you, I would never have met him."

I stopped messing with the notes now. "Me? Who are you talking about?"

"Why, Yang Quing, of course. That thick Portuguese accent of his bowled me over."

"I never suspected." While on an assignment in Brazil for Neil Welch of Delight Bottling, I worked very closely with Yang Quing. He spoke of coming to the United States one day. Eventually, a job opening occurred at a Minnesota plant, and he got the position. I hadn't seen him in a long time. "Well, congratulations to the both of you."

"Thanks. Oops, I'd better connect you to Dad, I mean Mr. Welch. I've got other calls to take. Bye."

"Bye," I said, and then I patiently waited for Neil Welch to come on.

I heard a click and then someone breathing. Neil must've picked up. "Hello, Matt," the president of Delight Bottling said in his deep baritone voice. "How have you been?"

"Just fine," I lied. I didn't want the owner of the largest pop bottling company in the world to know business wasn't doing that well.

"Did you ever get hitched to that lovely girlfriend of yours?"

"No, Miss Sinclair and I haven't tied the knot yet," I said in a disappointed tone. "Some things still need to be smoothed out."

Neil cleared his throat. "Sorry to hear that. I was positive you two had walked down the aisle by now. You're such a perfect fit. So, did Carol manage to share her good news while she had you on the phone?"

"Yeah, she did. That's wonderful."

"Well, I'm sure it won't be too long before you and Miss Sinclair have that wedding."

"I hope you're right," I said.

"Well, now, I suppose you're wondering why I'm calling you out of the blue like this?"

"I assume it's work-related?"

"Yes," the older gentleman replied. "I have a little proposition I'm hoping might intrigue you."

Welch paid me quite handsomely for the last job I did for him. I'd be a fool not to listen to him, especially with my financial woes. Eager to learn more I said, "I'm listening. I've got nothing major on my plate at the moment."

Chapter 54

Everything had to be perfect at Fu Yu's tonight, I told myself as I changed dress shirts for the umpteenth time. I was nervous like a kid on his first day of school. Rita was the teacher, and I wanted to do everything for her, except bringing her the well polished apple that is. In case Elaine's name cropped up, I had a strategy in mind. Circumvent the topic as fast as a sneeze.

I strolled into the bathroom now and checked myself out one more time in the mirror. Hair in place? "Check." Noticeable nicks from shaving? "None." Choice of dress shirt? "Perfecto." Hint of cologne? "Not yet." I plucked the bottle of Black Suede off the toilet tank, loosened the lid and allowed a few drops of liquid to collect on the fingertips of my right hand. Then before the cologne droplets had time to even think about moving too far south, I gently rubbed my fingertips together and patted my face.

I don't really know if it was the pressure of the fingertips on my face or the cologne that triggered it, but thoughts of the engagement ring surfaced for a second before I left the mirror behind. *Should I bring it?* I wagged my finger in the mirror and replied, "No. Absolutely not. Too risky a move." At this juncture, Rita and I were just navigating rough waters. If I went overboard too quickly, I could end up in the middle of the ocean without a life preserver, and everyone knows you can't make it back to shore from there without one.

Rita was my lifeline—my life preserver. Without her I was incomplete. She brought me out of my self-induced shell after Irene died. I know I can irritate her at times, but, on the whole, I like to think I'm a fairly decent guy.

Finished in the bathroom finally, I flicked off the light and went straight to the hallway to retrieve my Air Force trench coat that I wore to

Elaine's the other night. Once the coat was on and I had collected my keys off the nearby table, I waited silently for what usually came next.

Gracie didn't disappoint me. She came flying out of the kitchen right on schedule. Lucky for me, she put on her brakes before she knocked me against the wall.

"Okay, Girl, here's the drill. Mrs. Grimshaw offered to come over and give you some attention while I'm out. Why she felt she needed to do so I don't know. Anyway, don't do anything stupid."

The mutt's ears flapped up and down wildly, and then she let go of the most offensive yawn. It was clear she didn't think very highly of my last comment.

"I mean it," I went on. "Margaret's a super nice lady, but she's old and doesn't need to put up with your shenanigans."

"Wuff. Wuff."

"I'm delighted you understand, Gracie." I pointed to the kitchen now. "Go clean your bowl like a good dog."

Gracie glanced over her shoulder once as she softly padded back to where she had just come from. I suppose if I were her I'd want to make sure my master was really leaving too.

After the mutt reached her destination, I remained in the hallway long enough to make sure she followed through with my orders. Almost instantly, the recognizable sound of Alpo being pulverized was heard. "All right, Matt," I mumbled to myself, "Time to hit the road." Now I turned and quietly slipped out the door.

I left the apartment for Fu Yu's much earlier than was necessary, the main reason being that Rita and I weren't on better terms yet and I didn't dare risk being late. Seven o'clock was the scheduled meeting time. As I drove into Fu Yu's almost empty off-street parking lot, my wristwatch read quarter-to-seven. I took the first available slot nearest the entrance door. Hopefully, it would continue to be flanked by the two compact cars already there. I didn't want to come out later and find my only means of transportation squeezed between two monster trucks.

With the car parked now, I turned the ignition off and tried to decide whether I should go in yet or not. If I remained in the car until Rita showed up in a taxi or another means of transportation, I could escort her in. On the flip side, it might be better to go inside and find us a comfortable table first. I chose to go inside.

When I started towards Fu Yu's main entrance, I happened to glance at my hands hanging down at my sides and thought of Rita's. Mine were thick and tough and could handle almost anything. Her's were normally fine and delicate with well-manicured nails at the tips of them, but by now they must be damaged and fairly callused from all the wheel rolling she's been doing. Knowing my girlfriend the way I did, I was fairly certain she was using a manually operated chair. She was too thrifty for a motorized one.

I yanked on one of the restaurant's enormous, ornately-carved darkly-stained double-doors now and proceeded into the inner sanctum of my favorite eating establishment; the only place in downtown Minneapolis that offered almost a hundred different combinations of meals. They had Old Country Buffet beat by at least fifty meals or more.

Since no one had followed me into Fu Yu's, I had the perfect opportunity to stand in the center of the dark tiled lobby floor and carefully scan the entire eating area in search of Rita. Not one woman looked even remotely like her. Satisfied with my discovery, I inhaled deeply. A bad move. I was already famished before I left home, and now the fried and steamed aromas pouring out of the kitchen did an elaborate number on my nostrils.

The hostess, a small-framed Chinese female, mid-fifties with long, straight black shiny hair was busy giving instructions to one of the waitresses. Her long silk dress shimmered as she spoke. When she heard the door click shut she stopped talking and pivoted in my direction. "Ah, Mr. Malone. Nice to see you. Been long time since you come in, yes? Almost time for our Chinese New Year."

My jaw dropped significantly at her last remark. "What? It's time for your New Year already? I guess it has been a while, Su Lee. So, how's your father? Is he still overseeing the chefs?" Her father was in his late eighties, but he still wanted to be involved in every aspect of the restaurant business he started over forty years ago.

The gracious restaurant hostess permitted a miniature smile to form on her lips. "Yes, Father okay. Thank you. He never want to leave this place. I say—time to retire, but he no listen. He just wag his hand at me. "Her dark eyes drifted beyond me now. "Where the lovely Miss Rita? She not come with you tonight?"

I pushed my left shirt sleeve up an inch to have a clear view of my watch, and then I said, "She should be here any minute."

"Ah, good. I don't like see you by yourself." Then she patted my rough hand with her soft tiny one. "You like to be seated, yes?" Without waiting for my reply, Su Lee twisted her body halfway towards the hostess counter, quickly grabbed two menus, and then straightened to face me again.

"Yes," I replied, "but I need a table that can handle a wheelchair."

"I remember. Last time Miss Rita here she use special chair. She say she break her foot on vacation. Nice man from work bring her," she exclaimed, and then she stepped in front of me.

Chapter 55

Nice man from work. I cringed. It should've been me with Rita that night, not some other man. Not wanting Su Lee to see how upset I was, I swiftly shuffled my inner feelings to the back burner and politely corrected her in a soothing tone, "She broke her ankle."

"Ah yes, ankle," the restaurant hostess replied softly. "I see table girlfriend had last time empty. Plenty room for wheelchair. Comfortable for her. Come."

When we reached the table Rita had previously been seated at, I checked to make sure at least one chair had an excellent view of the main entrance. No way was I going to miss Rita's arrival. The seat facing east worked best. Fu Yu's entrance doors were right in line with it. I pulled the chair out and sat. "Thanks for suggesting this table."

Su Lee acknowledged my comment. "You like waitress to bring beer now, Mr. Malone?"

"No, thank you. I'll wait." I didn't dare share with the hostess the real reason for not starting a tab, that I feared my girlfriend wouldn't show. Nervous, I peered at my watch yet again: seven o'clock. Where are you Rita?

With our polite exchanges concluded now, Su Lee set Fu Yu's thick menus on the table and returned to her hostess duties at the front counter once again.

It was an hour past the time I normally eat supper and I could hear the menu calling to me, but if I started perusing it, I was positive I'd miss Rita's entrance—grand or otherwise. So I did what any dutiful boyfriend would do, I kept a watchful eye on the restaurant lobby instead.

By now, you're probably asking yourself why such a sweet person as Rita Sinclair would want to spend time with a jerk of a boyfriend, like me, who expects said girlfriend, wheelchair bound at that, to arrive at the restaurant on her own. What idiot does that, right?

Well, don't bother getting wound up like a ball of yarn. It's not healthy. Besides, this guy doesn't deserve to be boiled in oil. When these dinner arrangements were made, I offered to be Rita's limo driver. Her response, "I'll get there on my own."

Independent woman! Sometimes I think the women's movement has gone too far overboard. Many females of this generation now refuse any assistance from a male whatsoever. That truly irritates me. I mean, come on, didn't God create man for the sole purpose of providing for the woman? So, then, why the heck is it wrong for a guy to want to care for the woman he adores in every way he knows how?

The restaurant's one outer door swung open now, and a wheelchair crossed the threshold. The wait was over. Rita had arrived, but how did she get into the building, I wondered? Her arms were resting in her lap. Someone must've assisted her, but who? A taxi driver? Or maybe someone happened to be walking by when she got dropped off.

My answer came sooner than I expected. A tall, blonde haired clean-shaven gentleman immediately came into view after Rita had been pushed further into the lobby. The guy was around his mid-thirties, impeccably dressed and slimly built. At first I was taken aback to see who Rita had received assistance from, but then I soon realized I was mistaken. My neighbor, Rodney Thompson, was out of town on an FBI assignment, so it couldn't be him. When he gets back though, I'll inform him of his twin floating around town. He'll love hearing that gem. I shoved my chair out and stood now.

Rita's long, curly chocolate colored hair bounced back and forth against her red wool coat as she was wheeled forward. When she caught sight of me, her lips formed the teeniest grin, and then she motioned for me to stay where I was. Not wanting to spoil things, I obeyed. It was hard watching someone else maneuver my girlfriend around obstacles. I wanted to be the one assisting her.

Exactly what did this guy have that Rita chose him to escort her to the table rather than me, I wondered? I gave Rita's escort the once over. Better looking? Perhaps. Definitely makes more money—that fine suit of his says it all. And he is a bit younger than me. My palms began to sweat profusely. "Chill out, Matt." Money and looks aren't everything. Remember what Mom always said. "It's what the person has inside that counts." Hopefully, she was right and not just making something else up to help ease our youthful pains.

Rita and the stranger were at our small table now. "Oh, look, Rita," the radio broadcaster sounding voice announced. "You've got the same table we had when we had dinner together."

So this was the good-looking guy Su Lee and Margaret referred too. Great! I may as well take a hike. I can't compete against this beefcake.

"Okay, Lee," Rita said with a warm smile. "You can let go of the chair. I can scoot up to the table on my own now."

Lee ignored Rita. He stuck to her like a dog in heat. "You sure?" *Oh, my God.* He has puppy love written all over him. I wonder if Rita has been encouraging him in any way, you know to make me jealous.

My girlfriend's sparkling eyes hooked Lee's for a moment. "Positive. Thanks again for the lift."

"It was my pleasure," the tall blonde replied with his southern twang. "Okay, then. I'll just ask the waitress to get me a table in that corner over there," and then he pointed to the third table behind us. "Remember, when you're ready to leave just holler."

I momentarily shelved the fellow's comment about taking Rita home. I'd inquire about it later. Right now I had more important things on my plate, and it wasn't food. Who the heck was this guy? Somebody from Rita's past? I shook my head to clear out the clutter attached to the crevices of my brain. Nope. I didn't think so. The need to know would keep chewing away at me and ruin the whole evening if I didn't do something soon. I leaned into the center of the table now and said in a barely audible voice, "Aren't you forgetting something, Rita?"

She fluffed her hair as she glanced around the floor surrounding her wheelchair. "Like what?"

"Introductions."

Her naturally creamy-colored complexion reddened instantly. "Oh, sorry. It slipped my mind," she said. "Since getting back from vacation, my work load has increased along with my hours." I bet Boy Wonder is part of that workload too, I thought, and then I pictured the young buck escorting her everywhere she went. Rita twisted her head sideways now to catch Lee before he was out of hearing distance. "Lee. Can you please come back?"

The sharp dresser stopped in his tracks, snapped to the right and then proceeded in our direction again. When he reached Rita's side, he asked, "Is there a problem?"

"No, no." she politely replied. "I just wanted to introduce you two guys. Lee Swanson, this is Matt Malone, my boyfriend."

"Well, I'll be," Lee said drawing his words out severely. "So, you're the private investigator I've heard so much about?" He reached over and squeezed my hand so tightly it felt like it had been left in a vise overnight. Hmph. Works out too. Well, if he's in marketing, he's got the money to do it.

I promptly retrieved my hand and ignored the pain. "Nice to meet you too," I responded in a much chipper tone than I felt.

"PI work, is that as interesting a profession as shown on those TV shows?" Lee asked with sanctimonious under currents.

If I hadn't been in the presence of a true lady, I would've said, "You don't know how interesting, you little twerp. Why, I could run down all the dope on you in ten minutes flat if I wanted to." Instead I cooly said, "It can be," and then I hurriedly turned the tables and asked in a matter of fact tone, "and how do you know Rita?" I assumed they worked together, but it's possible they knew each other from somewhere else. I haven't been with Rita in a while. Even when I was, I wasn't with her every minute of the day.

"We work in the same department. She's been training me in."

Jealousy won out, and I heard myself loudly proclaim internally, *I bet she has.*

"Well, I'd better mosey on now, so you two can spend some quality time together. We don't get much of that with our hours, do we, Rita?"

"No, we certainly don't, Lee."

Rita's escort left us behind and immediately caught a waitress by the arm.

I was pleased to see that the waitress ended up seating him far enough away that he couldn't possibly hear our conversation. Now, I pulled my eyes off Lee, fixed them on my girlfriend's gorgeous face and innocently asked, "Why does he have to give you a ride home, Rita? I'm here for you?"

Her face flushed again. "The Topaz is a clunker."

Totally derailed by the unexpected answer I received, I dug deeper. "What does the Topaz's being a clunker have to do with it?" The Topaz and I had been around a long time together, shorter than my Air Force coat, but right up there all the same. Whenever someone makes a rude remark about the Topaz, I feel like they are actually commenting on my way of life.

"The front seats are too low, Matt," Rita replied in a non-confrontational tone. "It's always been a struggle for me to get in and out of that car. I'm sure I've told you that. Any passenger riding in Lee's new mid-sized car can easily pivot his or her legs out the door."

I ran my weather-beaten hand through my hair. Rita was right about the Topaz not being the best car to get in and out of. That's one of the reasons I help Margaret get out of the car when she rides with me, but it still stung when she said, "*Lee had a better car than me.*" What next? I was disliking the guy more and more. Not ready to call a truce quite yet, I continued with my questioning. "So, what make of car does Lee have?"

The tables were turned now, and Rita became flustered. "I ... I don't know. Do we have to get into this right now? Isn't it enough to know that his car gets me from A to B?

Okay, I know what you're thinking, but I couldn't let it go. It was a guy thing. My sweaty palms instantly shot up at the woman across the table from me. "Does Lee have to drive out of his way to take you home?"

"I thought we came here tonight to calmly discuss our situation, and not to drag other people into the mix, but I can see you won't stop digging until you get your answer. So here goes—Lee lives in my apartment building."

"Oh, oh, oh. Here she comes.
Watch out boys she'll chew you up,
She's a man eater . . ."
Daryl Hall and John Oates

Chapter 56

He lives in her building! Why ... I took a deep breath. *Control yourself,*
Matt. What if Rita only manufactured the story to see if you'd blow your cork?
For all you know Lee could actually live in Stillwater or Hopkins. I was going
to make a mess of this evening if I didn't watch my step. *Back up, Matt.*
Ease off the pedal. You've been so blindsided by Rita's escort you totally missed
what was sitting right in front of you. I shed the snakeskin covering my eyes
now and scrutinized the woman sharing the table with me as if I had just
become aware of her existence. "Let's start the evening over, shall we?" I
countered in a romantic tone. "Miss Sinclair, may I help you get your coat
off?"

Rita matched my mood now. "Why, yes, I'd appreciate that, Mr.
Malone," and then she nervously fumbled with her coat buttons while
I went to the back of her chair to better assist her. Once her coat was
opened, I grasped the shoulder area to alleviate any sleeve problems for
her, and then I hooked the upper part of her coat over the arms of her
wheelchair.

When I returned to my seat, I noticed how wonderfully the lantern
light above our table showed off Rita's emerald eyes. Her beautiful orbs
looked exactly like the jewel they were named for.

"What's on your mind, Matt? You look so intense."

"Oh," I said, "I was just thinking how stunning you look tonight,"
hoping those words would further dispel the previous mood that was set.

"Well, you look very spiffy yourself, Mr. Malone." You and I both
know spiffy and stunning aren't even in the same ballpark, but I took the
compliment anyway.

The waitress assigned to us mysteriously settled in at my side now.
She was wearing a long silk dress like Su Lee, but hers was bright red. Like
all the other waitresses, her feet were covered with what looked like white

stockings and black Mary Jane style shoes. "Excuse please. Order drink now, yes?"

I glanced at Rita. She quickly confirmed that she wanted something with a slight movement to her head. "Yes, I'll have a Bud Light, and the beautiful lady across from me wishes to have a glass of Zinfandel."

The young Chinese waitress bowed to her waist. "Yes, good choice. Bring soon," and then she backed away and scurried off to the bar.

Thinking all our distractions were out of the way finally, I settled in with small bits of conversation. "I see your foot's no longer wrapped in gauze but hidden in a boot. So, how's your ankle doing? Do you know when you can quit using the wheelchair?"

The woman of my dreams gazed at me lovingly. "My ankle's doing what it's supposed to be doing at this stage of healing. Bones can take anywhere from five to eight weeks to heal."

"Wow. I didn't realize bones took that long to mend. I've never broken anything."

"Lucky you," and then she continued. "That's not all. There's many, many weeks of therapy ahead." Now she shifted her hands to the top of the wheels on her portable chair and nervously tapped them against the wheels. "I'm not required to use this means of transportation while wearing the boot on my foot. Crutches or a walker work just as well."

"That's great news," I replied excitedly. "I was concerned that your lovely hands were getting abused by your wheelchair. You know—sore and swollen."

When Rita returned her fine hands to the table and gently rubbed them, I noticed she wasn't wearing the pre-engagement ring I bought her in Brazil. I hoped it was for practical reasons and not because she was still too angry with me. "Oh, they're sore."

"So, what are you using around your apartment to get from room to room? Your doorways are a lot narrower than mine."

"I'm using the walker you bought me in PV to get in and out of my bedroom and bathroom. Crutches didn't appeal to me. They look too uncomfortable to bother with."

Loud churning noises emanating from my stomach rudely interrupted any further discussion concerning Rita's ankle. Embarrassed, I shifted my eyes to the menus on the table and hurriedly asked, "Are you as hungry as I am?"

Rita actually let loose with a full blown smile this time. I forgot how much I missed seeing it. "You're asking if this woman's hungry? Hmm? Let's see. I haven't eaten since six-thirty this morning. Does that answer your question?"

"I think so." I handed her one of the menus now. "Here you go. Decide what you want."

"I bet I know what you're ordering," Rita said lightheartedly before she opened her menu. "Your usual, Moo Goo Gai Pan."

I braced my elbow on the small table for two and then rested my head in the palm of my hand. "Wrong. I thought I'd be adventurous and try a brand new dish."

Rita appeared totally confused. "And what may I ask brought this on?"

"Chalk it up to new beginnings. Expanding horizons and breaking old habits at the same time."

My girlfriend's oval face grew serious. "Well, it's nice to hear you want to turn a new leaf, but New Year's Day is long past for making resolutions, Mr. Malone."

"Ah, but that's not true. The Chinese New Year has yet to arrive." There, I hope that convinces her that I'm determined to change.

Rita opened her mouth to speak again, but our waitress interrupted her. "Wine for lady. Beer for man, yes?"

I barred my teeth as I gave her an appreciative smile. "A huh."

"Take orders now, yes?"

I set my huge menu down. "Sure. Rita, why don't you go first."

Her eyes swiftly scanned the open menu that was resting in her hands. "Let's see. I think I'll have an egg roll and the sweet and sour chicken with fried rice."

"And tea?" the waitress inquired politely.

"Yes, please."

Now the slim young woman turned her attention to me. "And for you?"

"Hmm. I think I'll have a helping of steamed dumplings and Szechuan chicken."

"Tea too?"

"No, make mine strong black coffee."

The shy waitress quickly took the heavy menus from us and hustled off to the kitchen to place our orders.

"They sure are efficient here, aren't they?"

Rita had lazily begun to absorb the scenery in the room as soon as the waitress left, but now that I had asked her a question, she dedicated herself entirely to me. "That's one of the reasons I like eating here, Matt. It's just a shame other restaurants around town couldn't be the same."

I was about to add another reason why Fu Yu's was probably so successful for so many years when the insufferable theme song on my cell phone began to play for our entertainment. Rita winced as soon as she heard the music. "I'm sorry," I offered apologetically. "I left the cell phone on in case you had to call and say you were running late."

"I thought your phone played Bruce Springsteen's song 'Born in the USA'?"

"It did," I acknowledged as I tried to ignore the phone's disruptive tune. "I just changed it recently."

"Oh? Well, aren't you going to answer it?" my girlfriend queried.

I glanced down at my coat pocket for a second and then shook my head. "Nah, I'd rather not. Whoever is on the other end can call back."

Rita persisted. "Take the call, Matt. It may be business related.," she said as she leaned across the table and grasped my hand. "I don't mind. Really."

In retrospect, I should've taken the call in a secluded setting away from the love of my life, but ever since Rita rolled up to the table I felt like I was in dreamland and any attempt to change the scenery would only banish the indescribable vision from my view. "All right, if you insist." Now I stuck my hand in my coat pocket and took out the cell phone. Once the slim phone sat squarely in the palm of my hand, I pressed the receive button. "Good evening. This is Matt Malone. How can I help you?"

"Matt," the intruder's voice pounced. "I hope I'm not catching you at a bad time, but I have something extremely important to share."

What rotten timing. *Do you mind, God, if I just ask what I did to deserve this? Was it a horrible crime in a past life? Oh, never mind! Catholics aren't supposed to believe in reincarnation, are we? Well, then couldn't this call have been from a legitimate client at least?* Since I didn't expect God to answer me through the use of a thunderbolt or an angel anytime soon, I took it upon myself to resolve the problem. I swiftly swivelled my lower torso from under the table to the back of my chair, and then cupped my left hand against my face. Hopefully this position was secure enough to keep Rita from overhearing the caller. Now in a calm, pleasant tone I said, "Sorry, I can't talk right now. Please call me tomorrow during office hours."

"Hey, don't cut me off like that," the female caller said in desperation. "What I have to say can't wait."

Both worried and irritated, I hastily replied, "This better be worth my time."

"It is," Elaine said. "Tonight at the supper table, Frank and I were talking about all the stupid messages written on the back of trucks these days when Sam piped up with, 'Jimmy and I saw a scary truck the night of your party.' Jimmy's the boy Sam spent the night with."

"Right. He lives across the street from you. So, can I hang up now?"

"No! There's more. Sam said the dark colored truck drove up and down our street a couple times. The back bumper was all lit up, and the back window had a white skull and wings painted on it. Jimmy told Sam it was the devil's truck."

I rubbed my temple. The truck canvassing the Best neighborhood struck a familiar chord. The only problem was I didn't see the decorated back window of the GMC I spotted in Java to Go's parking lot. The Topaz was stationed south of Ballad's business that evening. I twisted my torso just enough to get a glimpse of Rita. Good. She was sipping wine from her glass and didn't appear to be upset. She even smiled at me. I grinned right back, and then I raised my index finger and mouthed, "One more minute." Returning to the cell phone now, I ended my conversation with, "Okay, Joe, I'll see what I can do," and then I pressed the *end* button and resumed my previous position at the table.

But the party on the other end wasn't finished with me yet. All of a sudden Elaine's voice blared out of the cell phone. "Matt, who the heck is Joe? Are you feeling all right?" Yup, leave it to me to inadvertently press the speaker button.

Rita's attitude rapidly changed from being a demure, sweet, loveable kitten to a ballistic she-devil in an flash. She tore the cloth napkin off her lap and threw it across the table. "How dare you accept a call from her when we're trying to patch things up? Now, I know there was more than an innocent drink between the two of you."

"Rita, please, you've got it all wrong."

But Rita wasn't about to listen. She hollered for Lee and then grabbed her purse off the table.

Lee looked our way. He appeared to be in the middle of placing his order. "Be right there, Rita." As soon as the waitress left his table, he came straight to ours. "What's up?"

"I'm ready to leave."

"Okay, just let me grab my coat and cancel my order."

I tried to reach for one of Rita's tiny wrists while Lee was gone, but she wouldn't let me near her. She had shut me out. "For cry'n out loud let me explain."

Anger flooded her face now. "Save it," she tartly replied. "I don't want to hear it."

I ignored her directive. I needed to straighten things out. Save our relationship. "Please you've got to hear me out. There's nothing going on between the two of us. Honest."

Before Rita could dish out another nasty remark, our waitress appeared with our meals and announced, "Dinner for two?"

"Dinner for two, my foot," Rita spouted. "That's a cruel joke."

Rita's comment left the poor waitress dumbfounded. She didn't move a muscle.

Lee returned now and conveniently intervened on Rita's behalf. "Box hers to go," he commanded. "She's not staying."

The timid waitress nodded and set my lone order on the table.

When she finished her task, I shifted my eyes from my meal to Rita again and begged for mercy.

Unfortunately for me, no mercy whatsoever was offered, only hot, hateful words that burned me to the core. "I've been such a fool," Rita said bitterly. "I knew I shouldn't have come here tonight. How could I ever let myself think we still might make it down the aisle someday? I hope you stew in your juices forever, Mister."

The moment Rita snapped her mouth shut, Lee, Mr. Hunk to all the women out there, gallantly took control of her wheelchair and quickly pulled her away from the table. Of course, being a young stallion, he couldn't possibly leave my table behind without silently adding his own two cents to the mix. As he pushed Rita away, he glanced over his shoulder and displayed such an evil smile, I felt like the devil had just given me the kiss of death.

Alone now and embarrassed by Rita's unexpected outbursts, I, too, decided to have my dinner boxed and quickly signaled my waitress as she walked past. "Could you box my dinner and bring the bill?"

"Problem with dinner, Sir?"

I waved my hands back and forth. "No. Just my dinner companion."

Chapter 57

A couple of hours after midnight, my lone bedroom was brought to life by a shrill sound. "What the ...?" Feeling punchy and drained because of my terribly restless slumber so far, I wasn't able to connect the dots right away. Had I inadvertently set the alarm for the wrong time? I jerked my arms from under the covers and harshly slapped my thighs. Of course, Gracie took the sudden movement as her invite to leave the foot of the bed and come snuggle by my side.

After the mutt had taken advantage of the situation and licked my chops several times, it finally dawned on me what was happening. The noise continued. "Get out of here, Dog. Now!" I snapped and then I shoved Gracie out of the way. Once she was gone, I flipped on my side and turned on the bedside lamp. Heavy grit clogged my eyes as I stared at the alarm. "Three o'clock. Who the heck calls at three in the morning?" For just a second, the thought of Rita having a change of heart flashed through my mind.

I plucked the disturbing item from it's cradle now. "Yeah, this is Matt Malone."

"Mr. Malone?"

"That's what I said."

"It's Pedro Hernandez."

"Pedro?" Even though I was exhausted, my memory bank began to perform on all four cylinders. It's the artist? "What's up?" Aware of who I was speaking to now, I recalled quite vividly that I told him to call when he had spoken with Darryl concerning my interest in purchasing a fake painting, but a call this time of the morning was absurd. "Did you talk to Darryl about the painting?"

"You...you've gott'a come right away, Mr. Malone," he said. The young college student sounded like he was in a hysterical frame of mind. "I ..., I didn't know who else to call. There's been a terrible accident."

I shot up now and tried to clear my head of any remaining cobwebs. I should never have downed a few more beers after I got home from the restaurant. "What sort of accident?"

"Darryl's been shot in the head.."

"Give me directions, Pedro. I'll be there as soon as I'm dressed."

After asking pertinent questions of Pedro, I concluded that Darryl hadn't committed suicide even though the single hole to the temporal region of his head and the .357 Mag Revolver found in his hand suggested otherwise. Darryl, it turns out was left-handed. Whoever shot him didn't know that bit of information and placed the fired gun in Darryl's right hand as soon as he was cut down.

While Pedro dialed 911 on my behalf, I took advantage of the available time and searched through Darryl's personal belongings to see if I could resolve the mystery. There had to be information tucked away somewhere revealing what the dead man was involved with.

Starting in Darryl's single bedroom, I cautiously slid open his closet door. You never know what might be lurking on the other side, especially if you have one of Stephen King's or Dean Koontz's novels in mind. After I shoved several clothing items out of the way, I discovered Elaine's stolen picture leaning up against the back wall. "Well, I'll be. So, this is where they hid you." I brought the painting out into the lighted room now and flipped it over. The protective paper on the back of the painting had already been ripped off. Time to get tough with Pedro. I had asked him to remain in the kitchen, and now I yelled for him. "Pedro, get in here."

When the college student reached his friend's bedroom, he found me standing with my back against the closet door holding on to Elaine's painting. He recognized the picture at once but seemed to be taken aback by my find. "Where the heck did you find that, Mr. Malone?"

I studied the young college student for a moment, trying to figure out if he was as ignorant as he appeared.. "Pedro, did you know about this?"

"What? That Darryl painted duplicates? Yeah, sure, I knew about that."

I shook my head. "This isn't a duplicate, Pedro. It happens to be the one my friend purchased."

"But how could that be? Yesterday you told me hers was hanging on a wall in her home. What's going on? Was Darryl planning to touch it up for her?"

I could hear police sirens off in the distance now. My gut instincts told me Pedro knew nothing about Darryl's other business arrangements or he would've been quite agitated when I showed him Elaine's painting. "Pedro," I said in a non-confrontational tone, "how well did you really know Darryl?"

"Why are you asking?"

I glanced down at the picture in front of me. "Because this was stolen from Elaine's house this past Saturday."

Pedro immediately withdrew from conversation. He appeared genuinely shocked by my revelation. His face shifted from a bronze color to a milky tan.

"Perhaps you should sit down," I suggested.

The young college student took my advice to heart. He slowly dragged himself over to his friend's unmade twin bed and plopped himself down on the edge of it.

Concerned about his frame of mind I said, "Are you okay, Pedro?"

"Yeah, I think so. It's just hard for me to accept the fact that Darryl's gone and that he stole his own painting after he sold it. Why would he do that, Mr. Malone?"

"I don' know," I softly replied, and then I carried Elaine's painting over by the window, braced it against the wall and forged ahead. "Tell me, when did you first meet him?"

Pedro hung his head and thought about my question for a minute. "Our senior year of high school I guess. I crashed into him in the hallway on our way to art class. Not too long after that we started hanging out in my folks' garage. My dad said we could use it for a work studio. Darryl shared very little about his family, but I told him a lot about mine."

Suddenly recalling a tidbit of info Leonard Post shared with me about Darryl Hunt's family a few weeks ago, I decided to confirm if it was true or not. "Someone told me Darryl's father is a professor of art at a local college. Did he ever tell you which college?"

The young man's voice broke. "What? Who the heck told you that story?" Now his head violently jerked into an upright position. "My dad's the one who teaches art."

The sirens grew louder now. The cops would be here any second. If I wanted to know anything more, I'd have to speak with Pedro in private later.

Chapter 58

Knowing how much cops love to make private investigators squirm, I thought it best to skip out and leave Pedro holding the bag, but then at the last minute my conscience got the better of me and placed me in his shoes. Would I want a ton of cops breathing down my neck without some support person present? No way. So I did the decent thing. I chose to hang around and put up with whatever the cops dished my way.

Lucky for me, the first cop on the scene happened to be someone with many years of experience under his belt, a guy I've called on for PI info from time to time, Sergeant Murchinak, who works out of the police sub-station on Hennepin Avenue. He'd believe whatever crime theories I'd pedal. Married and father of five children, his mind was as sharp as a needle, but his jelly-donut belly belied his running track record.

Yeah, I know. People who live in glass houses shouldn't be throwing stones. My own stomach's been expanding at a phenomenal rate thanks to the nonagenarian chef living only three feet from my door.

"Hmm, must be something big going down if you're here, Malone. I didn't expect you to crawl out from your hole till spring."

Pedro stood by the door with his hands shoved in his pant pockets and studied the two of us.

I placed my arm on Pedro's shoulder and said, "Don't worry, Kid, I'll straighten him out. You keep talking like that, Murchinak, and you won't be getting any more free donuts from me."

The big cop laughed. "Whoa, look who is showing his fangs now." After he subdued his laughter, he turned his attention to Pedro, cocked his head and said, "You the one who found the vic?"

The college student cooly nodded his head.

"I suppose you'll have a decent alibi for me once I find out the exact time of death?"

Pedro removed his hands from his pockets and began cracking his knuckles, something I wouldn't advise a talented painter to do if he wanted to continue painting for many years down the road. "Why, yes, sir, as a matter of fact I do," he answered in a flash. "My girlfriend can vouch for me."

Murchinak plowed through us both now and went directly to Darryl's body. "How did you end up here, Malone? Was he a client of yours?"

I scratched my chin. I might as well be honest with him, I thought, or I'll be spending several hours at the sub-station which wasn't too appealing. "Nope. I met him and Pedro here when I was vacationing in Puerto Vallarta with Rita a couple weeks ago."

The sergeant offered a sly smile. "Oh, yeah? So how is that little gal of yours?"

"I'm not commenting on the grounds that it might incriminate me," I said sourly.

"That bad, huh?" The cop crouched down by the corpse now. "I told you not getting hitched to that gorgeous broad would be your downfall."

I faked a cough. "Can we get down to the topic at hand here, the dead man?"

Murchinak tilted his head towards me. "Sure, sure. So what do you think about John Doe here?"

"Your John Doe has a name," I replied sharply. "It's Darryl Hunt." I hated the reference to John Doe especially when we knew what the guy's name was. "As you can plainly see, the gun's enclosed in his right hand. He's cool to the touch, and rigor mortis has already set in his hands. I'd say he's been dead roughly six to eight hours."

"Your observations amaze me, Malone," the middle-aged cop said sarcastically.

I ignored his barb. We've known each other too long, and his remarks rolled of my back like good old vegetable oil. "Well, then please note that the deceased was left handed."

"Whoops. The guilty party made a major blunder."

"Hence, there was no suicide," I continued.

The cop stood and gazed around the room. "Obviously the killer didn't know Darryl, and therefore the murder must've been a random act."

I moved to the small olive and tan sectional couch now. "I'm sorry if I led you to that conclusion. The head honcho of this organization, the killer, definitely knew Darryl; he just didn't know him as well as he thought."

Murchinak shook his salt and peppered head in disbelief. "Are you suggesting this was a mafia hit? Because as much as I'd like to help you prove your theory pal, there are no kingpins living in Minnesota. They like what the good life's got to offer in Chicago, Vegas and Atlantic City too much."

And so this is where I let things hang. Let the cops think I'm crazy. I know better. I never suggested that the mafia was involved with Darryl's death. Once I proved what was going on, everything else would neatly fall into place.

Chapter 59

February

The police may be on their winding trail but paraphrasing a familiar song, this PI will, "Take the high road and they can take the low road, and I'll solve the crime before them."

Returning home now at 5 a.m., I kicked my grubby shoes off, tossed the keys on the table stand in the hallway and then headed to the bedroom, unzipping my jacket as I went. Something's going down at the Minneapolis Institute of Arts, and it involves the new art exhibit and Mexico. I glanced at the tiny calendar on my nightstand. We were into the first week of February already. That meant the new art exhibit was open to the public now. Perfect timing. I think I'll drive over there later this morning and snoop around. A PI can blend in where a cop can't.

The bedroom was in total darkness. No surprise there. I had left it that way. Not wanting to stumble over anything, I glided my hand up and down the nearest wall until my hand hit the switch for the ceiling light. Now that the room was lit, I peeled my jacket and clothes off and disposed of them in a heap next to the bed. The answering machine on the nightstand was blinking, but I didn't give a rip. It could wait till I got up again

My mind was still reeling all the events of the evening over and over like an outdated movie projector when I crawled between the cold, two-hundred thread count faded sheets, but after a considerable amount of tossing and turning, sleep finally hit me like a runaway truck The only problem with that was I got stuck in dreamland and wasn't sure if I'd ever find my way out.

The first dream had me and Rita in the deep dark jungle. She was Jane, and I was Tarzan. We weren't together very long when along came a huge hairy creature, probably a gorilla, and stole her away from me. I couldn't chase after them. Jane had offered me something to eat right before the gorilla had arrived, and I had lost my ability to fly from tree to tree via the plentiful vines. Another one had me skydiving over the glaciers in Alaska. I was a daredevil stunt guy. Rita was a top runway model waiting for me to land on the glacier she was on. We were scheduled to do a promotional event together. It never got off the ground. Something went terribly wrong, and I fell headlong into a cruise ship. The final dream brought me back to PV. I was a well-tanned beach bum relaxing in a comfy lounge chair underneath an enormous red and white umbrella reading the PV local newspaper. I had just begun reading about the annual art sale coming up when a good looking blonde screamed for assistance. Rita was absent from this scene.

I tried to get up and help her. My arms kept flailing wildly, but my body remained immobile. I finally shook my head hard and forced my eyes open. That's when I realized I had been caught up in the sheets, as well as, a dream. If it weren't for the last one though, I wouldn't have remembered the PV newspaper I had stashed in a side pocket of my backpack.

I turned on the bed lamp, threw off the covers, dashed to the closet and searched for the bag. Once I found it, I took it over to the bed and pulled the thick newspaper out of the pocket and paged through it. There it was in black and white.

Ninth Annual Grand Art Show and Sale.
Buyers come from all over the world to attend the annual Arts
Festival held in March.

When Elaine and I visited Darryl's and Pedro's stall, Pedro mentioned that PV had the largest art community in the country, and if a person had the time, there were forty galleries one could visit.

How ingenious. Darryl used Pedro, who has relatives in PV, as his means of smuggling art in and out Mexico, but something tells me the mastermind behind the stolen goods ring resides right under our noses in good old Minnesota. Who and how long it had been going on were only two of the questions that I hoped to uncover.

According to the article in the *Star Tribune* there were going to be about 150 pieces of Impressionist work on display at the Minneapolis Institute of Arts, but my gut instinct told me the art thieves were going after a Van Gogh this time around.

With a little luck on my side, I might be able to cut short whatever plan was in play for one of Van Gogh's famous paintings, even as early as tomorrow. I dropped the newspaper by the foot of the bed and then once again slid back under the covers. Eight o'clock would be here soon enough.

Chapter 60

I arrived at the Minneapolis Institute of Arts a little later than I planned, but being a work day there was no huge crowd bustling about yet. That would come during the lunch hour. A restaurant and coffee shop were both conveniently located here, offering food with an Italian flair. It was nice to know that my stomach could get instant gratification when it started its whimpering routine.

I stepped up to the counter now, located on the main floor in the lobby, and purchased a special exhibit ticket. The rest of the sights at the museum were free to the public. The young lady who helped me took my money with one hand and handed me my ticket and the brochure, created especially for this particular art show, with the other. I was surprised to see that many more artists were listed than I had anticipated, but works by Van Gogh were clearly the crown jewels.

As I walked up the few steps leading to the museum and then into the elevator, I began to peruse the beautifully designed brochure. Rita would've been pleased with the efforts of this marketing tool. A lot of thoughtful preparation went into the planning of its design.

The bright red and orange colors used for the background of the tri-fold pamphlet really made the printed words pop. Under the 1 by 1 photo of Van Gogh's *Starry Night* there was a blurb that stated Don Mc Lean's 1970 song *Vincent or Starry, Starry Night* was about the famous artist and his painting. Interesting. Even a guy in his forties can learn something new.

The elevator I shared with two other people in silence now stopped and yawned, allowing the three of us to step off and go our separate ways. While in the elevator I had decided to start with the first painting mentioned on the long list and try to follow the rest in numerical order. Heck, I had all day. Besides, the longer I hung around the building the greater my chances were of catching something out of the ordinary, right?

Due to ignorance, I assumed the artwork would be displayed according to the year it was created, but I quickly discovered I was mistaken. The art was categorized according to the artist which of course made perfect sense.

I am neither a connoisseur of fine wines nor fine art, but that doesn't mean I don't appreciate them both. Perhaps if I just kept going to things like this, I'd educate myself enough to do some major damage. Who knows.

Before I began my journey through the special art exhibit, I had to walk past a informational poster resting on an easel.

> *Unification of the Impressionists came about due to the artists strong desire to be free of the French Salon system which controlled exhibition of their work, training and sponsorship.*

I could relate to that. I've never liked being under any one's thumb.

> *Thanks to the cooperation of four other American museums, the Carnegie Museum of Art, the Nelson-Atkins Museum of Art, the St. Louis Art Museum and the Toledo Museum of Art, the Minneapolis Institute of Arts is proud to present the works of Manet, Degas, Pissaro, Cezanne, Monet, Toulouse-Lautrec, Renoir, Vuillard and Gauguin.*

Hmm. I've never heard of Pissaro or Vuillard. After I finished reading the information in front of me, I stepped back a few paces to move on and inadvertently crunched some person's toes. The injured party immediately squawked under his breath. Embarrassed now, I quickly spun around to make amends and found a familiar face staring back at me.

"Well, Mr. Malone," Leonard Post said, "You're the last person I expected to run into here today."

The man looked much better than the last time I'd seen him. "Ditto," I replied. "Sorry about your foot, Leonard, but I was so engrossed in what I was reading I didn't realize anyone had come up behind me."

Freddy Flat's friend hurriedly brushed my apology aside. "Ah, don't worry about it. I can still move it." He stepped to one side to demonstrate now. "See. So, what brings you to the art gallery on a work day?" the older gentleman inquired.

I briskly combed the side of my head with my fingertips. "That's the benefits of owning your own business. When the job's sluggish, I skip out and do what I want to do, like taking in this great exhibit." Okay, so it was a lie; it wasn't that far fetched.

"Well, you made the right decision. This art is superb." Now he lifted his hand to his chin. "It's nothing like what I've got on the wall back home. Say, is it true what I heard?"

"What's that, Leonard?"

"Darryl's going to do one of his Van Gogh paintings for you too?"

I swallowed hard. That million dollar question definitely caught this PI off guard. "I, ah, I haven't really committed myself yet," I answered cautiously.

Leonard flapped his hands in front of him rapidly. "Great artist. You'll be happy you chose him."

I stared at Freddie Flat's friend for a full second and then decided to fill him on the situation. "Look. It hasn't hit the newsstands yet, but Darryl's dead."

If Leonard already knew about it, he sure put on a good act for my benefit. His arms crumbled to his sides. "No? Such a young man. When did it happen?"

"During the night."

He stumbled back a little. "Really? Hit by a car?" and then his eyes scanned his watch.

Not wanting to release anymore info just in case someone was within earshot, I said, "Other means."

A lightbulb suddenly came on in Leonard's rather roundish head. "Oh, I got yeah. Such a shame. So many artists struggle with depression, but I guess that goes with the territory, huh?" I didn't answer. "Look at Van Gogh—when he painted *Starry Night* he was locked up in an asylum." Now he swung his hand out to me again. I took it. "Well, I'd better get going. I've taken up enough of your time and this is such a large exhibit to view."

"It was nice running into you, Leonard, under different circumstances."

Post laughed nervously and then stared at his watch again. "That was some crazy day in my apartment, wasn't it?

I sighed. "Yes, it was."

"I hope I'm never found like that again."

I turned my back on Leonard now, walked a few feet more into the room and then I stopped. I don't know what urged me to do so, but I quicky glanced over my shoulder to take one last look at Freddy Flat's friend and found he had vanished.

I shook my head. Strange! Why would he come to this floor and then not peruse the works of art that were of interest to him? And why did he keep glancing at his watch so much? "There you go again, Malone," I said under my breath. "Can't you stop playing PI for a couple seconds at least?" *Post has a daughter, remember. Maybe he was meeting up with her.* My stomach did a quick flop. Obviously, it didn't like that answer, or it was my darn curse again. I waited for more tummy action. None came, so I moved on.

Vuillard's works were patiently waiting for me now, and I swiftly cast my eyes on the first piece, *The Art Dealers*. The painting was of the two Bernhim brothers who commissioned and sold many pieces of art for Vuillard. Dealers in art. Dealers in antiques. Things finally fell into place for me, at least concerning Darryl. Maybe answers to Ballad's problem will soon follow suit. He left a message on my machine when I was out last night.

I rubbed my hands together. Back to the matter at hand, Malone. Get one puzzle put together, then you can master the other. What exactly did Leonard Post say to me, anyway? I quickly placed my brain on automatic pilot. Recall duty was extremely important. *He heard that I had talked to Darryl about a painting.* But I hadn't. Pedro passed the message on to him, which means Leonard had to have been in contact with Darryl after Pedro, like late afternoon or evening. *He mentioned how so many artists suffer from depression*—inferring Darryl committed suicide even though my words, "other means" could've meant a thousand other things, like he was drunk, fell and hit his head. He was robbed and stabbed. Someone shoved him in front of a bus or a train. There's no way Leonard could have chosen correctly the first time around unless he had firsthand knowledge of Darryl's death.

The two connecting up probably started innocently enough. Leonard Post met Darryl at a *Starving Artist* sale like he said. Impressed with Darryl's Van Gogh painting, Leonard convinced the artist that they should go into business together. Leonard would handle the sales end, and Darryl had to paint the fakes and transport.

Since he's not here to defend himself, I'd like to think Darryl didn't realize what it meant to hook up with someone like Leonard Post. Maybe at first he just thought he was creating paintings for a small group of

Leonard's elite antique clientele. I thought back to Darryl's conversation with me in PV. "You gott'a do what you gott'a do when scraping together enough dough for college tuition." Unfortunately, debt leads many a fine person down dark alleys. At some point, Darryl must've discovered what Leonard was really up to, but by then he had already dug his hole too deep.

Could Darryl's chance meeting of a PI in PV have instigated the flip? Scared, by my innocent shopping with Elaine, Darryl returned to Minnesota and reported his fears to Leonard; the art world was closing in on them. They should quit while they were ahead. Leonard refused.

Of course, my untimely request for a Van Gogh didn't help. The heat was definitely intensifying now. Time for Leonard to clean house. Darryl, an unsightly stain, had to be blotted out no matter what the cost.

That pulls everything together nicely. I just hope it's enough for the cops to make an arrest. Now I gott'a catch that creep before he disappears. Where the heck could he have hightailed it to, I wonder? More than likely he chased off to find his other accomplice, the one who replaces the originals with forgeries at art museums and galleries.

If I thought I had walked into a trap and I was supposed to be meeting up with my partner in crime, where would I most likely try to head him off at? he answer came easily enough, before he walked through the Institute's entrance or the parking ramp. Not wanting to lose what precious time was left, I slipped out of the exhibit hall and dashed to the stairwell.

Chapter 61

Tearing down the steps two at a time now, I ripped my cell phone loose from my outer jacket pocket, quickly displayed a frequently used number and hit *send*. "Yeah, Murchinak, this is Malone. Glad I caught you. Round up a posse pronto and have them swing by the Minneapolis Institute of Arts. What's that? You want to know if I've gone on a drinking binge. When the heck have I ever done that? Look, there's going to be a huge theft going down, and I thought your team would want to be in on the action. That's all." Then I gave him a detailed description of Leonard Post. Wish I could've given him the other guy's too, but I was clueless.

By the time I ended my conversation with Murchinak, I noticed that I was eyeballing the exit door that lead to the main level. I thrust my right hand out now to grasp the door knob. Contact made. I turned the knob slightly to the left and waltzed into the lobby to mix with those just entering the Institute.

Leonard Post was somewhere in the vicinity; I sensed it. He hadn't had that much of a head start on me, and his seventy-something gait was a lot slower than mine.

My brain cells momentarily took a detour and shifted from the man I was hunting to Gracie back home snoozing away on my bed. Too bad she wasn't born a bloodhound. That invaluable talent would've been greatly appreciated right now. *Time to forge ahead, Matt*

As soon as I cleared all thoughts of the mutt, a uniformed officer strolled in from the outdoors. When his eyes finally fell on me, I gave him a very slight nod. I didn't want to appear too conspicuous. He continued his quiet demeanor as he closed in on me. "You Malone?" I nodded again. "Have you seen him since you talked to Murchinak?" I shook my head sideways. "Okay, well, I'm going to take a look around. See you later."

While the cop was checking out the scene where I had just been, I decided to travel over to the parking lot only a couple feet away. That's one place I hadn't had a chance to look yet.

The lot was insane. Cars buzzed in and out on the ground level so fast I felt like I was playing a dangerous game of dodge ball as I maneuvered my body across the entrance and exit lanes. Lucky for me, I came away unscathed. Now that I was safely tucked away in one of the parking aisles, I'd survey the main floor first and then gradually work my way up the ramps. Why should I exert my body more than I had too? Besides, the cops should be showing up any second, and they're in much better shape than I am. Well, some of them.

As I jumped to avoid getting clipped by yet another car coming down the ramp, I thought I caught sight of a truck that closely resembled the one Elaine's son and I had seen. Since it was snaking its way up the ramp, I'd need to do some heavy hoofing in order to positively identify it as *the one.*

I was breathing hard and sweating profusely when I rounded the concrete pillar supporting the ceiling of the third level, but I'd found what I was searching for. There stood Leonard Post and his buddy. Post looked like he had overdosed on psychotic drugs. His mouth was contorted, his eyes were on fire and his arms swatted the air. Either he was having a meltdown, or he was ready to blow his cork. I chose anger.

The beefy-packed guy he was with stood with the back of his six-foot frame to me so I had no idea what age bracket he was in or what I was up against. If he was involved with the gas theft at Ballad's, I didn't recognize what I saw so far.

His head sat bolt upright on his shoulders and was topped off with a black knitted stocking cap. The upper torso was covered with a thin jean jacket, the lower was hidden by the car parked alongside him. Extending from his left hand was a brown mailing tube, the type used to ship rolled up poster-sized pictures.

I looked down at the level below me. Where the heck was Murchinak? My ears hadn't picked up on any sirens yet. I didn't know what to do. If I waited too long for back up, these two could be long gone.

I decided to wait one more minute and then I was charging in like a bull, with or without reinforcements. Now I angled my body near the pillar in such a way that Leonard couldn't possibly catch a glimpse of me, and then I exposed my wristwatch and started the count down in my head. "One, two, three…"

My hands were sweating as the last second ticked by and I still wasn't sure what I was going to do. I couldn't just mosey up and say, "Hi, Leonard." The stakes were too high. I had to be forceful, but what could I use to scare them? If only I hadn't chosen never to pack a gun, but that gave me an idea.

I rammed my hands into the pockets of my jacket. One of them held a thick pen. My right hand found what I was seeking. I wrapped my hand around the top part of the pen and positioned it tightly against the pocket lining. I glanced down at my pocket. It could pass. All right, I was prepared to make my move now.

I strolled out of the shadow and yelled, "It's over, Leonard. Give yourself up."

Leonard looked my way. "There's only one of you, Malone, and two of us."

I continued towards them. "Don't do anything stupid, Leonard. I don't want to use my gun, but I will if I have to."

The guy with Leonard whipped his body in my direction now. The shock of seeing his face stopped me cold. It was Chet Ballad. "The PI's a whimp," he announced.

Leonard cocked his head to one side and stared at Chet intently. "You know this guy?"

"Yeah, I met him at my brother's place a while back." He tugged on his knitted cap now as if that would hide his already revealed identity. "Don't worry Leonard, he ain't going to shoot us. He's just full of hot air."

"Don't be so certain, Chet," I snapped before I moved forward a couple more steps. "If I don't get you, one of the cops that are with me will."

Leonard spun this way and that looking for any clue of a cop. "You don't fool us, Malone. You're by yourself." Now he spoke directly to Chet. "Take him down."

Ballad rolled into action. He handed off the mailing tube to Leonard and then charged at me with all he had. His eagerness to attack his opponent, me, made me think of a college football player trying to impress pro scouts with his super tackling techniques. How apropos, I thought. All my problems started on New Year"s Day when the Purdue Boilermakers played the Washington Huskies. If only I could travel back in time.

Of course, entering a future portal right now wouldn't be so bad either especially since I don't want to be a goner any time soon. I crossed my left foot in front of the right like a line dance step. Wrong choice of moves. I tripped. Well, I never said I was good at dancing.

Chet reached his goal faster thanks to my being off kilter. As soon as his long arms touched my body, my backside went spinning to the ground. I tried to get him off me once I was there, but his hands kept slugging away at my face and my chest like I was his personal punching bag. "Why, Chet?" I managed to spit out in between punches. "You've got a good day job."

He spat on the blacktop. "You call driving a stupid coffee van around town all day a good job? There's no money in that. I have a kid going nowhere and a wife with a queen's life style. I needed more." Then he punched me again. I tried to grab one of his legs as they drew nearer to my head, but I missed my chance.

While the battle continued between Chet and me, I saw Leonard jump into the driver's side of the truck. Obviously he had what he needed. Chet wasn't a necessary commodity, he could be left to the hungry wolves. The black GMC with white skull and wings painted on its back window roared to life now, but not for long. A blend of voices rapidly shouting, "Police, you're surrounded," ended it all. "Turn the truck off, or we'll shoot." The truck went dead.

Once Chet Ballad and Leonard Post were cuffed and told their rights, Murchinak swaggered towards me like John Wayne used to do when he saved an old west town from the bad guys. "It's about time," I said still laying on my back and aching all over. "What the heck took you so long?"

"Sorry," Murchinak said with an impish grin. "From where I stood, it looked like you wanted to handle the problem for us." He leaned over and offered his hands to me now. I don't usually accept assistance, but this was one time I wasn't going to refuse. I was too sore.

As soon as I was on my feet again, I sensed a sticky wetness trickling from my nose. I swiped the back of my hand across my face, and then brought my hand into view. It was covered with blood.

Murchinak shook his round head. "You're one heck of a sight, Malone. You'd better clean up before heading home, or you'll scare the people in your apartment building."

"Very funny," I said half-heartedly, "but it's not my apartment dwellers you have to be concerned with."

"No, then who?"

"The guys down at your precinct."

Murchinak buttoned the top button of his coat. "Well, that's definitely one place that has plenty of clean-up materials on hand, but you're not expected to come down there right now. We can get your statement later."

"Oh, no," I said as I clutched my aching ribs. "I want to hear what those wise guys have to say. See if I aced the case."

Post pleaded innocent just like I expected him to, but once his buddy Chet Ballad blew his horn, everything fit together tightly.

Leonard met Darryl two years ago. Chet didn't appear in the picture until this past year. He met Leonard when they both wandered into the same watering hole. Ballad admitted that his tongue loosens fairly easily after several drinks, and he thinks that must've been when he let it be known that he was looking for some fast cash under the table. At the time, Leonard jokingly said he might be able to come up with something. A month went by before Chet ran into Leonard at the same bar again. When they chatted this time, Leonard told Chet he worked in the art world. Eager to share something they had in common, Chet spoke of the various jobs he had held at the local art museums since his college years. His last one being a part-time security guard on the weekends. A few weeks after that, Leonard made his move. He called Chet and asked if he was still interested in doing some jobs under the table for him.

Chet borrowed his coffee van several times to move stolen merchandise, but he always rigged the mileage count and replaced the gas. A couple times though, when he was forced to use the GMC truck for jobs instead of the van, he was low on gas and just siphoned what he needed from work vans. He never worried about getting caught. If anyone questioned him, he'd show them his company card and be on his way.

I didn't tell Chet I had already confirmed his performances at the bar the dates the gas was stolen, but he confessed he had long enough intermissions, forty-five minutes, to steal what he needed.

The big collector of Viking's paraphernalia had stolen Sam's football like I surmised after I discovered his involvement in the break-in. He said I could have it back. He told the cops that when he and his young helper didn't find what they were looking for at the Best's the first time around, they planted a bug under their kitchen table. That's how they knew where it was the night of the party.

Ballad was definitely tongue-tied when he learned of Darryl's death though. Murchinak put the iron gloves to him, to test the waters supposedly. It didn't matter. Chet swore he didn't have anything to do with Darryl's death, and I believed him.

After Murchinak finished with Chet, he invited me over to his desk. He said he had something he wanted to share with me. "Thought you might be interested in the most recent FBI report concerning art crimes since you solved one in my locale. He took an official looking document from one of his many piles now and handed it to me. "Take a look."

I grabbed the sheet of paper from him and began to read. "Man, oh, man! My friend, you and I are in the wrong line of business. According to this info Art crime is a $6-billion-a-year world-wide business."

"Read on."

"Ah, I see what you're getting at. Ninety percent of all art crimes committed are done by people working on the inside." Now I pointed towards the holding cell Chet Ballad was in. "And, Ballad's a prime example."

"I'm leaving on a jet plane,
Don't know when I'll be back again . . ."
Peter, Paul and Mary

Chapter 62

Thirteen Days Later

"Matt, open up," a soft, entreating female voice requested. "I know you're in there."

I ignored the pleading words that floated in from the hallway outside my abode and continued to sit at the kitchen table instead, where I had been passing the time drawing ever since eating breakfast an hour ago.

The visitor at my door didn't give up so easily, too set in her ways like me. "Matt, I mean it! Open up!", she demanded. Then every thing went silent for a moment. I didn't budge an inch. The determined woman didn't either. She came right back at the door and rattled it again. "You can't stay bottled up in that apartment of yours forever!"

Gracie threw me a sharp glance and then barked.

"What ever happened to a dog's loyalty to his master?" I whined.

"Matt, if you don't let me in right this minute, I'll be forced to get Mr. Edwards to unlock your door!"

I kept on drawing. The threat of our caretaker's arrival on the scene didn't scare me in the least. Sure he does a swell job of keeping the Foley neat and clean, but the man's also in his seventy's and if you pulled a feather out from under him he'd topple over like a house of cards.

The mutt yelped a couple times more and then she went into her whirling-dervish dance. She does that if I take too long to check out the ringing phone or noises outside our door. I ignored her too.

After trying to get me to unlock my door for the past five minutes, Margaret Grimshaw's concern for me now switched to pure irritation. "You crazy Irishman! Non capisco! I don't understand. Your behavior doesn't make sense. So, I go home to Petey now and take my plate of freshly baked caramel rolls with me."

I dropped my pencil. Did I hear caramel rolls? "Wait!" I yelled, "Don't go Margaret." As much as I was determined to block the world out, my stomach never could resist Mrs. Grimshaw's ooey, gooey rolls. Hers were right up there with my mom's who I thought were the best on this planet. "The doors unlocked, come on in."

The apartment door wailed now as it began to slowly swing back on its hinges. The mutt didn't wait for any orders from me, she flew straight to the entryway to greet our company. I hadn't been giving her the necessary doggie attention this past week that she deserved, so I'm sure she was excited to receive whatever she could from my neighbor.

"Well, Gracie, how's your master today? Is he being ornery to you too?"

"Wuff. Wuff."

"Is that so?" Margaret said, "Well, don't fret. I'll give him a good talking too. Just show me where he's hiding, Girl."

I listened as the two conspirators advanced towards the kitchen. It would only take about a half a minute for them to get to where I was. Since I didn't want Margaret to see what I had been up to lately, I quickly covered my serious doodling with a blank sheet of paper and then moved away from the table as fast as I could.

"Ah, there you are," Margaret said as she glided her bright pink slippered feet onto the outdated checkered linoleum floor. "Happy Valentines day."

"Yes, here I am in the flesh," I quipped. "I apologize for not coming to the door, but I just wanted to straighten up the kitchen for you." My neighbor scanned the messy counters but didn't say anything. "Now, let me at those world renown Grimshaw rolls you brought to my abode."

"Not so fast," the petite Italian warned as she held one hand out to stop me. "I want to know why you haven't been answering your phone or the door. Obviously you're down in the dumps, but about what?"

I swear, nothing gets past this elderly woman. I ran my pencil smudged fingers through my hair. She had me cornered, a position I've never liked being in. But this nonagenarian was a dear neighbor as well as a good friend and she deserved an explanation. "It's over Margaret," I said bluntly. "There's nothing more to say," then my body quietly fell into a *woe is me* mode.

Margaret set her plate of rolls on the end of the counter and then she clutched my right arm. "Now, now, Matt, it's not as bad as all that.

You can't let yourself get in such a tizzy every time your cases have been resolved. My mother taught me that there's always something new on the horizon,"she added cheerfully. "You just have to be patient."

Poor Margaret. She hadn't a clue what I was depressed about. I gently loosened her grip on me. "My strange behavior isn't about work."

The old woman blushed. "It's not? Oh, I'm sorry, I just assumed it was."

I sighed heavily. "Ah, don't worry about it. If I was in your shoes, I probably would've thought the same thing." My heart suddenly felt like it was going to burst out of my chest. "I meant it's over between Rita and me."

My revelation shook Margaret's small world. Her tiny pale hands flew to her hollowed cheeks. "What! Nonsense. I don't believe it. When did this happen?" she asked.

Before I gave my neighbor the answer she was seeking, I directed her to a chair. "Here, sit down. Let me get you a cup of coffee first, and then I'll tell you everything."

"You might as well grab the rolls while you're at it," Margaret said in deadly serious tone. "My mother always said it's easier to swallow a bitter pill with sweets."

"My sentiments exactly." I placed the plate of rolls on the kitchen table now, and then went over to the coffee maker and filled two coffee mugs just an inch short of being full to the brim. "Care for any sugar or milk in your coffee this morning, Margaret?"

"No thank you. I'll tough it out and drink it straight up like you today."

I returned to the table with the mugs of steaming coffee and set one in front of my neighbor. "There you are," and then I dragged a chair out from the table and sat.

Margaret's head had been tilted slightly down and now she lifted it. "Thank you, Matt. Now tell me how and when the break up with Rita came about."

I took a sip of coffee first, and then I began. "It happened when we met at Fu Yu's for supper."

"You poor boy. You've been keeping it to yourself all this time. Why didn't you tell me?" Margaret encased her coffee mug with her aged hands now. "No wonder you didn't want anyone bothering you."

It's hard repeating bitter memories out loud. What I needed before I continued was something sweet to smooth it over. I reached for a caramel roll and took a bite. "Everything was going along smoothly until I got a call on my cell phone. The darn mayhem in Mexico screwed things up royally for me," I said bitterly, and then my head slumped forward.

"I take it the call was business related?"

"Sort of. I told Rita whoever was on the other end could leave a message but she insisted I take the call. It was Elaine. I treated her like she was someone else and Rita didn't suspect a thing. I ended the conversation fairly quickly and then disconnected us."

"You mean Rita just guessed who you were talking to?"

I raised my head now and gazed into my neighbor's eyes. "No. I hadn't actually turned the cell phone off like I thought, and Elaine was still talking. Rita blew a fuse. She said she never wanted to see me again."

Margaret released her hands from her mug. "Oh, dear. I wish I would've been there. I know I could've calmed her down."

"I don't think anyone could've at that point, but I sure could've used your support," and then I took another bite of roll and stood up. "That reminds me, I should give you back your ring. I had planned to give it to Rita today."

My guest stopped me. "Matt, you'll do no such thing. You should always leave yourself open to new possibilities like the saying, 'When one door closes another always opens'." She picked up her mug and brought it to her lips now.

"You're right, Margaret," I said. "Thanks for reminding me of that. I bet there's tons of single women out there just looking for a guy like me."

Margaret gave me a Mona Lisa smile as she set her coffee mug on the table and shifted her attention to my neat little pile of paper and pencils. "What's this?" she quizzed. "A new case?"

My thoughts were still on Rita and I didn't respond at once. "What? Oh, no. Just some stuff I was fooling around with."

The Italian woman's thin eyebrows arched. "Is that so? Well, I want to see what you've been up to." Without waiting for my approval, she reached out and lifted the blank piece paper off what it was hiding. "Is this who I think it is?"

"Yup. It's my parents when they were a lot younger."

The elderly woman closely examined the drawing she had placed in front of her. "You're very talented, Matt. Did you just draw this?"

I laughed. "Are you kidding? This was started when I was in high school. It resurfaced recently when Mom sent a box of my personal belongings home for me to go through. I'm just tweaking it." Now I finished my roll.

"I'm surprised one of your high school teachers didn't suggest you continue in this venue," Margaret said. "Your work might have been hanging in a renowned art gallery by now."

I chuckled lightly as I picked up a pencil and twirled it between my fingers. "You know not everyone understands or likes Picasso's paintings, but he was one smart dude. He said, 'Every child is an artist. The problem is how to remain an artist once he grows up'."

"That doesn't just go for painting," my neighbor said. "Creativity of any sort seems to be lost when one nears the teen years. The imagination flees and we all get too serious about life."

"But you didn't lose your creativity, Margaret. You're always whipping up new dishes in your tiny kitchen."

The nonagenarian glanced at her deeply lined hands. "You have to work at it, Matt, or it slips away."

"Well, then, I'd say it's high time this guy got some fun and creativity back into his life. Maybe I'll sign up for art courses while I'm in Europe."

Margaret dropped my drawing. "Did you say Europe?"

I scratched my bristly chin. "Yeah. Oh, that's right I haven't told you yet, have I?" Margaret slightly moved her head from side to side. "Well, Neil Welch called me before I met with Rita. He had a job offer for me. Of course, at the time, I thought things would pan out for Rita and me and I didn't want to ruin our relationship again by taking on a job outside the country."

My neighbor's face turned sober. "I suppose you'll give up this apartment then?"

"According to Welch, I'll only be gone about four months and the salary is to be very generous, so I thought I'd keep the lease for now."

She quickly clutched a corner of her frilly apron and dabbed the tears that appeared on her face. "I'm going to miss you Matt," she said in a deeply hushed tone.

"Ditto," I added. Then I lifted my chapped hands off the table and gently set them on top of the elderly woman's smooth age-spotted ones.